Grief is the winter of the soul . . .
but with love comes the spring

1. Gipsies & Lovers

Chapter One

She stood looking out at the dull grey of a winter's day; the streets were wet and slippery beneath the feet of the people passing by – people with pinched faces and anxious eyes, muffled by scarves and coats against the bitter cold.

Would it never be spring again? She was so tired of seeing only grey skies, tired of all the pain and suffering she dealt with every day of her working life – of the deep, aching need inside her that never seemed to ease.

Where was he now – the man she loved? Loved so much that his going had left her with winter in her soul. Was he alive – or lying fatally wounded at the bottom of a muddy trench with the blood draining out of him?

She saw so much of it now, death and dying, and with every new intake of the wounded she found herself looking fearfully into the faces of the men she tended, always wondering if one day it would be him.

Sometimes she longed desperately for the country lanes of her home, for spring flowers and the sound of a lark singing high above in a clear sky. Spring had been such a joyous time of year when she was a child. She had believed that happiness was hers for the taking. All she'd had to do was reach out and . . . but she had let it slip through her fingers. Her bright dream had gone and now it was eternal winter in her heart.

'Nurse?' Sister Norden's sharp voice broke into her thoughts. 'Are you dreaming? I've asked you twice to prepare the dressings for the new amputation case.'

3

'Sorry, Sister.' She swung round guiltily, even though she had officially been on her break. 'I – I didn't hear you.'

She had been dreaming, of course – dreaming of a day long ago: of a time when she was still a child . . . naive, innocent and prone to foolish fancies, and to one particular, terrifying dream . . . a dream that haunted her even now.

'You – 'tis you who will bring the evil on us! Blood . . . blood . . . we are bound in blood!'

The girl screamed. There was blood all over her, in her hair, on her hands, in her eyes, in her mouth . . . blood everywhere . . . so much blood that she was drowning in it, suffocating . . . choking.

Sorrel woke from the old, familiar dream, starting up to look round her bedroom in fear, then, realizing it was just a dream, she lay back against her pillows and sighed. Would she never forget that morning she had first seen the gipsies? Sometimes she thought the memories would haunt her dreams for the rest of her life – that she was forever cursed.

Her trembling ceased and she breathed more easily, beginning to think about the dream. Why did it still haunt her? She'd been just a child when it happened, hardly old enough to be out on her own, but adventurous and spirited, forever into mischief – at least, that was what her mother always said when she was cross.

The gipsies fascinated her, with their dark faces and their strange ways. She had been warned not to go near them, of course, but that only made her more curious.

'Stay away from the camp, Sorrel,' her mother had told her before she went to pick blackberries that particular morning. 'Those gipsies are trouble. I've always said it – but of course no one listens to me.'

Sorrel hadn't listened either. She knew where the gipsies had camped on a piece of waste ground, just as she knew that blackberries grew in abundance nearby. She knew because she was a country child, bright-eyed, as quick as a monkey, and blessed with so much energy she could never be still.

As she neared the camp that morning she smelt wood smoke and heard the sound of dogs barking, children screaming as they played. It was a scene to colour the

4

imagination of any child, let alone a lively imp like Sorrel Harris.

Tall, dark-haired, swarthy-skinned men going about their business; ragged, dirty urchins darting in and out of the vans; and women in brightly coloured skirts, with long, tangled hair and gold rings in their ears – all chattering, screaming, laughing. Dark, mysterious and fascinating to an imaginative child.

One woman stood out from the rest. She was dressed in a bright crimson skirt, which was long and full with frills at the hem, some of which were torn and hanging loose, and she had a tight-fitting velvet jacket sewn with glass beads and gilt braid. Her hair was wild, hanging about her face in greasy coils; once it had been jet black but now it had streaks of grey. She seemed to be having an argument with somebody, her voice shrill with anger as she screamed a torrent of abuse.

Drawn towards the vibrant scene Sorrel wandered nearer and nearer, until she was inside the ring of gaily painted caravans, unhitched now from the horses that pulled them along country lanes, up hills and through deep valleys. Closer and closer so that at last she was near enough to hear what the woman was saying.

'You'll rue this day, Lorenzo,' she cried. 'If you'll listen to me, you'll move on to the next village.'

'Be quiet, woman,' a man replied sharply. He was a dark-skinned, foreign-looking fellow with black eyes and a gold ring in his ear. 'You're full of foolish talk. Aden Sawle is a good master and he's offering three weeks' work in the potato fields. Get on with your chores and leave me be.'

The woman tossed her head, her eyes flashing with anger, but she either feared or respected the man for her voice dropped to a low muttering. 'No good will come of it,' she said. 'He'll not heed me but . . .'

Suddenly she whirled round and, looking straight at Sorrel, lifted her arm and pointed. ''Tis you!' she cried in loud, ringing tones. 'You that will bring the evil on us. I curse you now as I shall curse you with my dying breath. I curse you and the whore who bore you!'

Sorrel trembled with fright as she looked into the gipsy's

5

proud face and dark staring eyes. What had she done to bring down this woman's wrath on her? Then, as she saw the way that cold, evil gaze travelled beyond her, she realized the curse had not been directed at her at all but someone who stood behind her.

She turned and saw a youth. He was some years older than her with thick, dark, curling hair and eyes that looked almost black.

'Hush your wicked tongue, Sadie,' he called, his expression softening as he met Sorrel's frightened stare. 'You've terrified the child. See how pale she is.'

'Then let her run away, back to her own kind.' The woman scowled at her. 'She's not welcome here. Her kind and ours never mix.' Sadie's eyes narrowed suddenly, their blackness lit by a queer silver flame. 'Get away, girl. For your own sake, go now and never come back. There's naught but death and pain for you here. Be warned . . . be warned.'

Sorrel gasped at the malevolence in the gipsy's eyes. She fell back in fear, then turned and rushed past the gipsy lad, her heart beating wildly. She heard the youth call after her but did not dare to look back.

She had run in fear of the nameless horror that threatened to overtake her if she stopped. Even now – years later – the memory of those terrible eyes was enough to set the chills running down Sorrel's spine.

It was such a silly thing to have haunted her over the years. She wasn't cursed . . . of course she wasn't.

Throwing back the bedcovers, Sorrel jumped out of bed and ran to the window to look out at the familiar scene outside. Everything looked normal, just as it should. There was no blood . . . just the farm cat strolling across the yard and some pigeons cooing in the trees across the road. Nothing to be frightened of . . . nothing at all.

Sorrel lifted her head to feel the warmth of the sun on her face and knew she was happy. Spring was such a joyous time of year with the new buds bursting and the hedgerows brightened by pale yellow primroses – violets, too, if you knew where to look for them.

She had grown up in the small Cambridgeshire village of

6

Mepal and knew all the best places to find wild flowers, or berries in autumn. She had been picking violets this bright May morning in 1909, loitering as she went about her errand; it was a Saturday, warm and sunny, and for a while she had escaped her usual chores. Her mother had sent her across the road to Five Winds with a basket of eggs for Rebecca Sawle, because Mrs Sawle's own hens were not laying as they should and she was making a batch of her sponges for the village fête that afternoon.

Mrs Sawle was a very important person in the village; she was attractive, though a little on the plump side, with reddish-brown hair, grey eyes – and a sharp tongue! She was the wife of Aden Sawle, who was the most prosperous farmer in the little community – though not quite so rich as he had been when the Sawles lived in a big house in the High Street. Something had happened when Sorrel was too young to know what was going on and the Sawles had moved back to Five Winds, forcing her own family – who had been living at the farm – to move into the tiny cottage across the road. May Harris had grumbled at the time of the move, though not so loudly that her husband noticed.

Sid Harris was Mr Sawle's head stockman and his closest friend. He would never hear a word against Aden, and though normally the most placid of men, could be roused to anger by idle gossip concerning his friend.

'How we're to manage in this place, I don't know,' May Harris had muttered crossly to her daughter, but in the end they had, and Mr Sawle had made it bigger for them as time passed and he began to prosper again. Sometimes Mr Sawle talked of building his wife another big house in the neighbouring village of Sutton but so far it had come to nothing.

Sorrel's mother said Rebecca had made up her mind not to move from the farm and apparently her word was usually law.

Sorrel belatedly remembered she was supposed to be delivering the eggs. Her mother had told her to be quick because Mrs Sawle wanted them 'specially – and that was at least fifteen minutes ago!

She hurried up to the kitchen door and knocked. It was

7

opened almost immediately by Rebecca Sawle, who looked at her with disapproval.

'You've certainly taken your time. I thought May would send you over straight away.'

'I came as quickly as I could,' Sorrel lied, and hid the violets behind her back. 'Ma said you wanted the eggs 'specially.'

Mrs Sawle's expression did not lighten. 'And how is your mother, Sorrel?'

The kitchen door was open just enough to allow the enticing smell of baking to drift towards her. She thought Molly must be cooking something special. Molly Green was the Sawles' daily help and she would have asked Sorrel in had she been alone – just as almost everyone else in the village always did when she called. But Rebecca Sawle did not like her.

'My mother is well, thank you, Mrs Sawle.'

'I'm glad of that. Be careful with that money – and tell your father that Mr Sawle has gone to Chatteris but will call to see him this afternoon.'

'Yes, Mrs Sawle. Thank you.' The door closed with a snap and Sorrel felt miffed as she turned away. Why didn't Mrs Sawle like her? She was friendly with her mother and father – so why did she look at Sorrel as if she were something unpleasant the cat had deposited on her doorstep? Had she done something to upset her – other than being late with the eggs?

'Sorrel! Sorrel Harris!' The challenging voice stopped her at the gate. 'Where are you off to in such a hurry?'

Sorrel's heart skipped a beat and she turned with a smile of anticipation as the youth came from behind the dairy.

'Hello, Jay,' she said, and waited for him to come up to her. 'Ma sent me over with some eggs for your mother. Her hens aren't laying as they should apparently. I'm going home now. Bob wants to visit his girl in Chatteris and I've promised to help him finish early.'

Jay Sawle nodded as her rather long speech ended. He was tall for his age and his eyes were grey like his mother's, his hair a soft brown and a little too long; it kept falling over his forehead and he pushed it back impatiently.

'Have you seen the tent going up in our top field?' he asked.

'No. I haven't been that way this morning. What's going on then? I thought the fête was in the vicarage garden as usual.'

'It's a circus,' he said, his voice lifting on a note of excitement. 'Dad arranged for it to come.'

Jay was nearly fifteen, but in his excitement he seemed younger than his age. They attended the same school and, though he could be arrogant and bossy sometimes, they had been friends ever since he had stopped some of the other boys from pulling her plaits. It had happened when he was just eleven and she not quite nine years old. There had been three of them tormenting her – the worst bullies in the school – but he had waded in without a thought for the consequences. She had watched the scrap fearfully but in the end he had emerged as the victor. He had walked her home afterwards with the bruises on his face going purple and his left eye slowly closing.

'A circus?' She stared at him. 'Here in the village? I've only ever been once.'

'Same here,' he agreed. 'Fanny hasn't been at all. Mother doesn't really approve – but Dad says we're all going this time. Not Richie, of course, he's still at boarding school until Easter. But he probably wouldn't want to go anyway.'

Jay pulled a face and she nodded, knowing that he and his elder brother didn't really get on very well. Jay was much closer to his sister. Fanny was a few months older than Sorrel and they had gone to school together until Fanny had had scarlet fever. After that Mrs Sawle had decided to finish her education at home, because she was too delicate to mix with other children.

Sorrel sometimes felt sorry for Fanny when she saw her sitting beside her mother in church. She always looked so quiet and pale. People said Mrs Sawle wrapped her in cotton wool because she was terrified of losing her.

'Mother thinks I should go away to school for a couple of years, to finish my education,' Jay said, kicking at a stone with a frown. 'But I should hate it. All I want is to go on the land with Dad.'

9

Sorrel nodded sympathetically. It wasn't the first time Jay had confided in her and she knew that all his hopes, thoughts and longings were firmly planted in the rich, dark soil of his father's land. His parents had argued over his schooling but in the end Aden had put his foot down. Jay had heard them arguing. From what he'd told her Sorrel thought they must argue a lot and she was glad her own parents got on most of the time – but then, Sid Harris was an easygoing man and her mother knew when she was well off.

'You'll be leaving school next Easter,' Sorrel said, a sigh escaping her. 'I wish I was. Pa has promised me a pony and trap so I can deliver the milk for him when I leave.'

Jay grinned at her. 'You're clever, Sorrel,' he said. 'Better at the book learning than me. You're the one who should go away to school.'

Sorrel shook her head. It was true that she often came near the top of her class in school; she was quick and bright and could work things out in her head when others were still scribbling away with a pencil and paper, but she didn't want to go away. She didn't want to leave her home and all the familiar things she loved. She had her own special dreams.

'You just mind your own business, Jay Sawle,' she said, tipping her head to one side as she gazed up at him. 'I don't need you to tell me what to do!'

He looked rueful and stuck his hands in his pockets. 'You've a mind of your own, I know that well enough – but you'll come to the circus, won't you?

'Maybe.' She gave a toss of her head, her heavy plaits swinging over her shoulder.

It didn't do to let Jay become too sure of himself. Sometimes he acted as though he were lord of the manor and then she had to take him down a peg or two – the funny thing was, he never seemed to mind what she said to him.

'I've got to go now. Ma will be waiting for me.'

'Sorrel . . .'

There was a note of exasperation in his voice and she laughed as she glanced back and saw him staring after her with a rueful expression on his face. Jay was her friend but she liked to keep him wondering.

* * *

Her father was scraping cow dung from his boots outside
the kitchen door as she ran into the yard behind her home,
her petticoats flying and her hair beginning to work loose,
straggling untidily about her face. Sorrel's hair was soft but
very thick; she had to be ruthless with it or it would have
been all over the place. At night she brushed it until it shone
and caught fire in the candlelight, seeming coppery instead
of the light brown it usually was. Her eyes were green like
a cat's, though in daylight they were often more hazel than
green – at least, that's what her mother said.

'You're passable, I suppose,' May was fond of telling her.
'But no raving beauty – so don't get beyond yourself, miss!'

'Ah, leave her be,' Sorrel's father always responded with
a smile for her when her mother scolded. 'She's the light of
my life. I bless the day she was born.'

He turned to her now with a loving glance, pausing to let
her catch up to him before going in. 'You're in a hurry,
lass?'

'Pa, oh, Pa!' she cried, sliding to a hasty stop. 'You'll never
guess what's happened. It's so exciting. You'll never guess
in a million years.'

'What's that then?' he asked, his eyes twinkling as he
hitched up his trousers. 'You wouldn't be meaning the circus
that's put up in Aden's top field, I suppose?'

For a moment she felt deflated but then she laughed and
nodded. 'Aden told you! I should have known he would. I
heard it from Jay just a moment ago.'

'Aden told me yesterday when he came to look at Daisy.
She's not giving milk and I think there's an infection in one
of her teats.' Sid lifted his cap to scratch his head. 'Beats
me why though – and she was one of our best milkers.'

Sorrel saw how worried he looked and nodded. Her father
was a large man with a red, weather-roughened face and a
huge belly that shook when he laughed. He was wearing
a stained tweed cap to cover his balding pate, a patched
jacket, trousers that clung precariously to his stomach –
they were always in danger of sliding off the mountain and
constantly needing to be hitched up – and heavy hob-nailed
boots. He carried a big responsibility as Aden's right-hand
man and she could see he was very concerned.

11

'You wouldn't want to lose Daisy,' she said as she followed her father into the large, warm kitchen. It had polished red tiles with rush matting laid in front of the sink and beneath the pine table. Her father's boots left a trail of mud as he went to rinse his hands under the tap.

'Sid – look what you've done!' May Harris muttered, giving him a look of disgust. 'Why I bother to keep this place decent, I don't know. Ted and Bob take their boots off when they come in from the yard – why can't you?'

'I thought I'd scraped them clean,' he said on a note of apology. 'Don't take on, May. I'll have them off now.'

'It's too late.' She scowled at him and then at her daughter. 'Get the cloth and wipe up that dirt, Sorrel. Shift yourself, if you please! You've been gone long enough and me wanting a hand with the dinner.'

'Sorry, Ma.'

Sorrel hastened to remove the evidence of her father's guilt, smiling as he winked at her behind May's back. She knew that she was his favourite, just as her brothers Ted and Bob were her mother's.

'Jay Sawle told me about the circus so I went to have a look at the tent they're putting up in Mr Sawle's field.'

'A circus? Well, I never . . .' May's scowl disappeared. She had a sharp tongue when she was cross but her moods never lasted long. 'Fancy that! It must be years since we last had a circus in Mepal. They've been regular to Chatteris and Sutton but not here in the village. In Aden's top field, is it?'

Sorrel went to the middle drawer of the big pine dresser that stretched the length of one wall, taking out a blue and white cloth to spread over the table. Her mother was particular about her linens and the cloth was spotlessly clean, starched and ironed. Sorrel smoothed it over the table, enjoying the crisp feel of it beneath her fingers.

She had begun to lay five places before she came out with what was in her head. 'I've only been to a circus once,' she said, glancing at her father. 'Can we go? Please, please, take us, Pa.'

'I only hope they haven't got lions and tigers,' May said with a shiver. 'I heard about a lion escaping from a circus once. It killed a farmer's best horse and ate it.'

12

'I've not heard there's lions nor tigers,' Sid said with a straight face but wicked eyes. 'Don't you worry, May. If a lion should escape it won't eat you – you're too skinny.'

'It will be *you* the lion eats, Pa,' Sorrel teased. 'More meat on you than the rest of us put together.'

'Don't cheek your father!' May snapped. 'He needs some flesh on him with all the work he does.'

Her father did work hard, Sorrel knew that. He and her brothers had a herd of fifty cows to milk morning and evening; there were thirty-odd bullocks out on the washes, which had to be counted twice a day, then Sid's own small herd of pigs to tend, and of course the horses – though these were mainly Ted's responsibility, for he was Aden's horse-keeper and took a huge pride in the great, noble beasts that did so much of the heavy work on the farm.

'Nay, don't scold the lass,' Sid said, hitching up his trousers and smiling at her. 'I don't mind a bit of leg pulling. Besides, she's right. I'd make two of you, May. You're a trim woman, as bonny as the day I wed you.'

May turned away to move a saucepan that was in danger of boiling over on the black iron cooking range. She was smiling. It was true that she had kept her figure better than most women managed – better than Mrs Sawle, Sorrel thought. Aden's wife had once been the prettiest woman for miles around, or so she had heard her father say, but Sorrel thought her mother had a better shape.

'Aden says there will be tickets for all of us,' Sid said. 'So you'll be going, Sorrel, don't you fret – and to the fête this afternoon.'

'Not until she's finished her chores, she won't,' May said tartly. 'Call your brothers in, Sorrel. I'm going to dish the dinner up now.'

Sorrel ran out into the yard. Her mother always got edgy if everyone wasn't at table when dinner was ready. During the week, of course, the men often came in at different times, but on Saturdays and Sundays they were expected to be punctual. Ted was already on his way but Bob was still in the sheds. Sorrel lifted her skirts and picked her way carefully through the mud, standing at the door of the milking shed to summon her eldest brother.

13

'Come on, Bob,' she called. 'Dinner's ready and Ma's on the warpath.'

Bob had been laying fresh straw on the compacted earth ready for the next milking session. He glanced at her anxiously over his shoulder. 'I wanted to get done,' he said, looking a bit shy.

He was a big, strapping fellow with a thick neck and wide shoulders, inclined to be bossy and sure of himself. Sorrel smiled inwardly as she saw his unease. It was amazing what love could do to a man!

'I'm meeting Mabel after dinner. You haven't forgotten you promised to go shepherding down the bank for me this afternoon?'

'Of course I haven't.' Sorrel shook her head at him. She was fond of her elder brother and knew this was a special day for him. 'What kind of a ring are you getting for Mabel then?'

'Whatever she fancies – within reason,' he said, slightly sheepish. 'We're going to tell everyone tomorrow – so you will keep this to yourself?'

'You know I will.' She retreated, hopping over a patch of mud to save her shoes. 'Hurry up or you'll be in trouble.'

Chapter Two

Sorrel bought herself a lump of peppermint humbug with the money her father had given her to spend at the fête. It was homemade, misshapen, and the stripes seemed to have got lost in the making, but it tasted ever so good. She sucked on it contentedly as she wandered round the other stalls in the vicarage garden.

She stared hard at the jar of beans on the stall Mrs Barlow – the vicar's wife – was presiding over, wondering if it was worth spending two of her precious pennies on hazarding a guess at how many beans there were inside.

No, she didn't really want a bottle of cooking sherry, she decided – though her mother might. She wandered on to the coconut shy, watched a few abortive attempts to knock down a nut by people she knew, shrewdly assessed it as being a hopeless task and went on to the hoopla. She had been lucky at that the previous year – and there were some pretty ornaments to be won.

She paid over her three remaining pennies and received three hoops, taking careful aim as she tried to get them over a tiny scent bottle she liked. Hearing a snigger behind her as each of her hoops missed the target, she glanced over her shoulder and saw a group of boys she disliked.

She scowled fiercely at one of them. 'Go away, Tom Robinson,' she said. 'Haven't you anything better to do?' Her remarks were greeted with hoots of laughter and jeers. Their behaviour made her angry but she knew better than to push them too far.

Sticking her head in the air, she walked off and left them.

She had spent all her money anyway, and it was time she kept her promise to Bob and went shepherding.

The lonely stretches of the washes held no fears for Sorrel. She had been born and bred to the fens and she loved them; loved the wide, flat fields of black earth, the endless skies that were never the same two days running, and the dark, murky brown water of the river with flirty little moorhens darting in and out of the bullrushes at the edges.

She sang to herself as she went in search of the bullocks. For once they hadn't gone too far and she counted them twice to make sure they were all there before turning homeward.

It was just as she turned that she noticed the girl kneeling on the ground, her head bent in concentration as she searched for something, her fingers moving almost feverishly in the grass.

Her hair was a wild tangle of dark curls and she was wearing a bright red skirt that spread around her on the grass like a little tent. She was a gipsy girl – probably with the circus – and for a moment Sorrel's heart caught with fright. She had been a bit nervous of gipsies, ever since that terrifying morning when the woman Sadie had seemed to put a curse on her.

Sorrel hesitated, not sure whether to stop and speak or walk past – then the girl looked at her with her clear blue eyes and Sorrel's fear subsided. She was only a few years older than Sorrel and not in the least intimidating.

'What are you looking for?' she asked.

'Four-leaved clovers,' the girl replied. 'They bring good luck.'

'I know. I found one last summer and the next day I came top of my class in spelling.'

The girl looked at her with a mixture of awe and scorn in her lovely eyes. She was so beautiful! Sorrel had never seen anyone like her before.

'You gorgios have your heads full of the book learning,' she said, 'but I bet you don't know how to make a potion that will cure almost anything – do you?'

'No.' Sorrel looked at her doubtfully. 'Do you?'

16

'Sadie taught me,' she said. 'I used to sell her cures at the farms and cottages we visited as we passed but now I'm with the circus.' There was a note of pride in her voice and her eyes seemed to light up as if something had come alive inside her.

'What do you do?' Sorrel asked. 'You're so lucky to be with the circus. I've only ever seen it once.'

'I ride Shima's horses,' she replied, 'and I help him to train them.' She smiled as if deciding that Sorrel was worthy of her notice. 'My name is Tarina – what's yours?'

'Sorrel Harris. My father is Aden Sawle's stockman. Mr Sawle is one of the biggest farmers in the district.'

'I know.' Tarina frowned. 'We've worked for him in the past.'

'Were you here some years ago ... for the potato harvest?'

'Yes.' She nodded, her wild hair tossing in a flurry of curls. 'It was hard work, and there were quarrels between the men. But that was before Lorenzo died ...' There was a look in her eyes then that might have been grief or fear.

'Was he your father?'

'No ... but my mother was his woman for a time.' Tarina's eyes clouded. 'After he died ... things changed ... so I ran away to join Shima in the circus.'

'What do you mean – things changed?'

The gipsy girl's expression darkened. 'That is not your business,' she said, and bent her head, her fingers scrabbling in the grass once more. 'I must find one ... I must.'

'You can't find them if you look. It's only when you're not really thinking about it that they come to you – it's magic.'

'I must find one for luck,' the girl said without looking up. She seemed to have withdrawn into her own world again.

'I hope you're lucky. I have to go now.'

The gipsy girl was focused on her search and did not seem to hear her. Sorrel wondered why she was so desperate to find the lucky charm.

'Goodbye.'

Sorrel walked on, beginning to sing again. It had been such a lovely day but the sun had gone behind a cloud and a breeze had suddenly sprung up, making her feel chilly. She increased her pace, eager to be home in the warm.

She had almost reached the farm when she saw the gang of boys coming towards her; they were the same ones she had seen earlier at the fête – except that now Lenny Browne was with them. She felt a spasm of fear as she realized they had seen her, her memories of bullying at their hands still strong.

These were the boys who had pulled her hair – the ones Jay Sawle had fought for her – and she knew they had been waiting for their chance to get back at her. Besides, Lenny was a lot older than the others and something about him disturbed her.

'Look who's here,' Tom Robinson jeered. 'Bin for a walk then?'

'I've been shepherding for Pa,' Sorrel replied, her chin jutting defiantly. 'Now I'm going home for my tea.'

'Too stuck up to talk to us,' he taunted. 'Suppose we don't want to let you go?'

She stood poised for flight, her heart thumping against her ribs. There were four of them altogether and she was only a girl. She couldn't fight them the way Jay had. And she had been warned that girls had to be careful of boys, though she wasn't exactly sure why. Her only chance was to outrun them. She was about to try when she saw her father standing by the river bank just behind the farm and relief flooded through her.

She waved and called to him. 'Pa . . . Pa! I'm coming . . . wait for me!'

Lenny glanced over his shoulder, frowned and said something to the others. She couldn't hear what he said but it made the rest of the boys turn away and walk past her without another word.

She ran to her father gladly, aware that she had escaped an unpleasant confrontation because he had come to look for her.

'Were all the bullocks there?' he asked, and she nodded, finding it difficult to catch her breath. Her father was frowning as he looked at her. 'Were those lads annoying you? I saw them go by and came out just in case. That

Lenny Browne is a wrong 'un. You want to stay away from his sort.'

'They were just teasing – but I was glad you were there.'

Her father was quiet as they walked back to the house together, then, just before they went in, he turned to look at her, a serious expression in his eyes. 'You're growing up, lass. Mebbe you ought not to wander about on your own so much. I always thought you were safe enough in your own village – but now I'm not so sure.'

'What do you mean, Pa? I didn't mess about near the river, honest.'

'It's not the river I'm bothered over,' he said. 'Listen to me, Sorrel. You're too young to understand yet but ... well, there's some boys ... men too ... they're not very nice. You've got to be careful. You stay near the farm where one of us can keep an eye on you in future. Your brothers can do the shepherding.'

Her father's warning gave her a peculiar feeling inside. She vaguely understood what he was saying. She had heard talk about some of the girls having a bad experience when the gipsies were in the village years before ... and there was something unclean about the way Lenny Browne had looked at her.

'Don't worry, I don't like Lenny,' she said, then as a thought struck her, 'Jay said he would take me to see the circus folk training the horses for the ring tomorrow morning after church. I'll be with him all the time. I can go, can't I?' She held her breath. If Pa said no she would die of disappointment but she wouldn't go against him, not for the world. 'Please, Pa.'

'Now that's one lad I do trust,' he said, and patted her cheek. 'You can go with Jay – but don't go wandering down the bank afterwards.'

Chapter Three

Tarina looked at the tall, handsome young man leading out the dancing ponies and felt her heart quicken within her. Shima was almost eighteen now; she was several months older but she felt that he had the strength and look of a man – a man who was ready to choose a woman for his own. Yet he had never looked at her once in that way. She knew that she was beautiful. She had seen hot desire in the eyes of other men – so strong and powerful was that desire in one man that she had run away rather than surrender to it.

She had discovered that Shima was with the circus and had walked for miles to find him; it had taken courage to do it and when she finally caught up with him, Shima had not been pleased to see her.

'You cannot stay with me,' he had told her, his dark eyes colder than she had ever seen them. 'You must go back to Sadie and Leyan.'

'You don't know what has happened since Lorenzo died and you left,' she had told him with tears in her lovely eyes. 'Black Jake has taken over as our leader – and he frightens me. Leyan is too weak to protect me, even though he is my half-brother, and Sadie does not care about anything since Lorenzo died.'

Once, long ago, Tarina had believed that Shima was Lorenzo's son and Leyan's half-brother, that he was the chosen one who would lead their tribe to good fortune – but Sadie had told her it was all a lie ... that Shima was truly the son of Aden Sawle, a rich farmer from Mepal. She had never dared to speak of it to Shima for she did not

20

know whether he had knowledge of it himself and would do nothing to hurt him.

She had loved him for as long as she could remember. Not as a member of her family but as the man she would one day choose for her own. Unfortunately, Shima still seemed to see her as a kind of sister, though they had no blood in common. He treated her kindly and with respect but showed no sign of wanting her as his woman – though he had sought permission for her to stay with the circus after she'd told him why she had run away from the gipsy tribe.

He had always had a gift for making horses do as he wanted; he could stand on their bare backs and ride round and round the ring with his arms stretched wide on either side, and he had trained his ponies to walk on their hind legs and bow down on their front. Tarina had begged to be allowed to help, and now she too could ride bare-backed around the ring. It had taken her a long time and she had fallen and hurt herself on many occasions, but now she was almost as good as Shima. Her position with the circus was secure but it still wasn't enough for her. She wanted to be Shima's woman. Why, oh why, wouldn't he look at her in that way?

'Where are you going?' he called to her as he turned and saw her watching him. 'I'm going to teach Brownie a new trick this morning. Don't you want to help me?'

'When I come back,' she promised, and waved to him. She would look for that four-leaved clover one more time. Perhaps if she found it . . . surely its magic would make him love her? It must . . . it must . . . because she was breaking her heart for him.

'Shima said we could watch,' Jay said as they walked towards the field in which the tent had been set up. 'He won't let anyone else see because it's like a free show and they might not pay for a ticket if they've seen all the tricks – but we can watch because Shima is my friend.'

'Shima?' Sorrel gazed up at Jay curiously, remembering the gipsy girl she had met down the bank the previous

21

afternoon. The girl had spoken of someone called Shima. 'Will Tarina be there, too?'

Jay was surprised that she should know the name so she told him what had happened and he nodded.

'Shima speaks of her as his sister but . . .' He frowned and hesitated. 'She isn't really, not even his step-sister, because . . . no, I'd better not say. No one is supposed to know. I'm not sure if Shima does . . .'

Sorrel's head went up and she gave him a very direct look. 'Are you saying I can't be trusted to keep a secret?'

Jay chuckled. 'Don't get on your high horse. It's not my secret – and I can't be certain, but . . .' He glanced over his shoulder as if he were afraid of being overheard. 'I think Shima might be my half-brother.'

'Oh!' Her mouth opened in astonishment. 'But isn't he one of . . . them?'

'One of the gipsies who came to help with the potatoes some years back?' Jay nodded and looked thoughtful. 'Yes. Lorenzo was supposed to be his father but I heard something . . .' His fingers closed around her arm, digging into her so hard that it hurt. 'You've got to promise never to tell anyone, Sorrel. I haven't told Fanny or Richie and I'm not sure – but I think Shima's mother used to work in the bar of a pub in Chatteris. It was called The Cottrel Arms when my mother's father owned it. She was having a child when she went off with the gipsies and died giving birth. Shima told me that Sadie wet-nursed him . . .'

'Did your father know Shima's mother when she worked in the pub?'

'It must have been just before he started courting my mother. I've heard Mother speak of a girl called Dotty Prentice who was carrying a child when she went off with the gipsies, and I heard my parents arguing over Shima once when the gipsies were here. I was supposed to be asleep and I couldn't hear everything but I'd crept downstairs to get a drink and . . .'

'And you think he's . . . ?' Sorrel's cheeks went scarlet. It was quite shocking and she didn't know what to think.

'You won't tell anyone, will you?'

'No, of course not.'

She wouldn't have dared to mention it at home. Her father would be shocked and upset. He thought the world of Aden – and he respected Mrs Sawle.

'Do you mind?' She looked at Jay curiously. 'That he might be your half-brother?'

'No. I told you, I like Shima.'

They walked on in silence until they reached the field. A tall gipsy was already working with his horses and they watched as he put them through their paces, applauding as they danced on their hind legs, bowed down and rolled over to play dead, then got up again and nodded their heads as if expecting a reward.

Sorrel was amazed. She couldn't believe that the gipsy could make them do all those wonderful tricks. He was teaching them a new one involving a lot of fancy steps, which seemed almost too difficult, but gradually they began to respond and she laughed as one of them butted Shima in the back until he gave it a piece of apple.

'That's one of the tricks you'll see in the ring,' Jay said admiringly. 'I wish I could be in the circus, don't you?'

'It looks fun – but I shouldn't like it when it's cold and the wind is howling in the trees.'

'They have camp fires.' Jay was obviously unwilling to give up his romantic ideas of life with the circus folk. 'What . . .' He was staring across the field and as Sorrel followed his gaze she saw a girl come running towards them. She was clearly in distress and Sorrel felt a prickling sensation at the nape of her neck as she recognized her. It was Tarina and, as she came closer, Sorrel could see that her white blouse was muddied and torn and her face scratched.

Jay took a step forward but Shima threw down his whip and ran to meet her. He caught her in his arms, holding her as she began to scream and cry hysterically.

'What's wrong?' he asked but she was sobbing wildly. 'Steady now, princess. I've got you – you're safe now.'

'They attacked me,' Tarina cried. 'There were five or six of them and he . . .' She choked and pressed her face against his shoulder. 'One of them tried . . . to pull up my skirt.'

Sorrel went white as she remembered her own fright the previous afternoon. 'I saw them yesterday,' she whispered to Jay. 'Tom Robinson and Lenny Browne ... they were after me until Pa ...' But Jay was listening to the others and didn't seem to hear her.

'What did this evil man do to you?' Shima demanded. 'Did he violate you?'

'He – he tried but I fought him.' Tarina's voice was thick with emotion. 'He ripped my blouse and thrust his hand inside and then he forced me to the ground.' She burst into tears. 'I feel so dirty.'

'It is bad enough,' Shima muttered, but there was relief in his face. 'We must be thankful that it was no worse.'

Tarina drew back from him, her expression one of pride mixed with anger. 'Is that all you can say?' she demanded. 'Will you let this gorgio dishonour me and do nothing?'

'Do you need to ask?' Shima growled. 'Describe this man to me. Did you hear his name spoken?'

'The others called him Lenny,' she replied. 'He was the leader amongst them.'

'His name is Lenny Browne,' Sorrel said, and for the first time Shima turned to look directly at her. His eyes were very dark, his hair a shining black curling crisply to his head. 'Lenny lives with his father in a cottage on the Chatteris road.'

'Sorrel,' Jay warned, 'be careful what you say.'

Shima was still staring at her and something in his eyes made her shiver. 'I have seen you before ... years ago ... at the camp. Sadie frightened you.'

She nodded, recognition coming as he spoke. He was the youth who had told the gipsy woman not to frighten her.

'Sorrel ... that is your name?' It sounded like music on his lips. 'Thank you, Sorrel. Rest assured, this man will pay for what he has done to my sister.'

His eyes had gone hard and cold and Sorrel drew in her breath sharply. 'I thought ... won't you go to the police? Pa said he would if they ...'

'We have our own way of settling these things.'

Jay took her arm and she saw he looked worried. 'I think we should go now. Your father will be wondering where you are.'

'Yes ... yes, all right.'

Jay hesitated, then looked at the gipsy. 'If you talked to my father he would see justice done, Shima.'

Shima shook his head. 'This can be paid only in blood.'

Jay nodded, his hold tightening on Sorrel's arm as he drew her away. He was silent, his expression grim and thoughtful; they walked without speaking until they reached the farm gate.

'It might be best if you kept this to yourself, Sorrel. I like Shima and don't want him to get into trouble over this.'

'I shan't say anything. What do you think he meant by blood? He won't kill Lenny – will he?'

'I don't think so,' Jay replied, but he didn't sound too certain. 'We can't do anything – but it's best not to say anything to anyone.'

'I won't. Lenny deserves a thrashing. I hope Shima gives him a good hiding, like your father did the day the gipsies upset Molly.'

Jay nodded and grinned. 'You should have seen Dad's face the next day. If *he* won, I dread to think what *they* must have looked like!'

She smiled, remembering the tales about the night Aden Sawle had met the gipsies at the bridge and thrashed the lot of them – some people swore there had been at least ten of them, but her mother said it was really only three. Whatever the truth, it had made Aden a local hero.

She watched as Jay walked off across the road. He was worried about the consequences to his friend if anything happened to Lenny Browne – a friend who might just be his half-brother.

Sorrel was eating her breakfast when her father came in that Monday morning. He washed his hands before taking his place at the table with the rest of them and her heart skipped a beat as she saw the look on his face.

'What's wrong, Pa?'

'You won't be going to the circus, lass,' he said heavily. 'Seems they changed their minds and went off during the night.'

'Oh.' She was disappointed but sensed that the circus wasn't all he had on his mind.

'And another queer thing . . . Lenny Browne has run off.'

She kept her head bent, hoping no one would notice her flushed cheeks.

'Run off?' May poured tea into a thick mug. 'Why would he do that?'

'Blessed if I know. His father stopped by the yard this morning. Said Lenny came in looking as pale as a ghost last night, grabbed his things and gabbled something about going for a soldier.'

'Well, I never,' May said, staring at him in surprise. 'Not that I'd shed any tears for that one. Good riddance to bad rubbish is what I say – still, it's queer. Why should he go off so suddenly?'

Sid took off his cap and ran a hand over his shiny scalp. 'Seems he was frightened over something.' He glanced at Sorrel but she was staring fixedly at her plate. 'I wonder . . .'

'Jay Sawle was looking for Lenny yesterday afternoon,' Ted said. 'Asked me if I'd seen him.'

'Had you?' Sorrel asked, then blushed as they all looked at her.

'As a matter of fact, yes. He was down the bank fishing – but Lenny wouldn't run off because of anything Jay had to say, would he?'

'Do you know what all this is about, Sorrel?'

Her cheeks were warm as her father looked at her. 'No, Pa,' she whispered, feeling awful. It was terrible having to lie.

'What would Sorrel know?' May asked. 'It stands to reason, Sid. That Lenny was a bad lot. He's in trouble with the law, you see if I'm not right. It's a wonder they haven't locked him up before this.'

Sorrel pushed back her plate, her appetite gone. Her mother looked at her sharply.

'What's wrong with that, miss?'

'I'm not hungry.'

'Waste of good food. I just hope you never know what it's like to go hungry, my girl.'

'Sorry, Ma.' She stood up. 'Can I go now? I don't want to be late for school.'

'Get off with you then.'

She picked up her books and went out but as she reached the front gate her father called after her.

'Just a minute, Sorrel.'

She waited reluctantly, her heart in her boots.

'I didn't press you just now – but you do know something about this, don't you?'

'I can't tell you, Pa. I promised Jay.'

'Lenny did something – he didn't touch you?'

'No, Pa, not me.' She bit her lip. 'I've got to go. I'll be late and get a black mark.'

'Go on then. Remember what I told you and come straight home after school.'

She nodded and ran off. The news of Lenny's disappearance had shaken her. What had made him take fright like that?

Jay was waiting for her at the school gate.

'Lenny has gone for a soldier,' she said breathlessly. 'Did you tell him Shima was after him?'

'I warned him, for Shima's sake. I was afraid he might kill him.'

'I'm glad Lenny has gone. I was afraid of him.'

'Why?' Jay's forehead furrowed as she told him and he cursed beneath his breath. 'If he had hurt you, I would have killed him myself!'

'Oh, Jay.' She gazed up at him uncertainly. When he was angry he looked a bit like Shima. 'Please don't say things like that. It's not worth it. I'm glad you scared Lenny off before Shima caught him.'

'I'm not sure I did. He just laughed and said he wasn't going to run away from a gipsy.'

'Then what happened?'

'I don't know. Perhaps we shan't ever know. I'm just glad Shima didn't kill him. I like Shima a lot . . . whether he's my half-brother or not.'

'Yes.' She looked into Jay's eyes. 'I liked him too – and I think you may be right. He does look a bit like you, and even more like your father.'

'It's a way they both have of looking straight at you, and his smile,' Jay said. Then as the school bell rang, he grabbed her hand. 'Come on, we're going to be late!'

27

She laughed as they ran for the classrooms, dismissing the disturbing thoughts about Lenny Browne and the gipsy. They were gone and she might never see either of them again. It was spring, life was good and she was happy. Jay was her special friend and one day – surely it would happen if she wished hard enough! – he might be more than that.

She had made up her mind, long ago, after he'd fought those bullies for her at school. One day, when they were both grown up, she was going to marry him.

Chapter Four

'Looks as though there's a change in the weather,' Sid said. 'If March comes in like a lion, it goes out like a lamb.'

'That's certainly true this year,' Aden agreed, striking a match and shielding it with his hand as he lit his pipe. He paused to draw on the tobacco. 'Anything I can bring you from Chatteris?'

'I can't think of anything we need – can you, Sorrel?'

Sid turned to his daughter with a lift of his eyebrows. She had been standing silently, listening to their talk, for the past twenty minutes or so.

'No, I don't think so.' She blushed as Aden looked directly at her.

'How are you getting on now that you've left school?' he asked. 'I expect May is pleased with an extra pair of hands in the house?'

Aden Sawle was a tall, well-built, handsome man with dark eyes and hair the colour of a raven's wing. Sorrel had noticed a few grey hairs at his temples of late but they only made him look more distinguished, and she thought it wasn't surprising that in his youth he'd had half the local girls setting their caps at him – much as Jay had now!

'Yes, it makes things easier for Ma,' she said in reply to his question, 'but I like helping Pa with the milking best.'

'She's a big help to me,' Sid said. 'Ted's teaching her to handle that grey pony we bought last summer. When she can manage it herself, I'll be sending her out to deliver the milk.'

'That will make things much easier all round.' Aden

nodded his approval at her. 'You're looking prettier than ever, Sorrel.' He turned to his friend. 'Before you know where you are, Sid, she'll be getting married.'

'I hope not – not for a few years yet. The light will go out of my life when she leaves home, and she's only fifteen, too soon to think of marrying yet.'

'They soon grow up. Jay won't be eighteen until the summer but he's already courted a few girls – no one his mother approves of, mind you.' Aden chuckled deep in his throat. 'Not that Rebecca would ever think any girl good enough for her sons – and I dread to think what she'll be like if Fanny ever decides to get married. She fusses over her all the time.'

Sid nodded, lifting his cap to scratch his head. 'Didn't you tell me that Richie was courting a girl from Chatteris?'

'Yes, nice girl. The daughter of a friend of Rebecca's. Her father owns a couple of mills . . .'

Aden moved towards the yard gate and Sorrel and her father went to admire the shiny new automobile he had recently purchased. It was parked outside in the road and, when it had first appeared, had attracted a lot of attention in the village.

'Yes.' Aden puffed at his pipe thoughtfully. 'Sally's not a bad lass but I'm not sure if anything will come of it – you can never tell with Richie. He's not one to let you know what he's thinking.' He smiled at Sorrel with his hand on the car door. 'I'm glad you're getting on well, lass. See you later then, Sid. I might call in on my way back if there's time – but Rebecca's got one of her dinners on this evening and I've promised not to be late.'

'Take care,' said Sid, frowning as Aden inserted the starting handle at the front of the car. 'I don't trust those things. Give me a horse and cart any day.'

'Horses can be temperamental too,' Aden reminded him. 'We've had our share of trouble with them in the past. Anyway, Rebecca will be driving this thing most of the time; I bought it for her sake.'

Sorrel stood by her father's side as the car drew away, then he went back to the cowsheds to finish laying fresh straw. The cows were still out in the pasture but Bob would be fetching them in an hour or so for the milking. Sighing, Sorrel turned reluctantly towards the house; her mother was baking and had asked her to finish rinsing some towels she'd left soaking in the copper.

'So you're back at last,' May said as she went in. 'I thought you'd stand and talk all day.'

'Aden came to see Pa. He spoke to me. It would have seemed rude just to walk off.'

'What was he on about then?'

May was always eager for any gossip and Sorrel knew she would be interested in her news.

'At first he was telling us about Mrs Sawle's trip to Paris. She and Fanny went with a friend of hers – Lady Celia Roth, I think he said. You know Fanny was ill again last winter? Well, apparently, the doctor said she ought to go to a warmer climate for a while. They've had two weeks at Lady Roth's villa in the South of France as well as three days in Paris.'

'Well, I never! The things some folk do,' May said. 'Paris – and her so strong for her good works. You wouldn't credit it, would you?'

'What do you mean?'

'Rebecca's always been against strong drink. She started a temperance movement locally after she'd been to one of those suffragette meetings – but Paris! They drink nothing but wine there, so I've heard.'

'Oh, Ma!' Sorrel laughed and began to rinse out the towels in the deep stone sink. 'I don't suppose Mrs Sawle drank wine all the time – and I'm sure Fanny didn't.'

Sorrel's eyes were drawn to the scene outside her window. It was familiar and dear to her but now she wondered what it would be like to travel abroad. Very few people in the village had been further than March Town – or Cambridge, the big university city some twenty-odd miles distant – but Rebecca Sawle wasn't like everyone else. Her father had owned substantial property in Chatteris and when he'd died she had inherited everything. People said that was how Aden got his start – but he'd done well for himself these past years too. Besides the farm at Five Winds and several acres in the fen, he now owned a corn merchant's business in Chatteris and various houses and cottages.

'Rebecca mollycoddles that girl of hers,' May went on thoughtfully. 'No good will come of it – it never does. Fanny will rebel one of these days, you mark my words.'

'She looks so sad in church sometimes.' Sorrel hesitated, then made up her mind to ask something that had bothered her for a while. 'Why doesn't Mrs Sawle like me, Ma? What have I done to upset her?'

'How should I know? What a thing to ask!' May made a sound of exasperation in her throat. 'You're the one to know the answer to that.' She gave Sorrel a hard stare. 'What makes you think she doesn't like you anyway?'

'She always keeps me standing outside when I take anything over. Molly asks me in if she's alone and wanting a gossip, but Mrs Sawle looks at me as if I were something the cat had dragged in.'

'Is that all?' May pounded a lump of dough with her fist and sniffed. 'She probably disapproves of your friendship with Jay. She wouldn't think you were good enough for one of her sons. I get on with her all right these days but there was a time ... thinks highly of herself, does Rebecca ... though after what happened with her father ...' May caught herself up and shook her head. 'Still, least said about that the better.'

'What do you mean?' Sorrel stared at her in surprise. 'What about Mrs Sawle's father?'

'It's an old story. Forget I mentioned it. Your father wouldn't like me gossiping about any of that.'

There was no point in asking her to explain. Once May had made up her mind to say nothing, that was it. Sorrel finished rinsing the towels and took them out to the line, still puzzling over the mystery. What had happened to Rebecca Sawle's father? There was obviously some old scandal but it must have happened a long time ago because Sorrel had never heard any gossip.

The towels were flapping in the wind as she picked up her basket and went to look out over the gate. Across the fens the sky looked grey and leaden but it wasn't as cold as it had been a few days earlier and she felt that spring was truly on its way ... and she longed for it after the cold, drab days of winter. She was always happiest when the fresh green buds were just bursting and the bulbs had begun to thrust their heads through the dark earth, heralding the warmer days.

As she stood staring at nothing in particular she heard the sound of hooves and craned her neck to see who was coming up the road. Her heart quickened as she recognized the smart black trap and the high-stepping pony – such a beautiful, mettlesome animal as it picked up its front hooves, so pretty to watch – and its driver looked every inch the squire's son in his fancy clothes!

Sorrel's smile faded as he swept by without so much as a glance at her. The devil! Just who did he think he was? She scowled as she turned away. Jay Sawle had changed since he'd left school, gaining a reputation for being a terrible flirt. He was no doubt on his way to see one of his mother's posh friends – some of whom probably had pretty daughters – and had no time to stop for a chat with Sorrel.

They seldom met these days unless he came into the yard for a few minutes, and then there was always someone else around. Jay had adopted a lordly attitude towards her, as if he were a man and she still a schoolgirl. He seemed to prefer talking to the other men and they were usually sharing a joke – the kind that wasn't considered fit for a young girl's ears.

His behaviour hurt her and sometimes Sorrel wasn't sure that she liked him anymore. Especially when he went by in that smart rig of his without a glance or a smile for her.

She kicked moodily at a stone and remembered the days when he had often asked if he could walk her home from school. He had been glad enough of a smile from her then, but now ... it seemed he had forgotten her.

May gave her a sharp look as she went in. 'What's the matter with you? You look as if you've lost a shilling and found sixpence.'

'Jay Sawle has just gone by with his pony and trap. He was in such a hurry he didn't even wave.'

'So that's it!' May put a tray of strawberry jam tarts in the oven, then straightened up with an old-fashioned look

33

for her daughter. 'You're wasting your time mooning over him, girl. He's not for you. You're too young to think of going courting yet, but when you do you'll be better off with someone like Tom Robinson.'

'I don't like him. He used to pull my hair in school.'

'That was years ago. He was a bit of a lad then.' May pressed a hand to her aching back and groaned. 'Tom likes you. Not that I'm saying he's the only one. I dare say you'll have your share of callers in a year or so. You've turned out prettier than I thought.'

Sorrel's eyes stung with tears but she was too proud to shed them. If Jay Sawle was too fine to be her friend now, she didn't care. She didn't care about any man!

'I'm going to see Mabel,' she said. 'I'll take that new coat you've knitted for the baby, shall I?'

'Yes, if you like.' May smiled the way she did when she thought about the new baby soon to be born. 'Go and get yourself changed. These tarts will be ready by the time you come down. You can take some for Bob and Mabel if you like.'

Sorrel walked past the churchyard with its mouldering gravestones, a basket full of the tarts and freshly made biscuits on her arm. The storm clouds seemed to have rolled away and her mood was brightening with every step, because she enjoyed visiting Bob's wife. Her brother had been married for more than two years now and Mabel was at last expecting their first child.

'Hello, Sorrel – where you going then?'

Seeing the two girls coming towards her, Sorrel quickened her pace. Mary Gilbert and Anne Rush were a year or so older than her and she had never been friends with either of them.

'To my brother's,' she said. 'I can't stop, I'm in a hurry.'

'One day you'll meet yourself coming,' Mary Gilbert retorted. She laughed and the two of them put their heads together, giggling and pushing each other as they passed by. Sorrel heard them whisper something about her father working for him . . . so they must be talking about Aden Sawle.

34

'Oh, Mary,' Anne shrieked, her voice loud and gleeful, 'you are awful. I'd never have said it if I'd known she was there . . .'

Sorrel glanced back over her shoulder, frowning as she saw the way they were clutching at each other in their mirth. Were they laughing about her? She didn't care if they were. They were both spiteful cats and she had never liked them.

She was almost at the end of the lane when she heard the muffled sobs. Puzzled, she stopped and looked for the source of the sound, then saw a girl leaning against a tree by the edge of the churchyard. She was crying and looked desperately unhappy. Sorrel hesitated; it was ages since they'd said more than a few words after church but she couldn't just ignore the other girl's distress.

'Fanny?' she said. 'What's wrong? Is there something I can do for you? You're not ill, are you?'

Fanny Sawle was a pretty girl but thin and pale-faced, her soft brown hair hanging in limp ringlets on the velvet collar of her fitted coat. She was as always dressed too fine for the village and her hair was far too fussy, making her look rather like a dressmaker's waxen fashion doll.

She glanced up with a startled expression. At first there was a flicker of apprehension in her eyes but she relaxed as she realized who it was.

'Sorrel . . . I thought it was those girls again.' She wiped the tears from her cheek with the back of her gloved hand. 'No, I'm not ill. It – it was nothing really.'

'It can't have been nothing or you wouldn't be crying.' Sorrel glanced back again but the other girls had gone. 'Was it something that Mary Gilbert said? You don't want to take any notice of her or Anne Rush. They were always spiteful at school.'

Fanny took out a pretty lace handkerchief and blew her nose. 'It wasn't anything they said to me. They were talking and didn't see me. I had been taking flowers to . . .'

'Your sister's grave?'

Fanny nodded, giving Sorrel a watery smile. 'Mother usually brings flowers once a week but she asked me to do it today because she has a chill.'

'You weren't crying for your sister, were you?'

'Oh, no, she was stillborn. I never knew her.' Fanny twisted the hanky between her fingers. 'Those girls ... they were talking about my father ... laughing in a horrid sort of way. They said he used to have a mistress in Chatteris and that it was my mother's own fault for being cold and only interested in her charity work. They said she was a sour-faced bitch and it was no wonder ...' She choked to a halt, her eyes brimming with tears.

'Oh.' Sorrel stared at her uncertainly. Jay had once told her that he thought the gipsy Shima might be his half-brother and that Shima's mother had been a barmaid in Chatteris before she went off with the gipsies, which was all very shocking, of course, but so long ago that it couldn't matter anymore. However, Fanny obviously did not know anything about the old scandal – and Sorrel wasn't going to tell her. 'I shouldn't let them upset you. Your mother isn't a sour-faced bitch – even if she is a bit short with folk sometimes – and I wouldn't believe a thing those cats say anyway.'

'I suppose not.' Fanny lifted her soulful eyes to meet Sorrel's. 'It's just that ... well, sometimes I hear my parents arguing, and it made me wonder if that was the reason ... but they always make up their quarrels and I think they love each other really.'

'Well, there you are then.' Sorrel felt a twinge of sympathy for the other girl. She must be lonely stuck at home with her mother all the time. 'I should forget what they said ... they're probably jealous because you've been to Paris and they haven't.'

Fanny's face brightened at the memory. 'It was such fun, Sorrel. We went with Celia ... Lady Roth is Mother's closest friend. She asked me if I would like to spend the summer travelling with her but of course Mother won't hear of it. She expects me to go visiting with her and it's so boring ... all those charity meetings.' Fanny broke off, looking guilty. 'I shouldn't be saying all this but I never seem to have anyone to talk to – no one I feel comfortable with anyway.'

'Don't you have any friends?'

'No friends I can talk to like this,' Fanny replied with a

shy look. 'I always used to envy Jay when he said he'd been talking to you.'

Sorrel pulled a face as she remembered the way he had swept by earlier without a glance. 'He doesn't have much time to talk to me these days.'

'Nor to me,' Fanny agreed with a sigh. 'He's always out with a new girl. Mother doesn't approve, of course, but my father says he's just sowing his wild oats and will grow out of it.' She looked self-conscious, her cheeks going pink again. 'I don't suppose I ought to have said that either.'

'So long as your mother doesn't hear you, it's all right.' Sorrel hesitated then said, 'I'm going to visit Bob's wife. She's expecting their first child. You could come with me if you like? Mabel is nice. She worked in a dress shop before they were married and she makes lovely clothes – even better than my Aunt Ruth. Mabel will show you the christening robe she's sewing if you ask her.'

Fanny's eyes lit up. 'I love babies, don't you? Would she mind if I came with you?'

'No, I'm sure she wouldn't,' Sorrel said. 'Come on, we'll walk together and you can tell me about your trip to Paris . . .'

Chapter Five

'Oh, Sorrel – just a moment! If you don't mind, I'd like a word with you, please.'

She swung round in surprise as Aden called to her. It was a pleasant, sunny morning in April and she had been collecting eggs from the various nooks and crannies in which the hens found to lay them, which meant searching under the hedges as well as in the haystack.

'Did you want something, Mr Sawle? Pa was here a few moments ago. Shall I see if he's in the house for you?'

'It's you I wanted to speak to,' he said, giving her a friendly smile. 'Fanny has a birthday this Sunday and she would be pleased if you could have tea with her.'

'Have tea with Fanny?' She looked so startled that her reaction made Aden frown. 'Oh, yes . . . yes, that would be lovely. I should like that,' she said hurriedly, not wanting to offend him.

'Good.' His expression cleared. 'She'll expect you at about half-past three on Sunday then.'

Sid was ambling towards them across the yard so Sorrel mumbled her thanks and escaped. Her mother looked at her curiously as she went into the kitchen.

'Aden was asking after you just now. What did he want then?'

Sorrel took the eggs to the sink to wash them. 'Fanny's birthday is on Sunday and I've been asked to tea.'

'To tea with Fanny Sawle? Whatever next!'

May looked more surprised than Sorrel felt. Despite her father's long friendship with Aden none of them had ever been asked to tea at Five Winds – though Aden gave a lavish harvest supper for all his people at the church hall each year.

'I suppose it's because I took her to tea at Mabel's two weeks ago,' Sorrel said, and her mother nodded agreement. 'She seems lonely. I don't think she has many friends of her own.'

'Rebecca is always having parties over there since Aden built the extra rooms on that cottage. Fanny must meet lots of young people.'

Sorrel remembered the look in Fanny's eyes when they'd met in the lane behind the church. 'Perhaps she doesn't like her mother's friends – or not all of them anyway.'

'No, perhaps not.' May was thoughtful. 'What will you wear on Sunday?'

'My blue dress – the one we made at Christmas.'

It was a simple style with a fitted bodice and leg-of-mutton sleeves but they had sewn pearl buttons down the front and added a pretty lace collar.

'Yes, that looks nice on you,' May agreed. 'Besides, we haven't time to make a new one. If she had said something earlier we might have bought some more material. We could have asked Ruth to get a new pattern in Cambridge.'

May's sister Ruth lived in Cambridge with her husband and six children. She had done well for herself when she left the village years before to work in a fashionable hat shop, eventually marrying the owner's nephew – who was a wealthy man in his own right. With such a large family she seldom had time to visit these days but still wrote to her sister and to Sorrel – and sent generous presents every now and then. It was she who had first taught Sorrel to make her own dresses and Sorrel looked a little like her at times.

'It doesn't matter,' said the girl, putting the eggs in a blue and white bowl and setting it on the dresser. 'I like my blue dress.'

'It will have to do. You can borrow my white bolero; it's about your size and I've hardly worn it – and there's a new lace handkerchief in my dressing-table drawer. You can wrap that in some tissue and take it as a present for Fanny.'

'Thank you.' Sorrel smiled at her mother. 'Don't worry,

Ma. I'm only having tea with her. It isn't one of Mrs Sawle's big parties. I shouldn't think anyone else will be there.'

Sorrel wasn't sure that she wanted to go at all but she had given her word to Fanny's father and couldn't change her mind now.

'You're to go through to the big parlour.' Molly frowned as she invited Sorrel in. She was wearing a smart black dress, starched white apron and cap, as if dressed up for the occasion. 'I'll show you the way.'

'It's all right, Molly. I'll do it.'

A young man of about twenty had come into the kitchen as she spoke. He was of a similar height to Jay with the same soft brown hair and grey eyes, but there the resemblance ended. Richie's chin had a hard jut to it and his mouth seemed to curl into a sneer as he smiled – a smile that did not reach his eyes.

Sorrel sensed a hardness in him, something hidden, as if he were constantly on his guard, hiding his true feelings, and it made her uncomfortable.

'You're Sorrel Harris, I suppose,' he said as she followed him into the first parlour, which was quite small and cosy with furniture that looked well used. It was part of the original cottage and led to a hall and a much larger room that had been built on later. 'Fanny is expecting you. You'd better come through.'

'Are you home for the holidays?' Sorrel felt a fluttering in her stomach. 'You've been to college, haven't you?'

'I've finished with all that,' he replied, his gaze flickering towards her with little interest. 'I'm going into business with my father.'

There was no time for Sorrel to inquire further for they had reached the parlour. It was a large, square room with a thick red carpet, that was soft to walk on, and a plush velvet suite of a rather hard-looking sofa and four equally hard armchairs. Various tables and cabinets stood about the room and were crowded with knick-knacks – little silver boxes, bits of china and photograph frames – and there was a piano in the corner. Sorrel was surprised to see a fire burning in the grate because it was quite warm outside.

40

Fanny jumped to her feet as Sorrel entered, smiling as she came to greet her, hands outstretched. She was wearing a very pretty pale blue dress of some silky material and had a string of large, creamy pearls about her throat. Sorrel thought they must have been a birthday present because she had never seen her wearing the necklace in church.

'I'm so glad you've come,' Fanny said. 'Let me introduce you to Sally – she's a dear friend of Richie's, and all of us.'

Sorrel had already noticed the girl standing by the window which looked out over the back garden. She'd had her back towards them but as Fanny spoke she turned and Sorrel saw that she was attractive, with a creamy complexion and masses of red-gold hair that curled naturally about her face and fell on her shoulders in a tumble of shining tresses. Her smile was warm and friendly as she came forward.

'I'm Sally Baxter,' she said, holding out her hand. 'Richie asked me to tea. I think I may be intruding and . . .'

'Of course you're not,' he said before she could finish. 'You know we all love having you here.'

Something in his tone told Sorrel that he considered *her* the intruder. She felt uncomfortable and was suddenly aware that her home-made dress looked cheap and shapeless compared with the elegant tea-gowns both Sally and Fanny were wearing. She had seen nothing like them, except on the pages of the fashion magazines her aunt sometimes sent her, and knew they must have been very costly.

'Come and sit down,' Fanny said. 'I thought we could talk for a while before we have tea.'

'I'll come back later,' Richie said, glancing at Sally with raised brows. 'You don't need me here.'

It was better when he had gone. Sorrel gave Fanny her present and she exclaimed over it in delight, saying it was one of the prettiest she had. Sorrel realized she must have a drawer full of such trifles and almost wished she hadn't brought it.

Fanny tucked the hanky into the sash at her waist. 'How is Mabel?' she asked, then turned to Sally. 'Sorrel's sister-in-law is expecting her first baby soon, isn't that exciting?'

Sally agreed that it was and went on to tell them that her cousin had just given birth to a darling little girl. She

41

described the child in detail, waxing lyrical over its tiny toes and fingernails. By the time the three girls had finished discussing babies the ice had been broken and Sorrel was feeling more relaxed.

Fanny rang the bell for tea and Molly struggled in with a three-tier wooden trolley laden down with a heavy silver service, delicate porcelain cups and masses of delicious-looking food.

'Would you pour for us, Sally?' Fanny asked. 'You do it so beautifully and I usually spill something.'

'I'm sure you don't,' Sally disclaimed, smiling. 'But I'll do it for you with pleasure.'

Fanny offered Sorrel a plate of tiny salmon sandwiches. They were so small that she hardly tasted them but she daren't take more than two in case it looked rude. They had graduated to the cakes when Jay and Richie walked in together. Sorrel thought how smart Jay looked in his formal grey suit, starched white collar and black silk cravat. Her heart raced wildly and she dropped her gaze, hoping no one would notice her flushed cheeks.

'I'm starving,' he said, and bent to kiss his sister's cheek. 'Happy birthday again, Fanny dearest. Save a piece of Molly's ginger sponge for me, won't you?' He straightened up, his gaze taking in her guests. 'It's nice to see you, Sally – and you, Sorrel.'

Sorrel mumbled her thanks and blushed even harder as he smiled at her.

'Fanny tells me she's been trying to persuade you to go up to London with her and your mother next week, Jay.' Sally spoke to him with the ease of friendship. 'Surely you will go?'

'Not me. I don't like London – besides, we're too busy for me to take time off just now. You and Richie should both go. Fanny would have far more fun with you there, Sally – and Richie could escort you to all the shops and museums you could possibly want to visit.'

'What a good idea!' Fanny cried, eyes lighting up. 'Please say you will, Sally?'

'I shall have to ask my mother but it would be very pleasant.' Sally looked pleased. She lifted the lid of the hot water jug and peered inside. 'Oh, we need some more hot water.'

'I'll fetch it,' Sorrel offered, springing up to take the silver pot from its stand.

Fanny's hand had been reaching for the bell. She hesitated and Sorrel was embarrassed as she realized she had been going to summon Molly.

'Yes, do,' she said, nodding to Sorrel. 'You're so thoughtful. Poor Molly always has so much to do. It's not fair to trouble her again.'

Sorrel's cheeks were burning as she left the parlour. She had acted instinctively but now she felt foolish. She ought to have realized that Fanny would send for Molly to replenish the water.

Molly filled the pretty jug from the huge copper kettle boiling on the range without a word. Sorrel carried it carefully back through the small sitting room and the hall, then something made her pause outside the door of the parlour.

'Why on earth you invited her, I don't know.' Richie's mocking voice carried to her through the partially open door. 'Honestly, Fanny! You know Mother doesn't approve. She's not our sort. You only have to look at that dress. Where on earth did she get it?'

'Richie, that's unkind,' Sally chided him. 'I expect she made the dress herself. I thought it was quite pretty. Besides, she seems a nice enough girl – and Fanny likes her.'

'Yes, I do,' Fanny said. 'So please don't say anymore.'

Sorrel walked in to a strained silence, set the jug on the stand and looked at Fanny awkwardly.

'It was nice of you to ask me to tea,' she said stiffly, 'but I think I ought to be going now.'

'Do you have to?' Fanny cried, and threw an angry glance at her elder brother. 'Won't you please stay a little longer?'

'I've got to help with the milking,' Sorrel lied. She needn't have gone because Bob was doing her chores for once but she couldn't stay there another moment, knowing they had been talking about her behind her back . . . laughing at her: 'I must go.'

'Perhaps you can come again another day?' Fanny said,

getting up to kiss her cheek. 'I'd like us to be friends, Sorrel. Really I would.'

'Perhaps.' She was longing to escape. 'Goodbye.'

'Wait for me,' Jay put in swiftly. 'I'll walk you home, Sorrel.'

'There's no need.' She lifted her chin proudly.

'I feel like a breath of fresh air.' He glared at his brother. 'Besides, I want a word with Sid.'

She turned and walked ahead of him in silence, her hands clenched in tight balls at her sides as they went out of the house and across the road. Clouds had obscured the sun and a chill wind had blown up but she was too angry to feel the cold.

Jay waited until they had reached her gate then caught her arm, swinging her round to face him. 'You heard Richie, of course.'

'I shouldn't have come. Fanny shouldn't have invited me. Your mother doesn't like me – that's why she didn't join us for tea.' She stared at him angrily, daring him to deny it.

'Mother was lying down with a headache. She often has them – and Dad is busy as usual. I can't make excuses for my brother; he is a snob and nothing I can say will change that. I'm sorry, but that's the way Richie is. Fanny really likes you. She was looking forward to your visit and will be upset now that you've walked off in a huff.'

'Oh, Jay.' She stared at him, her hurt pride forgotten. 'I didn't mean to upset Fanny – but your brother was right in a way. Your father is the biggest farmer in the district and my father works for him.'

'Now *you* sound like a snob,' he said with a frown. 'It's what Fanny thinks that matters. She doesn't have many real friends. You won't turn against her because of this – will you?'

Sorrel glanced towards the cottage that was her home. Until that afternoon she hadn't realized how different her life was from Fanny's. Aden's manner was always so casual and friendly; he never made any of them feel that he was the boss or in any way superior, and she had fallen into the habit of thinking Jay her friend at school – but really there was a wide gap between the two families.

44

'No . . .' she said, still hesitating slightly. 'I'll be friends with Fanny – if that's what she wants. I like her.'

'I'm glad she has you, Sorrel. She told me you took her to visit Bob's wife.' His grin flashed out, making her heart thump. 'She's knitting something for the baby but I wasn't supposed to tell you.'

'I shan't breathe a word,' Sorrel promised, tipping her head to one side as she gazed up at him. This was the old Jay – the Jay she had always admired.

'You were always good at keeping a secret,' he said. 'I often wonder what really happened between Shima and Lenny Browne that day, don't you?'

Sorrel thought about the tall gipsy, remembering the way his dark eyes had dwelt on her face so intently and the way he had spoken her name, giving it a kind of magic so that it sounded like the wind whispering through the trees on a soft summer eve.

'Shima must have scared the life out of Lenny. He has never come home since.'

'Shima hasn't been back either.' Jay sighed. 'It may be years before he comes – if he ever does.'

Jay obviously wanted to see his friend again but Sorrel wasn't sure it was such a good idea.

'If his being here causes distress to your mother, perhaps it's best if he never returns.'

'I know it hurt her once but she seemed all right when he stayed with us once for a few days.' Jay looked thoughtful. 'That was some years ago, when we were all children and there was a fire in the yard . . . do you remember?'

'I vaguely remember the fire,' Sorrel said. 'Was Shima here then? I didn't know that.'

'It was only for a few days – before he joined the circus. If only that rotten Lenny hadn't attacked Tarina, he might have stopped here longer last time.'

'Well maybe he'll come back one day,' she said, because he obviously wanted it so much. 'I've often wondered if Tarina ever found the four-leaved clover she was searching for that day.'

'Who knows?' Jay shrugged. 'Well, I'll be seeing you. You won't forget about being Fanny's friend?'

45

'Don't worry, Jay. She can come to tea at our house soon.'
She stood and watched as he went off in search of her father. What about her? she wanted to ask. He was concerned for his sister's feelings – but what about hers? Did he care how she felt?

'Oh, Jay,' she whispered softly. 'Tell me, are you still my friend?'

'You really are a rotten bastard,' Jay said, following Richie into the small parlour after he had come back from seeing Sally into her father's automobile. 'No matter what you happen to think about Sorrel, you had no need to say it then, knowing she might hear you.'

'Fancy her, do you?' Richie turned with a sneer on his lips. 'I suppose she's one of your little flirts . . .' He swore and staggered back as Jay's fist landed in his face. 'Damn you!'

'Take that back!' Jay demanded furiously. 'You've no right to say such a thing about . . .' He ducked as Richie swung at him, his fists coming up to defend himself. 'All right then, you've been asking for this for ages—'

'Stop it at once!' Rebecca's commanding tones made them both freeze. 'I've told you before, I will not have fighting in this house. For goodness' sake! Richie has only been in the house a few days and you're quarrelling already. What is the meaning of all this?'

Her sons turned to look at her defensively. Somehow their mother could still make them feel like schoolboys instead of young men.

'It was over Sorrel,' Fanny said, coming in behind her. 'Richie insulted her and she went home early.'

'Sorrel Harris?' Rebecca looked annoyed. 'I might have known it would be her.'

'She's my friend,' Fanny said quickly. 'It wasn't her fault – and I like her.'

'Richie hurt her feelings,' Jay said. 'I think he should apologize.'

'You certainly should not have insulted a guest,' Rebecca said reprovingly. 'Perhaps you should apologize, Richie.'

'You always take Jay's side,' he said, eyes glinting angrily.

'I have no intention of apologizing for saying what was only the truth.' He swept past his mother and up the stairs, leaving her staring after him in dismay.

'He's such a snob,' Jay said disgustedly. 'All right, Mother, I know I shouldn't have hit him – and I shall apologize for that – but I won't have him upsetting either Sorrel or Fanny.'

Rebecca's expression softened as she looked at her favourite son. 'Please don't fight with your brother,' she said. 'You know it worries me – and it makes things uncomfortable. Richie is . . . well, you know how touchy he can be.'

'I'm sorry.' Jay kissed her cheek. 'Is your headache better now?'

'Yes, much better,' she said, and turned to Fanny with a smile. 'Now, darling, what were you saying about Sally coming to London with us?'

Jay went through to the kitchen and then out into the yard. He was still angry with Richie. If his mother hadn't come in when she did, he would have given him the hiding he deserved. He and Richie had never really got on, especially since Richie went away to that fancy boarding school. Most brothers fought when they were young but grew out of it. In their case the animosity seemed to have grown stronger. Jay sometimes thought his elder brother really hated him, though he wasn't sure why. What he was sure of was that one day there would have to be a reckoning between them.

Chapter Six

Tarina hid behind a tree as the gipsy walked past her, hoping and praying that he had not seen her. He was tall, broad-shouldered and strong; his skin was dark and weather-roughened, his features as harsh as the nature of the man himself, his eyes as black as the devil's own. A man to be wary of, as she knew only too well.

She was afraid of Black Jake, afraid of the way he looked at her with his hot, lustful eyes – and of his evil temper. She sensed that he was determined to have her one day, and it was only her quick wits that had saved her from him thus far – her wits and (she suspected) the fact that he was a little wary of Sadie.

Sadie had once cursed a man and that man had died an agonizing death, which made the other gipsies respect her. Tarina was one of the few of her people who did not truly believe in her mother's powers but she wasn't above using other people's superstitions for her own purposes, especially against Jake. She hated him as much as she feared him and would rather die than submit to his lust – even the smell of his body was enough to turn her stomach, and the thought of being his woman made her want to vomit.

She ought never to have left the circus, of course, but done so in a fit of pique after Shima had refused to kill the gorgio for her.

'I've thrown a scare into him,' Shima had told her when he came back to his van that day. 'His face will bear the scar of my knife to remind him of what he did for the rest of his life – but I could not kill him for you, Tarina. He was no more than a lad.'

'So you care nothing for me!' she had cried, hiding her tears behind anger. 'I shall not stay with you. I shall go back where I belong.'

'Yes, perhaps it is best that you do,' he agreed, looking at her sadly. 'We are not blood kin and it is not fitting that you should live with me. You should go back and take one of your own people for your husband, Tarina.'

She had run from him then before the shaming tears could fall. She loved him – loved him so much that she would gladly have given her life for his – but he did not want her and her pride would not let her stay with him now that he had made his feelings so plain. She had left the circus a few days later, asking for news of her people from other travelling folk, camping with them for a while until she found her own tribe camped beside a river in a quiet Cornish village.

Sadie had stared at her from sullen eyes when she saw her that first day. 'So you've come back,' she muttered. 'Has he thrown you out then?'

'I came because I wanted to,' Tarina said, lifting her head proudly. 'I am a woman, not a child. You cannot tell me what I should do . . .' She recoiled as her mother slapped her face, refusing to cry or show any fear. 'Hit me then. Why should I care? You've never done anything else.'

'Slut!' Sadie raised her fist to hit her again but stopped as Leyan came into the van. 'This slut has come slinking back now that the bastard she has been living with has done with her – and I've a mind to send her off again.'

'Don't hit her,' Leyan said in a tone of command. He had grown since Tarina ran away and was almost a man. He would never be as tall and strong as Shima but she could see that Sadie was influenced by him. He had always been her favourite and, now that she was growing older, she had begun to rely on him more. 'Welcome home, Tarina. You can stay if you wish.'

Tarina felt the tears gather in her eyes. She had taken little notice of Leyan in the past but now she felt the warmth of kinship; they had the same mother and both their fathers were dead – neither of them had known much in the way of affection.

'Thank you,' she whispered. 'I'll work for my keep.'

'We all do that,' Sadie said bitterly. 'You were a fool to come back, girl. Black Jake is a devil. You would have done better to stay where you were.'

Now, Tarina came out from behind the tree and breathed a sigh of relief. Black Jake had passed by without seeing her. She was safe for the moment. But how she wished that she had never returned to the camp!

If only she had stayed with Shima. The happiest days of her life had been when she was with the circus, but she had been too foolish to realize how lucky she was then.

She shivered in the cool wind as she remembered her mother's warning on the morning of her return. Black Jake was truly a devil and she had lived every day since then in fear of him, as did many others of her tribe. He was ruthless and cruel, especially when he was drunk – and one day she would not be able to escape him. She knew that he would have her one day – whether she wanted it or not – and then . . . she would kill him.

Chapter Seven

It was autumn but still so warm that folk were talking of an Indian summer. Aden's people were threshing in the top yard and Sorrel had been sent with a basket of freshly baked bread, cheese, onion and a jug of beer for her father's docky. For a moment she paused at the gate to watch the frenzied activity.

A noisy, clanking monster, the traction engine ran the belt which kept the huge threshing drum churning. Several feet long and a marvel of pulleys and wheels, the drum required a small army of men to service its rapacious appetite. The heavy sheaves of wheat were passed from the stack to the man feeding the drum at the top; he cut the string and fed the loose stalks in a continuous motion. Below him, the wheat was separated into kernels, chaff and straw, an operation that kept at least three men at full stretch, filling sacks with corn or chaff and stacking the loose straw. The chaff and straw were the dirtiest jobs, often given to the younger lads, while the bagging took strength. Sacks of wheat could weigh as much as sixteen or eighteen stone and had to be carried on the men's backs to a nearby barn for storage.

As Sorrel drew nearer she could hear the men talking and laughing, and realized that a challenge was going on. It was often the way when they all got together at threshing time. They enjoyed pulling one another's legs, and the older ones would rib the young lads mercilessly, making their job as difficult as possible. A great joke was to put a cheeky lad in the straw jack and try to break his spirit by pressure of work, for if the youth took a breather the straw would be

51

sucked back and the machinery could be clogged up, bringing down the wrath of the master on the luckless lad's head. The real test of a man, though, was how much he could carry on his back.

Sorrel heard loud cheering and paused to watch what was going on. Jay was at the head of the drum. She saw him tough a heavy sack on his knees, weigh and tie it, then hoist it up on the sack winder so that he could rest it on his back. When it was secure he set off for the barn. The men began counting. 'One, two, three, four . . . five . . .'

Jay was passed on his way into the barn by an older man coming out, who reached the drum in time to tie, weigh and shoulder the next sack. 'Ten, eleven, twelve . . .' The counting went on as Jay came running from the barn and Sorrel suddenly understood. It was a contest between them to see who could carry the most sacks in a certain time. 'Fifteen, sixteen . . .' The excitement mounted as Jay filled his sack and started out again, this time disappearing into the barn before his rival came out. 'Forty-three, forty-four . . .'

'Who's winning?' Sorrel asked her father as he came out of the chaff shed with an empty sack.

'I'm not sure. It depends how much was in each sack. They're equal in numbers so it's down to weight.'

There was a burst of cheering behind them and as she turned Sorrel saw Jay being congratulated, the men patting him on the back and laughing in their excitement. The engine was being allowed to slow down as they all took a break for something to eat and drink.

'That last sack was a full eighteen stone,' she heard someone say. 'That will put some lead in your pencil, Jay – and from what I hear, you've need of it.'

There was a burst of coarse laughter and Sid frowned. 'Now then,' he warned. 'Watch your language, lads. We've got company.' He took the basket from Sorrel and glanced inside. 'This looks good, lass. You get back to your mother now.'

The men were dispersing to sit wherever they could find a pile of dry sacks or a straw bale, glad of a few minutes to rest. Sorrel was about to leave when someone called her name and she turned back, her heart racing as Jay came towards her. How handsome he looked – and how sure of himself! He seemed in especially good humour and she guessed he was proud of having won the contest.

'You won then?' she said, tipping her head to one side as she gazed up at him. 'I saw you carry that last sack. It must have been very heavy.'

'It felt like a ton,' he replied with a grin. 'So what are you doing here then? Come to give us a hand?'

Sometimes girls were employed in the chaff shed to tread it down and make room for more but it wasn't a job Sorrel relished. She liked caring for the stock and helping with the haymaking but treading the chaff was dirty, tiring work.

'No, thanks. I've got better things to do at home.'

Jay nodded, his eyes moving over her appreciatively. She was sixteen now and almost grown up.

'There's a dance on at the school on Saturday,' he said. 'I thought you might like to go?'

Sorrel held her breath, not quite sure what he meant. She was well aware that there was a dance being held in the village school; it was the big event of the year and every girl in Mepal hoped to be asked when they were old enough to start courting.

'Are you asking me to go with you?'

'Sounds like it.' Jay laughed. 'Well then, Sorrel – is it yes or no?'

'I'll think about it,' she said, struggling to hide her delight. 'I'll tell you later.'

Jay looked surprised. He had obviously expected her to jump at the chance. Any other girl in the village would have said yes at once but she wasn't going to fall into his arms just like that, especially after the way he'd behaved this past year or so – ignoring her as if she were a child! Well, she wasn't and the sooner he realized that the better.

'Don't take too long to make up your mind.'

'I'll tell you in the morning,' she said. 'After I've done the milk round.'

She smiled at him and turned on her heel with a little toss of her head, then ran out of the yard, leaving him to stare after her in bewilderment.

She was singing to herself as she walked home. It wouldn't

do Jay Sawle any harm to be kept waiting for his answer. To her way of thinking he had had rather too much of his own way. He only had to snap his fingers to have half the girls in the village running after him – Sutton and Chatteris too for all she knew. Jay had quite a reputation and was often known to disappear into the barn with a girl when the other men were working in the fields.

If Jay imagined Sorrel was like all the others, he was in for a surprise!

Sorrel went to Jay's house the next morning. He hadn't been into the yard and she wanted to give him her answer. It had always been yes, of course, and now she was anxious in case he'd changed his mind.

She knocked at the kitchen door; there was no answer so she waited for a few minutes before knocking again. Several seconds elapsed and then the door was opened by Molly.

Her mouth thinned as she saw Sorrel. 'Yes – did you want something? Only I'm busy . . .'

'I'd like to speak to Jay, please.'

'Master Jay is with his mother.' Molly emphasized the word 'master', her frown deepening to disapproval. 'Is it important? Only they have guests and I don't want to disturb them for nothing.'

'I would like to speak to him, please,' Sorrel persisted, her head going up. 'If it's not too much trouble?'

'Wait there then,' Molly said. 'I'll tell him you're here.'

She closed the door in Sorrel's face with a snap, leaving her standing on the doorstep. She might at least have asked her to wait in the kitchen! It wasn't as if she were a peddlar or a tramp. She was Fanny's friend – at least, they still met sometimes, though it was usually at Sorrel's home or Mabel's – she hadn't been invited to tea at Five Winds since Fanny's birthday, but this rudeness was unexpected.

Sorrel tapped her foot, her cheeks flushed with anger. So she wasn't good enough to be invited into the Sawles' house when they had guests! It was a while before Molly returned and Sorrel shivered in the cool breeze that had sprung up, heralding a change in the weather.

'Master Jay is busy at the moment,' Molly said when she returned. 'Would you please leave a message?'

Sorrel stared at her indignantly. If that was the way things stood, she would leave a message all right!

'Please tell Jay that Sorrel said no,' she said, and turned away.

'To what?' Molly asked, puzzled. 'Is that all the message?'

'He'll understand,' she replied, and walked off with her nose in the air. If Jay couldn't trouble himself to come to the door and speak to her, she certainly wasn't going to the dance with him!

'Have you seen that girl staying with the Sawles?' Mabel asked when Sorrel called to see her that afternoon. She was in her neat little parlour bending over her son's cot, and Sorrel went to stand beside her. Timmy was nine weeks old and growing more beautiful every day. 'I saw her when I took Timmy for his walk earlier. She was getting into a car with Richie.'

'No, I haven't seen her.' Sorrel flicked her heavy plait over her shoulder. 'I knew they had guests though. What's she like?'

'Very pretty, I'd say. She's one of those small, fragile girls with silver-blonde hair and pale blue eyes. She was wearing a lovely costume with a black velvet collar. It looked expensive, but then it would be, I suppose. They say she's Lady Roth's cousin and accompanies her all over the place since her father died.'

News travelled quickly in the village and no doubt everyone would soon know all about the Sawles' guests.

'Oh.' Sorrel turned away to hide her feelings. 'Can I pick Timmy up?'

'I shouldn't just yet,' Mabel said. 'I've only just finished feeding him and I think he'll sleep if we leave him to settle. Why don't you put the kettle on and we'll have a nice cup of tea?'

Sorrel went into the kitchen; it was quite large, spotlessly clean and comfortable. Mabel was a good housewife and proud of her home.

Sorrel filled the kettle and put it on the range, her

thoughts racing around like a puppy after its own tail. So that was why she hadn't heard from Jay! She had expected him to come round and ask why she wouldn't go to the dance with him but now she knew why he hadn't bothered to speak to her at the door. Once he'd seen Lady Roth's pretty companion he had probably wished he hadn't asked Sorrel in the first place.

She was angry and hurt but she wasn't going to show it. Bother Jay Sawle! She didn't want to go to the dance with him anyway.

The hall had been decorated with greenery and flowers to give it a festive air. Sorrel glanced round as they went in, feeling a surge of excitement even though she'd been in two minds about coming to the dance. This was Mabel's first real outing since having the baby. Bob had bought the tickets as a surprise for her and May was looking after Timmy. It had been Mabel's idea that Bob should get a third ticket for his sister.

'You're old enough to come now,' she'd told Sorrel with a smile. 'Don't think you'll be stuck with me and Bob all night; there's sure to be plenty of young men looking for someone to dance with.'

'But I haven't anything to wear.'

'We can soon fix that.' Mabel's eyes sparked with mischief. 'I've got two or three dresses upstairs that should fit you – pretty things I had when I was courting. I've put on a bit of weight since I married so you can take your pick.'

Sorrel chose an emerald green dress that fitted in close to her slender waist and swirled out in a flurry of frills just above her ankles. It was made of a silky material and had little puff sleeves and a dipped neckline. Her mother gave her an old-fashioned look when she came downstairs in it.

'It makes you look at least eighteen,' she said, but she didn't make Sorrel change out of it, merely instructing her to behave herself and do what Mabel told her.

'Of course I will, Ma,' Sorrel said, and kissed her. 'What do you think I am?'

'A sight too sure of yourself sometimes,' she replied, but gave her a dab of lavender water on her hanky.

Sorrel was feeling anything but sure of herself as she looked round the hall that evening. At the far end there was a long table laden down with sandwiches, sausage rolls and sponges baked by the Women's Institute members; the plates were flanked by jugs of lemon barley, fruit punch, cider and beer for the men.

'What do you want to drink?' Bob asked. 'Cider or lemon for you, Mabel?'

'Not cider, it might be bad for the baby,' she said. 'We'll both have lemon, won't we, Sorrel?'

'Nothing for me just yet,' she said, then turned in surprise as someone touched her arm.

'Will you dance with me?' Tom Robinson asked. 'Please, Sorrel.'

She hesitated, remembering that he had been one of her worst tormentors at school. He'd grown up now, though, just as her mother had said, and she realized he was quite attractive with dark, wavy hair and blue eyes – and his smile was rather nice.

'All right,' she agreed. 'If it's an easy one. I can't do some of those fancy steps.'

'I'll teach you,' he promised eagerly. 'My mother taught me the barn dance – and that's next.'

'Oh, I can do that,' Sorrel said with relief. 'It's just a few of the fancier ones I'm not sure of.' She gave Tom her hand as the music started again. 'Come on, it's easy.'

He took her hand, smiling at her in a way that told her that her mother had been right when she said Tom liked her. It gave Sorrel a little surge of pleasure and made her feel that she really was grown up.

As Tom led her on to the floor she caught sight of Jay from the corner of her eye. He was partnering Sally Baxter for the dance and Sorrel wasn't sure whether to be pleased or annoyed; it meant that she was sure to get a dance with him, because the barn dance was a progressive. At least it would give her a chance to show him what she thought of men who kept their friends standing on the doorstep!

As she went into Tom's arms she saw Richie talking to a very pretty girl; she was wearing a dress that outshone every other girl's in the room – including Sally Baxter's. Sorrel realized at once that she must be Lady Roth's cousin. Everyone knew her name now – Adele Carter – and she must have come to the dance as Jay's partner since Richie would have brought Sally.

Tears stung Sorrel's eyes but she blinked hard and stuck her head a little higher in the air. She couldn't care less who Jay chose as his partner.

She smiled brilliantly at Tom, who flushed a deep red and squeezed her hand before letting her pass on to her next partner. Jay was just three down the line and she took a deep breath, steadying herself for the encounter. He looked so smart and more attractive than any man had a right to be, which made her cross.

'You came after all then,' he said as she took his hand. 'I thought you didn't want to?' He seemed a bit put out, as if she'd ruffled his pride, and that made her feel better.

'I came with my family,' she said frostily. 'I know where I'm wanted – and where I'm not.'

'And what does that mean?' He flashed a look of annoyance at her.

'No one keeps me standing on the doorstep, Jay Sawle.'

'I've no idea what you're talking about.'

'And my name is Lillie Langtry!' she retorted with a toss of her head. Don't make out you don't remember. You couldn't be bothered to speak to me when I asked for you – that's the last time I come calling on you, Jay Sawle!'

He scowled ferociously but was prevented from continuing the argument as she moved on to her next partner. She turned her head away and smiled up at Joel Green, a man old enough to be her father. Let Jay make what he liked of that!

Tom reclaimed her as soon as the dance was over. He stood talking to Bob and Mabel until the music started, then asked her to be his partner for the waltz.

'She's going to dance this one with me,' Bob said, and grabbed her hand. 'You can dance with my wife this time.'

Bob smiled down at her as they joined the other dancers. 'Are you enjoying yourself, Sorrel?'

'Yes, thank you. It's fun,' she said, eyes shining like emeralds. 'Thanks for bringing me, Bob.'

'Mabel said it was time you had some fun – just don't let Tom monopolize you all the time.'

'No, of course not. Don't worry, I can keep him in his place.'

Bob chuckled. 'Yes, I reckon you can at that.'

After their dance ended she was surrounded by lads she had known all her life, all of them clamouring to be her partner for the next dance. She chose one and smiled at the others, promising them dances later in the evening. They kept her to her word and her popularity showed no sign of waning. So it was not until over an hour later, when the band went off for some refreshment, that she had a chance to pop outside for a breath of fresh air.

She was trying to escape from Tom for a little while; he had developed an air of possessiveness towards her and was getting a little aggressive in his efforts to keep his rivals at bay. He had gone to the men's cloakroom when she slipped out of a side door into the semi-darkness.

It was much cooler outside and after a few minutes she was ready to go back in. She was about to do so when she heard a girl's cry and then a sharp slapping sound.

Turning towards the source of the sound she saw a man and a girl standing in the shadows and felt shocked as she recognized them: it was Richie and Adele Carter!

'You shouldn't have kissed me.' Adele's voice was shrill and accusing. 'Gentlemen do not take advantage.'

'It was what you wanted,' Ritchie replied. 'You've been giving me a clear invitation all evening.'

'How dare you?' she cried. 'You suggested we should come out for a breath of air.'

I believed it was what you wanted – forgive me if I was mistaken, my dear Adele. You should have used your charms on my brother if you want more than a flirtation. I intend to marry Sally. Her father's businesses fit in very well with my plans. So while I am more than willing to indulge you in a little dalliance . . .'

'You are disgusting!'

She broke away from him and went rushing off into the darkness. Richie shrugged his shoulders then walked

59

towards where Sorrel was standing. He hesitated as he saw her, mouth drawing into an unpleasant sneer.

'I suppose you saw everything?'

'I wasn't spying on you. I just came out for some air.'

'Keep your mouth shut about this,' he said, giving her a threatening look. 'If Sally hears a word of this, I shall know who to blame.'

'Why should I tell her?'

'Just don't,' he muttered, and pushed past her into the hall.

Sorrel stood for a moment in the shelter of the porch. Something moved out in the shadows of the trees and she thought there was someone there but couldn't be sure.

'Sorrel . . .' Tom's voice called to her from just inside the doorway. 'Are you out there?'

'I'm just coming,' she said, and went to him with a feeling of relief. 'I was a bit warm but I'm fine now.'

'They're starting another barn dance,' he said, and caught her hand. 'What's wrong? You're shaking. You must have turned cold out there.'

'Yes, perhaps I did.'

Something about Richie had disturbed her. It wasn't such a surprise that he should have taken another girl outside and tried to kiss her, even though he was practically engaged to Sally – no, it was the underlying menace she had sensed in him, something dark and strange, that gave her goose pimples all over. She didn't like Richie Sawle very much. No, she didn't like him at all!

After her dance with Tom he offered to fetch her a glass of lemon and she stood watching the dancers for a few moments. Jay was dancing with Adele. She was laughing up at him as if she hadn't a care in the world.

'You wouldn't think butter would melt in her mouth, would you?' Sorrel turned to see Mary Gilbert standing beside her, a smirk on her mouth. 'Only you and me know better, don't we?'

'It was you . . . in the shadows. I thought I saw someone.'

'I went out for a breath of air like you. I wonder what that stuck up Sally Baxter would think if she knew her fella was kissing another girl?'

'You won't tell her?' Sorrel cried. 'She's not really stuck up at all, Mary – in fact she's nice. It would only hurt her.'

'Friend of yours, is she?' Mary sneered. 'Always have thought yourself better than the rest of us, haven't you, Miss Harris? Don't worry, I shan't tell her – but I bet it's all over the village by the morning anyway. I wasn't the only one out there.'

She walked off as Tom brought Sorrel's drink back. He handed it to her with a shy look.

'I suppose you wouldn't come out with me one night next week, Sorrel?'

'Come where?' She was surprised at his suggestion. He came round to the yard to talk to her brothers sometimes, but she hadn't thought he was interested in her, despite her mother's hints. 'Ma wouldn't let me go to the pub. She's against strong drink – besides, I'm too young.'

'We could go for a walk tomorrow afternoon.' He looked at her hopefully but she shook her head.

'I'm sorry, Tom. Pa says I'm too young for courting.'

'Maybe next year then?'

'Maybe.' She smiled to soften his obvious disappointment.

'Come on, Sorrel,' Mabel said from behind her. 'It's time we were leaving.'

Bob had fetched their coats. He and Mabel walked Sorrel home.

'Did you enjoy yourself?' Mabel asked as they reached the cottage. 'You seemed to dance with most of the lads.'

'It was fun,' Sorrel said, and giggled. 'Tom asked me to walk out with him.'

'The cheeky devil!' said Mabel. 'He knows you're only sixteen. You want to watch out for that one, Sorrel.'

'It's all right, I told him no. Ma wouldn't let me go to the pub and Pa would have a fit if I went down the bank with a lad.'

'So I should think,' Mabel said, 'but you could ask him to tea at mine – if you're interested?'

'I'll think it over,' she said, and kissed her sister-in-law's cheek. 'Thanks for taking me tonight.'

Sorrel was thoughtful as she went in. It had been fun and

she had enjoyed herself – but she was disappointed that Jay hadn't asked her for a dance.

By the following Monday the story of Richie and Adele Carter was all over the village. Sorrel heard her brothers discussing it as they were mucking out the cowsheds. They seemed to think it a fine joke, especially since Adele had been Jay's partner for the evening.

'It isn't that funny,' she said crossly to Ted. 'I think Richie behaved badly.'

'That's hardly a surprise. Richie Sawle is a swine. He always has been and always will be.'

'What do you mean?'

Ted shrugged his shoulders. 'When he was at the village school he used to bully the younger lads and make them do things.'

'What kind of things? Nasty things?'

'You don't want to talk about that,' Bob warned. 'It was a long time ago and best forgotten.'

From the closed expressions on their faces Sorrel realized she wouldn't learn anymore about Richie from them.

'It still isn't very nice of you to laugh at Jay,' she persisted. 'I thought you liked him?'

'We do,' Bob replied with a grin, 'but it's funny just the same. He fancies himself as a ladies' man and this makes him look a bit of a fool.'

She turned away in annoyance. She had been angry with Jay for keeping her standing on the doorstep but now she wanted to defend him. She knew he would hate being laughed at by the other village lads and it surely wouldn't be long before he heard what they were saying . . .

Jay knew what everyone was saying and it made him furious. It didn't matter that he had only taken Adele to the dance to please his mother – and because Sorrel had turned him down; he had been made to look foolish and he was angry with Richie, whom he suspected of doing it deliberately.

It wasn't until that evening that he managed to get his brother alone in the yard. Richie had been smoking a cigar there and turned to look at him, a flicker of mockery in his eyes.

'Come to join me for a smoke, little brother?'

'No, thanks.' Jay heard the mocking note and scowled. 'I wanted a word – about the other night.'

'So you've heard?' Richie's mouth curled into a sneer. 'I suppose it was to be expected. She isn't worth arguing over, you know.

'You had no right to behave in such a disgusting manner,' Jay said. 'She's Celia's companion and a decent girl . . . surely you can find enough of the obliging sort? Or don't you know the difference?'

'Quite the Sir Galahad, aren't you?' Richie murmured. 'You've cast me as the villain. Well, if that's what you want to believe . . . though Adele isn't quite the innocent you seem to imagine.'

'You rotten coward!' Jay flung himself at his brother. 'You need a thrashing.'

'Hey!' Richie cried, ducking to avoid Jay's fist. 'Watch out!' He cursed as the second blow hit him and he felt his lip split. He reached for his handkerchief and pressed it to his mouth. 'You've made it bleed.'

'Haven't you got the guts to hit me back?' Jay asked scornfully.

'I don't see the point in fighting over a girl who isn't really interested in either of us.'

'What do you mean?'

'Adele is looking for a rich husband,' Richie said. 'Lady Roth has given her a taste for the good life but she can't be sure of inheriting the money so she wants a husband who can provide her with all the things she enjoys so much.'

Jay stared at him. Secretly, he was in agreement with much of what his brother was saying but he was still too angry with Richie to admit it.

'We'll both inherit a decent bit – why shouldn't she be interested in us?'

'Because neither of us is ready to marry yet,' Richie replied. 'She was just trying her wings. She'll probably marry a man old enough to be her father, with more money than hair.'

63

Jay stared at him in disgust. Even though he knew Richie was probably right, he hated his callous manner. He was such a superior devil!

'You're a bastard,' he said, and walked off.

It was just as well that Richie would be living in Chatteris with Sally's people soon, because the feud between them was becoming impossible to live with – and sooner or later it would lead to more than a few angry words or a clash of fists!

Chapter Eight

Sorrel didn't know just how angry Jay was until Mabel told her the latest gossip a couple of days afterwards.

'Jay punched his brother in the face and split his lip,' she said. 'When Mrs Sawle heard about it she was terribly angry with them both – and she threatened to cut off Richie's allowance if he didn't apologize to Adele.'

'And did he?'

'I don't know.' Mabel shrugged. 'I heard it from Molly's mother and she only knew what Molly had told her.'

It was a nine-day wonder in the village and then it was forgotten as life moved on and people began to talk about other things. The papers carried stories of trouble in the Balkans, the renewal of the triple alliance in Europe and the controversial report on the new divorce laws.

'Mother is in two minds about the idea of making divorce easier,' Fanny told Sorrel as they met for tea one Sunday afternoon a week or so before Christmas. 'You know she supports the suffragette movement, even though she doesn't approve of women chaining themselves to railings or smashing shop windows? She is all for women having some redress against brutal husbands but thinks divorce is a charter for licentious living.'

Rebecca Sawle was well known for her strong views and interest in helping unfortunate women. She had tried to set up a temperance movement in the village, but it wasn't as successful as she had hoped – the pub was the most popular meeting place for the men after a hard day's work – but her refuge for battered women had been a godsend to many of the women whose husbands drank too much on a Saturday night.

'Women ought to have rights,' Sorrel agreed, looking thoughtful. 'But I'm not sure I agree with divorce. Besides, I often think Ma is the boss in our house. We all do more or less what she says.'

'But your father is such a kind man,' Fanny said. 'I doubt if he ever gets drunk, does he?'

'I've never seen him,' Sorrel admitted. 'What are you doing for Christmas, Fanny?'

'Oh, I expect we shall have the usual parties,' she said, and sighed. Then her face brightened as she looked at Sorrel. 'I've been invited to Aunt Celia's for a couple of weeks in the New Year.' She paused expectantly. 'I was wondering if you could come with me?'

'Me – come to Lady Roth's house with you?' Sorrel was so surprised that her mouth fell open. 'You never mean it, Fanny?'

'Yes, I do,' she said, and laughed. 'Mother has lots of her meetings arranged for January. She's going to a big conference in London and can't come with me.' Fanny gave her a look of appeal. 'She wouldn't hear of my travelling alone but if we went together on the train . . .'

'I've never been on a train.'

'You would enjoy it, I know you would,' Fanny said. 'Oh, please, do say you'll come? My father will take us to the station and Aunt Celia will send someone to meet us at the other end – but Mother says I can't go alone.'

'Wouldn't she prefer one of your brothers to go with you?'

Fanny's gaze slid away. 'Perhaps – but they can't. Richie is taking Sally to stay with her father's cousins and Jay says he's too busy. I think it's an excuse because he doesn't want to go to Aunt Celia's, but he won't be budged.'

'I don't know what Ma will say . . . or Pa either.'

Sorrel couldn't help feeling excited. She had never been further than Cambridge in her life, and that only once to buy her mother a new hat for Bob's wedding. Lady Roth lived somewhere in Hampshire in a great big house as fine as a castle – at least, that's what she'd heard. If she missed this chance she might never have another one.

'Can you get your father to ask mine?' she said. 'If Pa agreed to it, I'm sure Ma would let me come.'

'Yes, of course I can,' Fanny said, and smiled. 'I do hope you can come, Sorrel. We'll have such fun together.'

After Fanny had gone Sorrel ran upstairs to look through her wardrobe. Not many of her clothes were suitable for such a visit, but she knew Mabel would help her out. She had a lot of clothes she still couldn't squeeze into and would be sure to lend them if Sorrel asked. It had all seemed like a dream when Fanny first suggested it but maybe she would be able to go after all . . .

Sorrel's father agreed when Aden asked, just as she'd known he would. Her mother wasn't so keen on the idea. She looked at her across the supper table and frowned.

'Are you sure you want to go, Sorrel? Won't you feel a bit out of it – like you did when you went to tea at the Sawles'?'

'Fanny says Lady Roth is very kind. Ritchie won't be there and nor will Mrs Sawle.'

'Aden was telling me how fond Fanny is of you.' Her father looked at her with affection. 'This is a chance for her, May – a chance to see something of life outside the village. I think she should go. If she's unhappy she can write to us and I'll send Ted or Bob to fetch her home.'

'Please let me go, Ma,' Sorrel pleaded. 'I'm sure it will be all right – and Fanny can't go if I don't.'

'Jay could take her,' May said, still doubtful. 'But I suppose if you want to . . . we'll have to see about finding you some new clothes.'

'Mabel will lend me her grey costume and the blue silk blouse she bought for her honeymoon – and there's a lovely dress pattern in one of those magazines Aunt Ruth sent. If we bought some material this week, I could make it up in time for the visit.'

It was agreed that she should go. When Sorrel told Fanny, she was thrilled and offered to lend her some of her gloves and hats.

'I've far more than I need,' she said. 'I'll bring some round for you to try on.'

Sorrel began to be very excited. She went into Chatteris and bought some pretty material at the market. While she was deliberating over her choice she saw a girl watching her. At first she couldn't think who it was, then as the girl turned away she realized it was Tarina. She had given the stall holder her money and was unable to leave immediately; when she did the gipsy girl had disappeared.

Sorrel frowned as she searched up and down the rows of stalls in vain. She was almost sure it was the gipsy girl – did that mean that Shima was here, too? She wished she had been quicker. If she'd been able to speak to the girl she might have discovered something about his whereabouts.

If it had been Tarina she had had a nasty bruise on her face. Sorrel felt vaguely disturbed, though she didn't know why. She hadn't thought about the gipsies for a while now . . . she hadn't even had that dream for months.

She abandoned her search as useless and went home. There wasn't much time left if she was going to make the new dress before the visit to Lady Roth's house in the New Year.

Mabel had promised to make her a pretty lace nightdress as a Christmas present and her parents had been into Ely and bought her an expensive leather bag to pack her things in.

'We wanted you to have something nice,' Sid said as she exclaimed over it on Christmas morning. 'First appearances count.'

'Oh, thank you!' Sorrel cried, and flung her arms around him. 'I'm so excited, I can hardly wait.'

She and Fanny were to leave on 2 January and she was counting the days, but then, on New Year's Eve, something happened that was to change everything.

Bob and Mabel had invited the family to a little party at their house and he'd gone home early to help her get ready so Sorrel was startled when she looked out of the kitchen window just before teatime and saw Bob come running into the yard. He was still wearing his working things and looked in a state.

'What's wrong?' May asked as he came rushing into the house. 'You look terrible . . .'

'It's Mabel,' he said, his voice shaking. 'I think she's had a miscarriage. There's blood everywhere and she's bad – she's real bad, Ma.'

'I'll be round right away,' May said, glancing at Sorrel. 'You wait for your father and tell him what's happened, lass – and you can both come round when you're ready.'

'Will she be all right?'

Sorrel was frightened for her friend but her mother only gave a warning look and grabbed her coat, following Bob from the house without another word.

Mabel was upstairs in bed when Ted, Sid and Sorrel arrived at the cottage. The doctor had been and confirmed Bob's fears that she had lost her baby.

'She wasn't sure she was expecting again,' he said on a sob of despair. 'The doctor says it was too soon after Timmy and that's why she's so poorly. He says she mustn't put a foot to the floor for at least three weeks.' His fingers raked at his thick hair and he looked distracted with worry. 'If she does she might . . .'

'She's not going to,' May said firmly. 'You're not to worry about a thing, Bob. Sorrel will move into your spare room to look after her and Timmy.'

'But Sorrel's going to stay with that friend of hers.' Bob shook his head. 'No, we can't ask it of her. I'll manage somehow.'

'Sorrel?' Her mother looked at her hard and she swallowed her disappointment.

'Ma's right,' she said. 'I couldn't go away and leave you all in the lurch, Bob. Mabel needs nursing, the doctor said so – and Timmy is a full-time job. Besides, I wouldn't enjoy myself, knowing Mabel was ill.'

The look of relief in Bob's eyes eased her disappointment.

'Well, you can go another time, can't you?' he said. 'Fanny will understand when you tell her what has happened.'

'Yes, of course she will,' Sorrel agreed, but in her heart she wondered. Would Fanny think she was letting her down by putting her brother and his family first?

Her father sent a message round first thing in the morning and Fanny came to Mabel's just before noon. Sorrel was trying to wash out some nappies, keep an eye on Timmy

69

and prepare a light meal for Mabel all at more or less the same time.

'I had to come,' Fanny said as she invited her in. 'Surely you don't mean you can't come at all, Sorrel? Perhaps if we put it off a couple of days . . .'

'Mabel will be in bed for at least three weeks,' she replied, and glanced anxiously at the pot boiling over on the stove. 'She may not be strong even after that. I'm sorry, Fanny. I'm disappointed, too, but I just can't come with you. You'll have to ask Jay to take you. He needn't stay if he doesn't want to. He could take you and then fetch you back later, couldn't he?'

'My father said he would take me,' she admitted. 'But I was so looking forward to your coming with me.'

'I just can't, Fanny.'

'No, I suppose not,' she said, and looked at Sorrel coldly. 'Obviously your family means more to you than I do.'

'Oh, Fanny.' Sorrel gazed after her as she walked to the door. 'Please don't fall out with me over this.'

'I'll try to forgive you,' she said, 'but you've hurt me – you've hurt me deeply, Sorrel.'

She closed the door with a little bang. Sorrel stared at it in dismay, wondering if she ought to call her back, but Timmy started screaming and the pot boiled over on the stove, making it hiss and splutter.

'Oh, blow you, Fanny Sawle,' she muttered as she made a dash for the pot. 'You Sawles are all the same . . .'

She picked Timmy up from his cot and rocked him in her arms. Fanny had behaved like a spoilt brat. Sorrel was every bit as disappointed as she was but she'd had no choice.

She hushed the baby and laid him back in his cot. Her mother had been right. She was better off having nothing to do with the Sawles, Fanny or Jay. One thing was certain: she wasn't going to run after either of them in future. The next time one of them wanted something from her, they would have to do the asking.

Chapter Nine

It was foggy when she left the hospital to walk back to the nurses' hostel. She was tired and thought she might be coming down with a cold – except that she mustn't. Sister Norden would never forgive her if she let her down by staying off work now, just when they were so busy. She would simply have to make herself a hot toddy and hope the sore throat and aching had gone by the morning. She couldn't take time off at the moment, not with the wards overflowing with injured soldiers.

Hearing the sound of footsteps behind her she stopped and looked over her shoulder. The fog was a real pea souper and too thick for her to see anyone – besides, the footsteps had stopped. She was imagining things... it was like something out of one her nightmares, which she still had from time to time.

She started walking again then felt a thrill of fear as the footsteps began once more. She glanced over her shoulder, thinking that she could just make out a shape in the mist.

'Who is it?' she called. 'I know you're there. Who are you? I warn you, I've got a police whistle in my pocket and I haven't got any money...'

There was no sound, no movement of any kind. She began to walk faster and faster. Her heart was pounding fearfully even though the footsteps had stopped. No one was behind her... it was just the fear of being followed at night, something she had been warned about by the other girls at the hostel.

She saw the lights outside the nurses' home and began to

run, wanting to be inside in the warmth, with other people.
As she reached the safety of the hall she began to breathe
more easily. How foolish she was! It was because she spent
too much time brooding . . . thinking about the past . . .
longing for something that had gone and would never return.
For that time when she had been young and so much in love.

Sorrel halted as she saw the man standing with his back to
her. The gipsies had been camping here a day or so earlier
but she'd been told they had moved on or she wouldn't have
come this way. She was about to turn away when she realized
there was something familiar about the man and hesitated,
watching as he bent to thrust his hand into the ashes of a
fire the gipsies had left to die out when they moved on;
then, as he straightened up, his face half turned towards her,
she knew him. It was Shima – the gipsy Jay believed to be
his half-brother.

'Hello,' she said and he swung round as if startled, his
thoughts obviously still elsewhere. 'It is Shima, isn't it?'

His dark eyes studied her intently, as if searching for a
deeply buried memory. It was the autumn of 1913 and all
of four years since they had met. She was almost seventeen
now and she thought he had probably forgotten her.

'You're Jay Sawle's friend,' he said at last. 'I remember
you had a beautiful name . . . Sorrel, wasn't it?'

'Yes. Sorrel Harris.' Her cheeks went pink as he smiled at
her. He was very tall and broad-shouldered, a little like
Aden in his features but with more humour and softness
about his mouth. 'Are you looking for your people?'

'For Tarina and Sadie,' he replied, his dark eyes shadowed
by thoughts that were clearly bothering him. 'Have you seen
them? I've been following their signs across country for the
past week or so – but it seems that I've missed them again.'

'My father told me some gipsies were going to help lift
the potatoes this year but not in Mepal. I think they're
camping in Sutton Fen, on a piece of waste ground near Mr
Sawle's fifty acres. If you ask in Sutton village someone will
direct you.'

'I expect I can find them.' His smile flashed out again.
'Perhaps I shall catch up with them at last, thanks to you.'

'Have you left the circus?'

'The circus has been broken up and sold off.' His dark eyes became clouded with a secret sadness. 'We had a bad winter last year and this summer there was a terrible fire. Joe Saunders had no choice but to sell up.'

'Your lovely horses, too?' She thought with regret of the beautiful dancing ponies and the way they had responded to this man's gentleness.

'Joe was a good friend to me; he would have given them to me if he could but he had too many debts.'

'I'm so sorry.' She could see that it had hurt him to part with the horses and it made her think of the morning she had watched him training them – the morning Tarina had been attacked. 'Where is your sister? She was with you when you were here before . . .'

'Yes.' He paused, looking thoughtful. 'You remember how upset she was?' Sorrel nodded and a rueful smile touched his mouth. 'She went back to Sadie and the others because she was angry with me. She thought I should have killed Lenny Browne rather than just scaring him – but he wasn't much more than a lad. I am not sure that she has ever forgiven me.'

'Jay was afraid you would kill him,' Sorrel said. 'Have you seen him yet? He has spoken of you often and I'm sure he would be glad to see you again.'

'It has been a long time . . . perhaps too long.' Shima's words were more for himself than her. 'It might have been better if I had never . . . but fate brought me back.'

'I've just thought of something but I don't suppose you would want to . . .' Sorrel hesitated uncertainly, her brow wrinkling.

'Yes?' His dark eyes were intent on her face once more. 'You have something to tell me?'

'It's just that I heard Mr Sawle say he wanted more help with the horses. My brother Ted is his horsekeeper but he's been off sick for a few weeks and . . .'

'I'm sorry to hear that. Is it serious?'

'He fell off a straw stack and injured his leg. He'll be all right but he can't go back to work just yet.'

'That's hard for him. Has he a family to support?'

73

'Ted isn't married yet. He has been courting a girl from Sutton for years but he never seems to get round to asking her. I suppose he will marry Rose eventually – if she doesn't get fed up and find someone else, that is.'

'Some men take their time,' Shima replied, a faint twinkle in his eyes. 'That's as it should be. Marriage is for life and one should choose carefully.' Something in the way he looked at her sent little prickles down her spine. 'Thank you for telling me about the job, Sorrel. I may speak to Mr Sawle about it – but first I must see Sadie and the others.' He glanced at her basket. 'You've been picking blackberries. I saw some good ones back down the road. Shall I show you?'

For some reason she felt disturbed, vaguely unsure of herself. She lifted her chin as she saw a glint of amusement in his mysterious black eyes. 'Thank you, but I know where to look. I'm a country girl, Shima, and I've lived here all my life. Gipsies aren't the only ones who know these things.'

He laughed good-naturedly. 'It was merely a suggestion to repay you for your help. I must get off now. I want to find my people before it gets dark.'

Sorrel watched as he walked away, wondering why she had felt such an instant liking for him. He was a gipsy and she didn't usually care for them much . . . but if Jay's suspicions were right then he really wasn't a true gipsy at all.

Tarina was the first to see Shima enter the camp. She was sitting outside the van she shared with Sadie and Leyan, stirring the rabbit stew which was slowly cooking over a small fire. Her heart missed a beat. How tall and handsome he was – and how much she still loved him!

'Tarina.' Shima looked at her uncertainly, clearly remembering her anger the day she had left him to return to her own people. 'Have you forgiven me?'

Her heart was beating so wildly that she could hardly find the breath to answer him. 'Of course,' she said, her voice husky with emotion as she fought against the tears that would have shamed her. 'I am glad to see you again, Shima.

I heard the circus was finished and wondered if you would look for us.'

'I wanted to see you . . . and Sadie.'·

At the mention of Sadie's name, Tarina's lovely face clouded. 'She won't welcome you back,' she said. 'But no one listens to her these days. If you want to stay with us you must talk to Black Jake.'

'It was because of him that I came,' Shima said, his look of concern bringing a lump to her throat and almost oversetting her. 'You told me . . . has he forced you to become his woman?'

She shook her head, her tangled curls falling across her face. 'For a long time I was frightened of him – but now he has a woman. She is sixteen, but passionate and lovely. Since he took her for his own, he has not looked at me in that way.'

It was not quite the truth. Black Jake still looked at her with lust in his eyes but she had managed to stay out of his way; besides his new woman was a jealous little thing who was ready to fight for her man with the knife that hung from her belt. For months Marianna had managed to keep him from straying but now she was carrying his child, her body swollen and ungainly, and he had begun to look at Tarina once more.

'I am glad. It has worried me.'

'Not enough for you to come to find me before this!' Her eyes sparked with sudden anger. 'You think of me only now that the circus has finished, isn't that true?'

'You know it isn't, Tarina. I think of you often – and I have always loved you as my sister.'

'But I am not your sister!'

'No.' Shima looked at her sadly. 'Forgive me. I should not have come. I shall not trouble you again.'

As he turned away she sprang up and caught his arm. 'Do not go,' she said, the tears she had fought so hard gathering in her eyes. 'I *am* afraid of Black Jake. Stay with us for a while, Shima. I shall be safe while you are here, and once Marianna has given Jake a child, he will not bother to look at me.'

'If that is your wish,' he said, and smiled at her. 'Aden

Sawle is looking for temporary help with the horses. I shall work with you in the fields until you go and then I shall leave with you.'

'Sorrel!' She was on her way out of the yard when Aden called to her that morning and stopped to let him catch up with her. 'Have you got a moment, please?'

'Yes, of course.' She smiled up at him, tendrils of her soft hair escaping to curl about her face. 'Can I do something for you?'

'I believe you told Shima we were looking for help with the horses?'

'Yes, I did.' She was concerned all at once. Since the previous afternoon she'd had time to think and had realized she might have caused trouble for the Sawles, but then she saw Aden was looking pleased. 'Was – was that all right? I thought with Ted still laid up . . . and Shima so good with horses . . .'

'Yes, he always was, even as a child. It was clever of you to think of it, Sorrel. It is a bit of luck for us that he has come. He'll be a big help with the potato harvest. We're starting in the fen this morning.'

'Yes, I know. I've got some deliveries in the village, then I'll be taking my father and Bob some food down to the acres.'

Aden nodded then asked: 'Not driving your pony today?'

'Poor old Dobbin has an infected leg. The vet has been but the stuff he gave us doesn't seem to be doing much good.'

'You should ask Shima to look at it for you. He gave Jay something for his pony a few years back and it worked a treat.'

'Yes, Jay told me. They're good friends, aren't they?'

'So I believe.' A shadow passed across Aden's face. For a moment she saw such sadness in his eyes that it made her wonder. 'Well, I mustn't delay you any longer, Sorrel. I know you have things to do, but don't forget to ask Shima's advice – and Fanny is home again if you want to see her.'

'Yes, Mabel told me she'd met her in the village.'

Fanny had been travelling with Lady Roth again. Sorrel

hadn't seen much of her since their quarrel, though they spoke to each other if they met in the street. Mabel said it was silly to hold a grudge but Sorrel had been determined that the other girl should make the first move.

'You don't want to cut off your nose to spite your face,' Mabel had said only a day or so earlier. 'Why don't you ask her round here for tea like you used to?'

Sorrel had thought about it. Mabel was at last back to her normal self. They had been anxious about her during the first months of the year because she'd seemed susceptible to colds and chills, but she'd picked up in the summer and the doctor said there was no reason why she shouldn't start to think about another baby. Now, looking at Aden, Sorrel realized her sister-in-law was right. There was no point in harbouring grudges – and she liked being friends with Fanny.

'You can tell her I'll pop round later,' she said impulsively to Aden. 'Mabel said she would like Fanny to come to tea soon – if she would like to?'

He looked pleased. 'Fanny will be at home all afternoon.'

Sorrel was thoughtful as she walked on. Her mother had asked her to deliver eggs to some of her regular customers; the chickens were hers and the egg money gave her a little independence. Sid paid Sorrel a few shillings a week for delivering the milk, which enabled her to buy her own clothes and save for her bottom drawer, but with Dobbin unable to walk, it had temporarily brought a halt to the milkround.

At least Aden had seemed pleased that Shima was back but Sorrel had an odd feeling of unease. She wasn't sure why. Surely it couldn't be the vague memory of Sadie's curse? She still had the dream occasionally and had never been sure whether the gipsy woman had cursed her or Shima.

She shivered in the cool wind. She was being foolish! Nothing terrible was going to happen... it was all nonsense... and yet she couldn't get rid of the idea that a dark shadow was hanging over all their lives.

Chapter Ten

Sorrel borrowed her mother's bicycle, because it would have been too far to walk all the way to Sutton Fen and still be back in time to help Ted with the milking. His leg was sufficently well for him to be able to hobble about the yard but there was too much for him to manage alone and everyone else was out in the fields, desperately trying to get the potatoes up before the bad weather set in.

The last part of the journey was bumpy, the track cut up by cart wheels and horses' hooves, so she dismounted and wheeled the bike, feeling glad that she had wrapped up well with scarves and knitted gloves, because there was a chill in the air and the wind could be bitter as it blew across the fens. The land was so flat and there were hardly any trees or hedges thick enough to stop its force.

There wasn't much further to go now. She could hear voices, some of them raised as if in anger. As she reached the field where the men were working she saw that an argument was going on between Shima and one of the other gipsies. It seemed serious and she hesitated, looking for her father and brother. They were at the far end of the field with the cart, collecting up the bags of potatoes, and she decided to wait until they returned.

'Leyan hates Shima.' The woman's voice made Sorrel spin round in surprise but she recognized her at once. 'They always argued as boys, and now it is much worse. Leyan blames Shima for Lorenzo's death – though it was not his fault. When he was alive Lorenzo always favoured Shima and so Leyan hates him.'

'Who do you favour, Tarina?'

The gipsy looked at her, her eyes such an intense blue that they set little shivers running down Sorrel's spine. She felt a strong emotion flow from the other woman but wasn't sure whether it was love or hate.

'Leyan and I share the same mother,' she replied. 'Between Shima and I there are no blood ties. Leyan would have killed for me. Shima was too weak.'

'I don't think Shima is weak,' Sorrel said. 'What Lenny did was very wrong but he didn't deserve to die.'

'You are not one of us. You do not understand our ways. I was dishonoured. Shima owed me blood.'

She tossed her mass of curls and walked off. Sorrel watched her for a moment, saw her stop and talk to a dark-faced gipsy with eyes that had a cold, cruel expression, then looked towards the field and saw that the argument between Shima and Leyan seemed to have sorted itself out. Her father was standing with Shima and Sorrel waved to him. Sid smiled, said something to Shima, then began to walk towards her. She hurried to meet him.

'You look cold, lass,' he said. 'It was a long way for you to come. Tomorrow we'll bring our food with us.'

'You know Ma likes you to have fresh bread and a drink. We wrapped the bottle in a towel so the tea is still warm.'

'You're a good girl,' he said. 'Jay is taking the cart back to the yard in Sutton Gault. I should think he'll give you a lift that far. Wait a moment while I ask him.'

He went off before she could think of a reply. She watched him speak to Jay, saw Jay's eyes flick towards her and his little nod of agreement. She hadn't spoken more than a few words to him since the dance the previous year, though she had heard from Mabel that Adele Carter had married a man old enough to be her father.

She had wondered how Jay felt about that, but from things Ted let drop now and then she knew he was still chasing the local girls – though none of them was the kind he could take home to his mother.

Jay walked the horse and cart towards her. Sorrel lifted her chin, giving him a challenging look. She still hadn't quite forgiven him for what had happened the morning she was kept standing on the doorstep.

'Ready then?' he asked. 'I'll put your bike between the sacks and give you a lift up. I can take you as far as the Gault but you'll have to bike from there, because they need me back here as soon as I've unloaded.'

'That's all right,' she said. 'I'm going into Sutton to do some shopping before I go home.'

'Buying something nice?'

She was planning on getting a pair of silk stockings and a lace petticoat from the tallyman's shop but wasn't about to tell him that.

'You mind your own business, Jay Sawle. There are some things a woman doesn't tell anyone.'

'A woman!' he scoffed. 'It's not five minutes since you were in pigtails.'

'I'm almost seventeen,' she retorted, her cheeks pink with annoyance. She tossed her head as she saw the devilment in his eyes. 'Oh, you! Just you watch it. One of these days I'll get you back.'

'Maybe you already have.'

'What's that supposed to mean?'

She turned her head to study his face but his expression was bland, giving nothing away.

'You turned me down when I asked you to the dance last year – not many girls have done that.'

'What did you expect me to do? I came to your house and Molly told me you were too busy to come to the door to speak to me.'

'Lady Roth and her cousin had just arrived,' he replied. 'Molly spoke to my mother. I didn't even know you had been – until she gave me your message.' His mouth thinned. 'You don't think I would have done that if I'd known?' His eyes had lost their look of devilment. 'You do, don't you? That's why you said no.' Realization dawned in his eyes. 'I thought ...'

'It might have been my reason.' She gave him a hard stare. 'It certainly made me cross with you.'

'Honestly, Sorrel. I didn't know you were there. I was looking forward to taking you.'

'Were you?' She challenged him with a flash of her eyes. 'You didn't ask me for a dance.'

'Every time I looked you were dancing with someone – mostly Tom Robinson.'

'Yes, I was.' A little smile flickered over her mouth as she remembered. 'Perhaps I'll forgive you then.'

'Father told Fanny you were coming round to see her and she was pleased to get your message,' he said suddenly. 'She was upset because you couldn't go to Lady Roth's with her that time.'

'I couldn't let Mabel and Bob down. Bob was nearly at his wit's end as it was and they needed me.'

'No, of course you couldn't. That's what I told her.' He smiled. 'Anyway, she's looking forward to having tea with you on Sunday.'

'I heard she was having dancing lessons in Ely?'

'Yes, she is. Mother will be giving some coming out parties for her and she might take her to London in the summer. Fanny doesn't want to go.'

'Whyever not? I should have thought it would be exciting.'

The worst thing about living in a small village like Mepal was that there was very little to do, especially in the winter. In the summer they held various fêtes and bazaars but when the long dark nights drew on they mostly stayed in by the fire with a book or a piece of needlework. Sorrel loved music and when she read about the famous music hall stars in the newspapers she often longed to go to a show; she thought Fanny was lucky to be visiting London, where she would surely be taken to several theatres.

'Fanny doesn't care much for parties. She likes travelling with Aunt Celia and informal dinners with friends – but not the big dances Mother is planning to take her to next year.'

'Why doesn't she tell your mother that?'

'You don't know my mother.' Jay pulled a rueful face, then his expression became thoughtful. 'There's a fair on in Ely this week. I'll take you on Saturday afternoon, if you like?'

'Take me to a fair?' She stared at him in surprise. She had been to Sutton Feast a few times but never to the big fair in the neighbouring market town of Ely. 'How would we get there?'

'I'll take you in the trap,' he said. 'If you'd like, that is?'

She had always wanted to be taken for a ride behind that high-stepping pony of his but she didn't say yes straight away. She wasn't going to be easy to get like all his other girls.

'That would be nice,' she said. 'I'll have to think about it. Ma might not let me.'

She was prevaricating, paying him back a little for his remarks about her pigtails – and that dance. He knew it and his frustrated expression made her laugh inside.

'I'll tell you what, you come round this evening and I'll give you my answer then.'

'I can't come tonight. I've promised to go out for a drink with Shima.'

'If that's more important to you than . . .'

'Don't get on your high horse again! I'll come before I meet him but I shan't be able to stop long – will that do?'

At last he was responding in the way she wanted. 'Who asked you to stop? You can come for your answer tonight – or don't bother coming at all.'

Jay had slowed the horse as he reached the gates of the old farm house and yard his father had recently bought. Sorrel jumped down without waiting for him to help her, standing silently as he fetched her bike for her.

'I'll be there,' he said, and grinned. 'You're a minx, Sorrel Harris. One day someone will put you across their knee and spank you.'

'Not if I have anything to do with it!' she laughed up at him. 'Will you ask Shima if he will look at Dobbin's leg for me sometime? I would have asked him myself but he was having an argument.'

'With Leyan.' Jay nodded, looking sombre. 'That one is a troublemaker and he doesn't like Shima much. Yes, I'll have a word with him for you.'

She waved and pedalled off on her bike, leaving him staring after her with such a comical expression that it kept her in fits of laughter until she reached Sutton village.

* * *

Cycling home down the Witcham road she caught sight of the man just before he stepped out in front of her, making her swerve to avoid him. Her bike lurched to one side and some of her shopping fell out of the basket. She stopped and got off to pick it up.

'Look what you've done,' she said crossly. 'If Ma's shopping is ruined . . .' The words died on her lips as she suddenly recognized him. It was Lenny Browne and from the way he was swaying unsteadily on his feet she guessed he was drunk. She'd heard her father say he'd spent most of the past year in prison after having been thrown out of the army – but now he was back home!

He staggered to the edge of the road and slumped down on the wet grass, looking green in the face and obviously unwell. She hesitated, remembering her father's warnings, but compassion won. He looked as if he hadn't eaten a decent meal in weeks.

She leant her bike against the hedge and went over to him. 'Are you ill? I can see you've been drinking – but are you all right otherwise?'

There was a deep scar on his right cheek that looked as if it had been there for a while, and she suspected it had been made by a knife. Perhaps Lenny had paid in blood for his attack on Tarina after all.

He glanced up at her and she was shocked. His face was bloated and yellowish, his eyes red-rimmed. There were weeping sores at the corners of his mouth and he appeared much older than his years. Feeling sorry for him, she took a sticky bun from the bag in her bike basket and offered it to him.

'You might feel better if you eat something.'

He hesitated, then reached out and took the bun, cramming it into his mouth all at once. He chewed with his mouth open and spat crumbs as he looked at her properly for the first time.

'I remember you – you're the Harris girl.'

His leer made her nervous. She grabbed her bike and got on, pedalling away hurriedly. Her father was right. It was best to keep away from men like that. She had felt sorry for him but he wasn't the sort to appreciate sympathy; he would probably resent her for it – if he remembered when he sobered up.

It was all a little disturbing: the fact that Lenny had come back to the village at the same time as Shima and the gipsies.

Chapter Eleven

Shima was aware of dissatisfaction amongst the gipsies, but at first he wasn't sure what was causing it. He had noticed the sullen faces and caught a few grumbles but it was more than that. It wasn't until the Friday night, however, that Leyan spoke out.

'We're not bein' paid fair,' he said as Black Jake passed round the money he had collected that evening. 'We should 'ave bin paid piece work – the way Shima keeps us clawin' our guts out after the spinner ain't right.'

Several of the men murmured agreement, and though the women were silent Shima could see resentment in their eyes.

'We agreed to two and sixpence a day,' he said. 'We can't go back on our word now. Mr Sawle wants the crop up before the weather breaks. We can't let him down.'

'Why not?' Leyan scowled at him. 'Why should we care about these gorgios? I say we move on – look for work elsewhere.'

'No.' Shima met Leyan's angry stare unflinchingly. 'I say we stay. I'll have a word with Mr Sawle ... tell him we'll have to slow it down a little. Besides, we're moving on to the next field next week – it might be easier going.'

'We should move on.' Leyan's challenge was there between them, a tangible force that set the air crackling. 'We should move unless we're paid more.'

'We'll move on when I say.' Black Jake's voice cut through the tension like a knife. 'Stop whining, you feeble cur – or I'll stop your mouth for you.'

Leyan turned a queer putty colour. His eyes were dark

with resentment but like everyone else in the gipsy camp he was afraid of the man who had led them since Lorenzo's death. He hated him but had neither the courage nor the strength to challenge him – one or two had tried it and lived to regret their actions. Whispers told of a man dying of his wounds and now they all lived in fear of Jake's terrible temper.

Shima was surprised at the intervention. He had expected Jake to agree with the other men. He saw the gipsy staring at him, an evil leer on his face, as if daring him to challenge him.

'I'll speak to Mr Sawle about the money tomorrow,' Shima said as a sudden suspicion crossed his mind. 'Ask him if he'll let us change to piece work.'

'Damn you!' Jake clenched his fists and took a menacing step towards him. 'I'm the leader here and I'll take no interference from you or anyone else.'

Shima stood his ground, his suspicions hardening. The men had a right to complain, the money was poor, and he remembered Lorenzo saying that Aden Sawle had always been a generous master.

'Afraid of what I might discover?' he asked quietly. Jake's fingers moved towards the knife hanging from his belt. 'I wouldn't if I were you, Jake . . .'

'You cheeky whelp!' Black Jake met Shima's unflinching stare consideringly. For a moment they measured each other, then Jake smiled as if amused. 'So you're not afraid of me? You've red blood in your veins instead of milk – well, I like that, Shima. You've more guts than that spineless whelp of Lorenzo's. And since I like you, I'll let you live for the moment – but leave this to me. I'll see that we get three shillings a day from next week.' His chilling gaze moved slowly round the small circle of watchers. 'Will that satisfy you, you lazy curs?'

There was a murmur amongst the men, then they began to move away, back to their fires and their vans. If there were any who suspected, as Shima did, that he had been holding out on them they were not brave enough to say it out loud.

'He won't forgive you for that.' Tarina's voice made Shima

turn round. 'Be careful. If you turn your back on him in a dark place, he will plunge a knife into it.'

'Thank you for the warning.' Shima smiled at her. 'You need not fear for me, sister. I've learned a few tricks while I was away. Bullies like Jake do not frighten me with their threats and their empty bluster.'

'He has killed men for less,' she said, her eyes almost the colour of violets in her fear for him. 'He already hates you because . . .' Her words died away as she looked at him. She could not tell him that Black Jake hated him because she loved him – because he knew that she would willingly give to Shima all she had withheld from him. 'Just be careful, that's all.'

Shima nodded. He glanced at Leyan, seeing the jealousy in his eyes. Leyan hated him, he knew that. It had begun when they were children and Lorenzo had treated him as the favoured son while Leyan was either beaten or ignored. He would hate Shima even more now, because he had stood up to Jake – because he had forced him to give them the proper rate of pay for their work.

Black Jake might try to kill him in a fight . . . but it was Leyan who would plunge a knife into his back if he got the chance.

Chapter Twelve

The fair was in full swing when Jay drove into the stableyard behind the cattle market in Ely. He helped Sorrel down, arranged for his horse to be looked after, then smiled at her as if he liked what he saw.

'You look so pretty,' he said, bringing a flush to her cheeks as she slipped her arm through his. She was wearing a red coat, knitted scarf and tammy and yellow mittens to keep out the cold. 'What do you want to go on first?'

'I don't know – what do you think?' She was trembling with excitement as she clung to his arm and they walked through the crowds thronging the streets. The sleepy little market town had come to life all of a sudden. 'Isn't this fun?'

'Yes, it is,' he agreed. 'Shall we try the Jollity Farm first?'

'Yes, please.' Her eyes lit up with pleasure. 'I want to go on everything. Do you think we can win something to take home for Ma?'

'We'll have a good try,' Jay said, and grinned. 'Let's do all the rides first, then we'll chance our luck at the hoopla and the coconut shy.'

Afterwards, Sorrel would remember that afternoon as one of the golden days of her life. They began by riding the brightly painted horses that whirled them round and round until she was dizzy; from there they progressed to swings that made her stomach lurch as they almost turned them upside down in the air. She screamed and clutched at Jay's arm, then pushed him away as he teased her.

'You can't fall out,' he said with that superior look of his.

'Shall we go on the horses again, or have you had enough of the rides?'

Her head went up. 'Of course I haven't. Let's go on the mat next and then the horses again.'

They slid down the slippery, twisty slide, her skirts flying as she shrieked with pleasurable fright. As she got to her feet at the bottom she caught sight of Lenny Browne in the crowd. He was drunk again, swaying unsteadily on his feet as he pushed his way through the crowds of people enjoying themselves at the various stalls. She watched him, frowning and wondering what made him drink the way he did all the time.

'Is something wrong?' Jay asked. 'Who were you looking at just now?'

'No one,' she said. It was beginning to get dark and the lights of the rides twinkled in the gathering dusk. She breathed in all the exciting smells of the fair: popcorn, doughnuts and toffee, and fish and chips frying. 'Look, there's the toffee apple stall – shall we have one?'

Munching on the sticky, delicious sweet, she forgot Lenny and his problems as they went on the roundabouts again before moving on to the other stalls. Jay won a china fairing at his fifth attempt at the coconut shy and she finally managed to get her hoop over a tiny pink glass vase. She clutched it triumphantly.

'Ma will love this,' she said, smiling up at Jay. 'Can I have the fairing? I want to keep it so I shall always remember this afternoon.'

'I won it for you,' he replied. 'Have you had enough now? Only I thought we might have a fish and chip supper to round things off before we go home.'

'Can we go in and sit down?' she asked with all the innocent enjoyment of the child she still was at heart despite her burgeoning womanhood. 'With some lemonade, bread and butter – and squashy peas?'

'Pickled onions too, if you like,' he said, a teasing look on his face. 'Come on then, let's have our meal. I mustn't keep you too late on our first outing or your father will skin me alive!'

Sorrel felt a surge of happiness as she saw the look he

gave her. He was teasing her as usual but there was something new in his eyes – an expression that made her think he really liked her and not just as a friend. That he was beginning to see her as a woman and not simply the schoolgirl he had walked home so many times in the past.

Something made her think about Shima and his rather odd expression when he had teased her about the blackberries. It had disturbed her then but now she realized it was the same look as Jay was giving her . . . as if he found her very attractive.

'There's some poison in this fleshy part just above the hoof,' Shima said, and showed Sorrel where the horse's leg was swollen. 'I'll cut it and let the pus out, then you can apply this mixture once a day and it should heal quite quickly.'

'Poor old Dobbin,' she said. 'We've been putting poultices on and it hasn't helped a bit.'

'It probably brought the swelling to a head,' Shima said, 'but the poison has to come out before it can start to heal. Don't worry, Sorrel. I've done this many times with the circus ponies.'

She watched as he made an incision with his knife. It was a very distinctive knife with a sharp, pointed blade and a bone handle that had his name burned into it. An unpleasant-smelling yellow pus oozed out of the open wound and Shima washed it away, squeezing until the blood ran clean. He was quick and gentle and Dobbin merely snorted once, gazing round with docile eyes as if he knew that the gipsy was trying to help him.

'There, that should do it.' Shima wiped his knife blade and restored it to the sheath that hung at his belt. 'If it doesn't clear up completely, let me know and I'll come back and have another look at it.'

'I'm sure it will,' Sorrel said, admiring the way he had handled the pony. 'I can't thank you enough, Shima. Poor Dobbin was in a lot of pain and I was afraid we might lose him.'

Shima stood up, towering over her as he gazed down into her face, his expression warm and compassionate. 'You wouldn't want to do that,' he said, then, more hesitantly,

'Jay told me he was taking you to the fair – did you enjoy yourself?'

'Yes. It was such fun. We went on all the rides and then he took me for a fish and chip supper.'

Shima nodded, his manner becoming a little strained, as if he were hiding his feelings. 'I'd thought of asking you myself – but Jay got in first.'

'Oh . . . that would have been nice. Perhaps another time.' Her cheeks flushed as she realized that Shima rather liked her but she was saved from needing to say more as her father joined them. 'Look, Pa – Shima has squeezed out all the poison. He says Dobbin will be all right now.'

'That's good, lass,' Sid said, and hitched up his trousers. 'Your mother wants you.' He looked at Shima and frowned. 'Sorted it all out, have you?'

'Yes, sir. I was just telling Sorrel that she ought not to have any more bother – but I'll come back if it doesn't clear up.' He glanced at her as she started to walk reluctantly towards the kitchen. 'Bye, Sorrel. I'm glad you enjoyed the fair.'

'Thank you for helping Dobbin.'

He nodded, his dark eyes unfathomable as he gathered up his things to leave. Her heart fluttered, making her feel a little strange as she went into the kitchen. She liked Shima, and sometimes when he looked at her she had an odd melting sensation inside. It wasn't the way she felt about Jay – she had loved him ever since they'd gone to school together – but there was something about Shima that pulled at her heartstrings.

Her mother gave her a sharp look as she went into the kitchen, making Sorrel blush.

'I don't approve of your talking to that gipsy, Sorrel. Even if Aden did recommend him, it's not right. Not right him being here at all.'

From the tone of her voice Sorrel suspected she knew more than she was saying. It wasn't surprising. You only had to see Aden and Shima together to notice the likeness.

'You've heard what folk are saying, haven't you? About Shima being Aden's bastard.'

'Wash your mouth out with salt water!' May glared at her angrily. 'I'll not have you using that language.'

'But he is Aden's illegitimate son, Ma. Jay told me years ago. He heard his parents arguing about Shima and . . .'

'It's shameful, that's what it is,' May said, looking upset. 'Rebecca may be a sight too high and mighty sometimes – but this isn't right. Aden didn't ought to flaunt his by-blows in front of his wife. It's not decent.'

Her mother was a bit straitlaced sometimes but Sorrel couldn't help agreeing with her this time. She liked Shima and knew he was Jay's friend – but she had an uneasy feeling that his presence in the village might cause trouble, and not just for Rebecca Sawle.

'Jay says his mother doesn't mind about Shima now,' Sorrel said thoughtfully. 'But I think it must hurt her – especially when people gossip the way they do.'

'Of course she minds, even if she pretends not to. Think how you would feel in her shoes.'

Sorrel nodded. She was sure that Rebecca Sawle did mind even if she made out she didn't to her husband and family. It must hurt her – the way Sorrel sometimes felt hurt when she heard her brothers laughing about Jay's escapades with the local girls.

She heard a little more about Rebecca's feeling when she met Fanny for tea at Mabel's that afternoon. Fanny was rather quiet when Bob and Mabel were there but after they took the baby out for a walk she relaxed and turned to Sorrel with a heartfelt apology.

'I'm glad you asked me for tea,' she said, sounding a little awkward. 'I've been wanting to say sorry for being so awful to you that day. I know I shouldn't have said those things, Sorrel, but I was so disappointed.'

'So was I. You have no idea how much I was looking forward to seeing Lady Roth's house. It was much worse for me than it was for you.'

'Yes, I suppose it was.' Fanny was thoughtful for a moment. 'Perhaps you can come with me next year,' she said. 'Aunt Celia is spending the winter abroad but she'll be home in the spring. I'll ask her if we can both go and stay in the summer.'

'Not at harvest time,' Sorrel said quickly. 'I wouldn't be able to go then, Ma needs me to help her – perhaps in early-October, if that would suit you?'

'I'll write to her as soon as she's back,' Fanny promised. 'I wish I could go now. Mother is always so busy and I think she's upset about something, though she says she's not.'

'Because of Shima,' Sorrel said without thinking.

'Who is Shima?' Fanny looked puzzled. 'Oh – you mean the gipsies, I suppose? She isn't very happy about that, because one of them attacked Molly years ago. She and my father had an argument over it – that's why he sent them to Sutton Gault instead of letting them camp here.'

'Oh, I see.' Apparently, Fanny still didn't know that Shima was her half-brother and Sorrel wasn't going to be the one to tell her. 'Was your mother very cross?'

'For a while. She and my father made their quarrel up, of course – they always do – but . . .' Fanny looked unhappy. 'I hate it when they argue, Sorrel. I do wish sometimes . . .' She sighed heavily. 'Richie will be getting married next year and Jay will, too, one day I suppose – but I shall be stuck at home for ever.'

'Surely not? You will get married one day, Fanny – when you meet someone nice.'

'I don't think Mother will let me. She just wants me with her all the time, and if I say I don't want to go visiting with her, she looks as if I've committed a terrible crime.'

'You should have friends of your own.'

'That's why I want us to be friends.' Fanny looked at her earnestly. 'We won't fall out again, will we?'

'No – but you'll have to understand I can't always do what I want, Fanny. Your mother expects you to do what she wants and my family expect loyalty from me.'

'Yes, I know – but we can be together more often, can't we? I get so bored at home sometimes. Mother fusses over me so.'

'You're always welcome at our house, you know that, Fanny. And Mabel loves to see you.'

'I like her, too,' Fanny said, shedding her mood. 'I was wondering . . . We're having a big party soon for my coming out – would you come, Sorrel? Mother has hired the village hall and there will be nearly a hundred guests. I shall hate it unless you come.'

'Will your mother let you invite me?'

'If she doesn't, I shan't go myself.' Fanny's eyes suddenly sparked with mischief, making her look a lot like Jay. Sorrel realized there was a very different girl beneath the quiet, sad manner she normally displayed. 'Please, please, say you will come!'

'Yes, all right, I'd like to,' Sorrel said. 'But you must send me a proper invitation or Ma won't like it.'

'Yes, of course I shall.' Fanny looked happier. 'To tell you the truth, Sorrel, you and Sally Baxter are my only real friends. All the others are people my mother knows through her charity work or her social gatherings. Most of them look down their noses at me.'

'Oh, Fanny!' Sorrel cried. 'I'm sure they don't – how could they?'

'They do,' she insisted. 'That's why I shall never meet anyone I like. I want to fall in love with someone real – someone who is a bit like Jay but isn't my brother.'

'Yes, I do understand.' Sorrel saw the sadness in her eyes and was glad she had taken the initiative in renewing their friendship. Fanny was lonely and unhappy. Her mother was so protective of her that she was smothering her, squashing all the life out of her. She was doing it out of love and a fear of losing her, but it was draining Fanny of all the joy of life. 'You'll meet someone one day, Fanny. I'm sure you will – perhaps when we go to visit Lady Celia next year.'

'Yes, perhaps,' she said, and sighed. 'But if I like him, you can be sure that my mother won't.'

Chapter Thirteen

'I saw him, I tell you! He was in the village and he had been drinking. He looked at me ... laughed at me ... he was mocking me!' Tarina's eyes flashed with anger as she faced Leyan across the horse he was grooming. 'Do you think I could forget the man who tried to rape me?'

Leyan was silent as he continued to smooth the curry comb over the horse's back. Tarina had never accepted one of their number as her man, though more than one had offered for her.

'Why do you not bed with any man?' he suddenly asked, his dark eyes simmering with jealousy. 'Is it because you still hope that one day Shima will take you as his woman – because you still love him?'

'That weak-livered gorgio?' She glared at him, tossing her mane of curls defiantly. Shima had been with them for two weeks now, and though he was always gentle with her, he had never given any sign of caring for her as anything but his sister – and it hurt. It hurt so much that she wanted to strike back at him, to hurt him somehow. 'I would not be his woman if he begged me. I will be no man's until my honour has been avenged.'

She knew she was lying as she spoke; if Shima asked she would go to him willingly, but her pride had been bruised, her heart wounded. Shima's continued indifference to her beauty was hard to bear, especially since she could not see him without wanting to feel his arms about her. Sometimes her emotions were so confused that she was no longer sure whether she loved or hated him.

'You are my true brother, Leyan. It is you I care for – you I share blood ties with through our mother. Shima is nothing to me.'

'For years he stole my place as Lorenzo's eldest son.' Leyan's eyes glittered with hatred. 'But I thought you loved him? You ran off to be with him – you welcomed him when he came back – and I have seen the way you look at him.'

She lifted her head, eyes brilliant with the tears she was too proud to shed. 'Once, perhaps, I was foolish enough to love him, but now he is nothing to me. You are my only brother, Leyan. Shima does not share our blood. He is not truly one of us.'

His hand shot out, his thin, brown fingers curling about her wrist so tightly that she winced with pain. 'Do you swear to me that you care nothing for him?' She hesitated, a little frightened by the intensity of his look, then nodded. 'Then I shall do what must be done.'

'What do you mean?'

'Do not ask,' he said. 'I shall prove myself to you, Tarina – and then you will send Shima away.'

She felt chilled suddenly, as if a dark angel had spread its wings over her, and wished she could take back the words she had spoken out of pride. Her pride had been hurt the day she was attacked but in her heart she knew that Shima had avenged her humiliation. She did not really want the gorgio killed – all she truly wanted was for Shima to love her.

Yet she did not speak, and then as she looked into Leyan's eyes, she knew that it was too late.

Leyan hated the man in whose shadow he had been forced to walk for so many years. The more so since it had all been a lie. Shima was not Lorenzo's son: he was the bastard of Aden Sawle.

Father has no right to employ that bastard!' Richie said to Jay as he finished checking the load of bagged potatoes on to the merchant's cart. 'It's an insult to Mother – and to us.'

'Mother doesn't seem to mind Shima's being here,' Jay replied, frowning over his brother's words. He liked Shima but wouldn't care to see his mother hurt. 'It did upset her

once but now she seems to have accepted the fact that he's
Dad's son. I think she quite likes him.'

'Well, I don't, and I'm not willing to welcome him as a
brother.' Richie gave him a cold stare. 'I suppose you want
that gippo here? Have you thought what it means if he
stays?'

Jay looked at him uncertainly. What was eating at Richie?

'Are you worried that he might one day inherit some of
Dad's land? Surely there's enough for us all?'

'The land belongs to us – Father's legitimate sons. It
all splits up nicely. Five Winds for you and . . .'

'You get the corn merchant's and the fen land, I suppose?'
Jay's expression showed his disgust. 'My God, Richie!
You've got it all worked out, haven't you?'

'We don't want that gippo muscling in on things.' Richie
took a silver cigarette case from his jacket pocket, selected
a Player's and lit it. 'I intend to be rich one day – not merely
comfortable the way we are now – and I'm not prepared to
share my inheritance with that gippo.'

'If money's your god, good luck to you,' Jay said, a note
of scorn in his voice. 'All I've ever wanted is to make a
decent living from the land – and now, if you've finished,
I'm going back to work.'

He walked away as his brother finalized the details of the
load with the merchant's driver. Richie was a hard-headed
businessman, he had got them a good price for the potatoes
they had lifted so far but it had rained in the night and the
land was becoming saturated, which would make the going
harder. Jay knew the gipsies had been grumbling for days.
Shima had somehow managed to calm them but Leyan had
been stirring up trouble whenever he got a chance, and it
would make things awkward if they went off before the
lifting was finished.

Jay wondered if all brothers felt animosity towards each
other. This thing between him and Richie – was it just a
natural rivalry or something much deeper? He had known
for a long time that Richie heartily disliked him but had not
realized how much his brother resented Shima. Why? Why
did he hate Shima so? Jay rather liked having his half-
brother around; they got on well and it didn't bother him

that his father might decide to pass some of the land on to Shima one day – though he hoped it wouldn't be Five Winds.

The farm and cottage had been in his family for generations and meant more to him than all the rest put together, but they belonged to his father – and he wasn't about to die. Aden would probably live for another thirty or more years!

The thought brought a smile to Jay's face. He began to whistle as he climbed on to the box of the waggon he was about to drive back to the fields where Shima and the others were working. There was no point in worrying about something that might never happen. At the moment he had a valuable crop to get out of the ground.

Chapter Fourteen

Her father and brothers had been looking anxious for a couple of days now. Sorrel watched them as they stood together by the milking sheds; she knew what was on their minds, because she had heard them talking over breakfast. Leyan had been causing more trouble amongst the gipsies and they'd stopped picking for two hours the previous day, leaving the field with the work unfinished. With the weather so wet and changeable, that could mean that a part of the harvest might rot in the ground.

'Gippos were always lazy beggars,' Bob said, and scowled.

'Aden was a fool for taking them on. We'd have been better off with a local gang. But then he's always had a fondness for gipsies and we know why, don't we?'

'Watch your tongue,' Sid warned. He might privately agree with every word Bob was saying but he wouldn't stand for criticism of his old friend. 'I'll not have you speak about Aden like that. The gipsies aren't that bad. Shima got them back to work. He seems to be able to control them – though that fellow . . . Black Jake, they call him . . . I don't think he liked it much when they listened to Shima.'

'He's a nasty bit of work,' Bob said, taking off his stained cap and raking restless fingers through his thick hair. 'As for that Leyan – there's bad blood between him and Shima. There'll be trouble before we're finished, you see if I'm not right.'

'Aye . . .' Sid coughed and gave his trousers a hitch. 'I've seen that right enough. Shima's got his work cut out to keep the peace, but he seems a sensible man. It's that Leyan we've got to watch.'

'Tarina says he's jealous of Shima.' Sorrel blushed as her father and brothers turned to look at her. 'Because Lorenzo favoured Shima when they were children ... and because Leyan blames him for his father's death, though it wasn't Shima's fault.'

'And how do you know all this?' Sid's narrowed gaze made her uncomfortable.

'Tarina tells me things sometimes.'

'It will be a good thing when that lot move on,' Bob said, and this time his father didn't disagree. 'We can do without them – any of them.'

'I thought Shima was staying on to help with the horses?' Ted asked, looking puzzled. 'Leastways, that's what Aden told me.'

'It seems Shima hasn't made up his mind,' Sid said. 'He's promised Tarina he'll look after her ... Seems that ugly great fellow's got his eye on her and she's frightened of him.'

'Jake ... She's frightened of Black Jake,' Sorrel said, remembering. 'I saw him stop her once in the fields. She looked distressed, nervous – as if she hated him.'

'Well, you stay away from him – and the rest of them,' Sid muttered gruffly. 'And that includes Tarina. Take notice of what your mother says, Sorrel. She thinks they'll bring trouble – and I'm half inclined to agree with her.'

Sorrel nodded but didn't answer as she drifted back to the house. It wasn't fair of her parents to have a down on Shima just because he'd been brought up as a gipsy. He was always polite and nice to her and he'd cured Dobbin's leg, which made her feel kindly towards him. Besides, she liked him – she liked the way he smiled at her, as if she were special.

'And what's eating you?' May asked as she went into the kitchen. 'You want to watch the wind doesn't change or you'll look like you've eaten sour cheese for the rest of your life.'

'Pa was saying about the walk off down the acres.'

100

'Gipsies! I warned him there would be trouble, didn't I? I said no good would come of having them here.'

'Yes, you did.' Sorrel smiled at her mother winningly. 'Can we go to Ely market this weekend, Ma?'

There was now a new motor-bus that ran once a week on a Thursday all the way from Chatteris to Ely, stopping in the village to pick up passengers in the morning and drop them off again in the afternoon. They made use of it perhaps once a month, visiting the market town for supplies they could not buy in the village shop. It was much easier than driving in with the pony and trap, and warmer in the winter.

'You'll be wanting a new dress for Fanny's party, I suppose?' May studied her thoughtfully for a moment or two. 'I thought we might go into Cambridge on the train and buy a dress from a shop. We could meet your aunt and have tea together somewhere. She could help us pick something smart – the sort of thing Fanny and her friends wear.'

'Do you mean it?' Sorrel was incredulous. They always made their own clothes or bought them from the market in Ely. They had only ever gone shopping in Cambridge once and that was in a char-a-banc got up by the vicar as a church outing. May had only gone then because she'd wanted a new hat for Bob's wedding. 'We can really buy a proper frock in a posh shop?'

Some soup was bubbling on the hob, filling the kitchen with its rich, tantalising aroma. Sorrel went to move it off the fierce heat so that it simmered gently.

'Well, why not?' May's eyes were bright with the spirit of adventure. 'I've got a few pounds put by me – and you're a young woman now. You ought to have a decent dress or two. Ted can take us to the station in the trap and we'll go for the day. I might as well buy myself something, too. It will do us both good. Mabel can come round and hold the fort here for once.'

Sorrel had been about to ask if her sister-in-law could go with them but her mother was right: someone had to be at the cottage to look after the men and serve callers with eggs, milk and their special cheeses. The work wouldn't stop just because they had decided to take a holiday.

'We'll go the day after tomorrow,' May said, her cheeks

pink with excitement. When her eyes sparkled like that she looked young enough to be Sorrel's sister instead of her mother. 'It's ages since we had a day out.'

'Oh, Ma.' Sorrel laughed as she caught her mother's reckless mood. 'You're that good to me!'

'You deserve it,' she replied, surprising Sorrel. 'So do I, come to that. We both work hard and we deserve a treat – but it means we've twice as much to do today, so you'd best look sharp. Mrs Robinson wants eggs and cheese. You can take them round now but hurry back. I want this kitchen scrubbed to an inch of its life if Mabel's coming on Friday.'

'Yes, of course I will.' Sorrel grabbed her coat from the peg behind the door, her fingers all thumbs as she buttoned it to the neck. 'Don't worry, Ma. I'll do the kitchen when I get back.'

She fetched her basket, filling it with eggs and two of the small round cheeses her mother made and dried on little straw mats in the dairy. They tasted smooth and creamy, much better than anything the shops sold.

The wind was bitter as she started out and it stung her eyes. There was still a crunch of frost beneath her feet though it had begun to clear from the rooftops and some of the trees were dripping; if the thaw continued the paths would soon be slushy and slippery. It could even turn to rain and that meant the land, which had been saturated the week before, would become almost impossible to work – and that could make the situation with the gipsies even more difficult.

Sorrel walked quickly, delivering her goods to Tom Robinson's mother and stopping only a few moments for a brief chat before turning homeward. She was mindful of her mother's warning that they would have to work harder for the next day or so, to make up for the promised holiday, and she wanted to get on with scrubbing the kitchen.

As she reached the lane that wound past the churchyard she saw a woman bend to pick something from the hedge, and hesitated. Her father had warned her to stay away from the gipsies but she couldn't just walk past without speaking. Then Tarina swung round to face her and Sorrel sensed that she had been waiting for her.

102

'I thought I might meet you here,' she said as Sorrel stopped. 'I wanted to warn you . . .'

'Warn me of what?' An odd prickling sensation had started at the nape of her neck, sending cold shivers over her body. 'What's wrong, Tarina?'

Her eyes were dark and brooding, shadowed by some strange emotion that might have been fear – or even guilt. 'I saw that evil man,' she said. 'He was drunk.'

'Oh, you mean Lenny?' Sorrel nodded, thinking that she understood. 'I've seen him too. He seems to drink all the time these days.'

'Shima should have slit his throat when he had the chance. He owes me blood.' Now there was definitely a hint of guilt or defiance in her voice.

'Lenny has a scar on his cheek. I think perhaps Shima made him pay in blood after all.'

'It isn't enough.' Her eyes had the chill of black ice and Sorrel felt cold inside. There was so much raw passion in her that she felt the gipsy woman might be capable of anything. 'Once I loved Shima more than my life, but he betrayed me.'

Again Sorrel sensed a deep, dark emotion in her and she could not be sure whether it was love or hate. Perhaps it was a strange mixture of both, but whatever it was she felt it with all her being, all her soul. Sorrel knew instinctively that Tarina would be capable of loving or hating with equal fervour.

'Thank you for the warning,' she said, preparing to walk on. 'I'm sorry, I must go. Ma wants me to scrub the kitchen and she'll be cross if I don't hurry back.'

'I see danger for you,' Tarina said suddenly, eyes fixed in a wild staring look. 'Be warned, Sorrel Harris. The blood is coming and when it does it will touch your life . . . and mine.'

'What do you mean?' Sorrel's voice dropped to a hushed whisper. Her stomach was churning and she felt frightened. 'What danger – what blood?'

Tarina shook her head, looking bewildered. 'I don't know,' she said, and her face was ashen. 'The words came to me. You and I are linked in blood, that much is certain – but I don't know why or where.'

103

She brushed past Sorrel, running as if she feared the devil were after her. Sorrel was frightened, too, but not as terrified as the gipsy woman seemed to be. It was as if she had glimpsed the future, seeing something so horrible that it had scared her witless.

'Don't be daft, Sorrel Harris!' She spoke the words aloud to comfort herself. 'It was all a pack of nonsense.' She reassured herself as she started to walk home. Gipsy women made their living by telling fortunes but they invented all those stories of good or evil destinies. Yet both Sadie and Tarina seemed to have a strange power – the gift, or curse, of second sight.

Sorrel increased her pace. She had better things to do than worry about Tarina's warning. She and her mother were going shopping and she was about to ride on a train for the first time in her life.

'You – 'tis you that will bring the evil on us! You that will bring the blood . . . blood . . . nothing but death and danger for you here. Be warned . . . be warned . . .'

Sorrel sat up with a start, waking from the nightmare to find her nightdress soaked with sweat. She saw that it was almost light and threw off the bedcovers, jumping out on to the cold floor to run across to the window and look out. Thank goodness! It was a clear, dry morning and there was nothing unusual about the scene in the yard below . . . nothing to stop the promised trip to Cambridge.

It proved to be every bit as exciting to ride behind the huge, noisy steam engine as she had imagined, but then, their day out in the lovely old university city of Cambridge, with its pleasant greens and beautiful, ancient colleges, was a success altogether.

May's sister Ruth met them at the station with a taxi that took them into the centre of the town. She was dressed in a smart blue coat with a fur collar, and exclaimed as she saw Sorrel.

'You're all grown up,' she cried, and hugged her. 'And beautiful . . . really pretty.'

'Don't turn her head with that nonsense,' May said, but looked indulgently at her daughter. 'We're relying on you to help us, Ruth. Sorrel has been invited to Fanny Sawle's party, as I told you in my letter – and we want something special.'

'I know just what you're looking for,' Ruth said, an odd expression in her eyes. 'So Rebecca Sawle is still giving her parties then? She hasn't changed much, I don't suppose.'

'Now don't start all that, Ruth,' May said, a hint of warning in her voice. 'You ought to forget and forgive . . . it was years ago.'

'What was?' Sorrel was curious. 'Don't you like Mrs Sawle, Aunt Ruth?'

Ruth saw the look in her sister's eyes and hesitated. 'May is right,' she said at last. 'Me and Rebecca fell out years ago, but it was all a storm in a teacup – or a teapot!' She laughed at herself. 'Nothing for you to worry about, love. But we're going to make sure you look posh for the party.'

It was Ruth's determination that kept them going. They walked and walked through the narrow streets, round the cobbled market place, up and down the narrow alley of Petty Cury, along Regent Street and then back down Sidney Street and round to the market place again.

'My feet are dropping off,' May said. 'Let's have a cup of tea.'

They were laden down with parcels and bags full of exciting things – but they still hadn't bought Sorrel's dress, though May had got herself a new costume for Sundays and they had presents for all the family.

'We'll go back to that expensive shop,' Ruth said. 'You didn't want to go in, Sorrel, but I'm sure we'll find what we want there.'

'Won't it be too dear?' she asked anxiously. 'I don't want to cost Ma too much money.'

'Don't you worry about that,' May said. 'I've come prepared to get you a dress – and that's what I'm going to do.'

'You needn't worry about the price,' Ruth said. 'I've already made up my mind to buy it for you. And you needn't look like that, May. She'll be wanting other things – shoes and an evening stole . . . and pretty underwear.'

May argued but Ruth was adamant and after they'd finished their tea they went back to the shop in Regent

Street. It was carpeted throughout and so posh that Sorrel was still reluctant to go in but her mother pushed open the door and marched her up to the manageress, who was wearing a smart black dress with a little brooch fastened at its high neck.

'My daughter is going to her friend's coming out party,' May announced, not without a hint of pride. 'Miss Sawle is from a good country family and we want something suitable for a young lady.'

'I'm not sure we have anything . . .' The woman's cold eyes swept over Sorrel with an air of disbelief. 'And what price range is Madam looking for?'

'The price is of no account,' Ruth said sharply. 'We want something tasteful and of good quality.'

'Very well, I think we can serve the young lady.' The manageress snapped her fingers. 'Miss Mary will find you something suitable.'

The assistant she summoned looked more approachable and Sorrel sighed with relief as she smiled at her.

'I can think of three or four dresses that might suit you,' she said. 'With your complexion you can take a really rich colour . . . perhaps a deep blue or emerald.' She hesitated, looking uncertain. 'The emerald is the very nicest we have but a little expensive.'

'Bring it for her to try,' Ruth said decisively. 'We want the best you have.'

Sorrel loved the deep emerald colour of the velvet as soon as she saw the dress but she was afraid it might be too smart. It had long, tight sleeves, a high frilled collar of stiffened lace that stood up at the back of the neck but dipped to a deep V at the front, which, when she tried it on, allowed a glimpse of her white skin – and there was a short train at the back.

'You look beautiful,' the saleswoman told her as she came out of the dressing room and twirled in front of a large oval mirror on a wooden stand. 'Quite the sophisticated young lady.'

'Does it make me look too old?' Sorrel glanced at her mother anxiously, wanting her opinion. 'What do you think, Aunt Ruth?'

'It's perfect,' her aunt replied. 'But you must decide – it's your dress.'

May looked at her daughter long and hard, then smiled. 'You look like a young woman, Sorrel – but that's what you are now. It suits you. If you like it, I think you should have it.'

When the assistant named the price it took Sorrel's breath away and she saw her mother's face fall, but her aunt seemed to take it in her stride. She nodded to the assistant.

'Thank you, we'll take it. Please wrap it carefully. My niece has to carry it home on the train.'

'Are you sure?' Sorrel asked when the assistant took the dress away. 'I could have made three or four dresses with the money.'

'But not one like this,' her aunt said. 'Believe me, Sorrel, it will give me a great deal of satisfaction to know you'll be wearing this at Fanny Sawle's dance. I doubt if even she will have a better one.'

Again there was a hint of something secret as Ruth and May looked at one another. Sorrel was curious but daren't ask – especially as her aunt was being so generous over the dress. She felt guilty as she saw Ruth count out the crisp white five-pound notes. It was such a lot of money.

'Thank you so much,' she said as they all left the shop together. 'I shall never forget how good you've been to me.'

'Just have a good time at that party,' Ruth said. 'Now – we'd better go and buy all the other things you'll need.'

'Richie Sawle won't be able to sneer at you this time,' May said with satisfaction as she lashed out on new shoes and an evening cape with a little fur collar. 'I've been saving up for this for a while, and with Ruth buying you the dress, you're going to have everything you need to make you as smart as all the others.'

'With her looks, she'll be the belle of the ball,' Ruth said. 'That will be one in the eye for Rebecca. She won't look down her nose at my niece if I have anything to do with it!'

Ruth said goodbye to them after the shopping spree was ended and they took another taxi back to the station, loaded down with so many parcels that they could hardly carry them all.

'I thought Ruth might give you something,' May said when

107

they were settled on the train. 'But I never thought she would be that generous – it's because of Rebecca, of course.'

'Did they fall out or something?'

'It began when Ruth worked for her many years ago,' May said. 'She dropped Richie, and Rebecca sent her home in disgrace – then there was a silly business over a teapot Ruth won at the fête. It was all nonsense and best forgotten. It can't make any difference to you: it was too long ago to matter.'

Sorrel nodded. Her mother was right, it couldn't make any difference to her if her aunt and Rebecca Sawle had fallen out years before.

Ted met them at the station in Ely. He cracked his sides laughing as he saw them come struggling out with all their parcels.

'Bought the shop, did you?' he asked. 'Eggs must pay! I'll have to go into business myself.'

'I'll be saving for your wedding now,' May said, giving him a sharp look. 'It's about time you thought about settling down, my lad!'

Ted was silenced, his skin flushing a deep, dark red. It was the first time his mother had spoken out like that and Sorrel wondered if he would be shaken out of the rut he had fallen into.

She soon forgot about Ted and his girl, though. She could still hardly believe how lucky she was to have such a wonderful dress for Fanny's party and began to count the days. Surely nothing could go wrong to spoil things this time.

Chapter Fifteen

Shima frowned as he saw the man stop Tarina, deliberately holding her, preventing her from walking on. He was too far away to hear what was being said but it was obvious that she was upset and frightened. He started to walk towards them, calling her name aloud. Jake saw him coming, let her go and walked off.

'What did he say to you?' Shima asked as he met her. 'Was he annoying you again?'

Tarina was reluctant to meet his eyes. 'He ... he told me he wanted me,' she said in a low voice. 'That he would have me one day.' She brought her head up suddenly. 'He has looked at me before – but this is the first time he has spoken so plainly.'

'Then it's time I acted.'

'What do you mean?' Tarina's face was very pale, her eyes dark with fear. 'If you challenge him, he will kill you. He already hates you.'

'If Jake hates me it will come to a fight. Better it should be of my making than his.'

Tarina caught at his coat sleeve as he would have gone after Jake. 'Please don't,' she begged, her voice husky and pleading. 'I could not bear it if ...'

'I am not afraid of Jake.' Shima looked at her sadly. 'You were angry with me once because I could not bring myself to kill that young lad for you all those years ago – why will you not let me protect you now? I will fight Jake for you and kill him if it is necessary, though I think like all bullies, he will run rather than take a beating.'

Tears caught at her throat but she forced them away, lifting her head proudly. 'I want nothing from you,' she said. 'You should not have come back. When we leave you should stay here. You do not belong with us. You never have.'

Shima watched as she walked away, her back stiff with pride. He understood why she had tried to hurt him and did not blame her for her bitter words.

He was sorry he could not love her in the way she wanted to be loved . . . and she was right. He did not belong with the gipsies. He had known it in his heart ever since he'd come . . . but where *did* he belong?

Aden Sawle was his father. No one had ever told him so for certain, though years ago, after Lorenzo's death, Sadie had implied that it was so – but he did not need to be told. It was in Aden's eyes when he looked at him: a certain warmth, mixed with guilt and shame.

His father wanted him to stay on the farm; Aden had said it more than once but Shima wasn't sure. A part of him wanted to stay, to belong to the family at Five Winds . . . but something told him he must go. And go before it was too late.

Before he went, though, he must speak to his father – and someone else. He smiled as he thought of her, so soft and pretty with that shining innocence that made him want to protect her – to keep her safe from all harm.

Yes, he would walk across the fields to Mepal and perhaps, if he was lucky, he would see her for a few moments.

Ted was grinding the wurzels for stock feed when Sorrel drove Dobbin into the yard that morning, the empty milk churns rattling in the little cart behind her.

'Hey, Sorrel!' he called as she looped the reins and jumped down. 'Will you do something for me?'

'After I've rubbed Dobbin down.'

He nodded and went into the barn. Ted didn't often ask for favours but he had been thoughtful ever since he'd fetched his mother and sister from the station and Sorrel was fairly sure she knew what was on his mind.

'So what do you want?' she asked after she had settled her pony. 'What can I do for you?'

110

'Pa asked me to go shepherding when I've finished feeding,' Ted said, his cheeks turning bright red. 'But I was wondering . . . I'd like to get off to Sutton to see Rose . . .'

'Well, I've got to wash the churns and Ma wants me to help with the baking,' she teased, keeping him hanging on. 'Go on then, Ted Harris! Of course I'll do it for you. Just tell Rose I'd like to be a bridesmaid.'

She had never been as close to Ted as she was to Bob but she was fond of him and wanted to see him happy; she just hoped he hadn't been pushed into doing something he wasn't sure of. But he was old enough to know his own mind.

His colour deepened to brick. 'That's if she'll have me.'

'If I know anything about it, she's nearly given up hope of your ever asking. She must be potty about you or she would have found another lad long ago.'

Ted laughed and looked pleased. Singing softly to herself Sorrel went into the clean coolness of the dairy to wash the churns. Ted would be getting married soon and maybe, just maybe, it wouldn't be too long before there was yet another wedding in the family. Of course Jay hadn't said anything but once he'd seen her in that wonderful dress her aunt had bought her . . . why, anything could happen!

The bullocks were grazing just ahead of her. They had wandered further down the bank than usual and Sorrel knew that this was probably almost the last time anyone would need to come shepherding until spring. The grass was poor, thin stuff and the cattle would be taken into the home pasture for the winter feeding anyday now. She counted as fast as she could; it was getting colder and she thought longingly of the hot jam turnover waiting for her elevenses at home.

'Twenty-seven . . . eight . . . nine . . . thirty.'

They were all there. Satisfied, she turned and began to walk home. It was so cold! Her toes felt frozen inside her stout black boots and she could see white frosting on the grass. Across the river a ribbon of mist curled out towards her, making her look anxiously ahead to the farm. She prayed the fog wouldn't come down too thickly before she

111

was home; she wasn't exactly frightened but it was eerie and sounds became muffled in such weather. Tucking her head down against the wind, her hands thrust into her pockets for warmth, she walked as fast as she could.

Perhaps because she was concentrating on getting home she failed to see the man until he spoke to her. His voice startled her and her head came up, her heart beginning to thump madly as she saw who it was. As she looked at him her father's warnings came flooding back.

'Hello,' she said, not quite sure what to do. He was blocking her path, making it difficult for her to pass without going too near the edge of the bank. 'Cold, isn't it?'

She breathed in steadily and tried to reason with herself. Lenny couldn't mean her any harm. Why should he? Just because everyone said he was no good, it didn't mean he was dangerous. He would move in a minute. He was probably just being silly, teasing her the way men often did, asserting his masculine superiority. She got enough of it from her brothers; there was no need to be afraid, no need to feel so sick inside. Her tongue moved nervously over lips numbed by the chill wind and she shifted from one foot to the other, trying not to let her teeth chatter. Why didn't he say anything? He was just staring at her with those sullen eyes ... eyes that threatened and mocked her. She swallowed hard and took a step to the right. He moved to block her once more. She stopped then tried to go round him. He was ahead of her, a sneer of triumph on his mouth as he forced her to stop again.

'Please let me pass,' she said at last. 'I have to get home. Pa is waiting for me.'

She was praying that her father would come out to look for her as he had once before but she knew it wouldn't happen. Sid was in the yard, overseeing a load of potatoes that had been sold to a merchant from March. No one knew she had come shepherding instead of her brother so she would not be missed for some time. She hadn't told anyone because she didn't want to cause trouble for Ted. Her father had told him to see to it and would be angry if he knew Ted had asked her to do it for him.

'You always were a stuck up little madam,' Lenny muttered resentfully. 'Too good to speak to me now, I suppose. You wouldn't be seen with a jailbird . . . not Miss Sorrel Harris.'

'Don't be silly. It's too cold to stop talking, that's all,' she said, trying to sound calm even though by now she was really frightened. 'Please let me by. Pa will be worried.'

'And what if I don't want to?' He leered at her, his breath making little white clouds on the chill air. She was shivering but she wasn't sure whether it was the cold or the mounting fear inside her. 'What if I decide to keep you here?'

'My pa will come after you and so will my brothers,' she said, her chin jutting as pride overcame her fear for a moment. 'You'd better watch out, Lenny Browne, or you'll be in trouble.'

'Ain't afeared of your pa,' he said with an evil grin. 'Nor your brothers neither. I reckon I'll just have me a little fun . . .'

He made a grab for her. She screamed and jumped back. He laughed and lunged at her, grasping her arm. She screamed again, then kicked his shin. Taken by surprise, he gave a grunt of pain and let go of her. She seized the opportunity to dodge past him and started to run.

The cold stung her face, bringing tears to her eyes and blurring her vision. She was panting, gulping for breath, as she fled before him. Oh, please don't let him catch her! Please don't let him hurt her . . .

He came after her, and as she glanced back, she saw he was gaining on her. Desperation made her stumble and she felt rather than saw his flying tackle from behind. His arms were round her, imprisoning her in an iron grip as she tried to fend him off. Her terrified screams sent a flock of starlings winging into the air. She struggled violently, kicking, biting and yelling as loudly as she could.

Surely someone would hear? Someone would help her! But who would be out on a lonely river bank on a bitter day like this?

'You little hellcat!' Lenny swore as her nails scored his cheek. 'It's time you were taught a lesson.'

Sorrel screamed again as he forced her head back. She twisted and turned, trying to avoid his slobbering mouth as he pressed it over hers. His breath was foul and made her retch as he belched in her face. She wrenched away, freeing one hand and jabbing at his eyes with her fingers.

'Bitch!' he said, and cursed furiously. 'You deserve all you get!'

He struck her hard across the face. Her lip split and she tasted blood. He hit her again and again, making her ears ring. She cried out despairingly for help, then his hands were round her throat, squeezing and hurting her, making her choke and gasp for air. He put his leg round the back of hers, pulling it from under her. She was on the ground: it was wet and something hard pressed into the back of her head. Lenny was on top of her, fumbling with her clothes with one hand while the other still crushed her throat. She couldn't breathe. Her chest hurt and everything was going hazy. She thought that she was dying and tears welled up in her eyes.

The shouts seemed to come from a long way off, through a mist that filled her head, clogging her nostrils and her throat. She was drifting away . . . far, far away.

'You filthy devil,' someone said. 'I'll kill you. I should have killed you the last time . . .'

Lenny had been trying to get her knickers off. They were the thick knitted cotton sort with tight elastic round the legs and waist and had caused him some difficulty. Sorrel was vaguely aware that he was no longer pawing at her, though his weight was still crushing her to the ground. Then, all of a sudden, the weight was jerked off her and there was a lot of yelling, grunting and groaning as a struggle commenced. One small part of her mind recognized that somehow help had arrived but she could not make the effort to move until someone touched her cheek.

'Damn him. Damn his evil soul to hell!' The fingers stroked her cheek gently. She moaned, fluttered her eyelids, then gave a cry of fear as she began to come to herself. 'Sorrel . . . Sorrel . . . it's all right, my little one. Can you hear me? It's all right . . .'

Her eyes flew open and she screamed. Still in shock, she struggled against the hands that held her, fearing that she was about to be attacked once more.

114

'It's all right,' Shima said in the gentle voice he had used with his ponies, so caressing and soft that she instinctively remembered and was comforted. 'You're safe now, my little one. He has gone. I am with you. No one shall hurt you. It's Shima, Sorrel. It's all right. Hush, my sweeting, you're safe now.'

The soft, repetitive words worked as a soothing balm, calming her. 'Shima . . .' Her eyes filmed with tears. 'He . . . he . . .' Her voice cracked and she swallowed as she felt the soreness in her throat. 'He was strangling me . . . I couldn't breathe . . .' She trembled as the gentle hands stroked her hair, comforting and easing her. 'I . . . passed out . . . did he . . .?' She looked at him with pleading eyes. 'Did . . .?'

'He hurt you,' Shima said. 'I was in time to prevent rape.'

She glanced down at herself, suddenly realizing that her skirt was up around her waist and her knickers halfway over her hips. She flushed bright red and yanked the substantial undergarments back up, then pulled her skirt down. Shima stood up and turned away as she covered herself and struggled to her feet, but swung round as she gave a muffled cry.

'What's wrong?' he asked, looking concerned. 'Are you faint again?'

'I think I must have wrenched my ankle when I fell,' she murmured, and swooned.

She would have fallen if he had not caught her, sweeping her up into his arms to hold her protectively against him. Sorrel's face registered her pain as she struggled to contain her tears. Shima's dark eyes narrowed with anger against the man who had hurt her.

'Will you let me examine your ankle?' he asked. 'I want to see if anything is broken.'

'Yes,' she whispered, swallowing hard. 'It hurts when I try to stand.'

He lowered her gently to the ground once more, running firm, sure fingers over her ankles and untying her boot to slip his fingers inside and ease it off. He was as gentle as he could be but it made her wince.

'Nothing broken,' he confirmed at last. 'But it's a bad sprain. You'll have to keep off your feet for a few days.'

'How shall I get home?' She looked round anxiously. There was no sign of Lenny; he had obviously run off when Shima tackled him – but she was afraid he might come back. 'Don't leave me here, Shima. Please don't leave me.'

'I wouldn't dream of leaving you,' he promised her, and smiled. 'I'll carry you home.'

'You can't carry me all that way! I'm too heavy.'

'As light as a feather,' he said, and took her up in his arms once more. 'Put your arms about my neck and trust me. We'll get there. I won't leave you. I'll take you home and then your father can fetch the doctor to make sure you have no other injuries.'

'It's just my ankle and some bruises.' Her cheeks were burning with embarrassment. 'My throat hurts but I'm not sore. He – he couldn't have done anything . . .'

'I told you, I was in time.' Shima laughed, his white teeth gleaming against the weathered tan of his skin. 'It was probably those knickers that saved you. They call them passion killers and it seems he couldn't manage them.' His expression changed as she gave him a watery smile then choked on a sob. 'Don't worry, Sorrel, he won't get away with it – not this time.'

She twisted her head round to look at his face. His mouth was hard, his eyes like wet flints. She could feel the coldness of his anger and it frightened her. He had never shown her anything but gentleness but she sensed there was another side to his nature, a dark side that might be capable of anything.

'Don't do anything bad, Shima,' she begged in a whispery voice. 'Let Pa go to the police this time, please. They will put Lenny in prison where he belongs.'

A little nerve was flickering at Shima's temple, betraying the anger he was trying to keep in check for her sake. 'Of course,' he said, 'that's what I meant.'

But it wasn't. She knew it instinctively. Something in his eyes made her tremble inside. He could be gentle and kind but she sensed the iron resolve beneath the softness and knew that this time Lenny would not escape so easily.

Her father was standing talking to Jay and Bob when Shima

116

carried her into the yard, and for a moment they all turned to stare as if they couldn't believe their eyes. Shima was walking very slowly and half stumbled, his strength almost exhausted by the long walk up the river bank with her in his arms. Sid gave a cry of alarm and raced across the yard towards them, taking Sorrel hastily into his own arms. She gave a little sigh, her eyes filling with tears.

'Pa . . . Pa . . .'

'What have you done to my little girl?' he demanded fiercely as he saw the state she was in. 'Damn you! You filthy bastard . . .'

'What is it, Pa?' Bob was there and his temper flared as he too jumped to a hasty conclusion. 'I'll kill you – you dirty gipsy bugger!'

'What's going on here?' Jay sounded bewildered. 'Shima . . . you didn't . . .'

'The gippo's had a go at her,' Bob cried, and flung himself at Shima, who was recovering his breath and, taken off balance, went down on his knees in the mud. Bob aimed a kick at him but missed as Sorrel screamed.

'Stop it, Bob! Pa, make him stop. Make him stop! It wasn't Shima. It was Lenny Browne. Shima saved me . . . he saved me . . .' She was crying now, her emotions spilling over helplessly. 'Lenny would have . . . but Shima came and stopped him.'

Bob looked goggle-eyed as Shima struggled to his feet and stood there staring at him in silent resentment. Jay looked from one to the other then turned to Sorrel, his face flushed with a mixture of anger and concern.

'Are you all right?' he asked, then as she nodded tearfully, he turned to her brother. 'Say something, you fool. You heard what Sorrel said. It wasn't Shima. He's brought her home to you – you should thank him.'

'I thought . . . I didn't know . . .' Bob looked as though he wished the ground would open up and let him through. 'Sorry, mate. It was seeing her like that. I thought you'd done it and I wanted to kill you.'

'In your shoes, I should feel the same,' Shima said a little stiffly. 'She's had a fright and has hurt her ankle – but I got there before he could do anything worse.'

'You saw that bastard attack her?' Jay cried, his mouth twisting with sudden anger. 'I'll kill him. I swear I'll kill him!'

'I should have done it when he attacked Tarina,' Shima said, his face white and strained. 'This is my blood affair, Jay – not yours. He shall not escape this time, I swear it.'

For a moment the two men stared at each other, anger, pride and a hint of jealousy in their eyes. They were so alike then that Sorrel's heart caught with pain and she gasped. Her little cry seemed to spur her father to action and he turned away, carrying her towards the house so that she could no longer see their faces.

'They won't do anything silly, will they?' she asked him, her eyes filling with tears again. 'I don't want either of them to get into trouble because of me. Please, Pa . . . don't let them.'

'Don't you worry, lass,' he said gruffly. 'I'll sort them out in a minute. Once I've seen you safe with your mother.'

'Oh, Pa, she'll be so cross with me . . .'

'Nay, lass,' he said, smiling down at her reassuringly. 'Not this time. I reckon we all know who to blame for this – and he'll get what's coming to him. The law will see to that. With his record they'll throw away the key.'

'Don't be cross with Ted,' she begged. 'He didn't know this would happen. He didn't think . . .'

'Well, he should have,' her father said. 'He knew I didn't want you down that bank alone, especially with that Lenny Browne back in the village – but I'll go easy on him, for your sake.'

She closed her eyes as he carried her inside. Her throat felt as if it had been rubbed raw with a rasp and her ankle ached so much that she wanted to cry.

As soon as May saw them she started fussing.

'What's wrong with her?' she shrilled. 'What did that gipsy do to her? I told you there would be trouble with them here. I warned you . . . and I warned her not to go near them . . .'

'Hush your fussing, May,' Sid said. 'She's not bad hurt and it was the gipsy saved her from worse. I'll take her

118

upstairs and you can help her to bed. She's hurt her ankle. Once she's safe, I'll get one of the lads to go for the doctor.'

'And Fanny's party not two weeks away!' said May. She's not going to miss that. You'll stay in bed until you're better – do you hear me, Sorrel?'

'Yes, Ma.' The tears were slipping down her cheeks. It would be awful if she couldn't go to the party after all the money they'd spent on her dress. 'It wasn't my fault . . . honest it wasn't.'

'No need to tell me that,' May said in a softer tone. 'But you shouldn't have been down that bank alone. I'll have a few words to say to your brother when he gets back.'

Chapter Sixteen

Sorrel cried herself to sleep that night, though she didn't know why she was crying; she wasn't really hurt, except for her ankle. Lenny had frightened her but Shima had come in time to rescue her and . . . the look in his eyes had frightened her. That was why she felt so awful: she was afraid that he might do something terrible.

She wanted to get up the next day but her mother wouldn't let her – and no one would tell her anything. She needed to know if the police had arrested Lenny but when she tried to ask questions her family changed the subject, their expressions closed and secretive.

'There's nothing for you to worry your head over,' her father said. 'You just rest for a few days and everything will be fine.'

But it wouldn't be fine if Shima carried out his threat to make Lenny pay for what he had done to her.

It was a couple of days later that Fanny came to call. Sorrel was sitting in the parlour with her foot up on a stool when Fanny entered the room carrying a book and a small box of jelly sweets, which she laid down on the table beside her.

'How are you?' she asked, looking upset. 'I would have come sooner but Jay said you were still in bed.'

'Bored but otherwise fine,' Sorrel replied. 'I got up for the first time this morning. My ankle is much better but Ma won't let me do anything.'

'Will you be able to come to my party?'

'Yes, I'm sure I shall. The doctor said I would be all right in a day or so – the pain has almost gone already, and the swelling went down last night.'

'Good.' Fanny glanced over her shoulder as if to make sure no one was there. 'Jay told me not to say anything but I thought you ought to know – Lenny Browne has disappeared.'

'I hope he has gone for good this time. He's horrible, Fanny. You don't know what it was like.' Sorrel caught her breath on a sob. 'If Shima hadn't come when he did . . .'

'It must have been awful,' Fanny agreed, then looked at her hesitantly. 'They don't seem to think Lenny has run away this time.'

'What do you mean?' A chill ran down Sorrel's spine as she remembered the look in Shima's eyes. What had he done? Please, please, don't let him have done anything wicked!

'I heard our fathers discussing it,' Fanny said in a low voice. 'I was behind a door and they didn't realize I was there – they think Lenny may have been murdered.'

'Oh, no!' Sorrel's nails pressed into the palms of her hand and she felt sick. 'What makes them think that?'

'Both Shima and Jay went looking for him,' Fanny replied with a worried expression. 'They were both heard to say that they would kill him for what he did to you.'

'But Jay wouldn't . . .' Sorrel drew a shaky breath as she remembered his harsh words. 'I know he said things but he was angry and spoke without thinking. I'm sure Jay wouldn't . . . but Shima . . . Shima might . . . Yes, he might.'

'That's what our fathers are worried about,' Fanny said. She twisted her gloves in her hands nervously, then looked directly at Sorrel. 'Jay told me . . . that Shima is our half-brother, not a gipsy at all.'

'He shouldn't have told you,' Sorrel said, but Fanny shook her head.

'I'd half guessed from something my father said – but it makes it all much worse, doesn't it? Especially as Shima seems to have disappeared, too.'

'It's awful,' Sorrel agreed, a sob in her voice. 'But perhaps everyone is worrying for nothing. Lenny might have gone off again, just as he did last time, and Shima . . .' But Shima would not have gone off like that without good reason. Not without coming to say goodbye to her. 'Oh, Fanny,' she whispered. 'I wish it hadn't happened . . . any of it. I feel it's my fault. If I hadn't been there Lenny couldn't have attacked me and then none of this would have . . .'

'But that wasn't your fault. No one thinks that.'

'Some people will say it's my fault. They'll think I led him on . . . that I'm fast . . .'

'No, they won't,' Fanny said. 'Even my mother said they should lock him up and throw the key down a deep well.'

Sorrel tried to return Fanny's smile but she felt close to tears again. If Shima had murdered a man because of her . . . If he were arrested and then hung . . . she couldn't bear the thought. Suddenly, she remembered Sadie's warning all those years ago . . . and Tarina's strange words a few days earlier . . . she had seen blood but she had said it linked them. That they were linked in blood . . . but how could that be? How could what had happened link her with the gipsy woman? Except that Shima might have thought it time to avenge them both.

That night Sorrel prayed that nothing terrible had happened to Lenny Browne. She hated him and hoped he would never return to the village but she didn't want him to be murdered for her sake. She didn't want to be the cause of Shima's arrest and imprisonment.

Her prayers were in vain. The next morning Lenny's body was found by an eel fisherman; it had been caught in reeds in the river. Lenny's throat had been slit and, after a search, a blood-stained knife was found nearby on the grassy bank. The knife was very distinctive and had Shima's name burned into the handle.

Everyone was talking about the murder and blaming Shima. They said it was revenge for what Lenny had done to Tarina years before, but Jay didn't agree with the general opinion.

'It wasn't for her sake,' he said when he called round to see Sorrel that afternoon. 'If Shima did kill Lenny it was because of what he did to you, Sorrel.'

'Yes, I know.' She looked at him, her eyes large and

anxious in her pale face. 'What will they do to him if they find him?'

'He'll be arrested, of course. If they find him guilty . . . he'll hang. At best he'll spend the rest of his life in prison – and I think he would rather hang.'

'Oh, Jay,' she whispered as he finished. 'We can't let that happen. It mustn't happen. If Shima did it, it was to protect me. We have to help him, Jay. We must.'

He nodded, his eyes reflecting her own anxiety. 'I know. I'm going to speak to my father when I go home. I think I know where Shima may be hiding. If I can find him, I can give him money to get away.'

'Are you sure you should? Talk to your father, I mean.'

'Shima is my half-brother, Father's eldest son. I believe he will want to help him. Besides, what else can I do? Shima will need more money than I've got if he is to get away. He'll have to leave the country.'

It might be Shima's only chance. From all she knew of Aden Sawle, Sorrel believed he would be on his son's side – but would he think it better that Shima should give himself up?

'But where will he go?' she asked. 'He'll be a fugitive for the rest of his life.'

'Unless he can prove his innocence.'

'But they found his knife, didn't they? And everyone heard him say it was his blood affair.'

'We still can't be sure he did it,' Jay said, 'but I think he would find it difficult to prove his innocence. There's nothing for him but to leave the country.'

'Ask your father to help him,' she said in a choked voice. 'I can't bear to think of Shima in trouble – and it's all my fault.'

'Of course it isn't,' Jay said as he saw her distress. He stood up to leave. 'But I shall speak to my father. I'm certain he will help. Don't worry, Sorrel. I'll sort this out. If Shima is where I think he may be, we can get him away before anyone else finds him.'

There was hardly any light in the sky but Jay's eyes had adjusted to the gloom as he walked through the lonely droves. The place that Shima had once spoken of was deep in the fens, an old shed that had been used long ago for keeping pigs and had now tumbled into disrepair. It had been built miles from anywhere and was sheltered by a belt of ancient willows that screened it from the view of any casual passer by. Besides, in winter no one ever ventured this deeply into the fens, unless it was a wildfowler in search of game.

'What makes you think he might go there?' Aden had asked when Jay told him of his plan.

'It's just a feeling,' he replied. 'Shima said it was a good place for snaring wildfowl. He could live there for a while – until the heat has died down.'

Jay paused as he saw the clump of twisted willows. He hadn't been sure he could find the spot Shima had described and felt a sense of triumph. There had been a good chance that he might miss it, get lost in this isolated wilderness. The fens were lonely enough by day but at night they became sinister, eerie, the haunt of ghosts and spirits from ages past, places of mystery – and, yes, of a strange beauty that touched the soul – but they could also be treacherous for the unwary.

The clouds rolled away and for a moment the darkness was lit by a sudden shaft of moonlight, then the shadows fell once more and Jay was blinded by the night. He neither saw nor heard anything until the shadow crossed his path. A cry of alarm was on his lips as he half turned and was knocked to the ground, held there by a powerful body as the tip of a knife was pressed to his throat.

'For God's sake, Shima,' he croaked, knowing a moment of apprehension. Supposing his half-brother was a cold-blooded murderer? 'I've come to help you, not betray you.'

'Bloody fool,' Shima muttered and removed the knife. 'I could have killed you.' He got to his feet and gave Jay his hand, pulling him to his feet. 'How did you know where to find me?'

'You told me about this place,' Jay replied, his eyes adjusting to the blackness once more. 'Where did you come from? I never saw you.'

'I've been following you for a while but I didn't realize it

124

was you. What do you want? I'm not going back with you. I won't give myself up. I would rather be dead than caged.'

Jay strained to see his face in the gloom. 'I didn't come here for that. I want to help you get away.'

'Why?' He could feel Shima's hostility and sensed a deep anger and bitterness in his half-brother. 'You think I killed Lenny Browne, don't you?'

'I don't know – did you?'

'I meant to. He was dead when I found him.'

'Your knife was discovered near the body.'

'Yes . . . I saw it lying there.'

Jay was puzzled. 'Why leave the knife if you didn't use it? It's almost as if . . . as if it were meant to be found.'

Shima gave a harsh laugh. 'To point the finger of suspicion at me? Yes – what else?' There was controlled anger in his voice. 'The proof of my guilt.'

'You didn't kill him, did you?' Jay wished he could see his face. 'If it wasn't you, why leave the knife?'

'Because it should have been me.' Shima hesitated. 'I thought it might have been you. I lent you my knife a few days ago . . . to cut some string when we were bagging potatoes.'

'Did you? Yes, I remember. I left it on the sacks for you. But you thought I'd kept it and . . .' Jay swore loudly. 'Damn you, Shima! I wouldn't have done that to you. What the hell do you think I am?'

'No, I suppose not.' Shima sounded odd. 'I wasn't thinking very clearly that night. I'd gone in search of Lenny and I think I would have killed him if I'd found him first. I'm sorry, Jay. I should have known it wasn't you.'

'If it wasn't either of us – who the hell was it?'

Shima was silent for another moment, then: 'Leyan. It must have been him. He hates me because when we were young our father favoured me. Lorenzo was forever beating him but he still loved him . . . as I did in my way.'

'But you weren't Lorenzo's son,' Jay said huskily. 'You and I share the same father. He is very concerned for you. He gave me money . . .'

'But didn't come himself.' Again there was a hint of bitter-

125

ness in Shima's words. 'I may be his son but I'm only a bastard.'

'Don't judge him,' Jay said. 'He wanted to come with me but I persuaded him to let me come alone. You are my brother, Shima. Believe me, our father loves you – even if he has never shown it.'

'Perhaps.' Shima sounded odd, as if his emotions were at war. 'Tell him . . . tell him I said thank you.'

'Of course.' Jay hesitated. 'Can you prove it was Leyan who killed Lenny Browne?'

'Would anyone believe me when my knife was found with Lenny's blood on it? I doubt it.'

'Then you have to get away . . . go abroad. Father gave me money for you, enough to see you through for a while.' Jay took a heavy bag from inside his coat. 'It's mixed coin and some notes. Father said you would need some small change to avoid drawing attention to yourself. He said you should try to find work on a small trading vessel rather than travel as a passenger – it's less suspicious.'

'That's what I was thinking myself. Thank you for coming, Jay – and forgive me for suspecting you.'

Shima took the money bag from him. Their fingers touched and then they were suddenly clasping hands, hugging each other in a sudden expression of the closeness they had both felt for some time without ever speaking of it. Shima's voice was husky as he drew away.

'Take care of her, Jay. Don't let her suffer for this.'

Jay looked at him hard. 'You mean Sorrel, don't you?'

'Yes. I know she's yours. You've made that plain and I wish you both happiness . . . but I would have taken her from you if I could. I think you know that.'

'Is that why you thought I had killed Lenny with your knife?'

'Perhaps. I was a fool.' Shima smiled in the darkness. 'I should have known you had too much honour. Besides, it's you she wants. Even if this had never happened.'

'She thinks a lot of you,' Jay said, forcing the words out. 'She begged me to help you. I would have come anyway but she asked.'

126

'Thank you for that,' Shima said. 'Do what you can for Tarina, Jay. She has no one but Sadie . . . and Leyan.'

'I'll speak to Father about her,' Jay promised. 'I should go now. He won't rest until he hears that I found you.'

'Goodbye then – and thank you.'

'Where will you go?'

'To America perhaps – or Ireland.' Shima shrugged. 'It hardly matters, so long as I'm free.'

'God go with you,' Jay said. 'I shall pray for your safety – and that we shall meet again one day.'

Chapter Seventeen

Sorrel looked out of the window. It was a dull, grey day and she was so tired of being cooped up in the house. She hadn't seen anyone from the Sawle household for two days and was sick with anxiety. Had Shima got away? What was happening?

Her family were maintaining a determined silence over the whole affair; it was as if they had drawn together in a conspiracy to protect her – but it was tearing her apart. At last she could stand the silence no longer and decided to visit Fanny at home. Surely she had heard something? Someone must know what was going on!

Her mother looked at her suspiciously when she saw Sorrel wearing a coat and muffler.

'And where do you think you're off to, miss?' May challenged. 'I thought I told you to rest that ankle?'

'It's better,' she replied. 'Honestly, Ma. I thought I would go round and see Mabel. I need a breath of fresh air.' It wasn't a complete lie because she had every intention of calling to see her sister-in-law as soon as she had spoken to Fanny. 'I shall go mad if I sit about much longer.'

Her mother gave her a searching look. 'Off you go then – but keep away from those gipsies, and I mean all of them. I've heard some of them are camping ... just keep away, Sorrel. Do you hear me?'

'Yes, Ma. I hear.' She aimed a kiss at her mother's cheek. Her skin was as soft as a girl's, though she never used anything on it but soap and cold water. 'Shan't be long.'

The air was bitterly cold as she went outside, catching the

tip of her nose and making it tingle. Her father was talking to Aden near the barn; they were deep in a discussion of something or other and had their backs to her.

Fearful that they would order her straight back inside she slipped away unnoticed, taking the lane behind the church instead of the main road that wound through the village. Hung with fronds of shining white crystals, the trees and hedges looked less forlorn than they had of late, and the fields were carpeted with frost. From the dull, leaden grey of the sky it was obvious that the sun would not shine all day and it might even turn to freezing fog by the afternoon.

The thought of fog reminded her of the terrible events of the past few days, sending shivers down her spine. How horrible it had all been – and now Lenny was dead and Shima . . . Shima might soon be dead or in prison.

'Sorrel . . . Sorrel Harris!'

She had been lost in her own thoughts and the gipsy woman's voice startled her. She glanced guiltily over her shoulder, hoping that no one was watching her from an upstairs window. She couldn't ignore Tarina, no matter what her mother had said earlier. Besides, she might know something.

'Tarina . . .' Sorrel caught her breath as she saw how agitated the other woman was. 'What has happened? What have you heard?'

'The police came to our camp looking for Shima – they searched everywhere and threatened us with prison if we helped to hide him.'

Sorrel's heart thumped with fear and she could hardly breathe as she asked, 'Did they find him? Have they arrested him?'

'No.' Tarina moved closer, clutching at her arm. 'He had gone but they will find him . . . I know they will catch him.' Her eyes were wild with fear and pain. 'If they hang him it will be our fault – yours and mine.'

'They mustn't hang him!' Sorrel cried, and her stomach clenched with fright. 'Do you know where he is? Do you know where we can find him?'

Tarina shook her head, her grip tightening on Sorrel's

arm. 'No – but I know that he didn't kill that gorgio. It wasn't Shima.'

Sorrel stared at her in bewilderment. 'How can you know for sure? The knife they found belonged to Shima . . . it was stained with Lenny's blood.' The horror of it made her feel sick all over again. 'It had Shima's name on it and I've seen him using it.'

'That is not proof,' Tarina cried contemptuously. 'I thought you would believe me . . . believe in Shima's innocence.'

'I do,' Sorrel whispered, her lips stiff from a combination of fear and the cold. 'I want to believe it, Tarina. I want to help him – but what makes you so sure it was not Shima?'

'Because it was Leyan,' she said, and now her hand trembled on Sorrel's arm. She was wearing a tarnished gold ring and dirt had gathered beneath her long fingernails. 'I saw him come back to the van with the blood on his hands. Leyan stole Shima's knife. He killed that gorgio for me – to avenge me – but he wanted Shima to take the blame.' Her eyes glittered with anger. 'For that he must pay! I would have honoured him all my life if he had used his own knife – but it is coward's work to hide behind another.'

'We must go to the police.'

'No!' she cried in alarm. 'They would not believe me. Leyan must confess his guilt. There must be other witnesses to testify to his guilt.'

'Why should he admit it? He hates Shima, you told me so. He will never admit the truth – why should he?'

'I – I shall speak to Jake. He will make Leyan confess his crime.' She paused, eyes meeting Sorrel's and then sliding away. 'But I am afraid to speak out alone. Leyan is Sadie's favourite. She will try to protect him. If you are there she will not dare to attack me . . . not until later, and then it will not matter. I am used to her beatings. But I must save Shima. I must!'

There was such desperation in her voice that Sorrel was caught. 'You want me to come to the camp with you now?' Tarina nodded and Sorrel felt her stomach tighten with dread. 'You don't understand, I can't . . .'

'Coward!' Tarina accused, her eyes blazing with contempt. 'Will you let Shima hang, after what he did for you?'

Sorrel hesitated; her mother had forbidden her to speak to any of the gipsies and she was frightened of facing Sadie. Earlier memories of the old gipsy woman's curses still haunted her dreams, but as she gazed into Tarina's desperate eyes she was ashamed. Her mother might scold her but this woman was willing to risk far more. A beating from Sadie was the least she might have to face: gipsies did not tolerate those who betrayed their code – and she was about to betray her half-brother.

'You love Shima, don't you?'

'Once I adored him,' Tarina replied, a wistful smile softening her mouth. 'As a child I followed him everywhere. I thought that when we were grown he would take me for his woman, but he thought of me only as a sister.' There was anger in the lovely face – anger and guilt. Tarina had a wild, untamed beauty that matched her fiery temper. 'It is you he loves. I have known that for days – and you will not even try to save him! If he loved me, I would give my life for his.'

Her words stung and shocked Sorrel. 'Shima doesn't love me,' she said, 'but I shall help him, Tarina. I'll come with you now because . . . because Shima is my friend.'

'Come quickly then,' she urged. 'We camped on the Witcham road last night but this morning there is talk of moving on.'

They walked hurriedly, feeling a shared urgency. Sorrel wasn't sure that Tarina was doing the right thing – but she had refused to go to the police and if nothing was done it would be too late. Leyan would get away with murder . . . and Shima might hang for a crime he had not committed.

As they neared the gipsy camp it was clear something was going on. They could hear raised voices and paused, looking at each other in alarm. What was happening? Tarina put her finger to her lips, drawing Sorrel behind one of the vans so that they could hear and see without being noticed themselves.

Sorrel could see Black Jake. Close to she could see that he had a scar on his cheek and was even uglier than she

131

had thought – how cold and evil his eyes were! It was no wonder that Tarina was afraid of him.

'It's a lie ... a lie, I tell you!' Sadie cried. 'Leyan would not steal from you ... none of us would steal your gold.'

'Then what is this?' Jake thrust his hand under her nose. 'I found it beneath your son's bed – and someone has stolen what belongs to me. If this is not my gold, whose is it?'

'It's mine,' Leyan said. 'I picked it up after Sadie threw it at Shima years ago ... it was his mother's, the gorgio woman who gave him birth. He would not take it; he left it on the ground and I picked it up after he had gone. It is mine by right.'

'Blood money,' Sadie said, her face turning an ugly yellow colour. 'You should have left it where it was, Leyan. It was not yours and by taking it you have brought its curse on us all.'

'Then the money is mine,' Jake said, an evil leer on his face. 'You are a lazy, cowardly dog, Leyan. This money is my price for letting you stay here with us.' He was turning away as Leyan suddenly sprang at him. Jake laughed out loud. 'What? Challenge me, would you?' He swung his fist like a hammer, felling the younger man with one blow.

'Don't hurt him.' Sadie ran at Jake, catching at his arm as he was about to kick her son in the head. 'No, you devil. Let him be! Let him be!'

Jake brought his arm back hard, sending her flying. She fell to the ground and lay still, a trickle of blood running from the side of her mouth.

'You've killed her!' Tarina screamed, and ran to her mother, kneeling on the ground beside her, running her hands over the old woman's face. Her long hair had tumbled down over her shoulders in a mass of curls and her eyes glittered with tears as she looked up at her half-brother. 'This is your fault,' she cried accusingly. 'Your fault.'

She rose to her feet, staring at him with hatred. 'I accuse you of killing the gorgio Lenny Browne,' she said in a loud voice. 'You stole Shima's knife. It is you who will bring the law down on our heads – you who have brought trouble to us.'

'I did it for you.' The colour had drained from Leyan's

132

face. He was staring at her as if he had seen a ghost. 'Tarina, I did it for you . . . you know I did it for you! You told me you hated him. I did it for you . . . so that you would love me more than him.' His voice broke as he pleaded with her. 'Tarina . . . please.'

'Curse you! Curse the evil day my mother bore you!' She stepped forward and spat in his face. 'You are no longer my brother. I cast you out – I break all blood ties with you. You are cursed from this day forth until you die.'

Leyan backed away from her, his eyes swivelling this way and then the other as if he hardly knew what he was about. The fear was in his face, in his eyes, in his belly, turning it to water. He felt the hot sting of his own urine and knew that he had wet himself . . . as he had the bed so often in the past after a beating from his father.

'Tarina, I loved you.' It was a cry from his heart but she was a stone goddess, an avenging warrior queen with no mercy in her for him.

Watching from behind one of the vans Sorrel felt the sickness rise in her throat. It was like a scene from her worst nightmare and she wished that she had never come to the camp but was too frightned to move.

'I saw him with Shima's knife.' Black Jake spoke suddenly and Sorrel became aware of the other gipsies gathering in a circle about them, silent witnesses to Leyan's crimes and his shame. 'It was you – you who killed the gorgio.'

'Murderer!' Tarina stepped forward. She picked up a stone and flung it at Leyan with all her strength it struck him on the cheek, cutting the skin. 'Murderer . . . you killed that gorgio and now you have killed your own mother.'

'Murderer . . . murderer . . .' The cries were all around Leyan now. He touched his hand to his cheek, feeling the blood trickle from the cut Tarina's stone had caused. He began to back away as the others closed in on him. 'Murderer . . . betrayer . . . you brought the law on us. Cast him out! Cast him out!'

Tarina's stone was followed by another and then another from the crowd of watchers. Leyan put out his hands to ward them off, but they were too many and too angry. He began to back away, slowly at first and then running as the chant rose to a frenzied pitch.

Sorrel heard a moaning, gasping sound and saw the old gipsy woman twitch. She went to her, kneeling by her side as she opened her eyes.

'You . . .' It was a hoarse whisper but Sorrel heard it. 'You have brought the evil on us.'

The hatred in Sadie's burning gaze filled her with terror. She got to her feet and turned, running away from the camp and all the horror she had witnessed, towards the village and safety. She must get away from here – she must tell Aden what she had seen and heard. He would know what to do.

For once Fortune had decided to be kind. Aden was at his gate as Sorrel raced towards the farm. He turned to look at her in surprise as she called his name, his eyes so like Shima's at that moment that it caught at her heart.

'Sorrel . . .' He caught hold of her arm in his concern. 'Are you hurt? Has someone attacked you?'

'Not me . . .' She gasped for breath, her chest beginning to ache after her wild run. 'I have to tell you – about Shima. It wasn't him. He didn't kill Lenny. It was Leyan. He stole Shima's knife . . . left it on the bank so that Shima would be blamed, because he hated him. He has always hated him . . . it was Leyan, not Shima . . .'

Aden's eyes narrowed, then he nodded. 'It is as Jay thought. Shima knew it was Leyan but did nothing to defend himself.'

'Have you seen Shima?'

Aden hesitated as if considering how much to tell her, then shook his head. 'Jay went to find him two nights ago. It was deep in the fens and in the darkness he might never have found him – but Shima came to him.'

The fens could be lonely at any time but at night they must be frightening: Jay had been brave to go in search of his half-brother and the thought made Sorrel's eyes misty.

Aden's expression was grave. 'You know, of course, that they are half-brothers? That Shima is my son?'

'Yes. Jay told me a long time ago.'

'I thought perhaps he had. I never told Shima in so many words but he knows it now – when it is too late.'

'But it isn't too late!' Sorrel cried. The ache in her chest was easing and she had got her second wind. 'I've just seen Leyan confess to the killing in front of all his people. They stoned him, cast him out, because he brought the police down on them. Tarina threw the first stone. She thought her mother was dead but she was only winded ... Leyan ran away ... you have to stop him ... make him confess to the police ...'

'Calm down,' Aden commanded as the words rushed out of her in her eagerness. 'Tell me everything from the beginning, Sorrel. Where was all this – and how did you come to be there?'

She caught her breath, then related the whole story more slowly. Aden listened attentively, asked her several questions and nodded as if he had expected the answers. She told him about her previous meetings with Tarina, how the gipsy woman had felt betrayed by Shima but still loved him – and of Leyan's hatred for the man he had for years been forced to accept as his half-brother.

'So you see, Leyan has always hated Shima. He must have planned it very carefully ... so that Shima would be blamed and hung for the crime *he* had committed.'

'Yes, I do see.' Aden looked grim as she came to the end of her story. 'And the blame for all the pain and bad feeling lies with me. If I had only ...' He stopped and glanced towards his house. There was regret and grief in his eyes, an old grief that had lain festering inside him for a long time. Sorrel guessed that he was also thinking of the pain he had caused his wife when she first discovered that he'd had a child by another woman. 'This is my punishment for sending Shima's mother away and not telling the truth years ago. But I was afraid ... afraid of losing Rebecca.'

'You can't blame yourself for it all,' Sorrel said, sensing the deep sadness inside him. 'Others must have had a hand in it over the years. If Lorenzo hadn't favoured Shima, Leyan might not have hated him so much. And the quarrel between Black Jake and Leyan started over some gold ... gold that belonged to Shima's mother and was left lying on

135

the ground when Sadie cast him out of their camp years ago. She called it blood money and said it was cursed.'

'And so it was,' Aden said. 'Blood money... money I gave Dotty to buy her silence. I paid her in gold and she died having my child. Sadie is right, the money was cursed.'

'But it wasn't your fault,' Sorrel said again. 'Anymore than it was my fault that Lenny attacked me and brought all this to a head... it was fate. Something that was bound to happen one day.'

Aden's expression eased. 'No wonder Sid says you bring the sunshine into his life,' he said. 'Thank you for those kind words, Sorrel. We've all been thinking of you as a child – but you aren't, not anymore. I shan't stop blaming myself but you've made me feel much better.'

'What about Shima?' she asked, a little shy of the warmth in his face. 'Does this make a difference? Can you help him to prove his innocence?'

'Shima has gone. He may have left the country by now.' Aden looked thoughtful. 'But if we can clear his name... if we can make sure the blame for the murder is put where it rightly belongs... then he might come back one day.'

She saw the sadness in him, the regret for what might have been, and impulsively kissed his cheek, blushing furiously as he smiled at her.

'You get off home now,' he said. 'Leave everything to me, Sorrel. I'll see this mess is sorted out. I'm grateful for what you've done but I can manage now.'

'Yes, yes, of course.'

She turned away, feeling a sense of loss and disappointment. It had seemed so important to tell Aden as quickly as possible but if Shima had already left the country... but perhaps it was for the best. Yet she knew she would miss the young gipsy; she would miss his smile and his gentleness, and she was sad that he might be condemned to spend the rest of his life as an exile.

She wondered how he felt, knowing that he was Aden's son... knowing that all the years when he had wandered from place to place, enduring the hardships that were the constant lot of the travelling people, his half-brothers had

136

lived in ease and plenty. Was he angry and bitter? It would not be surprising if he were.

As she glanced towards the Sawles' house she saw a face at the upstairs window and realized that Rebecca was standing there watching. The window was slightly open and something told her that the older woman had heard every word.

Chapter Eighteen

Jay was frowning as he approached the gipsy camp. His father had not been easy to persuade but after some argument Aden had finally agreed to give Sadie and Tarina a piece of land as a permanent site for their waggons.

'They will probably throw your offer back in your face,' Aden had told him before he left the house that afternoon. 'But if you're ready for that . . .'

'I promised Shima we would help them if we could.'

'Aye . . . well . . . the land's there if they want it. A couple of acres more or less. Enough grass for the horses and screened from the road by a clump of trees, but I doubt they'll accept.'

Jay stopped walking, his thoughts abruptly shattered by the sound of a woman screaming. He spun round towards the source of the cries and saw her struggling to escape from the man who had her pressed against a tree and was quite obviously trying to force himself on her.

'You devil!' Jay charged in without hesitation. 'Take your filthy hands off her . . .'

The gipsy turned with a roar of rage to meet Jay's attack. Tarina screamed as Jake smashed his fist into Jay's face, sending him stumbling back. He rocked on his feet, swaying but managing to keep his balance. Shocked to discover that he had struck the son of the farmer who had recently employed him, Jake hesitated. In that moment of uncertainty Jay struck back, throwing himself at his opponent in a fury and taking him to the ground, where they rolled over and over on the damp grass, hitting and kicking at each other in a frenzy of blows.

Then they were on their feet again, both of them catching their breath, eyeing each other warily. Jay might have let it go then but Jake suddenly lunged at him and they went at it hell for leather, giving blow for blow, using their fists and their feet without regard for gentlemen's rules; it was a nasty fight, vicious and mean, far worse than Jay had ever been in before.

Jake went for his face, landing several swift blows and splitting his bottom lip. Jay was sent reeling back but the taste of blood in his mouth spurred him on and he caught Jake on the side of the head, seeming to stun him for a moment. The gipsy spat on the ground, shook his head and came back at Jay with a growl of anger and renewed fury. For a few moments it looked as if Jake was the stronger, his onslaught forcing Jay to retreat.

Tarina and the other gipsies, who had heard the noise and come out to watch, stood in huddled groups, their silence unnatural and strained. A fight would normally have had them cheering for one or the other – but Jay was not one of them and Jake was feared as much as he was hated, so they held their breath and waited.

Then, very gradually, little by little, it became apparent that Jake's swings were getting more and more wild. Jay was using his head now, ducking and weaving, thinking about it, popping a direct hit in when he got the chance and retreating out of Jake's way in-between punches. Jake's mouth and nose had begun to bleed, one eye was half closed; he was slower, more awkward ... beginning to stumble and sway on his feet. He had the brute strength of most bullies, but this time he was being out-fought by an opponent who had intelligence and skill as well as a wiry strength. Jake was bigger and heavier but Jay was like coiled steel – and he knew exactly what he was doing. There was a smile on his face now, as if he were taunting the gipsy ... playing with him, daring him to come at him ... and it made Jake lose his head so that he swore and cursed furiously every time his punch landed on thin air, missing the grinning face of his tormentor again and again.

'Kill him!' Tarina screamed suddenly. 'Go on, Jay Sawle. Hit him again. Knock him senseless!'

'She's right,' one of the men yelled from behind Jay. 'Teach the bastard a lesson, mate. Give him one for me.'

Jake was stumbling, obviously confused, only sheer will-power keeping him on his feet. He had clearly had enough but when he tried to retreat the men behind him pushed him forward, making him take the punishment. Now more voices were raised against him. To a man they were on Jay's side, their faces harsh with the lust for revenge. Jake had cheated them, terrorised them, shamed them. Now they wanted him humbled; they wanted him beaten into the dust . . . broken and battered . . . finished.

'Thrash the devil!'

'Kill him . . .'

'Hit him . . . hit him until the bugger stays down.'

There was a rumbling sigh in their throats as Jay's fists exploded in his opponent's face again and again. Jake's head snapped back, his eyes rolled and then his knees buckled, dropping him to the ground where he knelt with his head bent, dazed, bewildered, hardly aware of what had happened to him.

'Get up . . . get up,' the voices chanted. 'Up . . . up . . . up . . . up . . . up.'

Their voices were thick with hatred and a mindless blood-lust; they wanted him dead . . . torn to pieces. Jay stood over him for a moment, his fists at the ready; he was elated, triumphant, swept away on the tide of their hatred. Then, all at once, the red mist began to clear from his brain and he was conscious of the almost animal savagery the fight had aroused in these people . . . in him!

'Enough,' he said. 'He's finished . . . enough.'

In the ensuing and sudden silence Jake tried to rise but found it too much and slumped face downward on the ground. A young woman came suddenly from behind the others and knelt beside him. She was pretty but her body was swollen, heavy with child, and her face had bloated with an unhealthy pallor. Her movements were awkward and clumsy as she pulled at his shoulder, trying to move his body.

'Jake!' she cried. 'Jake . . . be you bad hurt? You must not be dead . . . not dead.' There was such fear and distress in her cry that Jay felt sympathy for her.

'He'll be all right,' he said. 'If he's your husband, I advise you to take him away from here as soon as you can.'

The woman's eyes were blurred with tears as she looked up at him and nodded. 'We'll go,' she whispered, her gaze travelling round the hostile faces and dwelling on Tarina's for a moment. 'Come on, Jake. Let me help you.'

'Get away, damn you!' He shrugged her hands off as she tried to help him. 'Leave me be!'

He pushed her away then struggled to his feet, swaying a little unsteadily as he stared sullenly at his opponent.

'Let this be a warning to you,' Jay said. 'I don't want to see you back here – ever. If I do, you'll find yourself talking to the constable.'

Jake's eyes flashed with resentment but he turned away without a word. For one moment he stared in Tarina's direction and Jay saw her face go white, but before he could say anything more it was over and Jake was shuffling off towards his waggon with his woman following a few steps behind, her head downcast as if in shame or fear.

'Are you all right?' Jay turned as Tarina spoke. 'Can I bathe your face for you? I know how to ease the bruising.'

Jay was silent for a moment, then he nodded. 'Thanks,' he said, and followed as she led the way towards her waggon. 'It does sting a bit . . . besides, I want to talk to you.'

The village was buzzing with all the excitement. Lenny's death, the banishment of Leyan and now the fight between Jay Sawle and Black Jake had given folk a feast of gossip – but the fight was what had them all laughing, because Jay was well liked and it had made him a bit of a hero.

'I should have loved to have seen it,' Bob said to Ted as they chuckled over it the next morning in the cowsheds. 'Jay has always been a scrapper but it sounds as if he thrashed the gipsy good.'

'They say it started over Tarina.' Ted threw back his head and roared with laughter. 'Well, can't say I'd mind a bit of that myself.'

141

'And you about to be married!' Bob shook his head in mock reproof. 'Jay's always had an eye for the lasses and you can't blame him if he . . .'

Sorrel turned away with a toss of her head. She knew that her brothers wouldn't be the only ones to think that there was something more to the fight than Jay's version. They were wrong of course. Jay wasn't interested in Tarina in that way – he couldn't be!

Her mother looked at her as she took her basket of eggs to the sink to wash them. 'And what's the matter with you, miss?'

'Nothing.'

'By the look of your face there's something.'

'Ted and Bob . . . they were laughing about Jay fighting with . . .'

'Gipsies!' May scowled. 'I've always said they're trouble. What on earth he wanted to get into a fight over that girl for, I don't know.'

'He couldn't let Jake hurt her,' Sorrel said, leaping to Jay's defence despite her own misgivings. 'He only did what Shima did when Lenny attacked me . . .'

'From what I heard, Lenny ran like a scared rabbit as soon as Shima pulled him off you,' her mother said, fixing her with a hard stare. 'Jay nearly killed that gipsy.'

'Well, he's gone now.'

'A pity the rest of them didn't go with him,' May muttered. 'You've heard that Aden gave a piece of land along the Chatteris road to a few of them as a permanent site for their waggons?' Sorrel nodded and her mother's frown deepened. 'That means they'll be in the village from time to time – so keep away from them. I mean it, my girl! You'll feel the back of my hand if I find out you've been talking to that Tarina again. I won't have you mixing with gipsies!'

Sorrel didn't say anything. Her mother had been furious with her when she'd told her what she'd seen at the gipsy camp the morning Leyan confessed to murder and was driven out by his own people. May had lectured her for ages, going on and on about it until Sorrel was sick of hearing about the gipsies.

142

'I ought to punish you,' her mother said now. 'I've a good mind not to let you go to Fanny's party.'

'Oh, Ma,' Sorrel cried. 'You can't mean it! Not go to the party – after we bought that lovely dress?'

'You don't deserve to go,' May said. 'I'll have to think about it – and I'll talk to your father. In the meantime you can start giving me a hand about the place. That will take your mind off gipsies!'

Sorrel was thoughtful as she went upstairs. She didn't believe her mother would stop her going to the party despite her threats, she was just upset and worried – worried that people would talk about her the way they were talking about Tarina.

Jay wasn't interested in her, was he? No, she wouldn't believe it! Jay was a flirt, there was no denying that – but he had a special feeling for Sorrel. She remembered the look in his eyes the afternoon of the fair and smiled. Lads always went a bit wild before they settled down to marriage.

'The police are satisfied it was Leyan,' Aden said, standing in the warmth of May's spotless kitchen. 'They're searching for him now and Shima is no longer wanted for questioning. He could come back now, if he wanted to.'

'If he knows,' Sorrel said, and wondered why she felt such a sense of loss. 'Thank you for telling me, Mr Sawle. I have been worrying about it all.'

'I knew you would be.' He smiled at her and then at her mother. 'I'm very grateful to Sorrel for coming to me. If it hadn't been for her, I might not have been able to sort things out as easily.'

'Will she have to give evidence?' May asked. 'Will she have to go into court?'

'I'm not sure. Perhaps if . . .' Aden broke off as the kitchen door opened and Sorrel's father came in. From the expression on his face it was clear that something was wrong. 'What is it, Sid? Something's up.'

'They've found Leyan,' Sid said, looking worried. 'He's dead . . . some days, they think. He had . . . cut his own throat and his body was half buried in the snow.'

Sorrel gasped and her mother frowned. 'Sid! You'll be giving the girl nightmares.'

'No . . . no, it's all right,' Sorrel said. 'I'd rather know the truth. I'm not a child anymore.'

'It's a horrible thing,' Aden said, looking grave. 'But a kind of natural justice. It will settle folk's minds – and it saves all the trouble and grief of a trial.'

'Yes, there is that.' May was relieved. 'Sorrel won't have to give evidence now, not in court anyway.'

'There may be a brief hearing,' Aden said, 'but I'll see she's kept out of it, May. I've got signed testimonies from Tarina and some of the others. At most Sorrel will be asked to put her name to her own statement.'

May nodded, then smiled at her daughter. 'It seems the worst is over,' she said. 'You've come out of it better than I'd hoped – just remember to keep clear of those gipsies in future.'

'You will let me go to the party, won't you?'

Aden looked at May sharply and she went pink. 'Of course,' she said. 'I was cross with you, Sorrel – but I'm not daft enough to waste that dress.'

'Fanny would be so disappointed if Sorrel wasn't there,' Aden said, smiling at her again. 'And so would someone else.' He chuckled as Sorrel blushed, then turned to her father. 'Now you're here, Sid, there's something I wanted to ask you about that new heifer . . .'

May waited until the door had closed behind them, then looked at her daughter. 'They say Rebecca was furious because he gave that land to Tarina and her mother. I hope it doesn't cause serious trouble between them . . . not like the last time.'

'What do you mean?' Sorrel stared at her curiously.

'Oh, nothing.' May hesitated, then shook her head. 'It doesn't matter. Did you hear what Aden said just now? He was meaning Jay, you know.'

'Yes.' Sorrel's cheeks felt warm. 'I – I think Jay likes me, Ma.'

'He would be a fool if he didn't,' her mother said. 'You're worth two of any other lass around here. I want to hear what Master Sawle says when he sees you in that dress.'

144

'Oh, Ma,' Sorrel said, and laughed. She darted at her mother and hugged her. 'I'm so excited. I can't wait!'

Chapter Nineteen

'Sid – will you look at her! She looks a treat in that dress,' May said as Sorrel walked into the kitchen. 'Aren't you proud of her? She's a proper young lady this evening.'

Sorrel's hair had been curled in rags all day and now it was brushed loosely instead of being dragged back into the usual plait; it suited her, curling about her face in pretty wisps and falling over her shoulders in soft waves.

'Sorrel is always beautiful to me,' Sid replied. He smiled at her and put on his cap. 'Are you ready then, lass?'

The party was being held in the village hall because there was to be dancing and too many guests for the Sawles to have it at home. Sorrel's father had promised to take her round in the trap and fetch her home later, even though she had protested that she could walk the short distance through the village.

'And get your pretty shoes muddy?' Her mother had been horrified at the idea. 'Your father will take you, Sorrel, and fetch you back at half-past ten.'

'But the party won't end until midnight.'

'I'll be there at eleven,' her father said. 'That's plenty late enough, lass. Don't forget you'll be up again by six the next morning.'

And he would be out in the yard an hour before her. Sorrel hadn't argued further. She couldn't ask him to wait up until past twelve for the sake of a party – and there was no way either he or her mother would let her walk home alone late at night.

She was trembling with a mixture of nerves and

excitement on the short drive to the hall. Tiny lanterns had been hung outside and there was a blaze of light spilling from the windows. Sid helped her down, frowning slightly as he felt her shiver.

'Now don't you be fretting,' he said. 'Your ma was right, lass, you are beautiful and a proper young lady. You're as good as anyone – and don't you forget it. We might not be as rich as Fanny's folk but we're not paupers and we've always been decent.'

It was a long speech for her father and it brought a lump to her throat. 'I love you,' she said, and kissed his cheek. 'Don't worry. I'm just excited.'

'Well, have a good time, lass.'

She smiled and nodded as he climbed back on to the driving box, then waved and walked towards the door of the hall. It opened as she got to it and Jay stood there, looking so handsome in his black evening suit and white silk shirt that it took her breath away. There were still a few faint bruises on his face but his hair had been brushed to one side with a deep parting and slicked down with oil, making him look every inch the gentleman. No one seeing him now for the first time could have imagined that he had recently been involved in a vicious fight with a gipsy.

'I was watching for you,' he said, and held out his hand to her with a smile. 'Come on, Sorrel. I'll take you in and introduce you to everyone.'

His strong, cool fingers closed round hers and she felt a thrill of pleasure. He was so sure of himself, so at ease, and his confidence lent her courage.

'You're beautiful,' he said, his eyes meeting hers in such a way that she felt little flutters in her stomach. 'I like your hair – and that dress suits you, especially the colour.'

He smelt different, sort of woody but with a fresh sharpness, as if he had used a fancy soap. As he drew her inside she saw that all the men were dressed more or less like him and the women had gorgeous, expensive gowns in pretty colours. Hers had probably cost nowhere near as much as most of them but it suited her and was stylish enough to bear comparison. Her mother was right. Richie Sawle would have no reason to sneer at her clothes this evening.

147

She saw him talking to Sally. He glanced at her, looking surprised and then annoyed, as if he resented her being there, but Sally smiled and waved a friendly greeting.

Fanny hurried over as soon as she saw her. 'Sorrel!' she cried. 'Where did you find that lovely dress? You look wonderful.'

'We bought it in Cambridge,' Sorrel said, and Fanny was impressed when she named the shop.

'Good evening, Sorrel,' Aden greeted her, coming over to join them. 'It's a great pleasure to have you here – you'll save a dance for me, won't you?'

'Sorrel is going to be dancing with me most of the time,' Jay said, 'but she might spare you one.'

It was said in jest but there was an air of possessiveness about Jay then that made Sorrel tingle with pleasure – until she glanced round and caught sight of his mother's face. Rebecca was staring at her with such coldness that she was jolted into remembering that Mrs Sawle did not like her. She felt a sinking sensation inside. Aden liked her and Jay seemed to be falling in love with her – but she sensed that Rebecca would never accept her into her family.

It worried her for a moment, then she forgot about Rebecca as Jay drew her on, introducing her to various acquaintances, people she had never met before who had come some distance to attend Fanny's dance. Most of them seemed friendly enough and she began to relax, to enjoy herself. She was in suffcient control of herself to smile when Rebecca came to greet her at last.

'Good evening, Sorrel. I'm glad you could come to my daughter's party.'

'Thank you, Mrs Sawle. It was kind of you to invite me.'

'Fanny was most insistent.' Rebecca nodded and walked on. 'Do enjoy yourself.'

Sorrel let out her breath in a sigh. Rebecca had greeted her out of politeness but there had been no warmth in her welcome.

The music had started and people began to dance. Jay took her out on the floor three times in quick succession, then she was claimed first by Aden and thereafter by several men she had met for the first time that evening, all of whom were so charming and complimentary to her that she laughed out loud again and again.

Jay danced with his sister and Sally but then he was back at Sorrel's side, his eyes simmering with jealousy.

'You've done your duty,' he muttered fiercely. 'You can spend the rest of the evening with me.'

'You look like a crosspatch,' she teased. 'I can't dance with you all the time, Jay – what will people say?'

'I don't give a damn,' he said, his eyes flashing with annoyance. 'You're my girl so they can say what they like.'

Her heart leapt in her breast and she could hardly breathe as she looked up at him. 'Am I your girl, Jay?'

He gazed down into her face in silence for a long moment and she swallowed hard, then he smiled, a shy, uncertain smile that made her want to hug him. 'You know the answer to that, Sorrel. You've always been my girl – the others were just a way of passing the time until you grew up.'

'Oh, Jay . . .' Her throat was tight with emotion and she wasn't sure whether she wanted to laugh or cry. She loved him so much, had always loved him. 'Jay . . .'

'Mother wants you!' a cold, clipped voice interrupted and they both turned to stare at Richie in surprise. 'She thinks you should dance with Amelia Burroughs. Besides, I haven't had the pleasure of Sorrel's company yet.' He grasped her hand as Jay reluctantly let go, squeezing her fingers so hard that she almost winced. 'Shall we dance, Miss Harris?'

He gave her no chance to refuse, compelling her to go with him. She sent an agonized glance in Jay's direction but he had turned away and a moment later was dancing with a pretty, plump blonde-haired girl.

'There's no need to look quite so much like a martyr about to be burnt at the stake,' Richie said, and as she glanced up, she saw that he was smiling. 'You've improved, Sorrel. I was wrong to say you were a hopeless case – you look pretty this evening and your dress is charming.'

She scowled at him. ' "Thank you for your kind words, sir, she said." ' She mocked him with the words of a popular ditty. 'You don't expect me to believe you, I hope?'

Richie laughed. At that moment he was attractive, as all the Sawles were, but something beneath his smile, something

149

lurking deep in his cold eyes, reminded her that he was not to be trusted. Even when he was trying to be pleasant, she had the feeling that this was a dangerous man.

'I admire your spirit,' he said. 'It seems I may have been seriously mistaken in thinking you just another dull village lump.'

Their dance had come to an end and she found Fanny at her side. Richie's sister laid a proprietorial hand on Sorrel's arm, lifted her chin and gave him a hard look.

'Sorrel is mine now,' she said, daring him to deny her. 'She's going to eat supper with me. I've hardly had time for a word with her all evening.'

'Of course, dear Fanny.' Richie inclined his head. 'I bow to your superior claim.' His mouth curved in that familiar sneer and Sorrel knew her instinct had been right. He didn't really admire her. He had probably been flirting with her in the hope of making Jay jealous.

Fanny tucked her arm through Sorrel's, drawing her towards the tables which were loaded down with all kinds of delicious dishes. There were crisp pastry cups oozing with salmon and chicken in rich sauces, fingers of toast with freshly made pâté, platters of cold roast beef, ham, tomatoes grown 'specially in a heated greenhouse, chutneys and potato salad with thick yellow mayonnaise, besides all kinds of sweet pies and biscuits.

'I do hope Richie wasn't upsetting you, Sorrel? You mustn't take any notice of anything he says.'

'He was paying me compliments.'

'Oh.' Fanny pulled a wry face. 'Well, don't trust what he says even when he's being nice. I don't. Poor Sally says he's asked her to marry him next summer – but she's far too good for him and I told her so.'

'Fanny! He's your brother.' Sorrel was a little shocked to hear her say such a thing, perhaps because she was so close to her own brothers. 'You shouldn't have said it – even if you think it.'

'I know.' Fanny squeezed her arm. 'I don't much like Richie – but Jay is different. I love Jay dearly. You like him too, don't you?'

'Yes. Yes, I do.' Sorrel's cheeks were warm as she glanced at her and then away. 'We've been friends ever since school.'

'I shan't tease you about it,' Fanny said, giving her another little squeeze. 'But I should be so happy if – well, you know what I mean.'

So Fanny had noticed. Sorrel was sure his mother would also have noticed that Jay was paying her rather a lot of attention – and she wouldn't be as pleased about it as her daughter.

Jay reclaimed her after she had eaten her supper with Fanny. He danced every dance with her after that, refusing to give her up to anyone but his father. She glowed in the warmth of his attentions even though she knew that he was making them the talking point of the evening. Everyone would be wondering what his intentions were and reaching their own conclusions.

Sorrel knew that some people would think her fast but she was so happy that she didn't care. They were having such fun that the evening sped by and Jay was disappointed when she told him it was almost time for her to leave.

'I could have walked you home,' he said with a flicker of annoyance. 'I was looking forward to it, Sorrel.'

'Perhaps that's why Pa was so determined to fetch me himself.' The burning heat in his eyes left her in no doubt of what he'd had in mind for that slow walk home. A delicious shiver ran down her spine and she knew he wanted to kiss her – wanted it rather badly.

'You're teasing me again,' he said as she tipped her head to one side and gazed up at him, the light of mischief in her eyes. 'Won't you please let me walk you home?'

'I must go with Pa – but maybe we could walk out on Sunday afternoon, if you want? Just through the village, though, not down the bank.'

'Or you could come to tea,' Jay replied, a smile tugging at the corners of his mouth as he caught on. 'Isn't that the way it's done? Proper courtin'.'

'You weren't suggesting anything improper, I hope?'

Jay chuckled deep in his throat. 'Would it do me any good if I were?'

'None at all!'

'I didn't think so.' The hot look was still in his eyes but his mouth was soft with humour. 'I'll have to sweeten you up, lass. Flowers and chocolates, is it?'

'You can try,' she retorted with a flick of her head. 'It won't get you far. You'll come calling and ask Pa's permission to walk me out – or I shan't come at all, Jay Sawle.'

He smiled and nodded but didn't say anything.

The time had evaporated somehow. When Fanny came to tell them, Sorrel couldn't believe her father was waiting for her already, and was reluctant to leave. It had been such a magical night – and yet Jay hadn't said anything definite, not really.

'Thank you so much, I've had a lovely time,' she said as Fanny kissed her and thanked her for coming.

'You must come next time, too,' Fanny replied. 'We must see each other more often, Sorrel.'

Jay walked her out to where her father had the trap waiting. It was cold but the rain had held off and there were a few stars in the sky. A storm lamp hung on either side of the trap, twinkling out of the darkness at them. Jay squeezed her hand as he helped her up on to the box seat beside her father, then stood looking at them and rubbing Dobbin's nose. The pony whickered a welcome, moving its feet restlessly as if surprised at being brought out of its warm stable this late at night.

'Take care of her, Mr Harris,' Jay said. ''Bye, Sorrel. I'll be seeing you soon.'

'Good night, Jay,' she called. 'Thank you for a lovely evening. And Fanny . . .'

She waved as her father clicked the pony on. He sat silently beside her until they had rounded the bend in the road, the clop of Dobbin's hooves echoing in the stillness of the gentle night – then he turned to glance at her, a mixture of curiosity and some odd, hidden emotion in his face.

'That's the first time Jay has called me "Mr Harris" since he left school,' he said. 'Now I wonder why he'd do that all of a sudden . . .'

Sorrel smiled at him in the flickering light of their carriage lamps but made no reply. Her whole body was wrapped in

152

a warm glow that emanated from somewhere deep inside her. It seemed that she had been waiting for this night all her life.

Jay loved her. He was showing respect for her father because soon, very soon now, he would be asking Sid if they could marry.

Sorrel lay in bed long after all the talk was over. Her mother had wanted to know everything and followed her into her bedroom, lingering while she undressed and brushed her hair. It was half an hour or more before she went to her own bed, but now Sorrel was alone and she could go over her wonderful evening again and again in her mind.

She was happy, happier than she had ever been, yet, just as she was on the point of falling asleep, a disturbing thought came to her.

Where was Shima? Did he have a warm, sheltered place to sleep in – and did he know that the police were no longer searching for him?

Remembering all the terrible things that had happened in the past few weeks made Sorrel uneasy. Life could be so very cruel at times. Was she taking too much for granted? Jay loved her but would his mother stand in the way of a marriage between them? She had never liked Sorrel and now she wondered if it was because Jay had always been her friend – if Rebecca had been afraid that it might one day come to this.

Did Rebecca Sawle hate her enough to stop them getting married?

For a while Sorrel tossed and turned restlessly as she wondered if all her dreams might come to nothing after all, but then, at last, she fell into a deep sleep . . .

Chapter Twenty

It was cold and drizzling with rain as she hurried through the darkened streets, wanting to be home after a day that had seen her almost reduced to tears by Sister Norden's scolding – and the death of a young flier who had been badly burned when his plane had been shot down.

Would the war never be over? At the start she would not have believed it could go on for so long... endless months and years of working in conditions that had broken girls with less spirit. Her feet hurt and her hands were so sore that it made her want to scream whenever she had to put them in water and disinfectant... but worse than all the rest was the aching emptiness inside her.

Would the sun never shine again? Would the spring never come? How she longed for it after the drabness of this terrible winter.

As she went into the nurses' hostel she saw two letters in her pigeon hole and took them out, her spirits lifting a little. It was always good to get letters from home.

She opened them as she walked upstairs. The first was a brief message scribbled on a card that made her smile, the second an invitation to a party that evening. She sighed as she slipped it into her pocket. The last thing she wanted that evening was to go to a party – but if she didn't, Fanny would be upset.

She went to her room, gazing longingly at her bed. She had been looking forward to a hot bath and an early night but she ought to make the effort... for her friend's sake.

Perhaps she ought to go anyway; if she didn't she would

probably only brood. She went to look in her wardrobe, wondering what she could wear and smiling as she saw the dress her aunt had bought her . . . the dress she had worn to Fanny's party that night. The night she had believed her dream was coming true.

'I'm thinking of asking Sorrel to marry me,' Jay announced over the breakfast table. It was the Sunday after Fanny's party and both his parents were present for once, which was why he had chosen the moment to speak out. He paused significantly to let them take it in then went on. 'I'm going to ask her father if I can walk out with her – and if she says she'll marry me, we'll get engaged in the spring and married next summer.'

'For goodness' sake, Jay!' Rebecca threw down her napkin in disgust. 'Have you lost your senses? A girl like that . . . you can't be serious.'

'Mother!' He looked at her reproachfully. 'Sorrel is a decent girl. She isn't like . . . well, I haven't even kissed her yet.'

'I didn't mean that exactly.' Rebecca gave him an odd stare. 'Though judging by the girls you usually take up with . . . but she isn't right for you, Jay. Not as a wife.'

'I want to marry her,' he said, a stubborn note in his voice now. 'I'm going to marry her, Mother – even if we have to wait until I'm old enough to marry without anyone's permission.'

'That won't be next summer. You're not twenty yet. You still need our consent – and I shall certainly not give you mine. Sorrel may be all that you say, but I had high hopes for you. I thought we might visit Celia in the summer. You were very taken with Adele Carter when she was here. Someone like that would be more suitable.'

'Adele was all right,' Jay said. 'I liked her – but I'm in love with Sorrel.' He shot a look of appeal at his father. 'Tell her, Dad – tell her I won't marry anyone but Sorrel.'

'Jay usually knows what he wants,' Aden said. 'I don't think we should turn our faces against this marriage straight away, Rebecca. Why don't you invite the girl to tea one day? It would give you a chance to get to know her properly.'

'I shall not ask that girl to tea.' Rebecca got to her feet. 'I don't like her and I never have. Let me tell you now, Jay – if you marry the daughter of your father's stockman, she will never be welcome in my house.'

'Rebecca!' Aden frowned at her. 'Think about this – he's your son. You can't just . . .'

'I'm going upstairs,' she said. 'Come along, Fanny. I want to go through your evening dresses.'

Fanny rose from the table. She said nothing but her eyes were full of sympathy as she gave her brother a nervous smile, then quickly followed her mother from the room.

Jay pushed away his uneaten breakfast and got to his feet. Aden rose too, his expression one of annoyance mixed with concern.

'You should have talked to me first,' he said. 'Let me reason with your mother.'

'She can't mean that, can she?' Jay ran his fingers through his hair in frustration. 'Why doesn't she like Sorrel? That business with Lenny Browne wasn't her fault – she isn't that sort. She didn't lead him on.'

'It isn't that,' Aden said. 'You know what your mother is like. She has always wanted the best for you.'

'What she thinks is the best!'

'Aye, well . . .' Aden sighed. 'Perhaps I was wrong to let you leave school when I did. Maybe you should have gone away as your brother did – seen a bit of the world before you settled down here.'

'I would have hated it,' Jay said stubbornly. 'I love the land – and I love Sorrel. All I want is to live here with her and raise a family. What's wrong with that?'

'Nothing.' Aden smiled. 'It sounds good to me. But we'll have to get your mother used to the idea.'

'I'm going to marry Sorrel.'

'Nothing would please me more – but your mother is right in one way. You *are* still only nineteen. There's no need to rush into things, Jay, is there?'

'I haven't got to marry her, if that's what you mean.' Jay's cheeks were an angry red. 'But I want an understanding so that she knows I mean to do right by her.'

'Go ahead and talk to her – but wait for a while before

you get engaged. If I know Sid Harris, he won't be anxious for you to steal her away too soon. Go courting . . . take her flowers and sit with her in church. Walk out in the village . . . not down the bank . . . then we'll see what your mother says. I'll bring her round in time. I usually can, you know that.'

'Yes, I know.' Jay smiled and relaxed. 'Find out why she doesn't like Sorrel, Dad. I'm sure Sorrel wouldn't have upset her for the world.'

'She'll come round, lad.'

Jay nodded. He wanted to protest that he couldn't wait until he was twenty-one. His feelings for Sorrel were too strong, too urgent, and he needed to be sure of her, sure that someone else wouldn't snatch her away. But in his heart he knew his father was right. Even if he were prepared to defy his mother's wishes, it wasn't likely that Sid would agree to the summer wedding he had hoped for.

'Flowers and chocolates?' he said, giving Aden a wry look. 'I shall feel daft. Can you imagine what Ted Harris will say if I turn up with a bunch of flowers for his sister?'

'If you're man enough to be thinking of marriage, you're man enough to take a girl flowers,' Aden said with a smile. 'Just remember this, son, the ladies like a little bit of fuss now and then. Kisses and sweet talk are fine, but respect and a few presents help to keep the smiles on their faces. I forgot it once and learnt to regret my mistakes.'

Jay nodded. He had been just a child at the time of the trouble between his parents but he remembered all the pain and grief it had caused. His mother still got angry some-times and she was very set in her notions of right and wrong – but she was no longer the cold and silent woman she had sometimes been when he was a small child. He knew that there was a deep love between her and his father, even though they often quarrelled, and he believed that Aden would talk her round to the idea of a marriage between Jay and Sorrel, in time.

'Yes, you're right,' he admitted. 'And I should have spoken to you first. I'm sorry.'

'Your mother has her ways.' Aden patted him on the shoulder. 'But she loves you, Jay. Never forget that. She'll

157

need a bit of sweet talking from me – but I'll have that invitation to tea for you before you know it.'

'Thanks, Dad.' Jay hesitated as his father turned away. There was another matter on his mind, something that had been bothering him since he'd seen the last invoice from the potato merchant Richie had dealt with personally. Jay was certain there had been eleven and a half tons in each of the three loads they had sold – but the bill of sale showed only thirty tons in all. 'I was wondering . . .'

'Yes, Jay? Something else on your mind?'

Richie had checked those loads himself and had confirmed the invoices as being correct. To raise any doubt about them was as good as calling his brother a liar. Jay had been in a hurry to get back to the fields at the time. Maybe he'd made a mistake.

'No.' It was best to say nothing if he couldn't be absolutely sure. 'No, it's nothing. I'm off to church now and I'll be seeing Mr Harris when I walk Sorrel home.'

Aden nodded, concealing his smile. Anything that got Jay to go to church without being forced into it by his mother had to be a good thing! Rebecca would see it once he'd had a word with her on the quiet.

'I see the Kaiser has banned his troops from dancing either the tango or the two-step – can't say I blame him.' Sid glanced up from his newspaper, a twinkle in his eyes. 'Some of these new-fangled dances are shameless – don't know what the younger generation are coming to.'

Sorrel smothered a laugh. It was a sly dig at Ted, who had been telling them about a dance in Chatteris he had taken Rose to as a celebration of their engagement. She met her father's eyes as Ted's face went bright red and he winked at her wickedly, making her splutter as the laugh came out despite her efforts to hold it back.

'Haven't any of you got anything better to do?' May asked. 'Weren't you expecting Aden this morning, Sid?' He nodded and stood up, she stared hard at Ted. 'I thought you had a mare about to foal?'

'Aye, I'd best be off.'

May looked at her daughter with satisfaction as they both

went out, laughing together because they were both under the petticoat rule, and Sorrel guessed that her mother wanted to talk about the letter which had been hand delivered by Molly Green that morning. It was an invitation to tea and had been signed by Rebecca Sawle.

'That must have taken some doing,' May said, picking up the letter and shaking her head over it as the door closed behind the men. 'I'll bet my last farthing it wasn't her idea.'

'Jay said something at Fanny's party about my going to tea one Sunday . . .'

'That was nearly two weeks ago.' Her mother frowned. 'He's been hanging around here so much lately, I'd begun to think he'd taken root.'

'He has been trying to get Pa on his own, so that he can ask him if we can walk out together. He's been trying for days but Pa won't let him say anything; keeps making excuses, making out he's too busy.'

'Jay will corner him soon,' May said. 'And when he does, I don't want you going down that bank. We'll have no shame brought on this family, Sorrel.'

'Ma!' She blushed furiously. 'As if I would.'

'Well, you've been warned. I've set my mind to a fancy wedding when you're eighteen.' May was thoughtful for a moment, then noticed Sorrel's expression. 'Your pa will need talking into that so you needn't pull a face. It won't be before harvest next year at the very earliest – more likely the following spring.'

'Jay hasn't even asked me yet,' Sorrel protested with a laugh.

'He will.' May's satisfaction showed. 'If it has taken two weeks for him to wangle an invitation from his mother, he's serious.'

She was right; Sorrel knew that Rebecca had been against it at the start. Jay had been in and out of the yard at least three times a day ever since the party. He'd told her that Aden was on their side and it seemed that he had finally won the argument. She had been invited to tea by his mother, which was a very different thing from having tea with Fanny.

It meant that – albeit under protest – Rebecca had

159

accepted Jay's intention to court her. Now all they needed was for Jay to get her father's permission, and that was proving more difficult than either of them had expected.

'If you've nothing better to do than stand there dreaming, you can take some of that calves-foot jelly I made yesterday round to Mabel. Timmy has had a bit of a cold and she'll find it useful to make a nourishing broth.'

Sorrel came out of her daydreams with a laugh. She took a large earthenware crock from the pantry and spooned some of the jelly into a dish, covering it carefully with clean muslin before putting it into her basket.

'I shan't need you for a while,' her mother said as she put on her coat. 'You can stay and talk to Mabel, if you like.'

'Thanks, Ma.' Sorrel accepted her mother's excuse gratefully. She too had seen Jay loitering near the yard gate and knew that he would walk round to her sister-in-law's house with her. 'I'll be back in time to help with the ironing.'

'Tell Jay to pop round when Sid comes in for his dinner,' May said. 'I'll make him sit down long enough to listen.'

'Make him say yes, Ma,' Sorrel said, and laughed as her mother nodded. 'I'll tell Jay to be sure and come today.'

She was still smiling as she ran out to the gate, reaching it just as Jay had given up and started to walk down the road.

'Wait for me!' she called, running to join him as he swung round to greet her eagerly. 'You can walk to Mabel's with me. I've got something to tell you . . .'

Sorrel knocked at the front door of Jay's house. He had offered to meet her but she'd told him she would come to the house alone. She'd made up her mind she wasn't going to be intimidated by anyone this time and smiled confidently when Molly opened the door to her.

'I've come to tea,' she said, her head up. 'Mrs Sawle is expecting me.'

'I know.' Molly looked at her uncertainly, obviously not quite sure what to make of the new situation. 'Only you're a bit early and she's not down yet. You'd better wait in the kitchen while I tell her you're here.'

Sorrel's cheeks flamed. Molly would never have dared to

speak that way to any other of Rebecca's guests. She was annoyed but didn't say anything as she followed her into the house. However, she refused to enter the kitchen, standing in the hall as Molly went off to inform her mistress.

She was back within seconds, looking like a scalded cat. 'Master Jay is in the best parlour,' she said, giving Sorrel a look that spoke volumes, showing plainly whose side she was on. 'Mr Sawle says to take you through at once.'

The sound of heavy footsteps made them both look round as Aden came down the stairs, still fastening his collar stud. The strong spicy scent of soap and hair oil wafted towards them. He smiled at Sorrel and straightened his cuffs.

'Here you are then,' he said. 'Rebecca won't be a moment. Please go into the parlour, Sorrel. Jay will look after you.'

'Thank you.' Not so long ago she had been in awe of him but since the trouble with the gipsies they seemed to have become friends. 'I'm sorry if I'm early.'

'Not at all, my dear. This is Jay's home and you must feel free to call whenever you wish – after all, it's likely that you'll be a part of the family soon. At least that's what my son tells me.'

His teasing smile made her blush but she put her head up as Molly gave a disapproving sniff and went off to the kitchen.

Jay was standing by the parlour window looking out at the garden. He turned as they entered, his face lighting up with pleasure, then he came to take Sorrel's hand and kiss her cheek.

'You look pretty,' he whispered against her ear. 'I love you, Sorrel. So very much . . .'

Her heart raced as she gazed up at him. What did it matter what anyone else thought when Jay loved her? He squeezed her hand then let it go as he heard a footstep in the hall. They all turned as Rebecca entered, her face wearing a fixed society smile which told Sorrel that she was not truly welcome in her house, even though she had been forced to accept her.

'Good afternoon, Sorrel,' she said, inclining her head imperially. 'Please sit down.'

'Good afternoon, Mrs Sawle,' Sorrel replied, matching her

161

tone and manners to those of her hostess. She sat primly on a straight-backed chair. 'It's a pleasant day, don't you think? Not as cold as it was earlier in the week . . .'

Hearing a muffled snort she glanced at Aden. His face was a picture. He was trying not to laugh and covering his mirth with his handkerchief, turning it into a cough as his wife shot a suspicious look at him. Sorrel felt a bubble of laughter well up inside her and suddenly she wasn't nervous anymore. If Rebecca was hoping to frighten her off with this display of coolness she would be disappointed.

Sorrel was going to marry Jay and no one could change that!

'No, Jay, no!' Sorrel cried breathlessly, breaking free from his hold. She gave him a little push as he tried to recapture her. 'I said you could kiss me but I'm not doing anything else. I've told you before . . . Ma would kill me if anything happened.'

Three weeks had passed since the teaparty at his house and, since her father had given his grudging permission, they had walked out together each Saturday and Sunday. Now they had stopped in the little lane behind the church on their way home from visiting Mabel. It was late in the afternoon and there was hardly anyone about: besides, their backs were to a sheltering tree and they were out of sight of any passers by – and the farm.

Jay stared at her a little sulkily, still breathing hard. 'Don't be such a prude, Sorrel. I only touched you over your dress. You know I love you, you know I want to marry you as soon as we can. I won't go too far, there's no need to be frightened. I know what I'm doing.'

'I'll just bet you do,' she said, her eyes challenging him. 'I've heard all about you, Jay Sawle. I know what you used to get up to with Polly Smith, Maisie Grant and . . .'

'All right, all right,' he said, laughing now. 'I've had a bit of fun with a few girls but none of them meant anything to me. It's you I love, Sorrel. You're the one I want to marry.'

'It's all very well your telling me that but promises mean nothing . . . not until you've spoken to my father.'

'I've tried, you know I've tried, but he always changes the

162

subject. He said we could go out together sometimes but he won't listen when I try to tell him I want to marry you. It's as if he doesn't want to hear about us getting married.'

Sorrel nodded, accepting the truth of his words. Her father had been giving her some odd looks of late and she'd sensed that he wasn't really happy about her seeing Jay. He still thought of her as his baby, even though she had turned seventeen.

'You'll just have to come right out and say it,' she told Jay. 'Once he knows you're serious, he'll get used to the idea. Ma says she'll make him let us get married in the summer if your mother agrees.'

'Dad's promised to talk her into it,' Jay said. 'I'll have another go at Sid this evening – ask him if we can get engaged at Christmas.'

'Will you really?' She looked up at him. Christmas was only days away. 'Oh, Jay . . . I do love you.'

'You're so lovely,' he said, and touched her cheek. 'I love you, Sorrel. I might not be clever with words but you're special to me. I'll always love you.'

'Jay.' She melted into his arms as he drew her to him, kissing her with such tenderness and passion that she felt her resistance ebbing. 'Jay . . .'

'Yes, my darling?'

'I . . . I know lots of girls do what you want . . .' Her cheeks burned and she couldn't meet his eyes. 'I suppose after we're engaged . . . but Ma would kill me if I got pregnant and Pa . . . I think it would kill him if . . .'

'It doesn't matter,' he said, tipping her chin so that she looked up at him. 'I shall probably try it on again, Sorrel, because I want you so much – but you just clip my ear if I do. We'll wait until we're married, that's the right way.'

'Are you sure?' She looked up at him anxiously.

'Just so long as you remember you belong to me!'

'Of course I do. I was always your girl – ever since that day you fought for me after school.'

'Do you mean that?' His gaze narrowed intently. 'There wasn't anyone else you liked a lot?'

'Who?' She was puzzled. 'I don't know what you mean.'

'Shima, of course.'

'Oh, Jay!' She laughed as she saw the flash of jealousy in his eyes, then the laughter died and she reached up to trace the curve of his jaw with her fingertips, feeling the slight roughness of his beard, even though he'd shaved that morning. 'It's you I want, Jay. Only you – always. Only you, my darling.'

'And I want you,' he said, his voice husky with emotion. 'Come on, let's get round to your house. I'm going to talk to Sid now before I lose my nerve again!'

'I can't agree to a wedding in the spring,' Sid said heavily. 'I'm sorry, Jay, but she's too young – and I don't think a long engagement is a good idea either. Perhaps if you ask me again next summer. When Sorrel is eighteen you could plan your wedding for the following summer.'

'But that's eighteen months,' she cried. 'Oh, Pa, you can't ask us to wait all that time. It's too long.'

'I was talking to Jay,' he said. 'Go on into the house, Sorrel. Give your mother a hand with the supper.'

She threw him a mutinous look but Jay nodded, his eyes telling her not to argue. Her feet dragged as she walked reluctantly towards the house and she felt close to tears. Jay would never wait that long; he was too impatient. She would lose him and it would be her father's fault!

'What's the matter with you?' May asked as she went in. She listened, frowning, as Sorrel told her what her father had said to them, then nodded. 'I expected this, Sorrel. Your father sets too much store by you, always has done ever since you were born. He doesn't want to lose his little girl.'

'He won't lose me. We'll be living nearby. He'll see me most days.'

'But it won't be the same for him.' A sigh escaped May. 'Leave him to me, Sorrel. I'll see if I can talk him into an engagement in the spring and a summer wedding next year.'

'Can you?' Sorrel looked at her hopefully. 'Jay's so impatient.'

'Then you'll just have to keep him in check, won't you?' May slapped thick yellow butter on to a slice of bread with an unusually heavy hand. 'Or not see him so often.'

'We only walk out on Saturdays and Sundays as it is.'

'But he's in and out of the yard a dozen times a day. Besides, two days a week is plenty. If you were in service you'd likely have just one day off a month, and then you might be forbidden followers. Think yourself lucky we've been so easy with you, Sorrel. I'll do my best with your pa but I won't have him upset, do you hear me?'

'Yes – yes, I hear you.'

There was no point in arguing further. Without her mother's help she knew she had no chance of persuading her father to let them marry sooner.

When Sid came in from the yard he was alone. Jay had left without saying goodbye to her and Sorrel guessed he wasn't very pleased about whatever her father had said to him after she'd left them together.

She had the good sense not to say anything to Sid. She could only hope that her mother would find a way of talking him round – and that Jay would be patient for a little longer.

Chapter Twenty-One

Richie saw the girl as he crossed the street and turned up past the Post Office in Chatteris. He was on his way to work in the office of Becket & Co., which was the name of the corn merchant's his father had bought a couple of years back, and he was already late. And that would bring another lecture from Aden when he heard about it from his spy.

Richie bitterly resented the fact that his father had put a manager over him in the office.

'It's just until you learn the business thoroughly,' Aden had told him at the start – but Richie knew the man was there to spy on him and report back.

His father didn't trust him to look after things properly, even though he could run rings round any of them. The spy thought he knew it all but Richie had his own little tricks. He was cleverer, quicker and sharper than anyone else – except perhaps his mother. She had a way of looking at him sometimes that made him feel as if she could see right into his mind . . . as if she could read his secret thoughts. Of course she couldn't – no one could – but it made him uncomfortable, just the same.

He couldn't afford any more black marks against him, especially just now. He didn't have time to hang around – but there was something about the way the girl walked, with her head up and her full, flared skirts swinging about her hips, that made him look at her twice.

It was a bright, crisp day and the sun was warm for the time of year; it seemed to bring out blue lights in the shining mass of black curls that tumbled halfway down her back.

She was a beautiful girl, though probably a gipsy and not worth his notice – and yet there was something that held him, something in those eyes and that proud face . . .

He wasn't sure why he paused, pretending to look in a shop window until she came up to him. As she did so he caught the fresh scent of her hair, which had obviously been washed that morning, and was suddenly aware of a desire so strong and urgent that it turned his loins to liquid fire.

'Hello,' he said impulsively. 'Haven't I seen you somewhere?'

She turned in surprise, a haughty look in her blue eyes as she studied him, then her expression softened and she smiled. 'Perhaps,' she said in a husky voice that made Richie groan inside. 'Are you one of the Sawles from Mepal? I know your family . . . I think you're Richie, aren't you?'

'Yes. I'm Richie,' he said, surprised in his turn. 'But I don't know your name – do I?'

'My people worked for your father a few times. I've seen you from a distance but you never looked at me. We live here now: Sadie, me and some of our people.'

Richie was silent. He had probably seen her on the land but taken no notice; dressed in her working clothes with dirt under her fingernails, she would have looked much as the others – and he didn't like gipsies. They were dirty, sly creatures: like that damned upstart who claimed kinship with him. If Richie had his way the whole lot of them would be shut up in a dark place and never let out again – yet this woman was so beautiful in her crimson skirt and blue velvet jacket, neither of them new but clean and respectable: clean and soft as her skin would be underneath them. Her skin looked like cream and roses. He wondered what she used on it to keep it so soft – like silk. He had never seen anyone quite like her.

'You must be Tarina' he said, his throat catching as desire rippled through him again. 'Your people have camped on a piece of Father's land.'

'Yes.' Her head went up at something in his tone. 'We're going to settle there and sell turf for lawns.'

'Does that pay?' Ritchie was always interested in business. 'Selling turf?'

'I don't know. Maybe.' Tarina shrugged. 'At least I shan't have to sell pegs round the doors.'

'Is that where you're going now?' he asked, his eyes moving over her with unconcealed lust. She was a fancy piece and no mistake. Her every movement set his loins tingling and he could just imagine how good her flesh would taste. 'Or are you shopping?'

Tarina's laughter rang out as she shook her head and the mass of curls quivered and bobbed about her shoulders. 'I'm going to pick herbs. Sadie makes things with them. Cures and . . . love potions . . . and scented ointments.'

'Is that why you smell so good?' Richie couldn't keep the hunger out of his voice. 'Good enough to eat.'

'Perhaps.' Tarina's eyes were bright and wicked as she looked at him. 'Do you know anyone who wants to buy some turf?'

'I might,' Richie said. 'Where can I find you if I do?'

'You know where to come.' Her smile tantalized him, teasing him, promising so much. 'Perhaps I'll see you again one day . . .'

'Oh, you will,' Richie murmured as she walked away from him, her hips swaying. 'You will, my proud beauty . . . you will.'

Tarina knew the man's eyes were following her as she walked on past him and it made her smile to herself. Something about him made her think of Shima, though they weren't really very much alike in looks – but they *were* half-brothers. She knew that for certain now. Jay Sawle had told her when she was bathing his face after the fight with Jake.

A slight shiver ran down her spine and she glanced over her shoulder as she still did whenever she thought of Jake. He and his woman had left the camp straight after Jay Sawle had thrashed him, but even as he drove away he had shouted threats at her in the language only her own tribe understood.

'What's he saying?' Jay had asked as her face went pale. 'What did he mean?'

'He threatened to make me pay for what you did to him,' she answered. 'He said he would settle his score with me one day.'

'I should have killed him,' Jay said regretfully. 'But you'll be safe enough if you take my father's offer, Tarina. I doubt that Jake will dare to come back to this area, despite his threats.'

At first she had been doubtful. They were travelling folk and she knew that for some of them it would be a fate worse than death to be chained to one place. She had agreed to ask the others that night, and to her surprise Sadie had been one of the first to agree.

'I've had enough of the road,' she'd said. 'We've always found work in Chatteris. I say we should take the offer.' She spat on the ground. 'I say 'tis owed us.'

She had looked at Tarina with such hatred then that the girl felt sick. Sadie would never forgive her for what had happened to Leyan. She had said nothing while Jake was with them, but after he'd left her grumbling had become constant – and she lost no chance to slap or curse her daughter. Only her failing health stopped her from doing more; she needed Tarina, though she would rather have died than admit it.

'Oh, Shima,' Tarina's heart cried out. 'Why did I leave the circus? Why did we ever come back to this place?'

If she had stayed with him perhaps none of it need ever have happened. They might still have been working and travelling together. Tears stung her eyes but she blinked them away. There was no room for tears in her life; they had never done her any good in the past and never would. She had always lived by her wits – and she would make them work for her now.

That look in the gorgio's eyes had told her what he wanted of her. She had kept her maidenhood for Shima – but he did not want her. It was unlikely she would ever see him again – and even if he should come back, it would not change things: he loved someone else.

'Richie Sawle.' She discovered she liked the sound of his name on her lips. 'Shima's brother.'

She would never lie in the arms of the man she loved . . . but she could have his half-brother as her lover. Perhaps . . . perhaps if she were clever enough she could have more than that. Men were ruled by their lusts. If she had given Jake

169

what he wanted, she could have queened it over every other woman in the camp . . . but she had hated Jake. The very smell of him had turned her stomach. She did not hate Richie Sawle. He made her think of Shima.

A little smile touched her mouth. Men always wanted one thing. It didn't matter whether they were of the true blood or not. If a woman had her wits about her there were ways of getting anything she wanted from the man who desired her. It was just a matter of playing his game and waiting.

Chapter Twenty-Two

It was unkind of her father to make them wait so long to get married! Sorrel spent a restless night, crying into her pillow and wondering if Jay would meet her after church as he usually did. When she came out with Mabel the next morning she saw he was there but one look at his face told her he was in a mood.

'It looks as if we'll have to wait until you're eighteen,' he said, kicking at a stone in his frustration. 'There was no moving your father.'

'I'm sorry. I never thought Pa would be like this.' She could sense his disappointment and her heart sank into her shiny Sunday boots. 'Ma says she'll talk to him in a little while – see if she can persuade him to let us get married next summer.'

'He won't budge.' Jay took her hand. 'I'm not sure I can wait that long, Sorrel. I know I said I could – but I wasn't expecting it to be eighteen months or more.'

'Are you saying you don't love me enough to wait? That you want to marry someone else?'

'Of course not.' He played with her fingers, his eyes avoiding hers. 'You know what I mean ... I want you so much ... it isn't fair of him to make us wait!'

She glanced over her shoulder, afraid that someone might hear him, but there was no one about. 'Jay ... I can't ... you know I can't ...'

'No, I suppose not.' He sighed in frustration. 'Maybe we shouldn't see each other so much.'

'Ma said the same.' Her eyes filled with tears. 'I can't bear not seeing you, Jay.'

'Don't cry, love.' He looked contrite as he saw how upset she was. 'I'm a selfish brute. We'll see each other once a week but it's best if we aren't alone too often. I might not be able to control myself.'

She nodded, swallowing her disappointment. Jay was a hot-blooded man and it must be hard for him to keep his passions in check. If she wasn't prepared to give into him she had to agree to his terms.

'All right,' she said. 'We'll meet at Mabel's on Saturdays and whenever you pop into the yard – but we won't go out alone.'

'Fanny's having some friends to dinner in the New Year. You can come for that.' He grinned sheepishly. 'We'll be safe enough with my mother there to keep an eye on us.'

She tried to smile but felt too miserable to respond to his teasing. It just wasn't fair of her father to insist on their waiting all that time. Anyone would think he didn't want her to get married at all.

They had reached the farm gate. Jay gazed down at her uncertainly, then kissed her cheek and turned away. She watched him walk back down the road, wondering how long he would wait. There were half a dozen girls she knew of who would jump at the chance to go walking down the bank with him.

Surely he would wait if he loved her enough? She knew that the next few months would not be easy for either of them but they were promised to each other and nothing could change that – could it?

Sorrel could hear the pig squealing as she finished washing the churns and walked to the door of the dairy. One of the sows had got out and her father was trying to catch it. As Sorrel watched he made a run at the sow but she butted his legs and he went down on his backside in the mud.

Sorrel was laughing as she ran to help him at the same moment as her brother appeared from behind the barn. They managed to corner the sow between them, shutting her safely in the sty once more.

172

'Betsy hasn't played up for a while,' Sorrel remarked, still smiling. 'She must think spring is in the air.'

It was the end of February but mild enough for spring, a hint of green already showing through the hedges and birds with twigs in their beaks beginning to court in earnest.

The small herd of pigs belonged to Sorrel's father. Aden allowed him to keep them in the yard behind their cottage and turn them out in the pasture for some free ranging before they went to market. Sid earned himself some extra money and in return supplied Aden with a side of pork when he had a pig killed for his own use. Sorrel knew her father was proud of the small herd – and of the independence it gave him.

Sid turned as he fastened the door of the sty but he wasn't smiling. Something in his eyes made her stomach churn. He had been acting oddly these past few weeks and she felt guilty, knowing that at least some of it was her fault. Her mother had been badgering him to let her at least get engaged to Jay and, two nights earlier, he'd finally given in. Sorrel had given Jay the good news and he was going to buy her a ring that Saturday.

'Have you finished your chores?' Sid asked, and, as she nodded, 'Then you'd best get in to your ma. She'll be needing a hand, I dare say. There's no need for you to hang around out here.'

His brusque manner hurt her. He had always been so warm and loving towards her, enjoying her company and keeping her with him as much as he could, and this new coldness made her want to cry. She turned away, her head going up. She wasn't going to let him see how upset she was.

When she went into the kitchen she saw Mabel sitting at the table. Her face was glowing with excitement and she couldn't wait to tell Sorrel her news.

'I've just told May,' she said. 'It's so wonderful, Sorrel. The doctor says I'm nearly three months gone.'

'That *is* good news!' Sorrel put her arms around Mabel's neck and hugged her. She smelt of lily of the valley and face powder. 'You've been wanting this so bad.'

'Mabel and me are going to Ely tomorrow,' her mother

said. 'I need a hat for Ted's wedding and there's some pretty ones in a new shop Rose was telling me about.'

'It's a shame you can't come, too,' Mabel said. 'But someone has to be here.'

'I don't mind. Jay is taking me out to buy a ring on Saturday.'

'May told me.' Mabel jumped up and kissed her cheek, getting lip rouge all over her and laughing as she wiped it off again. 'I'm so pleased for you, love. We shall be buying clothes for your wedding next.'

'Once Ted is settled we can concentrate on Sorrel,' May said, trying not to sound smug but making a poor job of it. 'It took some doing, I can tell you – but Sid has more or less agreed to September.'

That was only seven months away! Sorrel was grateful to her mother for what she had achieved but Jay was becoming increasingly impatient and they had almost quarrelled a couple of times when his hands had strayed further than they ought. So far she hadn't let him do more than touch her breasts – and she hadn't heard any whispers about him seeing other, more obliging, girls either – but it wasn't easy to deny him when she melted inside every time he kissed her. It wasn't just Jay who was eager for their marriage!

'You should know I wouldn't go with anyone else,' he had said, looking angry when she'd hinted that he might. 'That's all in the past. It's you I want, no one else.'

They had kissed and made up that quarrel but she had sensed his frustration. He wanted much more than the frantic kisses they snatched behind a tree on their way home from her sister-in-law's house. Sorrel didn't blame him for being annoyed over it. If Jay had had his way they would have been married at Christmas.

She sighed as she left her mother and Mabel gossiping and went upstairs to turn out the bedrooms. What did other girls do to keep their men at bay during this awkward time – or did they all give in to persuasion? Was she wrong to hold out against him? She was doing what she had been taught was right but it didn't seem fair when the very people she was trying to please were denying her the right to happiness.

174

Maybe it would be best if she just did what Jay wanted – what they both wanted. Why shouldn't she? Maybe . . . maybe next time she would . . .

Sorrel held out her hand for Jay to slip the ring on her finger: it was a beautiful diamond cluster shaped like a daisy and Jay had bought it in a shop in Ely. She knew it was one of the most expensive on offer and she stared at it in awe as it twinkled on her finger.

'It's lovely,' she whispered. 'Thank you, Jay. I love it.'

'I love you,' he said huskily. 'Sometimes I lie awake at night and it hurts because I want you so much. I want to be able to hold you in my arms. I'm afraid that if I don't marry you soon it will be too late – something will happen to part us . . . you'll never be mine.'

'Don't be daft,' Sorrel said, reaching up to kiss him gently on the lips. 'I'll always be yours, Jay. Ma says we can be married in September. That's not so very far away, is it?'

'I suppose not.' A wistful smile tugged at the corners of his mouth. 'It's just a feeling . . . but I'm being stupid. It's because I want you so much.'

'I don't see why we shouldn't . . .' Sorrel was almost paralyzed with shyness. 'Soon anyway . . . so long as we're careful.'

'Sorrel!' His breath shuddered against her ear as he held her. 'Are you sure?'

She was trembling inside as she saw the burning look in his eyes. All her instincts told her that it was wrong to go against her mother's warnings but she loved Jay so much – and it *was* her father's fault. If he had agreed to a spring wedding Jay wouldn't have been so impatient. He needed her and she wanted to make him happy. She wanted to know what it was like to be truly his.

'It's not warm enough to go down the bank yet . . .'

'There's the farmhouse down the Gault,' he said. 'Dad was talking about having it done up for us. I could get the key next Saturday, if you're sure?'

Sorrel came to a decision. Jay was more important to her than anyone else, even her parents. 'Get the key, Jay. I'll

175

think of something to tell Ma. We'll spend the afternoon there together.'

'I'll look after you,' he promised, eyes glowing with love for her. 'I won't get you into trouble, Sorrel. Besides, we'll be married in a few months.'

'Yes.' She reached up to kiss him. Surely it couldn't be wrong when they loved each other this much? 'By September at the latest.'

He gave her a long, lingering kiss. 'Never forget that I love you, Sorrel.'

'I won't.' She glanced at the ring on her finger and smiled inwardly. Jay loved her and she loved him. Nothing could part them now.

Sorrel caught the stink of whisky on her father's breath as he handed her a basket of eggs and was shocked. It was the middle of the afternoon and he never drank more than a glass of beer with his lunch.

'Is something the matter, Pa?' she asked. 'You haven't got a chill, have you?'

'There's nothing wrong with me,' he said, and glared at her. 'Mind your own business, Sorrel, and leave me to mine.'

'Pa . . . don't be angry with me, please.'

For a moment something flickered in his eyes but then he turned away and walked into the barn. Sorrel was crying as she went into the kitchen and May gave her a sharp look.

'What's eating you?'

'It's Pa. He has been drinking whisky. I asked him if he had a cold and he snapped my head off.'

'He's feeling sorry for himself, that's all.' May pulled a face. 'He'll get over it, but in the meantime that's the price you'll have to pay for getting your own way over the engagement.'

It was three days since Jay had put the ring on her finger and her father's mood had seemed to get steadily worse from then on. He avoided looking at her and spoke only when necessary.

'Jay is taking me out again this Saturday,' Sorrel said, more determined now to go through with her promise after

176

her father's behaviour. 'I want to look for a dress to copy for the wedding.'

They had talked it over and decided that she should spend her money on good material and make her own gown. Mabel had promised to help and she would be able to have more clothes for her honeymoon than if she bought her wedding dress.

Her mother turned back to her baking. There was already a tray of fruit buns in the oven and the kitchen smelt warm and spicey.

'You can deliver some eggs and cheeses for me,' she said. 'The list is on the dresser.'

Sorrel picked it up, then went to the cool larder to pack her baskets with the various orders. Her mother was still busy as she went out and there was no sign of her father in the yard as she walked to the gate. His attitude had really hurt her. If he loved her as much as he said – surely he would want her to be happy?

After making her deliveries she took the path behind the church home, stopping in surprise as she saw the woman waiting for her. She had a basket over her arm and had been picking bits and pieces from the hedge but Sorrel sensed that the herb-gathering was just an excuse to be there. Tarina was waiting for her and there was an air of excitement about her.

'Tarina . . .' Sorrel stopped reluctantly. 'How are you – and Sadie? I heard you were living near Chatteris.'

'We've land just outside – given us by Aden Sawle,' she said, something flickering in her eyes. 'I've been hearing about you – you're to wed Jay Sawle, aren't you?'

'Yes . . . who told you?'

'Never you mind,' she said, and there was a hint of malice or mischief in her voice. 'I told you our lives would run together, didn't I?'

'I don't understand you.' Sorrel was puzzled by her manner. She was very pleased about something. 'Tell me what you mean, don't talk in riddles.'

'Maybe I shall one day,' said Tarina. 'It is not certain yet. I came only to tell you that I have heard from Shima.'

'From Shima? How? Where is he?'

'He sent me word in our way – a traveller passing through. He was in Ireland and now he has gone to America to make his fortune.'

'Does he know he could come back here if he wanted?'

Tarina nodded. 'He knows but he won't come. Why should he?'

'I don't know.' Sorrel had an odd feeling of loss. 'I suppose there's no reason. Has he asked you to join him?'

Tarina's eyes glittered like broken glass. 'I would have followed him once but not now. I have better things to occupy me.'

Again Sorrel sensed an inner gloating. Tarina wanted to tell her something and yet she was holding it back, almost as if she were taunting Sorrel.

'What do you mean? You never say anything straight out.'

'Our destiny may be much closer than you think,' she said with a smirk. 'You'll find out one day, Sorrel Harris.'

'I've had enough of this,' she said. 'I must go now, Tarina. I'm glad you've heard from Shima. I'll tell Jay when I see him.'

Tarina's eyes were wild and angry as Sorrel walked away from her. 'We're bound together,' she called after her. 'Remember that . . . there's no escaping it.'

Sorrel felt ice trail down her spine but didn't look back. Her mother was right; it was best not to have anything to do with Tarina or her people. And yet she was glad to have news of Shima. She knew Aden had sent his son a large sum of money, money that could take him to America and a new life. It would probably be years before he returned. If he ever did.

Sorrel sensed something was wrong as soon as she walked into the house. Her mother had left a pile of dough on the table and there was blood on the floor, a badly stained cloth lying nearby. Someone had been hurt. Accidents were not uncommon in the yard but this looked serious.

'Ma . . .' she called. 'Ma, where are you?'

'Up here . . . just a minute.'

Her voice came from the floor above. Sorrel rushed up

the stairs and met her coming from the bedroom. May's expression was so shocked that Sorrel felt sick.

'Your pa has had an accident,' she said, her face white. 'He was chopping wood and . . . the axe blade flew off and cut his arm. I've managed to stop the bleeding for the moment but he'll need the doctor. It may want stitching.'

'Shall I go?'

'Ted's already gone for help.' May caught her breath. 'It's a nasty cut, Sorrel. When he came in, I thought – but he'll be all right.'

'How did it happen?'

'It was an accident,' she said, stressing the word. 'Could have happened to anyone. The head of the axe had worked loose and it just came off.'

'But it wouldn't have happened if Pa had taken more care, would it?' Sorrel felt ill as she saw the answer in her mother's face. 'It's my fault . . . my fault he was hurt.'

'No, of course it wasn't,' May said, and sighed. 'It's his own fault, Sorrel. You mustn't blame yourself. He's being very silly.'

'Can I do anything to help?'

'I was making a pie for supper. You'll have to see to that. I'll have my hands full looking after your father.'

Sorrel nodded and turned back to the kitchen. It hurt to think of her father lying up there in pain and she wanted to do something for him – but her mother would look after him. He wouldn't want her fussing over him, not in his present mood. He was angry with her – angry because she wanted to get married.

Ted brought the doctor back and they were upstairs for nearly half an hour. The pie was in the oven by the time the doctor came down.

'How is my father?' Sorrel asked fearfully. 'Will he be all right?'

'In a few days, though he'll need to rest for a while – if your mother can keep him in bed. It was a nasty wound but he was lucky. He won't lose the arm.'

'Thank you.' She was close to tears but didn't want to cry in front of him. 'Would you like a few fresh eggs, doctor, and a cheese?'

'That's very kind of you, Sorrel.' He accepted the gift and patted her shoulder kindly. 'Now don't you go worrying. Mr Harris is a strong man. He'll be up and around again soon enough.'

She forced a smile as he went out, but of course she couldn't stop worrying. Her father could have lost his arm . . . he might have died. It was all her fault. He hadn't wanted her to get engaged and it had upset him when Jay bought her the ring. If he hadn't been drinking, the accident would never have happened.

She told Jay the next morning when he called to see how her father was. He looked at her uncertainly, his eyes narrowing.

'Are you saying you want to call it off?'

'No, of course not,' she cried. 'I love you and I want to marry you . . . but I don't think we ought to go down the Gault on Saturday. Ma can't spare me, she's that much to do with looking after Pa.'

'You're feeling guilty.' Jay was annoyed. 'This is just your way of getting out of it, isn't it, Sorrel? You've changed your mind.'

'No, that's not true . . . but we have to wait for a while. I can't do anything now, not while Pa is ill.'

'I see all right,' he muttered. 'But don't expect me to be happy about it.'

He started to walk away but she ran after him, catching at his sleeve. 'Don't go like this, Jay. Please! You know I love you. I wish we could be married tomorrow – honestly, I do.'

He hesitated, some of the annoyance fading from his eyes. 'I'm not angry – not with you. I think Sid did this on purpose, just to upset you.'

'That's a horrible thing to say.' She stared at him in distress. 'Pa wouldn't do that, Jay. He wouldn't!'

'I think he might do anything to stop you getting married. He wants to keep you at home with him.'

'That's not fair,' she said, tears stinging behind her eyes.

'No, I don't suppose it is,' Jay agreed. 'But at the moment it's the way I feel. I'll see you around, Sorrel – when you've got time.'

He walked off and she let him go, her heart feeling as if it were being torn in two. Perhaps her father wasn't being fair but neither was Jay. She loved them both and this was so painful she could hardly bear it.

Chapter Twenty-Three

Richie looked down into the face of the woman lying beneath him on the ground. It was the first real summer day of 1914 and more than three months had passed since he'd first seen her. He had needed all his powers of persuasion plus several expensive presents to break down her resistance, but it had happened for the first time a week ago and since then he had had her six times.

The first time he had been astonished to discover that she was still a virgin. He had never dreamt that he would be her first lover; if he had known he might have thought more carefully about seducing her, but it was too late for caution now. Besides, she was better than any other girl he had ever had. Her enthusiasm and passion more than made up for any lack of experience – and he enjoyed teaching her how to please him.

'Was it good for you?' he asked, bending to kiss her ripe, full lips as she pouted up at him. 'I've never had a woman like you before, Tarina. You're so full of fire.'

'Perhaps it is because I have the true blood,' she said, and laughed. 'You are used to milk-and-water women.'

'I wouldn't say that exactly,' Richie murmured, mouth moving down to suck on her dark-edged nipples. She tasted like wine and he felt light-headed, intoxicated. 'Just that you're the best.'

Tarina tipped back her head, moaning as desire rippled through her and she arched her body towards him, inviting the exploration of his tongue and mouth. His tongue trailed down between the valley of her breasts, over her taut navel to the mound of soft, damp hair and the quivering flesh between her thighs. She opened to him, offering herself to his devouring mouth, writhing and moaning in anticipation of the pleasure he could give her.

'You're insatiable, aren't you?' he groaned as his manhood begin to harden and burn once more. 'I can't understand why you haven't had lovers before this.'

'Perhaps I was waiting for you,' she said. 'Don't talk, Richie. I want to feel you inside me again. I want all of you . . . now!'

He moaned deeply, then lifted himself and plunged into her. She was hot and slippery and he lost his head, thrusting into her violently in a frenzy of excitement, again and again, until he spent himself inside her and collapsed on to her naked breasts, their sweat mingling.

'Richie,' Tarina whispered, her fingers tangling in his hair, 'I love you. Say you love me. Say it now.'

'I love you,' he muttered against her damp flesh. 'I love you, Tarina.' Her perfume enveloped him, filling his senses so that he could think only of her, of her softness and her pliant, yielding body. 'I'll never have enough of this . . . never . . .'

'And we shall be married in the way of your people?'

He stiffened, lifting his head to look into her face. Her smile disturbed him and he suddenly realized that for the first time he had not pulled away at the last moment. The satisfaction in her eyes told him that she had planned it that way, driving him mad with lust so that he had forgotten to be cautious.

'Marriage?' he said, drawing back from her. 'I never promised you marriage, Tarina. You can't say I did.'

Her eyes flashed with sudden temper and she sat up, pushing back her long hair. 'I am not one of your milk-and-water women, to be tossed aside when you've done with me,' she said. 'Your seed is inside me, Richie Sawle. I am carrying your child.'

He stood up and pulled on his clothes, beginning to feel uneasy as he saw the wild look in her eyes. Gipsies were unpredictable and she might be capable of anything – but he wasn't going to be blackmailed into marrying her. His plans had been set for a long time and he was not prepared to change them – even if she did stir him in a way no other woman ever had.

'You can't be sure about that, Tarina.' He gave her a hard, resentful stare. Damn her and her tricks! No woman was going to trap him – even this beauty whose very scent was enough to drive him mad with longing. 'I've been careful most of the time. The odds must be against it happening just like that.'

She shook her head, a smile on her lips. 'I have been taking Sadie's potions to make me conceive,' she said. 'I have your child, Richie – and I shall have you.' Her eyes narrowed to menacing slits. 'Remember what happened to Lenny Browne? Leyan is not the only one who would kill for me . . .'

When the time for her monthly cycle came and went without the usual bleeding Tarina knew that she was carrying the child of Richie Sawle but she waited for another two months before going to him at the place of his work. He saw her standing outside his office and came out to her, taking her arm and hurrying her into one of the sheds where the corn was stored before delivery to the miller. All the sheds were empty now, swept clean in preparation for the new harvest that would soon be gathered.

There was both anger and apprehension in his face as he looked at her, his fingers digging into the soft flesh of her upper arm so hard that it almost made her wince. 'Why have you come? I told you never to come here during working hours.'

'And I told you I was carrying your child.' Her eyes flashed with triumph as she saw him turn pale. She placed her hand over her stomach, which was just beginning to show a slight curve. 'Now you know that I did not lie – so when will you wed me?'

'Never!' Richie cursed himself for a fool. 'I'm not going to marry you and that's final . . . anyway, that could be anyone's brat. How do I know you haven't been with half a dozen men? Men of your own kind. I've seen them looking at you when I ordered turf a couple of times. You could have been with any of them.'

'But I have not,' Tarina cried. 'They know that and so do you. I was a virgin when you first lay with me and the child I carry inside my womb is yours. If you will not marry me, I shall put a curse on you.'

Richie laughed as her eyes sparked with anger. 'You're so beautiful when you look like that, Tarina. It almost tempts me to give you what you want . . .'

'You do love me. You will marry me.' She threw herself into his arms, winding hers about his neck. 'Make love to me, Richie. I want you now – here in that straw.'

He unwound her arms, looking uneasily over his shoulder, afraid that someone might come in and see her. This was the first time she had come to his place of work, though he had met her several times at their secret hollow. Each time he had meant to finish with her, but each time he had given into his lust, taking her with a feverish passion – though he had never been careless again. He was angry with himself for falling into her trap. He had known she was pregnant even before this despite his denials, just as he knew it was his child. He wanted her now, wanted her so much that he could feel himself hardening and his breath coming faster. With difficulty he pushed her away, fighting the urge to throw her down and take her fully clothed as she was.

'I don't care if the brat is mine,' he said harshly. 'You can curse me all you like – and I'm not afraid of your menfolk. I doubt if any of them would risk murder after what happened to Leyan. He killed for you – and you drove him out. Oh, yes, I know what you did to that poor fool . . .'

'You devil!' The blood left her face and she went for him with her long nails, scoring his face before he caught her wrists. 'I hate you. I shall kill you myself.' She tried to reach the knife that hung at her belt but he twisted her arm behind her back then thrust her away so that she fell to the ground and crouched there, glaring up at him. 'I swear I'll kill you, gorgio.'

'You can try,' Richie said with a flicker of a smile. 'Or you can be sensible. I like you, Tarina, and I'm willing to be generous. I'll give you money for the baby and for yourself.

185

If you keep your mouth shut and don't cause me any trouble, I'll always look after you. I'm going to be rich one day and . . .'

She got to her feet and stood looking at him in silence for a moment, then she spat in his face.

'Pig! Keep your filthy money. I don't need it.' She flounced away from him, her hair tossing, skirts swaying. 'I'll kill your brat, gorgio pig. It will never draw breath – and one day I'll kill you.'

A chill went through him as he saw the wild look in her eyes. 'Don't be silly,' he said, taking an uncertain step towards her. 'There's no need for this, Tarina. I told you I would look after you and the child. I can't marry you but . . .' He stopped abruptly as she took the knife from her belt and held it threateningly. Her eyes had the fire of sunlight dancing on blue ice and she laughed as his face drained of colour. 'Don't be a fool . . .'

'Coward,' she cried scornfully. 'I hate you, Richie Sawle. I only lay with you because you were Shima's brother – but you are not half the man he is. I wouldn't marry you if you begged me – and your child will die today.'

Richie felt the sickness churn inside him. He hadn't thought of the child as a living being but now he suddenly realized it was his own flesh and blood.

'We could still see each other . . .' He stiffened as she laughed derisively. 'Tarina . . . don't do this. I'm not a monster and I do care for you. I'll give you money . . . anything except . . .'

She looked into his eyes and he felt the ice of her contempt, then she was gone. He discovered that he was shaking. A marriage between them was impossible, of course, but her fury had stunned him, leaving a nasty taste in his mouth. He wasn't feeling regret . . . no, no, that would be stupid. He couldn't marry a gipsy; it would ruin all his plans . . . his whole life . . . everything he had worked and schemed for would be lost. And yet when he'd held her in his arms he had felt more warmth, more love, than he had ever known before . . . as if they were in some strange way bound to each other. A sudden aching sense of loss swept over him and he felt cold – cold and empty, as if a chill wind had blown over his life. What had he done?

'Tarina . . . please . . .'

What was he asking? Richie took a grip on himself; he had almost lost control, slipped into that dark abyss he knew was there . . . waiting. What kind of nonsense was this? And over a woman! Let her go – what did it matter? She didn't mean it. She was bluffing. He began to breathe more easily as he convinced himself that she had made empty threats to frighten him. She wouldn't kill her own child – no woman would do that. It was possible, of course. He'd heard of women drinking hot gin and sitting in hot baths . . . and her mother knew a lot about herbs . . . but she wouldn't.

It was just another of her tricks to snare him, just as she'd led him on for weeks before letting him seduce her. She had played with him like a cat with a mouse, all the time planning to snare him in her trap. She would be back again tomorrow or the day after, pleading with him to marry her. He would be nicer to her the next time, he decided, smiling as he began to feel better; they would come to some arrangement – an arrangement that meant he could keep her as his lover and still marry Sally . . . sensible, safe, rich Sally.

Tarina stared at the bottle of dark liquid she had stolen from Sadie's trunk. She knew what it was and what it would do, because she had seen her mother give it to women who wanted to get rid of their unborn babies often enough. It wasn't only gipsy women who asked Sadie for help. At the fairs they had visited on their journeys up and down the country Sadie had sold cures for coughs and rheumatics openly, but there were many other potions in her store cupboard. Women came to buy the cures and then spoke in whispers of their secret desires. Some wanted to conceive a child, others to get rid of the one they carried. Tarina had listened and watched, and of course it was she who had scoured the hedgerows looking for the wild plants and berries Sadie infused into her potions.

Tarina was trying to remember how much of the liquid she needed to drink to be sure of aborting the child. She was afraid to ask her mother because she knew Sadie would

187

take a stick to her if she guessed the truth. It was bad enough that she was with child ... but the fact that the father was a gorgio who had refused to wed her would make Sadie more angry. These days she never ceased to grumble and complain, no matter what Tarina did to please her.

'It was your fault Leyan killed that gorgio,' she cried when Tarina protested at her unfairness. 'It is because of you that my son is dead.'

Tarina knew that her mother hated her. She was twisted up with bitterness and the pain in her joints that was growing gradually stronger so that even her own cures could not ease it. Her blows and curses had made Tarina's life almost unbearable and she had hoped to escape when Ritchie took her as his wife. She had liked him ... she might have loved him in time ... perhaps did love him a little ... but now it was too late.

What a fool she had been to have anything to do with him! The bitterness burned inside her, eating away at her like a canker. She no longer wanted to marry Ritchie. The only man she had ever really wanted was Shima and she wished desperately that she had never taken a lover.

All she wanted now was to be free of this child in her womb – then she would go to America and look for Shima. Even if he did not want her as his woman, he would look after her, he would care for her as his sister. America was a big place but she would find him somehow. Even in America her people had that special fraternity which wove a web about their hearts and kept them in touch through the signs they could all follow. Yes, when this gorgio brat was dead she would go in search of the man she loved.

She opened the bottle and smelt its contents, then tasted a drop on her finger and shuddered. It was very bitter but she must swallow it. Tipping back her head, she drained the contents. Better to be on the safe side and take it all ...

Jay tethered his horse outside the gipsy camp. He had come to see if Sadie's people were interested in buying some turf from his father's bottom field, which they were about to plough up, then he thought he would go into town and see his brother. Aden wasn't sure whether they should sell the corn as soon as they'd harvested it or keep it in the stack until the prices went up.

There were rumblings in Europe, talk of war and trouble to come; it all seemed very far away to Jay on this pleasant summer day but his father was worried. If it really did come to a war this time, the price of corn could rocket and Aden wanted to be sure of getting as much as he could for their crop. He wasn't sure whether to sell or hold but Richie would know: he had an eye for business.

Jay paused for a moment to breathe in the fresh air and the scents of summer, his eyes moving over the low-lying countryside. The sun was shining and it was a peaceful scene, the gaily painted vans each set in their own little space.

Dogs and children were playing some way off behind the vans and Jay could see ponies grazing ... but where were the men and women? The place seemed to be deserted, except that several of the vans were open and there were fires dotted about the camp.

The children's cries were the only sounds as Jay walked into the centre of the camp. The silence struck him as unnatural as he glanced round. Where were they?

He had begun to walk towards Sadie's caravan when he heard a terrible scream from somewhere behind it. Something was happening! He broke into a run, and as he rounded the corner of the waggon, he stopped and stared at the strange sight that met his eyes.

Several of the women were gathered in a semi-circle watching something on the ground. Moving closer, Jay saw a girl writhing in agony. Her skirts were up around her waist and her white petticoats were stained crimson with blood. Before his shocked eyes the girl screamed in agony as a mass of slime and tissue slithered from between her legs and was swiftly gathered up by Sadie.

The vomit rose in Jay's throat. He turned aside and wretched into the hedge. Behind him the gipsy women had become aware of his presence and began to mutter. Suddenly, he felt a hail of missiles and something struck him in the back. He swung round and saw that Sadie was on her feet, staring at him with such hatred that his blood ran cold.

'Sadie ...' he cried, putting out his hand to protect his

face as another stone hit his cheek. 'I'm Jay Sawle. I've come to offer you some turf . . .'

Silence fell as she held up her hand. She stepped closer to him, peering at him as if trying to see his face, then thrust the bloodstained bundle under his nose. He jerked back, feeling the bile in his throat again.

'Curse you, son of Aden Sawle. May the blood of my daughter be on your head and all your kin!'

'Tarina?' Jay's face went white. 'That's Tarina . . . shall I get the doctor to her?'

Sadie's look was terrible as she stared at him. 'She's dead,' she muttered. 'As dead to us as her child . . . the child your brother planted in her belly.'

'My brother . . .' Jay gasped. 'You mean . . . Richie? Richie did this to her?'

'His name is cursed.' Sadie spat on the ground and some of the spittle landed on Jay's boots. 'I curse him and all who bear the name of Sawle.'

'Did he rape her?' Jay met the menacing stare of the old woman. 'Let me look at her. If she . . . if that was her child, she needs medical attention.'

'Leave her be,' Sadie muttered. 'She has been harmed enough by your folk.'

'If I leave her to you she will die,' he said. He took a deep breath and stepped forward determinedly. 'I'm taking her to a doctor. Get out of my way, Sadie. If you try to stop me I'll have the law on you.'

The women began to murmur again and one threw another stone. Sadie glared at him, her black eyes burning with a deep hatred. Jay felt the anger and bitterness directed at him but refused to be intimidated. As he moved closer to the girl Sadie suddenly shrugged and stood aside.

'Take her if you want,' she said. 'I've finished with her.'

Jay pushed his way through the hostile women until he reached Tarina. She was still lying in the same place with her bloodstained skirts pulled up and her eyes closed. He knelt down and covered her decently. As he did so she moaned and opened her eyes, giving a little cry of fear.

'It's all right,' he said gently. 'Trust me, Tarina. I'm Shima's friend, you know that. I shan't hurt you. I'm taking you to a doctor and you'll be looked after until you're well again. When you're better my father will give you money so that you can go away from here.'

Tarina's eyes closed. Jay wasn't sure whether she had heard him or not. He bent down and gathered her into his arms, picking her up from the ground and standing upright. The women stared at him silently, their hostility so strong that it was a tangible thing. They drew back as he walked forward, drawing away from him as if he were contaminated, and several of them spat at him as he passed. Ignoring them, he carried Tarina out to where his pony and trap were hitched to the fence, laid her in the back and covered her with a blanket, then untied the reins.

It was more than an hour later that Jay found Richie in one of the store sheds. He was talking to another man and examining some grain. He half turned as Jay approached, surprise in his eyes. Then, as if he had somehow read Jay's mind, his face went ashen. He took a faltering step backwards as Jay strode towards him. Jay's fist landed plumb in his mouth, causing him to stagger and then fall to the ground.

'What's the matter?' Ritchie gasped. 'Have you gone crazy?'

'Get up, you bastard!' Jay yelled furiously. 'Get up and fight like a man or I'll whip you like the mongrel cur you are!'

Ritchie hesitated, then got slowly to his feet. Jay knocked him down again, then caught hold of his coat and dragged him to his knees, almost choking him as he hit him again and again across the face. Richie seemed stunned, making little effort to protect himself, almost as though he knew he deserved a beating. Sickened by his brother's cowardice, Jay let him drop to the ground.

The other man had been watching silently, his face shocked. Now he made a movement as if to help Richie, but he held out his hand to ward him off and struggled to his feet.

'Get out, Bill,' he said. 'This is between my brother and me.'

191

The man hesitated, then left hurriedly. Richie wiped the blood from his mouth, waiting until the man had gone before speaking.

'So you know,' he said at last. 'I suppose she told you. Does Father know? What did he say?'

'Is that all you care about?' Jay's mouth curled in scorn. 'Doesn't it matter to you that Tarina is lying close to death at this moment after aborting your child?'

'Tarina ... close to death?' Richie's face blanched. He looked as if he'd seen a spectre. For a moment there was something in his eyes – a wild, blind look – that scared Jay. 'I didn't believe her. I didn't think she would really do it. Believe me, Jay. She wanted me to marry her. I offered her money, anything except ...'

'She refused your money,' Jay said. 'What did you expect? She was always proud and wild, Richie.' His eyes narrowed as he sensed this had hit Richie hard – harder than he had expected. 'Why did you do it? Surely there are plenty of women willing to have a bit of fun without ... haven't you ever heard of being careful?'

'I was ... most of the time.' Richie eyed him resentfully. He was back in control, holding himself on a tight rein. 'Why did she have to be such a fool? I would have looked after her. I might even have set her up in a place of her own ... visited her sometimes ...'

'You make me sick,' Jay said, any sympathy he might have had evaporating. 'I'm ashamed to have you as my brother. If Father knew he would disown you.'

'Are you going to tell him?'

Jay saw the fear in his eyes and felt a surge of disgust. 'I ought to,' he said. 'It would serve you right if I did – but I'll make a bargain with you. You'll pay all Tarina's medical expenses out of your own pocket, and when she gets well – if she does! – you'll give her five hundred guineas.'

'Five hundred!' Richie swore furiously. 'That will take most of what I've put by for ... damn you, Jay! You and your notions of honour. She was willing and more than willing!'

'I don't care if she lay down and begged you,' Jay said coarsely. 'You knew who she was and what you were doing.

I'm warning you now, you give Tarina every penny of that money or I'll tell Father everything – and I don't mean just about Tarina either. There's a little matter of some missing potatoes . . .'

The fear in Richie's eyes hardened into hatred. 'Damn you,' he muttered. 'I'll do it. I'll do it – but I shan't forget this. One day I'll make you sorry you interfered in my affairs.'

'You can do what the hell you like,' Jay replied, his mouth twisting in scorn. 'I can take care of myself, Richie. Just remember, I've got a long memory, too.'

As Jay looked into his brother's eyes he knew they had reached a turning point in their relationship. They had never been friends but they were enemies now.

Tarina let her gaze drift round the long, narrow, depressing ward of the infirmary. It was a hospital now but not so long ago it had been a workhouse and still showed signs of its origins in the dull green walls and tiny windows that shut out most of the light. She had never been in such a place in her life and she hated it. She hated the stifling atmosphere and the smell of sick people. She hated being made to lie in bed and being scolded by the sharp-tongued Sister – and she hated herself for ever having lain with Richie Sawle.

'Time for your medicine,' Sister's voice broke into her thoughts. 'Sit up and take it like a good girl.'

'I do not want it.'

'You must take it. Doctor prescribed it for you.'

Tarina stared at her in sullen defiance. Why had Jay Sawle brought her here? If he had not interfered her mother would have left her to bleed to death. It would be better if she were dead. None of the men in her tribe would want her now; she was an outcast, just as Leyan had been.

'Stop being a foolish girl and take your medicine!'

As the stern-faced Sister pushed the glass towards her Tarina suddenly struck it from her hand. It fell to the floor, splintering and spilling its contents on the clean surface.

'You wicked, ungrateful girl!' Sister cried. 'I won't put up with this behaviour. 'You will take your medicine or . . .'

'What will you do?' Tarina's eyes sparked angrily. 'I hate

you and your medicines – and I've had enough of you, you old cow!'

'How dare you!' Sister lost her patience, administering a sharp slap to her face. 'You will do as you're told.'

'You can't make me,' Tarina cried, and leapt out of bed. 'I didn't want to come here and I won't stay.'

She evaded Sister's grasp and sped down the length of the ward on bare feet, past the astonished gaze of nurses and patients alike.

'Come back here this instant!'

Hearing the shout, one of the junior nurses tried to catch Tarina. They struggled for a few seconds, then the nurse gave a cry of pain as the gipsy bit her. She let go, staring at her hand in bewilderment as Tarina ran off.

'She bit me . . .' the nurse whimpered as Sister came up to her. 'She bit me . . .'

'She's nothing better than a wild beast,' Sister said, pursing her lips primly. 'Let her go then. We couldn't have kept her here much longer anyway. She'll go back to her own kind – that sort always does.'

It was dark now and the camp was silent; the fires were smouldering, almost out, the dogs sleeping. Tarina had waited and waited until she was sure that Sadie would be asleep. She knew that her mother drank one of her own potions every night to stop the pain from her swollen joints; once asleep she would not waken until morning.

It was time now. Time for her to creep into the van and take her things – the things she would need for her journey. For a while she had wanted to die as she lay in that hospital bed but since escaping her natural resilance had reasserted itself. Why should she die when Shima was alive? He was all she had ever cared for, all she loved . . . the only one to show her true kindness. She would search for him and when she found him . . . perhaps he would want her this time . . . perhaps he had forgotten that other one.

The sound of Sadie's snores made her pause. She stopped to look down at her mother for a moment and was surprised to feel pity. Sadie would be alone now. She would find it hard to earn her living without her daughter's help.

194

Perhaps ... but no, she would not stay to be beaten and cursed. Sadie would have let her die if Jay Sawle had not come.

Gathering the few things she possessed, Tarina crept from the van once more. She would dress when she was well away from the camp; it was not safe to stay here any longer than necessary in case someone woke and discovered her.

The night was no longer dark, the sky streaked with a strange pearly glow that allowed her to see her way with ease. She crept behind the hedge and put down her clothes, the knife she always carried at her waist and a few trinkets Richie Sawle had given her ... things she would sell to help pay her fare to America.

She reached up to pull the hospital nightgown over her head, her white flesh gleaming like pure white silk in the strange light. She was so glad to be free of the coarse garment which smelt of disinfectant and sickness. She would have liked to scrub herself clean but there was no time. She must leave here before anyone stirred.

'Got you at last, you little bitch!'

Tarina gasped as someone grabbed her from behind, catching her arm and swinging her round to face him so that she could smell the foulness of his breath.

'Jake ...' she cried, and shuddered as she gazed up into his evil eyes. 'You're drunk. Let me go. Let me go, Jake – or I'll ... I'll tell Marianna!'

His mouth curled into a sneer. 'To hell with that cat. Her brat died of a fever and she ran off and left me weeks ago. It's you I want – you I've always wanted. You kept me dangling on a string, pretending to be such an innocent – but now I know you for the whore you are. You can give me what you gave to that cocky young whelp.'

'No!' Tarina tore herself from his grasp. She was naked and shivering as his eyes devoured her feverishly. 'I won't. I won't let you use me as you did Marianna. I hate you, Jake – do you hear me? I hate your black soul ...'

He cursed loudly and lunged at her. She turned and ran across the rough patch of grass, hoping to reach the vans, to get help before he caught her – but he was too fast for her. A cry of despair escaped her as she sensed he was close, then he launched himself at her, bringing her down. He was lying on her naked body, hands moving over her at will, mouth slobbering against her throat. She fought wildly, using her nails to gouge his face, twisting and turning beneath him as she screamed for help.

'That's right, fight me,' he muttered thickly. 'I love it when you bitches fight, it makes it more fun.'

'I hate you,' she cried, and spat in his face. 'I hate you ... hate and despise you, you filthy pig!'

He struck her with the back of his hand, cutting her lip. She tasted blood as he forced his mouth over hers, her stomach heaving as she caught the foul stench of his breath; then as he thrust his tongue inside her mouth, she bit down hard.

He cursed and hit the side of her head so fiercely that it made her ears ring. The second blow rendered her almost unconscious so that she ceased to struggle and lay in a daze as he forced her legs apart, his fingers invading her tender flesh, opening her for his savage thrust. He jabbed into her in a frenzy of mindless lust, grunting and moaning until he was spent, then slumped against her, crushing her, almost smothering her with the bulk of his body.

Tarina lay still. She was numbed, frozen by a kind of fatalistic despair. She had always known this day would come, and in the end no one had been able to save her from his savagery. The physical pain he had inflicted on her already ravaged body was as nothing to the mental agony she was enduring, even though she could feel a slow trickle of blood between her thighs.

Jake seemed to have fallen into a stupor. She pushed at him, managing to roll his body to one side. That was better. She could breathe, she could think ... but something was cutting into her leg. She reached out and touched the cold hard metal of the knife that had come half out of its sheath and was pressing into her flesh. Jake's own knife.

She drew it gently from its sheath, half afraid that he would stir and stop her, but he did not move and she knew that he was fast in a drunken stupor. He was no threat to her now but in the morning ... it would never happen again! She would never allow him to use her like this again. She stared at the sharp blade in the strange pearly light, then something snapped in her head and she gave a cry of savage delight, plunging the knife into the side of Jake's neck. The blood spurted instantly, covering her face and her hands; it was in her eyes, in her mouth, in her nose. She struck again and again, wildly, in the grip of a terrible madness that would not let her stop even after she knew that he was dead.

She had killed him! It was justice. She felt a rush of heady pleasure in knowing that he could never touch her again, then she shivered as she realized what she had done. They would hang her . . . but not until she had endured months of anguish at being locked away in a dark cell.

She would rather die in the river . . . the river! She must wash away the blood . . . she must wash his blood off her . . . she must wash away the blood . . . so much blood . . . the blood she had seen in her dreams.

She stood up and began to walk very slowly, her mind confused, her body seized with a fit of uncontrollable shuddering. She must go to the river . . . the river would cleanse her of this horror. The river would take her and she would be free of this nightmare and the blood . . . the blood was choking her . . . the smell of it making her want to vomit. She had to be clean . . . clean and free of his blood.

What was she doing? She looked about her in a daze, fear and horror so jumbled in her mind that she hardly knew what she was doing. Then, seeing her clothes and the nightgown she had disgarded earlier, she bent to pick them up, though she did not know why she had done so. There was nothing for her now but the river . . . nothing but a death of her own choosing . . . the lesser of two evils. Yes, she would go to the river . . . she must wash away the blood.

Now at last the river was ahead of her, a streak of shining silver in that strange, eerie light. She dropped the nightgown, then her clothes, stepping into the cold water. She could feel mud beneath her feet, squelching between her toes as she walked out until the current claimed her; she let go, giving herself up to the water, her mind drifting away as her body sank beneath the surface, down and down into the murky depths and oblivion.

'Oh, Shima . . .' she thought as the green darkness closed around her. 'Shima . . . I loved you so much . . .'

Chapter Twenty-Four

'You're upset about something.' Sorrel looked at her sister-in-law anxiously. 'You're not worried about the baby, are you?'

Mabel was seven months gone now and feeling the strain of carrying her second child. Because Bob worried about her, Sorrel had fallen into the habit of popping round every day to give her a hand with the housework and make sure she was all right.

'No, Sorrel, it's not that.' Mabel glanced away, refusing to meet her eyes. 'Don't worry about me, love. I've got something on my mind, that's all.'

She was bothered about something, that much was certain. She had been in an odd sort of mood all that morning but it was obvious she didn't want to talk about whatever was worrying her.

'If you're sure you're all right?' Sorrel kissed her cheek. 'I'd best get home then.'

'It was good of you to come.' Mabel suddenly hugged her. 'I'm that fond of you, Sorrel.'

She saw a suspicion of tears in Mabel's eyes and sat down at the kitchen table. 'You'd better tell me,' she said. 'I'm not leaving here until you do.'

'Bob said I wasn't to . . .' Mabel hesitated. 'I think you should know . . .' She took a deep breath then came out with it. 'It's just that they're saying that gipsy girl drowned herself in the river not far from here.'

Sorrel felt the cold trickle down her spine. 'Gipsy? You mean Tarina, don't you?'

Mabel nodded. 'I don't know all of it, Sorrel. Only that she'd been in the infirmary and . . . her nightgown was found by the river. They say there was blood all over it and one of the other gipsies was found stabbed to death near their waggons. The one they used to call Black Jake.'

'Black Jake . . . stabbed?' Sorrel felt sick. 'Tarina drowned?' She stared at Mabel in shocked disbelief. 'Why was she in the hospital?'

'I don't know,' Mabel said. 'Bob didn't say.'

Sorrel stared at her hard. She had a feeling Mabel was lying but didn't know why she should. 'Have they found her body yet?'

'No – but if there was a tide running it might have been carried further downriver.'

Sorrel nodded, knowing that what she said was probably true. The whole of the fens was covered by a system of drains and pumps; if water had been pumped down from one of the stations it could have swollen the river and the current might have carried Tarina's body a long way.

'Yes, I expect so.' Sorrel stood up again. It was a shock and it had made her feel a bit strange but she didn't see why Mabel was so upset: she didn't even know Tarina. 'Are you sure that's all of it?'

'All I know,' Mabel said. 'You won't tell Bob I told you? He was most insistent you shouldn't know.'

'No, of course not, though it's bound to be in the papers, so why he didn't want me to know . . .' She shrugged her shoulders as she went out, still puzzled by her brother's attitude. 'See you tomorrow then.'

The sun was warm on Sorrel's head as she walked home, her thoughts and feelings all muddled up in her head. Tarina dead . . . drowned . . . and a man stabbed to death! The gipsy girl hadn't really been her friend but Sorrel felt as if she had come to know her quite well, and she was so beautiful. The thought of her body lying at the bottom of the river or caught amongst the reeds somewhere made Sorrel's eyes sting. Poor, poor Tarina! What had happened to make her take her own life like that? Sorrel shivered despite the warmth of the sun: it was all so horrible! And why hadn't

Bob wanted her to know about it? Was there something more, something they were hiding from her?

Thinking about it, she realized all her family had been giving her odd looks for a couple of days now – and Fanny had been the same when she'd spoken to her after church that Sunday. Sorrel had wondered why she was in such a hurry to get home but she'd accepted her friend's excuse that her mother was expecting company.

The months had gone much quicker than she'd expected. Not long to wait for the wedding, though they hadn't set the date for certain yet. Jay had been so busy recently that he hadn't been round to call for her in nearly two weeks. He was sure to come this weekend, though, and when he did she was going to ask him to talk to the vicar about putting the banns up soon. Her father still wasn't happy about their getting married that year but appeared to have accepted the inevitable.

Sid's arm had healed well, though it was still a bit stiff and he couldn't use it as easily as before the accident. Sometimes Sorrel saw him rubbing it with liniment and knew it must ache. He was also drinking more than he ought. Her mother had gone on about it a few times but it didn't seem to make any difference.

'He's got a taste for it,' May had told her once when they were alone. 'When a man gets that way there's no reasoning with him. I've warned him but he won't listen so he must take the consequences. I just hope he doesn't bring the rest of us down with him.'

So far Aden hadn't said anything about Sid's drinking. He was still doing his work and Ted covered up for him if necessary. Ted and Rose had moved into the cottage with them after they were married. It made things very crowded but it was only until the cottage Aden had promised them was ready, which shouldn't be long now.

Her mother seemed to enjoy having Rose in the house and it made the work easier, but Sorrel wasn't as fond of Rose as she was of Bob's wife. Rose had a sharp tongue and used it on Ted more than Sorrel liked to hear.

As Sorrel walked into the yard behind the house she saw her brothers in a huddle by the barn. They appeared to be worried about something but, when she called a greeting, Bob waved and smiled at her.

'How was Mabel then?'

'She's fine,' Sorrel replied. She would have gone over and asked him why he hadn't wanted her to know about Tarina, except that she had given her word to her sister-in-law.

She went into the kitchen. Her mother and Rose were sitting over a cup of tea. They had obviously been talking earnestly about something but they stopped as Sorrel entered and she was conscious of the strained atmosphere . . . as if they had been talking about her.

'What's wrong then?' she asked. 'What's happened?'

'Nothing,' her mother said, and gave Rose a warning look as if to silence her. 'We were having a brew and a nice gossip, that's all. You'll have had your meal with Mabel, I expect?'

'Yes.' Sorrel looked from one to the other, annoyed by their guilty expressions. What had they been saying that she wasn't supposed to hear? Sometimes her mother still seemed to think she was a schoolgirl! The news about Tarina was shocking and it had upset Sorrel but she wasn't going to be silly over it. Why should they think she wasn't old enough to be told the truth? 'I'm going upstairs to finish the skirt of my dress – unless you want me for anything?'

May shook her head. Rose looked as if she were bursting to say something but another glance from Sorrel's mother stopped her.

'Mrs Robinson brought some nice new magazines round,' she said after a moment's pause. 'You might like to look at them later, Sorrel.'

'Thank you. When I've finished my sewing perhaps.'

Sorrel was puzzled as she walked upstairs. Rose seldom went out of her way to be nice to her. Was it imagination – or had she seen pity in her sister-in-law's eyes?

The sun was shining through her bedroom window. She stood looking out for a moment over the fields behind the house and, in the distance, the shining streak of the river. She would miss this view when she married. The house in the fens was miles from anywhere and all she would see would be acres of rich black soil and the endless skies – but it wouldn't matter because then she would be Jay's wife. She could hardly wait for her wedding day and was singing softly to herself as she took her dress down from its hanger, smoothing the white satin lovingly with her fingertips. She still had the skirt to hem and the sleeves to set but it was coming on well.

It was about an hour later that she heard heavy footsteps coming along the landing. They stopped outside her door and then someone knocked.

'May I come in, Sorrel?'

She pricked her finger as she heard her father's voice, sucking it at once so that she didn't get blood on the satin and mark her wedding gown; she didn't want to spoil it after all the work she had put into making it.

'Yes, Pa, of course.'

The door opened slowly. Her father stood on the threshold looking at her awkwardly and seeming as if he didn't quite know what to do next. He was wearing a checked working shirt and the familiar patched trousers but had taken off his cap and looked as if he had washed his face in cold water. Sorrel realized he was nervous. Something was wrong! She had sensed it all day now, as she looked into his eyes, she was certain.

'Why are you looking at me like that?' Her heart was thumping wildly. 'What have I done?'

'It's not what *you've* done, lass.' Sid's voice cracked with emotion and she knew why he'd washed his face before coming up to her: he had been crying. 'I don't know how to tell you, Sorrel. I'm sorry, so sorry ... but it has to be done. You have to know.'

'Pa?' The look in his eyes terrified her. 'Pa ... what are you saying?'

'When I first heard I didn't believe it ...' He sighed heavily, his eyes moist as he looked at her. 'But it's true ... it's true, lass.'

Her stomach was churning and she felt sick. 'What didn't you believe, Pa? Please tell me.' She stood up, the satin gown slithering to the floor at her feet. 'Don't keep me hanging on ... tell me!'

'It's about Jay and that gipsy girl ... the one you were friendly with.'

'Tarina?' Sorrel could scarcely breathe. She had known there was more to the story than Mabel had dared tell her.

Her father nodded, his eyes loving but sad. 'I'm not enjoying this, lass, believe me. I know I asked you to wait for a while before you got married, but I didn't want this ... I'm so sorry.'

'What about Jay and Tarina?' She cut him short as the fear whipped through her. 'I know she was drowned in the river ... at least, they found her nightgown, but ...'

'So you've heard that?' Sid nodded. 'I knew you would hear rumours – that's why I have to tell you myself. Tarina was having a child. They say she took something to get rid of it – one of her mother's vile potions, I shouldn't wonder.'

'A child?' Sorrel felt a pain in her chest. 'She got rid of it ... that's why she was in the infirmary?'

'Jay took her. She was lying there bleeding on the ground so I've been told. He had gone to the camp for some reason or other ... he took her to the infirmary and they cared for her. Then she ran off and ...' His eyes narrowed. 'How much have you heard?'

'Just that a man was found stabbed to death near their camp and her nightgown was caught in the reeds.' Sorrel gasped. 'What has all this to do with Jay? What are you trying to tell me?'

She felt as if she had been kicked in the stomach. Why was her father staring at her like that? As if he were afraid to go on – of hurting her. He couldn't mean ... he couldn't mean that Jay ... For a moment the room seemed to spin round her and she thought she was going to faint. Her father grabbed her as she swayed, holding her pressed against him. She could smell the fresh straw on him and his own familiar musk. Once it would have comforted her but now she pushed him away, staring at him wildly as she fought against the rage and pain warring inside her.

'What are you saying? It wasn't Jay's child! I don't believe you. It couldn't have been ...'

'It's what folk are saying.' Sid sighed heavily. 'Even Aden seems to believe it, though he was reluctant at first. He

204

asked Jay for the truth but he refused to answer. Just stared at his father then walked off without a word.'

It couldn't be true. She wouldn't believe it. Jay wouldn't do this to her.

Yet even as she denied it she was remembering his impatience, his frustration because she wouldn't let him make love to her – his anger when she'd changed her mind about going to the house in Sutton Gault after her father's accident. He'd continued to come round most Saturdays as if nothing had happened and had stopped suggesting more than a chaste kiss or two on the way home from Mabel's. She had believed that he'd decided to be patient for her sake, because they had no choice, but now . . . now she was remembering the sly look in Tarina's eyes the last time she had seen her.

'Our destiny is a lot closer than you think . . . we're bound together. Remember that . . .'

She had wanted to tell Sorrel something. She'd had that gloating expression in her eyes, as if she were very pleased about something. Had she wanted Sorrel to know that Jay was her lover – that he had lain with her?

No! It wasn't true. It couldn't be. Mustn't be.

'Jay would never betray me like that,' whispered Sorrel, but images of Tarina's face crowded into her mind. Then she remembered: hadn't Jay's father done something similar? Like father, like son, wasn't that what they said? Blood will out . . . but Jay loved her! He loved her. 'He wouldn't, Pa.' Her breath shuddered as she held back the tears. 'He wouldn't. Jay loves me. I know he does.'

'I'm sorry, lass.' Her father's eyes were misted with tears and she knew he was blaming himself. 'If I'd let you wed in the spring as he wanted . . .'

'No!' She lifted her head with a flash of pride. 'If he couldn't wait a few months he's not worth having.'

'Sorrel, I had to tell you. We couldn't let you hear it from anyone else.' Her father looked at her pleadingly, begging for forgiveness – but she couldn't say the words that would ease his conscience.

'Please,' she whispered as her throat tightened, 'I should like to be alone if you don't mind. Just for a while.'

'Yes, of course. Remember we all love you.' He hesitated a moment longer, then went out.

She closed and locked the door after him, leaning her back against it as the wave of grief washed over her.

'Jay,' she whispered, the tears beginning to well over and run down her cheeks. 'Jay – how could you? How could you?'

That night was the longest of Sorrel's life. She stayed locked in her room, ignoring her mother's repeated requests to come down for her supper. She wept until the tears ran dry and she was left with an aching emptiness inside. Her dreams were in tatters and it hurt, it hurt so much that she wasn't sure she could bear it, but in the morning she knew what she must do. No matter how damning the evidence was she must not condemn Jay without a hearing. He must tell her himself. She wanted to hear it from his own lips, then she would accept that it was all over – that he had never really loved her.

Her mother looked at her as she went down that morning. She didn't say anything about Jay and when Sorrel announced she was going to Mabel's, just nodded.

Once Sorrel was out of the yard she ran across the road to the farm. She was in such a state that she hardly knew what she was doing as she pounded on the kitchen door. All her thoughts were centred on Jay. He had to tell her that this terrible rumour was a lie!

She was shocked when the door was opened by his mother. For a moment they stared at each other in dismay, then Rebecca stood back to invite her in.

'Will you come through to the parlour, please?' Rebecca said. 'I think we should talk alone.'

Sorrel followed her into the small, comfortable parlour. It was a pretty room, decorated in shades of yellow and green; Rebecca's sewing lay on one of the tables, her books open on another, as if she used the little parlour often. Sorrel's knees were shaking and she felt dizzy, unable to control her nerves or to communicate with Jay's mother. Rebecca seemed to realize what a state she was in and took a decanter from the sideboard, pouring some of the contents into a glass and handing it to her.

'Sip a little of this brandy. It will steady you.'

Sorrel did as she was told; the fiery spirit stung her throat and made her cough but it stopped her shaking so much. After a while she was able to speak.

'I have to see Jay,' she said, her body stiff with tension. 'Please! I need to talk to him now.'

'So you've heard?' Rebecca's voice was soft with sympathy. 'I am so sorry, Sorrel. Believe me. I was against the marriage between you and my son at first – but I would not have had this happen to you. I am furious that Jay should have behaved so badly . . . though I blame his father for harbouring those wretched gipsies here in the first place.'

'Then it's true?' Sorrel gasped, her face going white. 'I came to ask because . . . I wanted to hear Jay say it.' She choked and could not go on.

Rebecca looked at her in silence, then sighed. 'It seems that history has a habit of repeating itself. Something very similar happened to me soon after I was married. I saw Dotty Prentice one day. She had worked for my father in his pub for a while and when I saw her again she was carrying my husband's child.' Rebecca paused, the shadow of an old grief in her eyes. 'When I asked Aden about it he lied to me, just as I fear Jay will lie to you if you ask him about this gipsy girl. In time I forgave my husband but it caused me much grief. It takes a special kind of love to accept and understand a man like that. Like his father, Jay is generous and charming – but they both do things sometimes that give pain. If you marry Jay you will have to accept that, Sorrel.'

'No!' She put down the glass of brandy she had hardly touched. 'I wouldn't have him now if he went down on his knees and begged me!'

'Sorrel, please consider. Think about this carefully, I beg you.'

Rebecca's pleas fell on deaf ears as Sorrel turned and fled from the room, through the kitchen and out of the house. Tears were blinding her as she ran out of the farm yard and down the road. Jay had betrayed her with Tarina. She had conceived his child . . . and aborted it.

What had caused her to do such a wicked thing? Had she believed Jay would marry her? If she had then it meant he had betrayed them both.

Tarina had seen something terrible in the future . . . something that frightened her so much she had run from it in fear. Had she seen her own death? After Leyan died Sorrel had thought it was his blood that Tarina had seen – his blood that bound them as she had foretold – but now it seemed that they were bound by a betrayal that was far worse. The blood that bound them was Tarina's own: the blood of her child.

'We are joined by the blood . . . it will touch both our lives.' She had said it and now it had come true.

She was dead and Sorrel's life was in ruins.

Sorrel went for a long walk. She needed to be alone, to sort out her thoughts without advice or pitying looks from her family. Did she still love Jay? Would she marry him now if he still wanted her?

She wasn't sure. All she knew was that she was hurting so much she felt as if she wanted to die. How could Jay do this to her? He had ruined everything for the sake of a roll in the hay! He had always been a flirt but had sworn to her that that was all over . . . that he loved her.

She walked and walked for ages but at last she knew she must go home. Her mother would be worried about her – they would start looking for her if she didn't go back soon.

As she walked into the yard she heard an argument going on and her heart caught as she saw Jay and her father; they were shouting at each other, both of them obviously in a rage – and she knew at once that it was over her.

'Pa!' Sorrel called and they both swung round to look at her. 'What is it? What's going on?'

'You leave this to me, girl.' Her father's face was a mottled red and purple. 'I'll sort this bugger out.'

'Sorrel!' Jay's cry tore at her heart. 'I have to talk to you . . . please.'

'She doesn't want to see you,' Sid said. 'Not now – not ever. Not after the way you've let her down.'

'Damn you!' Jay glared at him angrily, then looked at her. 'Sorrel? Don't listen to his lies. You know he never wanted you to marry me.'

Sid growled with rage and went for him; they wrestled as Jay tried to fend him off without hitting him. Sorrel gave a cry of alarm and ran towards them, pulling at her father's arm.

'Stop it, Pa. Stop this at once,' she cried. 'You can't fight Jay. He's Aden's son.'

Her father was breathing hard, his face a dark red, but he drew back, looking at her uncertainly. 'He's no right to come round here asking for you after what he's done.'

'It's all right, Pa,' Sorrel said. 'I want to talk to Jay. I'm glad he's come.'

'Sorrel?' Sid looked at her uncertainly. 'Are you sure this is what you want?'

'Yes. I'm going to walk to the gate with Jay, Pa, and I don't want you or anyone else to follow us. I shan't be long.' Her head went up, eyes flashing with pride. 'I'm not a child. I can speak for myself.'

'I shall hear her if she calls,' Sid warned, looking angrily at Jay. 'Lay a finger on my girl and I'll kill you!'

'I'll be all right, Pa. Jay isn't going to hurt me. We'll walk as far as the gate and talk, that's all.'

She glanced at Jay as he walked silently at her side, his face white and strained. Sorrel crossed her arms over her breasts, holding herself on a tight rein so that she wouldn't start shaking and give herself away.

'Why have you come?' she asked as he remained silent. 'Why now and not a week ago – before all the talk started?'

'Why are you like this?' he asked. 'I couldn't come sooner. We've been busy on the land and . . .'

'No, I don't suppose you've had much time to spare. You've been busy elsewhere, haven't you?' Her voice was sharp with pain and an underlying bitterness.

'What is that supposed to mean?'

'Don't pretend you don't know. Everyone is talking about you and . . . Tarina.'

'I see.' His voice was dangerously soft, his lips white-edged. 'So you believed him? I didn't think you would listen to tittle-tattle, Sorrel. Your father . . . I expected that. But not you.'

She rounded on him then, her temper flaring. 'What am I supposed to think? You hardly come near me for weeks and then . . . You refused to answer your own father when he asked for the truth. Even your mother is sorry for me because of what you've done!'

'You've spoken to my mother about this?' Jay's eyes had taken on the quality of flint. 'Without asking me? You went behind my back?' He glared at her angrily. 'You believe it was my child, don't you? Don't you?'

Sorrel was silent. It was on the tip of her tongue to say she would believe him if he denied it but the words wouldn't come. She was hurting so badly inside, crying tears no one could see.

'That's it then, isn't it?' For a moment longer he stared at her, his face white with anger. 'Thanks for nothing, Sorrel. It's just as well we found out what we really think of each other before it was too late, isn't it?'

'What do you mean?'

He didn't answer her, his expression so haughty and arrogant that it shocked her; then he walked past her and out of the gate, his back as straight and stiff as a board. She watched him go, her heart aching.

'Oh, Jay . . . Jay,' she whispered, but she didn't call him back. Her foolish pride wouldn't let her.

2. War & Friends

Chapter Twenty-Five

She glanced over her shoulder but there were no lights and she could not see much in the gloom of the foggy winter evening. She'd had an odd feeling that she was being followed several times recently but whoever it was obviously meant her no harm. She thought it might be one of the young men she had nursed on the wards; he was probably seeing her safely home out of a sense of chivalry, watching over her like a good angel.

The men often called her an angel, telling her she had given them the strength to carry on when all they really wanted was to lay there and die. She was constantly being asked out by men she had helped nurse back to health. They were often lonely and secretly afraid of going back to the mud and filth of the trenches, because they knew that next time they might not be lucky enough to come home.

Sometimes she went out in a foursome with another nurse she had become very friendly with, but she always made it clear that she wasn't available for long-term relationships. The pain inside her wasn't as sharp as it had been – but now there was this sense of loneliness, this emptiness . . . this feeling that her life had become a barren waste. All her energy, all that she had to give, had been given to the sick and dying; she was drained of emotion, tired and empty . . . so empty.

She needed to be loved, to feel someone's arms around her, holding her close. She wanted to feel like a woman . . . to be kissed, touched, loved.

Had she ever been the naive girl who had believed in

perfect love? If she had that belief had been shattered into a thousand pieces when he walked away from her.

The days following her break-up with Jay were the hardest of Sorrel's life. She cried into her pillow every night, tossing and turning restlessly until she was exhausted, and waking with an awful numbness about her; she was going through the motions of living, shutting the pain out of her mind as if it were all a bad dream. A part of her wanted to find Jay and tell him she was sorry, that she didn't believe he had betrayed her with Tarina, but somehow she couldn't. Her pride held her silent – and then it was suddenly too late.

At the end of June something happened that meant little to her at the time, even though she'd heard her parents discussing it. She had been in the kitchen when her father read out the news of the Archduke Franz Ferdinand's assassination.

'Isn't he the heir to the Austro-Hungarian throne or something?' May asked and Sid nodded agreement. 'Poor man. It makes you wonder what the world's coming to, doesn't it? Still, it's typical of foreigners. We're different here. It couldn't happen here – it's all that spicy food and wine, makes them foreigners a bit mad, if you ask me.'

'Aden says the whole of Europe is like dry tinder just waiting for a spark to set it off. He thinks it will lead to a war – and we'll be dragged into it.'

'Never!' May cried, looking alarmed. 'Why should we care if some foreigner has been murdered?'

'It isn't just a case of that,' Ted said. 'It's a question of treaties. Germany has an alliance with Austria and if Austria breaks off relations with Serbia – which it will – then the Csar won't stand by and see Serbia invaded. And if Russia fights, France will be drawn in, and that means we . . .'

'For goodness' sake!' May cried. 'Don't go on so, Ted. I can't understand a word you're saying, and what's more I don't want to. The King won't let us go to war with the Kaiser and that's that.'

Sid gave Ted a warning glance and he shut up but Sorrel had seen the expression in her brother's eyes – a look that might have been excitement or fear. Perhaps both.

At the time she'd wondered if Aden was right but she hadn't been very interested in far-off rumblings. She had been thinking about her own plans then, and what to wear for Richie's and Sally's wedding, which had been arranged for the middle of July. It was to be a lavish affair and she'd been looking forward to it, but of course she wouldn't be going – not after the quarrel with Jay. That had changed everything.

Her own problems had driven everything else from her mind since then. She was so desperately unhappy that she hardly noticed what was going on around her, let alone in Europe. The papers might be full of stories about meetings between the heads of various countries and jingoistic talk of war but to Sorrel it seemed far away and unlikely to affect her or their sleepy little village.

It took all her courage to get through each day, and she could only be grateful that Jay was staying well away from her. Her father had told her there was no need for her to go across to the farm; he loaded her little milk cart himself every morning to make sure that she did not bump into Jay.

Her whole family was being tactful. No one had mentioned Jay and she hadn't seen Fanny for weeks. It might have gone on that way for much longer if the rumblings in Europe hadn't suddenly errupted into something much more serious.

It was as the British people returned to work after the annual summer bank holiday that war was declared; it was a cruel awakening, which shocked those who had not believed all the talk would come to anything.

The next morning Sorrel's father read out the newspaper reports of excited crowds cheering in Downing Street and outside Buckingham Palace.

'War. Oh, Sid.' May's face turned pale and she sat down with a bump opposite him. 'Why were all those people so excited? Don't they know what it means? Men injured and killed . . .'

'Don't take on so,' he said. 'I doubt it will come to much – they say it will be over by Christmas.'

'Does it mean . . .' They both turned to look at Sorrel as

215

she spoke. 'Will people . . . young men from the village be joining up?'

'No doubt some of them will be fool enough,' her father said with a frown. 'Not lads that work on the land, though. Land work has to go on no matter what, unless they want us all to starve. Aden will see to it that his sons don't get called up. So if you're worrying about Jay, you can stop. Though why you should bother your head over that rotten little so-and-so . . .'

'Sid!' May gave him a hard look. 'She was bound to wonder. They were friends for years before . . .'

Sorrel felt the tears catch at her throat. She grabbed a tin of polish and a duster and went upstairs before they spilled over.

Wars meant that men got killed. No matter how much Jay had hurt her she couldn't bear the thought of him being injured or killed. Her father was right, though. Aden could get him out of it, and he would. Men who were needed on the land didn't have to join up if they didn't want to, at least, that's what she'd heard.

Sorrel rubbed hard at the top of her dressing table, making the wood shine until she could see herself in it. Why did Jay's betrayal still hurt so much? Why couldn't she forget him?

'Sorrel.' Her mother came into the room, making her jump. 'Fanny is downstairs. She wanted to see you so I asked her to wait in the parlour. Do you want to see her or shall I tell her you've gone out?'

'I'll see her.' Sorrel glanced in the mirror and tucked a wisp of hair behind her ear. 'I can't hide from everyone, Ma. Besides, it's not Fanny's fault. I still like her.'

'That's what I thought,' May said, giving her an approving look. 'You've got to live in this village, Sorrel. The sooner you face up to things the better.'

'Yes, I know.' Sorrel's face was pale but set as she went downstairs. She had to speak to Jay's sister one day so she might as well get it over.

Fanny was staring out of the parlour window. She swung round as Sorrel entered, looking tense and uncomfortable.

'You don't mind my coming? I've wanted to before this

216

but . . . my father said I should give you time to . . .' She caught her breath. 'I'm so sorry, Sorrel.'

'Please don't,' she said, turning her face aside so that Fanny shouldn't see how close she was to tears. 'How was the wedding? Did Sally look pretty?'

'Yes . . . very.' Fanny sounded as if she were on the verge of tears herself. 'Jay didn't go. Mother was furious with him but he said he was ill and stayed in bed all day.'

'Oh.' Sorrel bit her lip. 'I wonder why?'

'I'm so angry with him,' Fanny burst out suddenly. 'I can't believe he would be such a fool and I've told him so. How could he go with that girl when . . .'

'Please, Fanny,' Sorrel begged. 'I don't want to talk about that – it's over.'

Fanny nodded, her mouth trembling. 'I know I shouldn't but I love you – and I love Jay, despite what he's done.' She took a deep breath, then met Sorrel's eyes. 'I came to tell you he has joined the army. He was one of the first from the village to sign on.'

'Jay . . .' Sorrel felt a cold dread catch at her heart. She suddenly realized that until that moment she had still been hoping it would all come right, that Jay would come to her and somehow they would make up their quarrel. Now he was going away and she might never see him again. He could be killed! 'But he didn't have to.' Her eyes pleaded with Fanny. 'Pa said Aden would get him out of it.'

'My mother was cross with him. She said he was a fool to volunteer – but my father said he was proud of him, said it was for the best in the circumstances.' Fanny twisted her gloves nervously in her hands. 'They've made up their quarrel, Sorrel. Couldn't you . . . before he goes?'

'No.' Sorrel's stomach clenched. 'I can't. I'm sorry, Fanny. If Jay wants to see me he knows where I am.'

'He says it's over,' Fanny admitted, tears in her eyes. 'But I thought . . . I know he still loves you. Before he leaves, Sorrel, you could at least say goodbye to each other. You've been friends for so long. Couldn't you forgive him enough just to say goodbye?'

Sorrel felt the tears trickle down her cheek. She brushed

them away with the back of her hand. 'When – when does he leave?' she asked in a choking voice.

'In the morning.' Fanny took a step towards her, laying a hand on her arm. 'He's so unhappy, Sorrel. You've no idea how he has suffered since . . . I'm not excusing what he did, don't think that. It's just that I care for you both so much.'

'I'm not sure if I can,' Sorrel said. 'I'm grateful to you for coming, Fanny, but I have to think about this. For a little while.'

Fanny nodded, hesitated, then said what was on her mind, 'Will you come to Aunt Celia's with me in October? She's thinking of turning a part of her house into a convalescent home for the wounded and I've promised to help her get things ready.'

'For the wounded?' Sorrel swallowed hard. 'Oh, Fanny, it's all so horrible. To think that lads we know may be hurt or . . . killed.'

'Yes, I know. Jay said several others were signing up when he was at the recruiting station. Some of them probably won't come back. That's why . . .'

'Please don't,' Sorrel begged. 'Don't say it. I can't bear it, Fanny.'

She was silenced but the look in her eyes told Sorrel that she understood. 'I'll go now – but think about what I've said.'

Sorrel nodded but made no reply. After Fanny had gone she was tortured by her own thoughts. Supposing Jay was badly injured or killed? How would she feel then? Would she regret not seeing him before he left? She still loved him . . . perhaps she would always love him.

At last she could stand it no longer. She had to see him – had to say goodbye to him. Her mother looked at her as she went into the kitchen wearing a fresh dress.

'Where are you off to? Dinner will be on the table in a few minutes.'

'I need a breath of air. I shan't be long.'

She walked out of the yard and then ran across the road to Jay's house. The urge to see him had become stronger, a tide of panic rising inside her so that by the time she arrived at the farm she was so worked up that she could hardly breathe. She knocked at the back door.

Aden answered it himself. His sleeves were rolled up to the elbows and he had earth on his hands as if he had been working in the garden.

He looked at her oddly. 'What can I do for you, Sorrel? Won't you come in? Is it Fanny you've come to see or did Sid send you for me?'

'Is – is Jay here?' She took a deep breath to steady herself. 'I – I would like to see him please.'

Aden's expression changed, became grave. 'I'm sorry, lass, you're too late. I took him to the station earlier. His train left an hour ago.'

'But Fanny said he was leaving tomorrow morning...' She was too late! For a moment she wanted to scream or cry but she held her grief inside, staring at Jay's father in dumb misery. 'She said it was tomorrow.'

'He decided to leave today ... said it would give him time to sort himself out, before he had to report to his unit.'

'Oh.' Sorrel blinked hard, holding the tears back. 'It doesn't matter. I just wanted to say goodbye ... to wish him luck as a ... friend.'

Oh, Jay, Jay, her heart was crying. Jay, I loved you so. Why did it happen – why?

'I'm sorry, Sorrel. More sorry than I can say.'

'It's all right.' She lifted her chin proudly, knowing that he was upset for her. 'Another time perhaps.'

'I'll tell him you came when I write – or perhaps you would like to write yourself?'

'No. Please ... don't say anything. When he comes back perhaps ... they say it will soon be over, don't they?'

'That's what some people say.'

'But you don't think so?'

'I don't know, Sorrel, and that's the truth of it. We can only pray it comes to a speedy end, for all our sakes.'

'Yes, yes, of course.' The tears were very close now. 'I must go now. Goodbye.'

'Sorrel.' She glanced back and saw the sadness in his eyes. 'Whatever Jay did, I know he loves you very much. If you could forgive him ...'

'Please . . .'

She fled across the yard as the tears welled up and overflowed. It was foolish of her to have come. Nothing had changed. How could she have thought it might? Jay had betrayed her with Tarina – and because of it the gipsy girl was dead. Her shadow would haunt them all their lives.

Sorrel's special dream was over. She had to forget Jay, to forget she had ever loved him.

Yet how could she forget when his image was in her mind day and night? He had gone away to war and she knew she would never know another moment of true peace until he was safely home again.

'Have you decided?' Fanny asked when they met for tea at Mabel's three weeks later. The new baby had been born a week previously and Sorrel was staying in the house to care for her sister-in-law and the children until Mabel was over the birth. 'Aunt Celia says she is looking forward to having us both to stay, and there will be lots for us to do there.'

She sounded excited, her eyes bright with anticipation. Sorrel looked at her thoughtfully.

'In three weeks?' she asked, and Fanny nodded as she finished preparing a tray to take up to Mabel. 'I shan't be needed here by then. Mabel already feels much better. She would get up if the doctor would let her.'

'She has a lovely little girl,' Fanny said. 'I wouldn't ask you if she really needed you but she doesn't, does she?'

Fanny looked so anxious that Sorrel smiled. 'She won't in another week or so, and Ma has Rose to help her now. I'm not really needed at home either.'

Ted had surprised them all by joining the navy two weeks before he and Rose had been due to move into their new home. Neither his mother's tears nor his wife's scolding had moved him. He told them it was done and nothing either of them could say would stop him. Sorrel suspected that it was Rose's sharp tongue that had driven him away. His marriage wasn't as happy as Bob's. His mother had pushed him into it and in his heart he had regretted it ever since, though of course he'd never said so straight out – but Sorrel knew.

After Ted left Rose had decided to make her home with

her mother-in-law. Sorrel wasn't particularly pleased about that but May got on with her well – and it meant that Sorrel would be free to go with Fanny. They had been invited for a long visit with Lady Roth; she had told them she hoped they would stay for at least a month, perhaps more.

'Yes, I'll come,' Sorrel said. 'It will be a relief to get away for a while.'

She had been restless ever since Jay left to join the army, and there were times when her home seemed like a prison, holding her trapped in a life she no longer enjoyed. She needed something different and new, something to challenge her mind and ease the ache in her heart.

Fanny looked at her uncertainly when she came back from taking Mabel's tray upstairs.

'How is she?'

'Fine – but fed up with being in bed.' Sorrel paused. She sensed that Fanny had something on her mind. 'What is it? What don't you want to tell me?'

'This is from Jay,' Fanny said, taking a white envelope from her pocket. She held it out. 'Would you like to read it?'

Sorrel hesitated, then took the letter from her. Her heart was beating so fast that at first her eyes wouldn't focus and she could hardly see the words let alone read them.

Dear Fanny,
Just a few lines to let you know what I'm doing. They've kept us on the hop ever since we got here so I haven't been able to write before. It's all a bit of a muddle. We haven't got uniforms yet, or weapons. We train with pitchforks or shovels over our shoulders and one man brings his dog on parade – which makes for a laugh. You should have seen the Sergeant's face when it started howling every time he gave an order!

Sorrel laughed, turning the page eagerly as Jay gave details of his life in camp. His letter was so typical of him that she could almost hear him speaking the words aloud. As she read on she realized that it wasn't really much fun even

221

though he made it sound amusing; the food was often inedible and it was impossible to get hot water for washing.

Some of the chaps' hands are covered in blisters. All we do is dig trenches. You should see the poor blighters who used to work in offices or shops. At least I'm used to manual work, though it isn't easy even for me. Luckily, I think I'm going to be transferred soon. One of the officers asked if I would like to work with the horses so of course I jumped at the chance . . .

Sorrel looked up, her throat tight with emotion. 'He seems to be coping well.'

'Yes.' Fanny was uneasy. 'Read the postscript at the bottom, Sorrel.'

She looked at the letter again, reading aloud this time: 'Don't worry about me, Fanny. I'll be fine. I'm sorry we quarrelled and glad you kissed me before I left. I want you to know that Tarina's child . . .' Sorrel caught her breath and read the words a second time to make sure, 'Tarina's child wasn't mine. I can't tell you any more but please believe me. If Sorrel ever asks, you can tell her.'

She closed her eyes, blinking away the stupid tears. 'Oh, Fanny,' she whispered in a choking voice. 'Oh, Fanny . . . Fanny. Why didn't he tell me?'

'He's too proud to beg – you should know that, Sorrel. We all thought he was guilty, every one of us. He was too stubborn to deny it, but I think he wanted me to know the truth now in case . . .'

'He should have told me.' Sorrel wiped her hand across her eyes. The pain in her chest was so intense that she could hardly breathe. She felt as if she were dying and wished that she would. 'But I didn't give him the chance. I was so hurt, Fanny. And angry. Everyone was feeling sorry for me . . . my pride was hurt, too. But I should have listened to him . . . I should have . . .'

'How do you think Jay felt then?' Fanny was in tears herself. 'He expected us to believe in him, Sorrel – you and me if no one else. Besides, I think . . .' She broke off, flushing.

'What were you going to say?'

222

'No, I shouldn't.' Fanny bit her lip. It would be wrong of me to say when I have no proof . . .'

'Please, if it's about Jay and Tarina, you must tell me. Please, Fanny. Please!'

'Jay went to their camp to inquire about some turf,' Fanny said. 'That much of it is true. I know because I heard him telling Father what he was going to do earlier that day. Tarina was in terrible agony having just . . . well, you know. She was losing a lot of blood and if he hadn't got her to the infirmary she would probably have bled to death. He did what any decent man would have done, Sorrel.'

'I wouldn't blame him for that, Fanny – any more than I did when he had that fight with Black Jake.' Sorrel's hand trembled as she folded the letter and put it back in its envelope. 'Everyone was so sure it was his child, even your father and your mother. Why didn't he deny it? Why accept the blame if it wasn't true?'

'I'm not sure,' Fanny said. 'But Jay has always had funny notions of honour. He would never split on the rest of us when we were children. I think . . . I think he may have been protecting Richie.'

'Richie!' Sorrel stared at her in shocked disbelief. 'Richie and Tarina? I don't believe it. Richie and a gipsy . . .' Yet even as she spoke the words she was remembering the way he had tried to seduce Lady Roth's pretty companion. Adele had been outraged and run away from him but perhaps Tarina . . . She might have been persuaded to give him what he wanted in return for – what? Perhaps she had thought he would marry her. Perhaps that was what she had been hinting at that day in the lane behind the church. She had been excited, as if she wanted to tell Sorrel but was afraid of speaking too soon. 'If it was Richie it explains so much.' Sorrel quickly told Fanny what she meant. 'So it all fits, doesn't it?'

'It's hard to believe, isn't it?' Fanny said thoughtfully. 'You would expect him to look down his nose at her, wouldn't you? He's usually such a snob. But I saw her once. She was very beautiful – poor girl.'

'Yes, she was.' Sorrel hesitated. For a while she had hated

223

Tarina but now she was able to think of her without bitterness. 'Very.'

'It was terrible that she should die like that.'

'If she is dead.'

'What do you mean?' Fanny stared at her in surprise. 'She drowned in the river. Everyone knows that.'

'They've never found her body, have they?'

'No . . . but her nightgown was there in the reeds by the river and no one has seen her since.'

'She wouldn't stay here if . . .' Sorrel shook her head. 'No, I'm sure you're right. Her body must be at the bottom of the river somewhere.' She handed Jay's letter back to Fanny. 'What made you think it might have been Richie's child? No one else thought of it.'

'Jay and Richie had a fight after Tarina was taken to the infirmary. Neither of them would say what it was over – and of course it wasn't the first time they had quarrelled.' Fanny wrinkled her brow. 'But Jay wouldn't go to the wedding and that was strange. He said he didn't want anything to do with Richie, though he sent Sally a lovely present. And I heard an argument between Richie and my mother after Jay joined up. She threatened to tell Father something and then Richie came out into the hall and slammed off in a rage. I'm not sure exactly what the argument was about, but I did hear my mother say that he owed it to Jay to tell the truth.' Fanny gave a little shudder. 'Richie looked so . . . strange.'

Sorrel didn't notice Fanny's odd manner. She was thinking about Jay; it would be like him to take the blame rather than shame his brother. He had given Richie a thrashing and considered the matter closed – but he'd reckoned without the tide of gossip that had swept through the village, carrying both him and Sorrel with it and wrecking their lives.

'Fanny, if it was Richie . . .'

'I know.' Fanny looked at her unhappily. 'Jay should have told you. But he was always peculiar about things like that – pride and honour and all that nonsense men set so much store by. But he ought to have told you the truth.'

'I wanted to believe him. If he had just said it . . . but he didn't even try to deny it.' Sorrel caught her breath. 'Oh,

Fanny, he must have felt so miserable. That's why he went off to sign up as soon as war was declared.'

'Yes, I think that's why he did it. He couldn't bear to stay here knowing that you . . .' Fanny stopped as she saw the pain in Sorrel's eyes. 'What will you do now? Will you write to him?'

'I don't know.' Sorrel swallowed hard. Jay hadn't tried to see her before he left. She had hurt his pride by believing everyone else rather than trusting him. Perhaps it was too late to mend things now. 'I just don't know, Fanny. I don't know what to do.'

The more Sorrel thought about what she and Fanny had discussed, the more convinced she became that they had all wronged Jay. She spoke to her parents about it that evening after supper. Her mother looked doubtful but her father nodded sorrowfully.

'It was my fault,' he said. 'You would have been wed long before this if it hadn't been for me. I should have known the lad wasn't to blame. If I hadn't been so stupid you might have worked it out between you.'

'It was six of one and half a dozen of the other. Jay should have told us the truth – but men are all fools.' May gave her daughter a straight look. 'What are you going to do about it, Sorrel? Shall you write to him?'

'I'm not sure. He might not want me to.'

'You mean your pride won't let you.' May sniffed with disapproval. 'If you're in the wrong you should do something about it. Suit yourself, miss, but a bit of humble pie now and then never killed anyone. Mind your pride doesn't choke you.'

Sorrel felt confused and uncertain. She wanted badly to tell Jay she loved him – to let him know that she was sorry for not having given him a chance to explain – but she was afraid he would despise her for it. He must feel that she had let him down by not trusting him and she couldn't blame him for that – but did he still care enough to want to hear from her?

She tried writing to him but kept seeing the proud, arrogant stare he had given her before he walked away from her. He had been hurt and angry, perhaps so angry that he no longer cared what she thought of him. And yet he had told Fanny she could tell her about Tarina's baby if she asked.

'Oh, Jay . . . Jay,' Sorrel whispered in the privacy of her bedroom. 'Forgive me . . . please forgive me.'

All she could do was write her letter and hope that he would understand what was in her heart. Several attempts found their way into the fire but finally she managed a few lines.

Please forgive me if I misjudged you. I was so hurt that I couldn't think clearly – and you didn't deny the child was yours. Why couldn't you have told me, Jay? I wanted so much for you to say it but you didn't. When Fanny told me you had joined up I came to see you and wish you luck. Your father told me that he had already taken you to the station, so I was too late. Am I too late to say sorry? Take care of yourself, Jay. I miss you.
Your friend Sorrel.

It wasn't what she longed to write. If she had written what was in her heart she would have told him that she loved him, begged him to come home safe for her sake, and the paper would have been wet with her tears, but as usual her pride held her back. She couldn't bring herself to beg – anymore than he could. And she couldn't blame him if he had stopped loving her.

He should have told her! He should have told her the truth! The words went round and round in her head as she lay sleepless, watching the light slowly gather and then heard the birds begin their dawn chorus. She hadn't cried into her pillow this time but the ache was there inside her, reminding her of what she had lost.

Each day after that was the same, a slow blur of muted pain, every hour dragging by as she struggled to hide her misery. Her father was also very quiet. He had shed his anger towards her and seemed sunk in remorse. Whenever he looked her way his eyes were full of pleading but without hope, as if he could not expect forgiveness.

He raised no objection to her going away with Fanny. One day he came into the kitchen when she was rinsing some towels at the sink and laid some money down on the drainer beside her.

'That's for you – to take with you next week.'

Sorrel looked round and saw that he had given her fifty pounds in crisp white five-pound notes. 'That's far too much,' she said. 'I shan't need all that. Take some of it back, Pa.'

'You keep it,' he insisted. 'Just in case you want something while you're away.'

He was trying to ease his conscience. Sorrel felt a pang of sympathy for him. She had done all she could to show him that she didn't blame him for what had happened, but he couldn't forgive himself for making her unhappy. He just kept saying that if it wasn't for his selfishness she would have been married, and Jay would not have volunteered.

He pored over the newspapers and took every report of casualties in the ranks personally, his shoulders seeming to bow under the weight of his guilt. Sorrel told him that Jay was still training, that he hadn't been sent overseas yet, but Sid seemed to expect bad news at anytime. She thought he was blaming himself because Ted had joined up as well – and perhaps wouldn't have done it if Jay hadn't first.

Sorrel was worried by her father's manner and at last she spoke to her mother about it. 'He looks ill, Ma,' she said. 'And he's lost weight. Don't you think he should see the doctor?'

May shook her head. 'It's just his conscience eating away at him. He'll get over it – and he can afford to lose a bit of weight.' They were packing Sorrel's clothes the night before she was due to leave for Hampshire. 'I'm glad you're going with Fanny. So long as Sid can see you looking so pale and miserable he'll go on whipping himself. Maybe he'll pick up when you've gone.'

'Oh, Ma.' Sorrel sighed deeply. 'I don't want him to feel like that. It was as much my fault as his. I should have trusted Jay, asked him for his side of it instead of believing other people's gossip.'

'You still don't know the facts,' her mother pointed out.

227

'It's only what Fanny thinks. You don't know for sure that it was Richie's child.'

Sorrel didn't argue with her. In her own heart and mind she was convinced of Jay's innocence. Now that she could think about it more sensibly she had come to the conclusion that Jay would have married the girl if the child had been his. Tarina would not have needed to get rid of the baby, because Jay would have done the right thing. He would have told Sorrel it was over between them and then married the mother of his child. It would have been the honourable thing to do – and Jay had always stood by his friends. She ought to have known the rumours were lies. She ought to have trusted him.

Sometimes the ache in her heart was almost more than she could bear. Why . . . why had she listened to her father and Jay's mother? Why hadn't she been strong enough to believe in Jay despite them all?

Chapter Twenty-Six

Sorrel was at the window when Aden stopped the car outside the front gate. He was taking Fanny and her to the station and they would be met by someone at the other end of their journey.

'He's here,' Sorrel said, and turned to kiss her mother's cheek. 'I'll write every week.'

'Behave yourself – and have a good time,' May said, giving her a quick hug. 'Take care of yourself, love.'

'I'll carry your bags,' Sid said gruffly, and picked them up. 'Take your time, lass. Aden will wait a minute.'

'She's ready,' May said, then, as he went out, 'Forgive him if you can, Sorrel – for my sake?'

'Yes . . . of course. I already have.'

Sid had put her bags in the car. He turned as she came up to him, staring at her uncertainly. She went to hug him, her eyes smarting as his arms closed around her.

'I love you, Pa. Take care of Ma – and yourself.'

'I love you, lass.' His pale eyes watered as he stood watching her get into the car. He cleared his throat then gave his trousers a hitch. 'Write to us often.'

'I will,' she promised, and waved as the car drew away. "Bye.'

'Isn't it exciting?' Fanny asked as they settled down. 'I thought today would never come, didn't you?'

Sorrel nodded. Fanny's eyes were glowing and she seemed to have shed her usual reserve. She hardly stopped talking all the way to Ely and then she flung her arms around her father, thanking him as he saw them both settled on the train. He had bought both girls magazines and sweets for the journey and just before he left he pressed two five-pound notes into Sorrel's hand.

'In case you need anything, Sorrel.'

'Pa gave me money.' She tried to return the notes but he wouldn't take them.

'A small gift,' he said. 'Please accept it, Sorrel. I want you to have it. I shall always think of you as the daughter I nearly had.'

After that she could only thank him and accept.

The train journey was interesting but uneventful, until they were joined a few stations from their destination by a group of young soldiers in uniform. Four of them sat on the opposite seat and several more stood outside in the corridor. They were all very young – most of them obviously volunteers – and excited about going over to France to fight. They made jokes amongst themselves and laughed as they settled down, throwing more than a few curious glances at the two girls.

After a while one of the soldiers took out a silver cigarette case and offered it to Fanny and then Sorrel; they both smiled and refused.

'Do you mind if I do?' the young soldier asked. 'I'll go out in the corridor if it will upset you?'

'No – no, of course not. My father smokes a pipe sometimes and I like the smell of the tobacco,' Fanny said. 'I've never tried a cigarette. My mother doesn't approve of women who smoke, especially in public.'

'Nor does mine,' he admitted with a smile. 'She doesn't really approve of my smoking either but all the chaps do it.' He hesitated then, added, 'I'm John Parkinson. I've been in the army for a bit longer than most of my friends . . . almost expected, really. The second sons in our family usually go into the army or the church, and I'm not cut out for anything that needs too much in the way of brains.'

'I'm sure that's not true,' Fanny said, a faint flush in her cheeks. 'I'm sure you're very clever. You're wearing the uniform of a captain, aren't you?'

'Oh, that's nothing,' he replied. 'We're expendable. They

have to have some poor devil to lead the chaps over the top. So as long as you can command a little respect they give you a captaincy and let you get on with it.'

'Don't you believe him, miss,' one of the other young soldiers said with a cheeky grin. 'He knows what he's doin' all right.'

'Well, we shall find out soon enough, Jackson,' the captain said. 'Would it be too rude of me to inquire where you young ladies are going?'

'To stay with Lady Roth at her house in Hampshire,' Fanny said, and at an exclamation from him, 'Do you know her?'

'Very well,' he replied, looking pleased. 'My parents visit quite often when she's at home. I hear she is thinking of turning part of Rothsay Hall into a convalescent home for the chaps.'

'We're going to help her get things ready,' Fanny said. 'Shall we see you while we're there? We shall be staying for a month or more.'

'Then I expect we shall meet.' He seemed delighted at the prospect. 'We have a few days' leave before going back to our units.'

'Then we shall look forward to seeing you, shan't we, Sorrel?' Fanny glanced at her and then back to Captain Parkinson. 'I'm Fanny Sawle and this is my friend, Sorrel Harris.'

'Pleased to meet you both.' He leant across to shake hands with each of them, then introduced the other young men, saying jocularly, 'This is our lucky day, isn't it, lads?'

Sorrel watched Fanny come to life as she talked to the young man. He was attractive rather than wildly handsome with short dark hair, grey eyes and a gentle manner – but his smile was full of warmth and there was something about him that vaguely reminded Sorrel of Jay.

Fanny remarked on it when they left the train after saying goodbye to the young soldiers. She looked thoughtful as they climbed into the back of Lady Roth's large, comfortable car.

'Wasn't he nice?' she said to Sorrel, her eyes glowing. 'When he smiles he makes me think of my father – or Jay.

231

He doesn't look like them, it's just something in his smile. Did you notice it?'

'Yes, I did,' Sorrel agreed. 'I thought he seemed very agreeable.'

'Yes, so did I.'

Fanny lapsed into silence as they were driven through the town. Sorrel glanced out of the window but couldn't see much more than a blur of tall buildings because it had started to pour with rain.

It had stopped by the time they arrived at Rothsay Hall, however, and she was able to appreciate the full splendour of the old house. She had expected something grand but it was far more beautiful than she had imagined: a classically elegant mansion built of butter-coloured stone, with long sash windows and terraces trailed with masses of climbing roses and ivy. It was a fairytale palace set in lovely parkland but she thought it must be far too big for one person.

Fanny smiled when she voiced her thoughts. 'Aunt Celia often says the same thing. Her husband bought it for her when they married so she can't bear to part with it, but she finds it lonely since he died. Of course she has no children, which is very sad because she and her husband wanted an heir. I suppose that's why she travels so much . . . to see her friends. She does have a lot of friends.'

Sorrel nodded but didn't say much. She was feeling nervous of meeting Lady Roth and her mouth was dry as she followed Fanny into the large drawing room, which was furnished with the most beautiful things she had ever seen. The walls were covered with a pale green silk paper, and there were several mirrors and paintings in gilt frames hanging round the room. The curtains were dark green velvet and the three massive sofas were upholstered in a silk brocade which picked up the shades of both pale and dark green and were edged with a thick gilt beading; pale satinwood cabinets, tables and elbow chairs stood about the room and there were several lamps, exquisite arrangements of fresh flowers, porcelain figures and two splendid bronzes in alcoves at either side of the fireplace.

It was a very feminine room, a fitting setting for the

lady who came to greet them as they entered, her hands outstretched in welcome.

'Fanny, my darling, here you are at last.'

Lady Roth was a tiny, fragile-looking woman with silvery hair that had once been pale blonde; she had a gentle, rather sad face and faded blue eyes. However, as she spoke her air of fragility vanished and Sorrel saw that she was a warm, friendly person.

'So Fanny has brought you to me at last, Miss Harris – or may I call you Sorrel, my dear? My dearest Fanny has told me so much about you that I feel I already know you.' She smiled again as Sorrel nodded. 'And you must call me Aunt Celia, as Fanny does.'

Her hands clasped Sorrel's with surprising firmness. Sorrel liked her at once and any lingering doubts about the visit disappeared.

'You are very kind, La ... Aunt Celia.'

Sorrel blushed and Lady Roth laughed. 'No, don't be shy, my dear. I want us all to be comfortable together. I know how fond Fanny is of you and I'm so happy to have you both here. It was good of you to give your time to help me – and I promise you it will not be wasted. We are all going to be very busy.'

Having decided that a large part of her house could be put to better use, Celia Roth had lost no time in making her arrangements. Her personal and most loved possessions had been removed to the smaller wing on the south side, where she had a wonderful view of the gardens right down to a pretty little stream and the lake.

'My housekeeper has had the maids opening up rooms that have not been used in years,' she told them as she took them on a brief tour of the house. 'Most of the cleaning has been done – but there is so much more to do. Now this is the nurses' wing and they will have the exclusive use of the walled garden when they want to be private. We shall keep to our own. And the patients will have the use of all the rest of the grounds.'

'What about the park and the lake?' Fanny asked. 'Will you allow them the use of the boathouse?'

'I think that should be available to all of us,' Celia said.

233

'Matron will keep one key and I shall have the other.' She paused, a little frown wrinkling her smooth brow. 'We expect our first visitors within two weeks. You've heard how our poor boys are suffering over there, of course? Our hospitals are already finding it difficult to cope and it is going to get much worse. The patients they will send us will be suitable cases who need a rest and some peace rather than intensive nursing.'

Sorrel and Fanny looked at each other. The news of the war had for some time been grave, hammering home the awful reality; those who had been carried away on a tide of jingoisitc pride were now realizing that it was unlikely to be the short, sharp struggle they had predicted.

At home on the farm it had hardly seemed real to Sorrel, even though the newspapers carried pictures of wounded men and devastation in Belgium and France. Now, listening to Celia and seeing the preparations she was making, she could no longer shut her mind to the truth.

Over the next few days she thought more and more of the men who were out there fighting for their country; it was of Jay she thought most, of course. He hadn't answered her letter but Fanny hadn't received a reply to her last three letters either. She believed he had probably been moved to a new unit – perhaps to join the British regulars who had been fighting from the beginning and were in urgent need of new recruits.

'Our letters will catch up with him all at once,' Fanny said to Sorrel when they sat talking one evening after a hard day's work. 'Then he'll write to us both. You'll see, Sorrel. He will write to you, I know he will.'

'Don't you think he would have let you know if he were being sent to France? They usually get leave first, don't they?'

'Perhaps he didn't want to come home ... if he hadn't received your letter,' Fanny faltered, not quite meeting her eyes. 'Sometimes they only get a few hours ... and he wouldn't be allowed to tell us where he was being sent in a letter in case it went astray.'

'No, I suppose not.' Sorrel yawned and stood up. 'I'm tired. I think I'll go to bed, if you don't mind?'

Celia hadn't been joking when she'd said there was a lot to do and they had been working hard to get the house ready for their guests, as Celia liked to call them. A consignment of single beds had arrived that morning and had been set up, two to each of the larger rooms and up to six in what had once been elegant reception salons. All the beds had had to be made up with clean linen, and an endless supply of towels was needed for the various bathrooms and cloakrooms. Long lists had to be made and checked, cupboards cleared, unwanted items removed for storage.

New baths and showers had been installed and it was strange to see the beautiful proportions of the lovely old house turned upside down by modern plumbing. Sorrel had thought it might be upsetting for Celia but when she'd mentioned it her hostess had laughed.

'It's just what this place needs, my dear – to be useful again. If we can help those poor boys just a little it will all have been worthwhile.'

It had seemed an almost impossible task, but somehow they had got everything done and the house was just about ready. Sorrel yawned again. It was surprising how tired she felt, because she was used to hard work.

'I'm sorry. I can't seem to stop. Are you coming?'

'You go up,' Fanny said, looking a little self-conscious as Sorrel stood waiting for her answer. 'I have something to do first . . . but I shan't be long.'

Sorrel wondered about the look in Fanny's eyes but didn't dwell on it long as she went to say goodnight to her hostess in the little sitting room down the hall, then up the stairs to her own very comfortable bedroom.

She undressed and brushed her long hair, then got into bed and turned out the light, whispering the little prayer she said every night before going to sleep. Wherever Jay was – whether he had got her letter or not – she prayed he was safe . . .

The night before the first patients were due to arrive Celia gave a party to introduce the nurses and doctors to her neighbours. It was the last time she would be able to use the magnificent library, which was in the main part of the

235

house and would soon hold a billiard table and dart boards for the use of the convalescents.

'Isn't this fun?' Fanny said, her eyes sparkling. 'Mother's parties were never like this.'

She had started to wear her hair in a simple knot at the nape of her neck because it was easier than her usual ringlets and took less time in the mornings. It suited her, making her look older and attractive rather than fussily pretty. She was enjoying being useful and Sorrel wondered how she would feel when it was time to go home – back to the everyday round of visiting and sitting at home with her mother.

'Yes, it is nice,' Sorrel said. 'It was clever of Celia to use this evening as an excuse for us all to get to know one another. I've met most of the nurses – and Matron. She's a bit of a dragon but I suppose she has to be.'

Fanny nodded and moved on. Sorrel noticed they were running short of sausage rolls and mentioned it to Celia's parlour maid, who went off to the kitchen to fetch some more; Sorrel turned as someone touched her on the shoulder.

'Miss Harris?' She stared for a moment then smiled as she recognized the young man. 'Do you remember me – from the train the other day?'

'Yes, of course.' The maid had returned with the sausage rolls and Sorrel encouraged him to try one. 'Do help yourself – they're very good.'

'If you recommend them.' He took one and bit into it. 'As you say, very good.'

Sorrel noticed that he seemed to be looking at something across the other side of the room, then smiled inwardly as she realized that it was actually someone: Fanny.

'Have you seen my father by any chance? Or perhaps you haven't met him – Sir Gerald Parkinson?'

'Yes, I have met him. He's on the board of governors for Celia's home. She told me he had helped her cut through a lot of red tape so that it could be set up quickly.'

'Celia has been telling me how hard you and Fanny have worked these past few days.' His eyes seemed to follow

Fanny about the room and Sorrel sensed that he was very interested in her friend.

'Fanny is enjoying herself very much,' she said. 'At home she is often bored because she has so little to do. I think she would like to stay on and help Aunt Celia with the patients.'

'Father says they'll need all the help they can get,' he replied. 'There is only a very small staff of nurses and they won't have time for everything . . . writing letters, arranging flowers . . . you know, the sort of thing that makes so much difference when someone is ill.'

'Yes, of course,' Sorrel agreed. 'It sounds useful.'

His eyes were continually following Fanny around the room. Sorrel smiled to herself. John Parkinson was obviously smitten with her friend.

'Why don't you take Fanny for a little walk in the garden?' she suggested. 'It's time she had a break and I'm sure some air would do her good.'

His skin went slightly pink. 'Is it so obvious?'

'Only to me, because Fanny is my best friend. I think she would enjoy that walk – in fact, I'm sure she would.'

'Do you really think so?' He was so eager and yet so unsure. 'I haven't been able to stop thinking about her . . .'

' "Faint heart never won fair lady," as my mother would say.' Sorrel laughed as his eyes lit up. 'Ask Fanny – what harm can it do?'

'By George, you're right!' he said and grinned at her. 'Will you excuse me please, Sorrel?'

'Of course.'

She smiled to herself as he went off in pursuit of Fanny. She looked surprised when he spoke to her but nodded eagerly. Sorrel watched them leave the room together with satisfaction. John Parkinson was nice and it was time Fanny had a little fun.

Fanny came to Sorrel's room as she was undressing later that night. There was such a glow about her that Sorrel knew the walk had gone well.

'You look happy,' she said. 'I suppose I can guess the reason.'

'Oh, Sorrel,' Fanny cried, her eyes sparkling like diamonds

237

in the light of the lamps. 'You do like him, don't you? Please say you do. I couldn't bear it if you didn't approve.'

'He's very nice, Fanny. I like him – and I'm sure he likes you a lot. He couldn't take his eyes off you at the party.'

'We're in love,' she said, looking shy. 'We've met twice since that day on the train, when he called here on errands for his mother. And I phoned him the other evening ... after you went to bed.'

'And you didn't tell me!'

'There wasn't anything to tell – until this evening. We had just said hello ... you know, all the usual things. Both of us felt the attraction but neither of us dared to think the other did. But John is going to Belgium soon and ...'

'How soon?'

'He can't say exactly, of course, but he has another week before he has to report back so ...' Her cheeks went pink. 'He ... has asked me to go away with him for a couple of days, to the sea.'

'Will you go?' Sorrel looked at her doubtfully. It was a tremendous decision to make. Fanny had only just met Captain Parkinson and to go away with him on her own was very daring – even shocking.

'I – I think so.' Fanny was obviously nervous. 'I know you must think me very forward, Sorrel, but supposing ... supposing something happened and ...'

'You mustn't say things like that – and I don't think you're forward or wicked.'

'Sorrel dearest.' Fanny kissed her cheek. 'I knew you would understand. I shall tell Aunt Celia I'm going with a party of friends. You won't tell her the truth, will you?'

'Of course not.'

'And you don't mind my leaving you for a few days?'

'Don't be silly, Fanny. I am quite happy here. I shall go for some long walks, and it will be interesting to see the patients arriving. I hope I can be of some help to the nurses, but I mustn't get in their way.'

'You won't tell anyone about John and me, will you? Not in your letters home. If my mother knew I was ...'

'You know I won't. It's your affair, Fanny, and I wish you

lots of luck. You deserve some happiness. Besides, I think you are very brave.'

Fanny laughed and hugged her again. 'Yes, I am, aren't I? I can't believe I've agreed to go with him – but I've never felt like this about anyone before. I know my mother would not approve of what I'm doing but . . .'

'You don't have to justify yourself to me, Fanny. If I were you, I would do the same.' Tears stung Sorrel's eyes but she held them back. 'If Jay were here now, I would go anywhere with him.'

Fanny's glow dimmed a little. 'He will write to you when he gets your letter, I know he will. He loves you.'

'Yes . . . he did once.' Sorrel made an effort to forget her own doubts and fears. She smiled lovingly at her friend. 'Anyway, we shan't think about any of that now. You go off with your John and enjoy yourself.'

Chapter Twenty-Seven

'I'm glad you're having a nice time,' Sorrel said into the mouthpiece of the telephone in Celia's sitting room. 'I'll tell Aunt Celia you rang and that we shouldn't expect you home until tomorrow then.'

'I know I said this evening but we've decided to stay one last night.' Fanny laughed nervously. 'It's lovely here in Hastings, Sorrel – and it has stopped raining at last.'

It had been raining for days but as Sorrel looked out of the window she saw the sun had come out. 'It's nice here, too,' she said. 'I think I shall go for a walk.'

'See you tomorrow then. Bye.'

Sorrel smiled as she said goodbye and hung up the receiver. She had been about to go out when Fanny rang and scribbled a note for Celia before putting on her coat: 'Fanny says she thinks there's something wrong with the line. She has rung before but couldn't get through – she'll be back tomorrow.'

Sorrel was thoughtful as she went out of the house. She had written a letter to her mother and wanted to walk down to the village to post it; she could have left it in the hall for collection with the others, but a long walk would do her good, blow away some of the cobwebs. Because of the rain she hadn't been able to get out as much as she would have liked and was looking forward to some fresh air.

A large black car had pulled up in front of the house. Sorrel paused to watch as a young nurse helped the soldier inside to get out. For the past two days men had been arriving in ones and twos, some in ambulances, others in private cars or taxis. Most had minor injuries and were able to walk unaided to their rooms, but this soldier had a thick bandage round his head and over one eye; his right arm was supported by a sling. There was something about his pale, strained face that made Sorrel think he was still very ill.

As she watched he suddenly stumbled and fell to the ground. Without stopping to think she ran to help the nurse as she bent over him.

'I think he has fainted,' the young nurse said, giving Sorrel an anxious glance. 'He wouldn't take my arm.'

The soldier was stirring. His eye flicked open and he looked up at them with such anger that Sorrel was shocked.

'Don't fuss so,' he muttered. 'I can manage myself.'

'You fainted. I should call a doctor . . .' the nurse said, fluttering like a trapped moth as he shrugged off her offer of help again, insisting on struggling to his feet unaided. 'Perhaps a bathchair . . .'

'Do that and you'll regret it. Just leave me alone and stop fluttering, girl.' He grabbed hold of Sorrel's arm, his fingers digging into it so hard that she had to bite her lip to stop herself wincing. 'Are you a nurse?' He glared at her from beneath heavy black brows. 'You don't look like one.'

'That's because I'm not. I'm staying with Lady Roth – and I help out where I can be useful.'

'You can help me then. And you . . .' He fixed his harsh stare on the unfortunate nurse. 'You can go away.'

'Major Bradshaw,' she said nervously, 'Matron instructed me to look after you.'

'And I'm telling you, I would rather have this young woman.' His one good eye glared at Sorrel. 'What's your name? I suppose you've got one?'

'Sorrel Harris,' she replied. 'I believe you're in room twelve, sir. It's one of the single ones so you will have privacy. I'll take you there if you wish?'

'Come on then, don't keep me hanging about.'

Sorrel turned and walked towards the house, his hand gripping her hard as he leaned heavily on her. The nurse hovered behind them as they went into the house but she was obviously intimidated by his manner. He was a man of perhaps thirty-seven or so and from his bearing Sorrel thought he must be regular army, one of the dedicated soldiers who had been in the thick of the fighting since the very beginning.

He walked very slowly and she sensed that it was only his iron will that was keeping him going. When they reached his room – which was one of the better ones, reserved for officers – he sank down into the armchair and leant back his head, clearly exhausted. Sorrel was about to leave when he looked up, fixing her with a glacial stare.

'Would you get me a glass of whisky, please?'

Sorrel glanced at the nurse, who shook her head emphatically. 'That isn't permitted until the doctor has seen Major Bradshaw.'

'I'm sorry,' Sorrel said. 'I don't think I can do that – not without authority.'

'Damn you! Do you think I'm a child or an imbecile? If I say I want a drink, I want a drink.'

'No, sir. I don't think you're an imbecile or a child,' Sorrel replied. 'But I am not allowed to give alchoholic drinks to guests, unless authorized by Matron.'

'Quite right, Miss Harris.' Matron's crisp tones made Sorrel look round. 'Thank you for your help. You may go now. I shall see to the Major myself.'

'Yes, Matron.' Sorrel obeyed without question but smiled at the Major as she left. He looked completely drained and she could sympathize with his desire for a stiff drink.

After leaving the house she went for her walk to the village, coming back across the fields because it was quicker and Celia would be expecting her for tea. She stood for a moment on the old wooden bridge that straddled the stream, watching as the clear water bubbled merrily over a tumble of small boulders. There were tiny fish darting in and out of the rocks and once in the early morning she had seen a heron standing in the shallow water at the edge. The lake was much deeper, of course, and she thought it might be pleasant to take a boat out – if the weather was warmer. But she wouldn't be here in the spring.

Looking round at the beautiful parkland, Sorrel knew a moment of regret. How peaceful it all was. Celia was very lucky to have such a wonderful home – and she was lucky to have been invited to share it, if only for a short while. She began to walk towards the house, feeling relaxed and happier than she had been since her quarrel with Jay. Celia had been so generous in making it possible for men like Major Bradshaw to come here; it would be good for him to rest in such tranquil surroundings as these. If it had been possible she would have liked to be able to help him and all the others, but of course it wasn't. Her visit would soon be over and then she would have to go home.

Celia was about to have tea when Sorrel walked in. She welcomed her with a smile and picked up the pretty silver teapot.

'I was just beginning to wonder where you were,' she said. 'Did you enjoy your walk, dear?'

'Very much, thank you. It is so beautiful here. I shall miss it all when I go home.'

'I was hoping to talk to you about that,' Celia said, handing her a delicate porcelain cup filled with a fragrant liquid. 'Matron popped in to see me a few minutes ago . . .'

'Oh?' Sorrel put her cup on the table beside her. 'I hope she wasn't too cross? I didn't mean to interfere. Major Bradshaw fell and I went to help – then he insisted that I take him to his room and . . .'

'Quite the reverse, Sorrel.' Celia offered her a plate of macaroons but she declined. 'Matron told me that she was impressed by the way you handled a difficult situation. She wondered if you would be interested in helping the nursing staff? They need sensible girls to take on some of the work the trained staff just don't have time for.'

'What kind of things?'

'Fetching and carrying. Scrubbing bedpans. Taking the men for walks in the grounds – those who can go out but need help with crutches and things. Keeping the rooms tidy, of course. Everything other than the tasks that require further training.'

It was much the same as Sorrel had already been doing but with some of the less pleasant jobs added on, and on a more permanent basis. The rooms were rapidly filling up and she could see that the nurses would be rushed off their feet once all the patients had settled in.

'I'm not sure . . .'

'Of course you must think about it. I wouldn't expect you to decide at once – but you would be very welcome to stay on if you wished.'

'I think I should enjoy it. It would make me feel as if I were really doing something to help. But I should have to talk to my parents first. They might not want me to be away any longer than we agreed.'

'Yes, I do see. You would need their permission.' Celia sipped her tea, then looked thoughtful. 'I expect you hope to marry one day.'

She glanced at Sorrel's left hand but it was a long time since she had worn the ring Jay had given her, though she still had it safely put away at home. He hadn't asked for it back and she had been too upset even to think of sending it to him.

'Perhaps . . . I don't know.' Getting married to the man she loved had always been Sorrel's special dream but now she was no longer sure of anything.

'It occurred to me that you might like to train as a nurse – once you are eighteen, of course. You are the kind of girl they need, Sorrel. But perhaps the idea doesn't appeal?'

'I have thought about it recently,' she said, surprising herself. 'I didn't think it was possible but I suppose it might be – while there is a war on and they need more nurses.'

'I think we shall be needing them for a long time,' Celia said gravely. 'Give the idea some consideration, my dear. I don't want to push you into anything but . . .' She paused and smiled. 'At what time should we expect Fanny tomorrow?'

'I'm not sure. She thought it might be in the afternoon but it depends on . . . her friends . . .'

'Yes, I see.' Celia nodded. 'I was just wondering . . .'

She broke off and they both turned as someone opened the door and walked in. Sorrel didn't know which of them was the most shocked to see Rebecca Sawle standing there. Celia sent an agonized glance at Sorrel, then jumped to her feet and went to greet her friend with a kiss.

'Rebecca, my dear,' she said. 'Why didn't you let me know you were coming? I would have sent the car for you.'

'It was a sudden decision,' Rebecca said. 'I was in London

for a meeting but it was cancelled at the last minute so I decided to catch the train. I tried phoning from the station when I arrived but I couldn't get through.'

'We've had some trouble since they installed all the new lines,' Celia said. 'It doesn't matter. You are always welcome, of course. Come and sit down and I'll ring for some fresh tea.' She rang the little brass bell at her side, clearly agitated by the unexpected arrival of Fanny's mother.

'Sorrel . . .' Rebecca acknowledged her with a polite smile. 'I hope you've settled in well?'

'Yes, thank you, Mrs Sawle. No one could help liking it here – and Aunt Celia has been very kind to me.'

'Yes, I'm sure.' Rebecca glanced round the room. 'It seems odd not to be using the main salons, doesn't it? This is so much smaller than you're used to, Celia.' She patted her hair, tucking a stray wisp into place. 'Where is Fanny?'

'She – she's out,' Celia said. The expression on her face gave her away and Sorrel realized that she must have guessed there was more to the trip than Fanny had told her. 'With friends.'

'I shall see her this evening then. You can put me up for the night, Celia? I know you haven't as much room as you had but . . . what is wrong? Why are you staring at me like that? If I'm putting you to too much trouble I can stay in the village.'

'Of course there's room.' Celia sent a signal for help. 'It's just that . . .'

'Fanny is away staying with friends.' Sorrel came to her rescue. 'She should be back some time tomorrow.'

'Staying with friends?' Rebecca's eyes stabbed at her. 'What friends?'

'Some people she knows from staying with Lady Roth before,' Sorrel replied as Celia gasped. 'Sir Gerald somebody or other and his family.'

'Parkinson,' Celia put in, looking slightly green. 'Very good family, Rebecca. I'm sure you must have met Sir Gerald here . . .'

'I think I may have done – but I'm not sure that I approve of Fanny's going off without asking my permission. Though I suppose if you know the family . . .'

'Oh, yes. Very respectable. Good friends of mine.'

Looking at Celia, Sorrel could see that she was terrified of being pressed for more details but Rebecca seemed satisfied and the subject was dropped as she began to ask questions about the nurses and patients – and how Celia felt about having her home invaded by strangers.

Celia did her best to answer but was clearly upset. Sorrel felt sorry for her. Rebecca Sawle's unexpected arrival had placed her in an embarrassing situation.

Sorrel felt awkward herself, as if she were part of a deliberate plot to deceive. Why did Fanny's mother have to turn up unannounced today? If they had only known she was coming they could have warned Fanny when she rang. As it was they could only cross their fingers and hope that Rebecca wasn't looking out of the window when Captain Parkinson brought her daughter back in his car.

'I think I shall walk as far as the village to inquire the times of the trains,' Rebecca announced after breakfast the next morning. 'There's still some crackling on your telephone, Celia. You should have it seen to.'

'Yes, I will,' she agreed. 'Wouldn't you rather take my car to the village, dear? It is a long way to walk.'

'It's a pleasant morning. Aden is always telling me I don't walk enough these days; the exercise will do me good.'

Celia turned to Sorrel in relief after she had left the room. 'We must hope that Fanny returns while her mother is out,' she said. 'Not that I wish to deceive Rebecca, of course, but she does tend to treat Fanny as though she were still a child and might get upset if . . .'

'Yes, I know. I'll keep an eye out for Fanny and tell her her mother is here,' Sorrel promised. 'But I'm going to see Matron this morning, and I thought I would take a few of your books for Major Bradshaw to read, if that's all right?'

'Yes, of course.' Celia nodded approvingly. 'I dare say he will be glad of a little company.'

Sorrel visited Matron first. She greeted her kindly and asked her to sit down.

'It isn't that we are short of volunteers,' she said. 'We've had offers from more young women than we can possibly take on but most of them have never done a day's work in their lives – and they are no help at all with the difficult patients like Major Bradshaw. Men with his temperament terrify most of my nurses, let alone the young ladies who volunteer to help with the teas and flowers.'

'He doesn't worry me,' Sorrel said. 'I think he's just tired, and frustrated by his own weakness. He can't bear to be fussed over. What he needs most is peace and quiet.'

'Exactly.' Matron nodded her approval. 'We must be there when he needs us but not intrude too much.'

'I thought I might take him these books.' Sorrel had chosen from the works of Thomas Hardy, Rudyard Kipling and H.G. Wells, thinking that they might appeal to a man like the Major.

'He has probably read them,' Matron said. 'But it's the thought that counts. Don't expect to be thanked, though.'

Matron was right. The Major cast a jaundiced eye over the books when Sorrel offered them to him a short time later.

'I read these long ago,' he said, 'but leave them – a couple of them may be worth a second look. There's little else I can do.'

'You could join some of the others in the library for a game of cards,' Sorrel suggested. 'Or perhaps a walk in the grounds, when you feel up to it.'

'I prefer to ride. Once I'm feeling better, as you put it, I shall take myself off – preferably back to my quarters.'

'Won't you go home, to see your family?'

His black brows knitted in a frown. 'My sister, you mean? Victoria is married with a horde of ungovernable brats. My home is a room at my London club or army quarters.'

'You're not married then?'

He laughed gruffly. 'Never found a woman fool enough to take me on – nor one that I could stand to wake up next to for the rest of my life.' He studied her from beneath his heavy brows as if expecting her to blush. When she didn't he looked amused. 'Sensible girl, ain't you? You may visit me now and then if you like. I don't suppose you play chess?'

'No, I'm sorry I don't – but I've played whist or gin rummy

247

with my brothers. I could give you a reasonable game at cards.'

'Hmmm – we'll see.'

Sorrel was smiling to herself as she left the main part of the house. Major Bradshaw was beginning to feel a little better and his temper had definitely improved. When Fanny came back she would tell her about him. Fanny played chess with her mother. Which reminded her to keep an eye out in case Fanny and Captain Parkinson arrived before Rebecca came back from the village.

Chapter Twenty-Eight

Fanny laughed as she braked hard and the little roadster screeched to a halt in front of the inn. She glanced at her companion, a teasing look in her eyes as he covered his face in a show of mock horror.

'There – I told you I could drive,' she said. 'I've won. You have to pay a forfeit.'

'Anything.' John leant towards her, eyes bright with mischief and something more – something that made Fanny catch her breath. 'How about a kiss? Will that do?'

'For a start,' she said, and smiled up at him. His lips caressed hers with the tender sweetness that made her want to melt with love for him. 'Oh, John, I do love you so.'

He stroked the soft curve of her cheek with his fingertips. 'I love you, Fanny. These past couple of days... they've meant so much to me. I shall never forget, my darling. When I'm lying out there in the trenches and things seem black, I shall close my eyes and think of you.'

'Please don't,' she said in a husky voice. 'We have until this evening – don't let's think about tomorrow.'

'No, we won't,' he said, 'but I wanted you to know you will always be with me. And now . . .' He grinned at her, the mischief back in his face. 'I'm going to buy some cigarettes and then I'll drive back to Lady Roth's.'

'Oh, you!' Fanny pouted at him. She was smiling as she watched him walk into the inn. She had never been this happy in her life and wasn't going to let anything spoil it, not even the nagging dread of John's departure the next day.

She took out the little silver compact he had bought her while they were at the seaside, looking at herself in the mirror as she touched her hair. She had never worn make-up in her life, but she didn't need it; her complexion was a perfect combination of cream and rose, her skin as soft as silk – at least that was what John had told her when he'd held her in his arms that last night ... Something caught the corner of her eye and she turned her head to look as someone came up to the car. Her heart took a frightened leap and she trembled inside as the door was suddenly wrenched open.

'Mother!' Fanny felt sick as she saw the anger in her mother's eyes. 'Where ... why are you here?'

'You little fool,' Rebecca cried. 'So that's why Celia seemed so odd when I arrived. I suspected she was hiding something from me. How could you behave in such a disgusting manner?'

'What do you mean?' Fanny asked, her stomach tying itself into knots as she looked into her mother's eyes. 'I don't know what you're talking about. I haven't done anything wrong.'

'Don't play the innocent with me,' Rebecca snapped. 'I saw you kissing that soldier. You've been away with him, haven't you? Celia said you were with friends – but it was him, wasn't it?'

Fanny got out of the car. She stood staring at her mother, her mouth dry with fear. She knew it was useless to try and explain, her mother would never understand how she felt – the sense of urgency that had driven her to do something she knew would be seen as unacceptable.

'John and I ... nothing happened. We didn't ... it was just to be together because we ...'

'You little slut!' Rebecca slapped her face. 'My own daughter behaving like a tuppeny whore! If I hadn't seen it with my own eyes, I should not have believed it.'

Fanny was shaking as she put a hand to her cheek. She felt sick and the tears were stinging her eyes. Her mother had always been so strict with her, keeping her at home, never letting her have the freedom many other girls had.

She had always tried to be obedient, never deliberately flouting her mother's wishes – but this was different.

'Fanny?' John's voice broke the silence. 'What's going on here? Are you all right, darling?'

'John . . . this is my mother. She saw us . . . just now and . . .' Her voice broke. 'She thinks . . .'

'Mrs Sawle.' John's shoulders stiffened. 'I know what you must be thinking but it wasn't like that. I love Fanny and I want to marry her.'

'Then you should have behaved in a decent and proper manner,' Rebecca said, her voice icy. 'How dare you ruin my daughter's reputation?'

'But no one knows . . .' Fanny stopped as her mother looked at her. 'John has to go away soon and we . . .'

'Go up to the house please, Fanny. I shall talk to you later. I have something more to say to this young man.'

'No. I'm staying with John. I'm not a child and I won't be treated as one.'

'You are not yet nineteen,' Rebecca said. 'And you will do exactly as I tell you or . . .'

'Do as your mother says,' John said softly. 'Go on, Fanny. I'll see you later.'

'But I want to stay with you.' Her eyes were brimming with tears. 'She has no right . . .'

'Later,' he said. 'Let me talk to your mother alone – please, darling.'

Fanny looked at her mother, who nodded, her expression so forbidding that Fanny's heart sank. She knew it was hopeless; her mother would not listen to a word John said – she had already made up her mind that he was a vile seducer.

'Promise me you won't leave without telling me?' Fanny's face was pale and tense. 'You won't go without saying goodbye?'

'I promise,' he said, and smiled. 'Go on now – it's best.'

Fanny hesitated, then began to walk slowly away, turning every few steps to look back at them. Tears spilled over and ran down her cheeks. Suddenly she could bear it no longer.

'I'll be waiting for you,' she cried. 'Don't let her spoil it, John.' Then she began to run, through the village street and across the fields. There was a crushing pain in her chest and she was sobbing now. 'Please . . . please don't let her spoil it . . . don't let her spoil it!'

Outside the inn John met Rebecca's flinty eyes. 'What you've done is unforgivable,' she said. 'You are never to see my daughter again – do you understand me? I forbid you to speak to Fanny ever again.'

Sorrel was standing by the stream when she saw Fanny running towards her. Her manner was so desperate and wild that she knew something terrible must have happened and hurried to meet her, grabbing hold of her arm as Fanny started to scream and cry hysterically.

'She's ruined it all . . . she always spoils everything!' Fanny wept as Sorrel put her arms around her. 'I love him so much and she . . .'

'Hush. Hush, my dearest,' Sorrel said, stroking her hair. 'Tell me what happened. Was it your mother? Did she see you with Captain Parkinson?'

Fanny drew back. Her face was streaked with tears, her hair falling in lank wisps about her neck and shoulders.

'Yes.' She gulped for air. 'We had stopped in the village for John to buy some cigarettes and . . . we kissed in the car. He went to the inn and Mother . . . pulled open the door. She said such terrible things . . .'

'It must have been a shock to her.' Sorrel could imagine the scene and Rebecca's reaction. 'We had told her you were staying with Celia's friends. What did she say?'

'She called me a slut – and she hit me.' Fanny was shaking. Sorrel put an arm around her waist. 'She said wicked, awful things to John. I'm not a child, Sorrel. And whatever she might think, we didn't do anything wrong.'

'No, of course you didn't.'

'No, really, I mean it. John wanted us to be alone for a few days but he loves me too much to – well, you know.' She blushed. 'I would have if he had asked but he said it wouldn't be fair to me, not the way things are. He wants us to get married on his next leave.'

'Did you tell your mother that?'

'He tried to but she wouldn't listen.' Fanny's feelings

252

errupted in a passionate outburst. 'I hate her, Sorrel. She has ruined everything. I shall never forgive her. It was all so beautiful and now . . .'

Sorrel tried to soothe her but Fanny broke away from her and ran towards the house. She obviously wanted to be alone, to cry out her grief and pain in the privacy of her own room. Sorrel let her go. Fanny would feel better once she had calmed down.

But what would Rebecca have to say when she returned to the house? She was bound to be very angry.

'I want you to come home with me,' Rebecca said. 'After speaking to Captain Parkinson – who was very frank with me – I am willing to accept that you did not go so far as to . . . have intimate relations with him, but I cannot condone what you did. Going away with a man . . . alone! And letting him kiss you in public. Your behaviour has shocked me, Fanny. Shocked and hurt me.'

Sorrel looked at Fanny's white face. They had been sitting on her bed talking together when Rebecca came into her daughter's room.

'Perhaps I should go.'

'No – please don't leave me,' Fanny begged, catching hold of her arm. 'Stay with me, Sorrel. Please.'

Sorrel nodded. 'If that's what you want.'

Fanny stood up, twisting her handkerchief between nervous fingers. 'I am nearly nineteen, Mother. You still think of me as a child but I'm not. You can't make me come home with you. You can't stop me seeing John.'

'I assure you that it is very much within my power to compel you to return home if I so wish,' Rebecca replied. 'You are my daughter and I expect you to behave as a decently brought-up young woman ought. I am very disappointed in you, Fanny.'

'I shall run away if you force me to come home,' Fanny said. She raised defiant eyes to meet her mother's glacial stare. 'I'm not ashamed of what I've done, and I shall see John again.'

'You may see him this evening,' Rebecca said. 'I am not unfeeling, Fanny, whatever you may think. You may talk to

253

him, providing that Sorrel remains with you. He will come to the house at five o'clock and you may have half an hour with him.'

Fanny looked stubborn, as if she were about to refuse her mother's offer. Sorrel laid a hand on her arm, giving her a warning look.

'Fanny, maybe it's best.'

'All right,' she said at last. 'I'll meet John here and Sorrel can be with us – but I shan't come home with you. I hate you for what you've done. You've spoiled everything, made it seem ugly . . .'

'Very well.' Rebecca inclined her head. 'I shall give you a little time to come to your senses. Please remember, Fanny, your father and I can make you come home if we wish – we have the legal right to compel you should it be necessary.'

'But Father wouldn't,' Fanny replied, her eyes glinting with anger. 'He would have listened to us . . . he wouldn't have made it dirty.'

'Fanny,' Sorrel warned, 'stop it. You mustn't. Your mother was angry. She didn't mean to . . .'

'Thank you, Sorrel,' Rebecca said with more dignity than anger, 'but I can speak for myself. I shan't see you before I leave, Fanny, but – if you disappoint me again, if you continue to defy me – I shall disown you.'

She walked from the room, her back straight and stiff. Fanny stood staring at the closed door, her face very white.

'Fanny, why don't you go after her?' Sorrel asked. 'Tell her you're sorry. Try to make her understand how much you love John.'

'No!' Her face was pale but determined. 'I've made up my mind. I shall stay here with Aunt Celia, and I shall write to my father and ask him for permission to marry John on his next leave.'

There was no arguing with her in her present mood. Fanny had changed, grown up. Sorrel admired her for her courage but could see it was costing her dear. In her heart Fanny knew that her mother was strict because she loved her – because her various illnesses as a child had made her more vulnerable than other girls – but she was hurt and frightened.

Frightened that John was going away and might never come back.

Their leavetaking that evening nearly tore the heart out of Sorrel. She would have left the room if she could but John asked her to stay.

'I gave my word to Mrs Sawle that this meeting would take place in the presence of a third person,' he said stiffly. 'This unpleasantness is my fault, Fanny. I was selfish. I should never have asked you to . . .'

'Don't!' she cried, her hands trembling as she held them out to him. 'Please don't say it. The few days we spent together were the happiest of my life. Whatever happens now I shall never forget them . . . never.'

'Nor I,' John said, his voice husky with passion. 'Fanny . . . my dearest love.'

Sorrel stared out of the window into the darkness as he moved to take her into his arms. Tears of pity for her friend slipped down her cheeks and she could taste salt on her lips.

Why did life always have to be so cruel? Fanny was being forced to say goodbye to the man she loved in the presence of a third person, and she might never see Jay again.

It was so unfair!

Afterwards, when John had gone, promising faithfully to telephone her as soon as he could, Fanny wept in Sorrel's arms.

'What am I going to do?' she asked. 'Oh, Sorrel, I can't bear it. Supposing he . . .'

Sorrel hushed her with a kiss. 'You mustn't, my dearest. I know how you feel, but you mustn't torture yourself.'

'Yes, you do know, don't you?' Fanny said, clinging to her. 'You understand. You don't condemn me for what I did, do you?'

'You know I don't. I'm glad you had a little time with John,' Sorrel said, stroking her hair. 'One day perhaps your mother will understand and . . .'

'I shall never forgive her for ruining our last day,' Fanny vowed. 'Never.'

'Oh, Fanny.' Sorrel sighed as she saw the stubborn set of Fanny's face. 'She's your mother.'

Sorrel sympathized with her friend but Fanny *had* broken

255

the rules and her mother was bound to be upset. Besides, despite their quarrel, Fanny must still care for her. She could not really want a permanent rift with her mother, could she?

Rebecca asked to speak to Sorrel before she left the next morning. Fanny was locked in her own room and had refused to answer anyone's call.

'Please tell Fanny that if she behaves sensibly and comes home I shall not mention this incident again. I know she listens to you, Sorrel. I am prepared to forgive her this once – and to give consideration to a marriage between her and Captain Parkinson if he applies to her father properly. Celia assures me that his people are respectable and, though she may not think it, I can understand what prompted Fanny to behave as she did – even though I was deeply shocked and hurt.'

'Fanny did nothing wrong, Mrs Sawle, not really.'

'That may be your opinion, it is not mine. They hardly knew each other. To go away like that ...'

'But they are in love.'

Rebecca's look silenced her. 'Please give my message to Fanny. Now you must excuse me. I have a train to catch.'

She was driven away in Celia's car, leaving a subdued silence in the house. Fanny came down a little later, but her eyes were red from weeping and neither Celia nor Sorrel knew what to say to her.

She stayed in her room most of the evening but the following morning Celia went to tell her there was a call from John and she came out in a rush, eyes suddenly aglow.

'He says he will write to my father today,' she told Sorrel afterwards, looking happier than she had since the quarrel with her mother. 'He will explain everything and ask for Dad's permission so that we can get married when he comes home on leave.'

'I'm so glad,' Sorrel said, and hugged her. 'Don't worry, love. I'm sure it will all come right in the end.'

'Yes, perhaps.' Fanny gave her a watery smile. 'I'm glad I've got you, Sorrel. I don't think I could bear it without you.'

256

'We're friends,' she said, and squeezed her arm. 'I shall have to go home next week, though. I promised my mother.'

'Have you thought about staying on here?' Fanny asked. 'I shall, no matter what anyone says. I shan't go home, and my father won't let my mother force me.'

'Oh, Fanny.' Sorrel looked at her sadly. 'Wouldn't it be better to make up your quarrel with her?'

'No.' Fanny's expression was so stubborn that Sorrel would have laughed if it hadn't been so sad. Fanny loved her mother and must be hurting over their quarrel even if she wouldn't admit it. 'Never.'

'It's up to you, of course.' Sorrel sighed. 'I should like to stay here with you and do what I can to help, but I shall have to ask my mother. If she says I can come back then I shall.'

'Shall you mind travelling home alone?'

'No, I don't think so.' Sorrel smiled at her. 'I'm almost sure my mother will let me come back, Fanny, but I have to ask before I make promises.'

'Yes, of course,' she agreed. 'But hurry back, Sorrel. We shall all miss you.'

Chapter Twenty-Nine

Jay opened his letter from Fanny and smiled as he saw the photographs she had enclosed of herself, then his smile faded as he saw the one of Sorrel. Sorrel . . . looking more beautiful than ever. He ran his fingers over her face, trying to remember the scent of her skin and the sound of her voice. Did she ever think of him? Had she discovered the truth . . . or didn't she care anymore? He had hoped she might write to him, even if it was just to wish him luck, but he hadn't had any letters for weeks until one from Fanny had arrived this morning.

It was November now and a few weeks since he'd been sent to France. The war had settled into a kind of stalemate with little real work for the men to do amongst the mud and the barbed wire that protected the trenches – trenches that stretched endlessly from the North Sea as far as Switzerland, so they said, though he'd seen little of them, stuck here at base camp. Some of the lads played football to overcome the boredom, while others dared each other to crawl as far as the enemy lines, fire a few shots and get back without being injured or losing their weapon.

Jay thought the men who indulged in such escapades were mad. There was no point in risking death or injury unless it was on a direct order. It hadn't taken him long to realize that war wasn't the adventure he had expected; the constant pounding of the guns, the filth and the stench when wounded and dying men were brought back from the front lines, was sickening, becoming a nightmare that haunted him while he lay sleepless at night.

He thought about Sorrel all the time, wondering if she had forgiven him – and why he'd been such a damned fool. Why the hell had he walked away from her like that? Why hadn't he told her the truth? His pride had been hurt and he'd been angry but afterwards he had wanted to see her so badly ... but somehow he had never got round to making the first move; then the war had come along and he'd thought it was a fine adventure, volunteering in a spirit of bravado, thinking how Sorrel would cry if he died a hero. Now he knew there were no heroes, only dead men.

He put the photo of Sorrel in his breast pocket and began to read Fanny's letter again. In another hour he was on duty. A convoy of waggons loaded with ammunition and other supplies needed to be taken up to the forward positions and he would be driving one of them.

The roads had been reduced to little more than cart tracks, churned up by a succession of wheels and horses' hooves and turned into mud by the heavy rain that had fallen of late. Ahead of them was what had once been a pretty village but was now a wasteland of ash and rubble. The guns were quiet up at the front line that morning; it was strange how you got used to the sound so that you began to worry when all you could hear was a bird singing. Almost like having a nagging toothache that had temporarily abated and knowing it would be all the worse when it started up again.

Shouting and cursing could be heard from the head of the convoy and Jay pulled hard on the reins as he was forced to stop. One of the waggons seemed to have lost a wheel, blocking the narrow road and making it impossible to pass because of the craters and ruts on either side.

'Typical, ain't it?' his companion said. 'I've got a date tonight with one of them Belgian nurses and we're stuck here in the middle of nowhere.'

'I'll see what's going on,' Jay said, handing the reins over. 'Keep a look out. And if you see a Jerry kite coming at you, get the hell out of it.'

Attacks from German planes were rare even this close to the forward lines, but there was always the possibility that one could suddenly zoom out of nowhere and start shooting

259

up a convoy. And that was no fun when you were sitting on top of an ammunition waggon.

Jay walked towards the scene of the confusion. The road was nothing but a series of deep ruts, its rough surface forever causing breakdowns, and the hazards of a trip like this were a fact of life.

Tempers had begun to fray as the drivers and their mates swore at one another and argued about whether the waggon should be abandoned or unloaded and repaired. Jay took a look at the damage and decided it wasn't too bad.

'I could fix it,' he offered. 'What have you got on the back, mate?'

'Supplies, that's all I know.'

'Well, I reckon we'd best unload and get the waggon off the road. My mate can take over from me and I'll give you a hand. I'll fetch my tools and sort it out with the corporal.'

Jay walked back down the line of irritated men and restless horses, returning a few minutes later with the box of tools and spare bits he had learned to carry with him for emergencies. The other drivers had combined to unload and push the offending waggon to one side. Jay helped clear the road for the rest of the convoy, watching as they rumbled by before setting to work on the wheel.

'Are you sure you can fix it?' The driver of the broken waggon glanced over his shoulder. 'My name is Sam Bates by the way. I've seen you around but we ain't spoken afore this.'

'I'm Jay.' He began hammering nails into the splintered spokes. 'We learnt to cope with breakdowns on the farm,' he said. 'It won't be a pretty job but this metal plate will hold long enough to get us there and back.'

It took him half an hour to repair the wheel and his clothes were covered in mud, the trousers soaked through by the time he'd finished. Sam offered him a swig of whisky from a hip flask and Jay drank it gratefully. It was cold and he would be glad when they had deposited their load and were on their way home. They had almost finished reloading the supplies when they heard an odd spluttering sound and looked up, startled. A small plane was flying low and coming towards them, its engine making a peculiar whining noise as it narrowly skimmed the tops of a small stand of trees a short distance away.

'Bloody hell!' Sam cried. 'It's a Jerry!'

'Yes.' Jay shaded his eyes. 'The so and so is shooting at us. Get down, you fool!'

As the plane came zooming towards them, Jay pushed Sam to the ground and flung himself on top of him. A hail of bullets ripped into the earth on either side of them, then there was a terrific explosion as one hit the waggon. Jay felt himself tossed into the air and then he blacked out. Just before he lost consciousness he wondered if Sorrel would cry when they told her he was dead.

'I told you Fanny would rebel one day,' May said as they sat talking together in the kitchen long after everyone else had gone up. 'Rebecca has tried to keep her on a leading string for far too long. It was bound to happen – not that I'm agreeing with the way she behaved, mind.' She fixed her daughter with a hard stare. 'I should have something to say to you if you went off with a lad you hardly knew, miss.'

Sorrel pushed her hair back out of her eyes. 'She didn't do anything, Ma. They had separate rooms at the hotel and he had the bill to prove it, which was the reason Rebecca agreed to let them meet at the house. It was just a chance for them to be on their own. You can't blame them, not with him having to go away so soon.'

'No, I suppose not – and there's many a lad *would* have taken advantage of the situation. Rebecca should have given them the benefit of the doubt; it wasn't fair to make them say goodbye with you there as a gooseberry.'

'I know. I did my best to be invisible but it wasn't easy. You can't blame Rebecca in a way, though. She and Fanny had a terrible quarrel. I thought Fanny would give in and go home with her mother in the end, but she was so stubborn. She's grown up.'

'As you have,' Sorrel's mother said, studying her thoughtfully. 'So you want to stay on at Lady Roth's then?'

'For a while,' she replied. 'I believe I can be useful – and I don't think I could settle at home, not while there's a war going on.'

'Your father will miss you. He has been looking forward to having you home again.'

Sorrel met her mother's eyes. 'He seems better . . . is he?'

'Yes, I think so. He isn't drinking so much anyway.' May turned her wedding ring on her finger several times. 'I'm not going to make the decision for you, Sorrel. You must make up your own mind. We can manage without you if you want to do this – but you can come home whenever you like. We shan't hold it against you if things don't work out as you expect.'

'Thanks, Ma.' Sorrel got up to kiss her cheek. May smelt faintly of lavender water and baking. 'I think I shall go back – at least for a while. And I shall think about training as a nurse when I'm eighteen.'

May nodded, as if she had known all along what her descison would be. 'So you've not heard from Jay then?'

'No, but Fanny hasn't either. She says the letters are probably being sent on to him at his new posting, wherever that is. You don't think anything has happened?'

'If he had been killed we should have heard,' May said. 'In a case like this no news is probably good news. Your letter may have been lost in the post like hundreds of others. Why don't you write to him again?'

'I might, but I'll wait for a while, see if Fanny has heard anything when I go back to Rothsay Hall. There might even be a letter waiting for me.'

'Yes.' May was thoughtful. 'You know, sometimes these things are meant for the best. If you'd married Jay you would probably have stayed in the village all your life. This time away has been good for you, Sorrel. You've learnt from it and that can't be bad.'

'You're a wise old bird, Ma,' she said, and smiled at her. 'I know you're right – but I'd give everything to be married to Jay, to know that he's safe and that he loves me.'

'Then you'll just have to be patient until he comes home, won't you?' May yawned and stretched. 'Well, I'm for my bed, it will soon be morning.'

'I shall help Pa with the milking. I'll talk to him then, tell him what I want to do.'

'Yes, it would be best coming from you. Goodnight then,

Sorrel.' May looked at her for a moment, then touched her hand. 'For what it's worth, I'm proud of you ... proud of what you're doing and the young woman you've become.'

Sorrel spent a week at home with her parents. It was a pleasant, happy time and there were no harsh words between them. Her father accepted her decision, telling her he loved her and that she had made him even more proud of her than he'd always been.

'You were lovely as a little girl,' he said, his eyes moist. 'But you're a beautiful woman, Sorrel – and it isn't just skin deep.'

His words made her want to cry but she laughed and shook her head at him, telling him he was an old flatterer – but when he gave her a hug, she hugged him back twice as hard.

The day before she was due to leave she had tea with Mabel.

'We shall all miss you,' she said as Sorrel nursed the baby while Timmy pulled at her skirts and demanded that she kiss his battered, one-eyed teddy. 'But you're doing the right thing. I think you'll make a good nurse.'

'That's if they'll have me.' Sorrel pulled a face. 'I might not get in – but I can always stay at Celia's if I don't. I'm useful there.' She stroked Timmy's head. 'Yes, darling, I can see Teddy needs a new eye. We'll sew a button on, shall we?'

'You'd make a good mother, too,' Mabel said, looking reflective. 'I suppose there's no one else?'

'No.' Sorrel smiled a little too brightly. 'You'll keep me in touch with everything, won't you? Let me know if I'm needed.'

'Of course, love. Don't worry about your pa. Bob will look out for him.'

'I'm so glad he isn't joining up,' Sorrel said. She had been afraid he might want to go, despite the fact that he was needed for the vital work of feeding the people. As yet the war hadn't eaten into the nation's resources too much but it was only a matter of time before they were stretched to the limit. Food was important and men like Bob were badly

263

needed in the fight for survival, but it couldn't be easy for him to stay at home when so many of his friends were leaving the village. 'Is Bob restless? Does he feel out of things?'

'Sometimes,' Mabel admitted with a sigh. 'But Aden told him he couldn't be spared and he knows it's true.'

'Richie hasn't joined up either, has he?'

'Apparently he told his mother that he thought it his duty to stay here and help his father. But . . .' Mabel shrugged. 'I suppose she was pleased; she didn't want Jay to go, did she?'

'No, she didn't.'

Sorrel was thoughtful as she walked home after tea. From things her mother had told her she understood that Rebecca saw very little of her eldest son these days. With Jay in the army and Fanny at Rothsay, she must be feeling a little lonely.

Sorrel wondered if perhaps she ought to try and see Rebecca before she left for Hampshire. If they talked Rebecca might give her a message for Fanny. There could surely be no harm in trying?

She called at Five Winds on impulse. Molly answered the door, inviting her into the kitchen. She looked subdued and anxious as she went off to ask if Rebecca would see Sorrel but was back within a few minutes.

'Mrs Sawle thanks you for coming, but she has a headache and can't see you. I'm sorry.'

'It doesn't matter. I'm sorry to have troubled her.'

As Sorrel turned away Molly caught her arm. 'I'm worried about her. She's been in such a mood lately – and Mr Sawle is too busy to notice. They've always had their ups and downs but . . . she set so much store by Miss Fanny. There's been no word from Master Jay for weeks and that other one . . .' Molly pulled a face. 'He's no son to her at all and never has been. If you ask me he's . . .' She stopped as if realizing she had said too much. 'To tell you the truth, I think she may be sickening for something.'

'What can I do? Shall I go up and talk to her?'

'Oh, no!' Molly was horrified. 'She would never forgive me. I shouldn't have said anything but it was kind of you to call and . . .' Molly sniffed and wiped her eyes with her apron. 'I'm a fool. It's just that I'm so fond of her. People think she's hard, but they don't know what she's had to put up with.'

'Yes, I know what you mean – at least I know some of it.' Sorrel pressed her hand. 'She'll be all right, Molly. Don't worry. Rebecca is very strong, and I'm sure she and Fanny will make it up soon.'

'I hope you're right. Rebecca might be strong but she hurts on the inside like everyone else – she just doesn't show it much.'

Sorrel was thoughtful as she crossed the road to go home. She had no particular reason to like Rebecca Sawle after the way she had stood out against her marrying Jay, but she couldn't help feeling sympathy for her. Her husband was stretched to the limit by the shortage of labour on the land, and she had lost one of her sons to the army and now was estranged from her daughter. She must be feeling very alone just now.

Aden insisted on taking Sorrel to the station himself. He asked her if she was all right for money and she assured him she was.

'If there is ever anything I can do for you, Sorrel, you will let me know?'

'I have all I need, thank you, but I shan't forget your kindness.'

'Give my love to Fanny. I've written to her but...' He looked regretful. 'Her mother was wrong, Sorrel, but she won't admit it. I've never interfered between them and I can't force Rebecca to make up their quarrel, but she's suffering. I hope in time Fanny will find it in her heart to forgive her and come home.'

'I'll talk to her but I can't promise anything. Fanny has changed, she's more determined now ... stronger.'

'You will let us know how she is? If she is in any kind of trouble ...'

'Yes, of course.' Sorrel hesitated, then reached up to kiss his cheek. 'I'm glad you persuaded Bob to stay on the farm. Pa needs him.'

'Bob is a good worker. I couldn't afford to lose him.' Aden smiled down at her. 'If I hear from Jay I will let you know.'

'Thank you.'

She waved to him from the train.

Aden was worried because no one had heard from Jay for weeks. Like everyone else he was pretending to believe that their letters were simply en route to wherever Jay had been sent but in his heart he was afraid that his son might have been injured.

'Oh, Jay,' Sorrel whispered to herself as she sat back in her seat and watched the station disappear into the distance. 'Where are you and why haven't you written to anyone? Please . . . please be safe.'

Fanny had come with the car to meet Sorrel at the station. She was learning to drive and full of new ideas.

'When I can manage it, I'm going to drive an ambulance,' she told Sorrel after she had hugged and kissed her. 'You should learn, too, Sorrel. Matthews will teach us both.'

Matthews was Lady Roth's dedicated chauffeur. He admitted to sixty-eight years but was probably older and would have retired long since if he had been less fond of his employer. Sorrel was sure that the last thing he wanted was the task of teaching two young and inexperienced women to drive but when she said as much he assured her it was no trouble.

'It would be a privilege, Miss Sorrel,' he told her. 'Lady Roth wants you both to be happy with us – besides, cars are the thing of the future. It's all going to be very different when the war's over, you take my word for it.'

'Well, if you're sure you have time it would be fun to learn,' Sorrel said and thanked him. 'Of course I shall be busy most of the time from now on.'

'Major Bradshaw was asking for you,' Fanny said. 'He's such a crusty old thing but I quite like him. We play chess together sometimes.'

'Rather you than me,' Sorrel said, and laughed.

Fanny's laugh echoed hers. She was pleased to see Fanny in better spirits and when they were alone later that day she discovered the reason. Aden had given his permission for her to marry Captain Parkinson.

'Of course it may not be for ages,' she said, 'but it gives me something to look forward to, doesn't it?'

'Yes, it's wonderful news,' Sorrel said, and then hesitated. 'What about your mother?'

Fanny's mouth hardened. 'I haven't heard from her. She thinks I shall apologize but I shan't. I still haven't forgiven her for what she said to John that day.'

'Couldn't you write to her?'

'Don't ask me to do that, Sorrel. She was wrong. It's up to her. She wouldn't listen to me and now I don't want to speak to her.'

This new Fanny could be every bit as stubborn as her mother. She had begun to look more and more like Rebecca must have as a young woman, and it seemed terrible to Sorrel that they should be estranged, but there was no point in arguing. Fanny had made up her mind. She was determined that the first move should come from her mother and there was no swaying her.

'I'm so glad you've come back,' she said, tucking her arm through Sorrel's. 'I wanted us to be together.'

'Yes, I know.' Sorrel tucked a wisp of hair behind her ear. 'It may not be for long, though, not if I apply for nursing training.'

'Well, we'll make the most of it, and you'll have leave. One of us can always get on a train. We'll keep in touch, Sorrel. You're like a sister to me.' Her face flushed and Sorrel's instinct told her she was trying to hide something from her.

'Have you heard from Jay? You have, haven't you?'

'Yes.' Fanny went still. 'You mustn't get upset, Sorrel. He's all right.'

'He has been injured, hasn't he? I've been afraid of it for a few days. Why didn't you tell me at once?'

Fanny's eyes slid away guiltily. 'The letter only came this morning. I was going to let you read it but . . .'

'What? Is he badly hurt? He's not dying!' Sorrel's heart raced fearfully but Fanny shook her head.

'It was just a scratch really, not bad enough for them to send him home.'

'Then why are you looking so odd? What don't you want to tell me?'

'You had better read it for yourself.' Fanny took an envelope from her pocket and handed it to her. 'I'm sorry. I don't understand Jay, I really don't.'

Sorrel's hands shook as she opened the letter and began to read Jay's unsteady hand.

Dearest Fanny,

I'm sorry I haven't written for a while but your letter didn't catch up with me until just before I caught one. We had been on the move for ages and then, it was just a bit of bad luck really. I've got a piece of shrapnel in my arm, nothing much but a bit sore. I'm in a small hospital back at base. It used to be a nunnery but the nuns have opened it up for the wounded and it's not bad; they do their best for us, bless their hearts.

Don't panic, Fanny. I'm all right. It was just a flesh wound in my upper arm and a few cuts. Louise says I'll be as good as new in a couple of weeks. It was a bit of luck I was brought here instead of one of the field hospitals. Louise is a Belgian but she speaks pretty good English – and you'll never guess what! Her father is a farmer. She has invited me to stay with them when I leave here. I shall probably get a couple of weeks' leave before they send me back so I might as well go. Louise is a good sort and I like her . . .

Sorrel folded the letter and replaced it in its envelope before giving it back to Fanny.

'He couldn't have got your letter,' Fanny said. 'It must have got lost as several of mine obviously have. He wouldn't go home with this girl if . . .'

'Wouldn't he?' Sorrel asked with a flash of anger. 'Your letter reached him, why shouldn't mine? He hasn't answered me but I think I have my answer anyway. Jay doesn't want me. It's over.'

Fanny was upset. 'I shouldn't have shown you the letter.'

'I'm glad you did. It has saved me from making a fool of myself. I was going to write to him again.'

'But now you won't? Oh, Sorrel.'

'There isn't much point, is there? It's over between Jay and me. His letter makes that clear.'

'Sorrel, I'm sure Jay wouldn't . . .' Fanny looked as if she were about to cry.

'Please don't say anymore. I just want to forget. I have to forget Jay. If you're really my friend you will let me do that, Fanny.'

She nodded miserably. 'Of course. If that's what you want – but I'm furious with Jay. I shall tell him so in my next letter.'

'Please don't. You mustn't be angry with him, Fanny. You know how fond you are of him. Besides, Jay needs you. He and I quarrelled and it's over between us – that's not your fault.' Sorrel squeezed her hand. 'Don't be upset.'

'I care about you . . .'

'I know. I'll be all right.' Sorrel smiled at her a little wearily. 'I think I'll go for a walk if you don't mind.'

She left before Fanny could say anything. For weeks she had lived in dread of something like this. At least now the worst had happened and she knew where she stood. Jay didn't love her. He had found someone new. She sighed as the wind cut through her clothes; it was so cold . . . such a dull cold winter's day.

Would it ever be spring again?

Chapter Thirty

Sorrel didn't cry for Jay this time, nor was she angry. Their relationship was over and he had a perfect right to go home with any girl he liked: knowing that didn't stop it hurting of course, but it was a numb ache rather than the sharp pain of their first parting.

'What's wrong with you?' Major Bradshaw asked her one morning after she had been tidying up his room. 'You look drained. Are they working you too hard here?'

'I enjoy my work,' she said. 'It gives me something to occupy my mind.'

'You've had bad news, I suppose.' His voice was gruff but with an underlying note of sympathy. 'I'm sorry. This wretched war has a lot to answer for.'

'It wasn't that kind of news,' she replied, 'but you're right in a way. The man I loved – he found someone else.'

'You're young enough to get over it. You'll find someone else in time.'

'Yes, of course. It's just that I've loved him for as long as I can remember.'

'He must be a damned fool!' The Major glared at her from steely eyes. 'You know I'm leaving here soon?'

'Matron said another week or ten days.'

'Sooner if I can wangle it.' He paused, clearing his throat. 'I'm expecting company this afternoon. I've been assigned a new batman. Reynolds was killed when I caught this little lot – good man, been with me for years.' He glanced up at her. 'I asked them to send the new one down here so that I can break him in gently before we get out there.'

'Will you be going back to active service?' She could see that he was affected by the loss of his former comrade but thought it best not to say anything: he would not appreciate sympathy.

'I most certainly shall, the sooner the better. Never could stand being idle.' He glanced at his pocket watch. 'Keep an eye out for my man, won't you? We'll have tea in my room please.'

'What's his name?'

'They haven't told me yet but you'll know him. He's a new recruit and bound to be wet behind the ears – though he has a way with horses. At least, that's what I've been led to believe.'

'I'll try to bring him here myself,' Sorrel promised. 'I have to go now but I shall see you later.'

She met Matron as she was leaving his room. They stopped for a few words and Sorrel told her about the visitor Major Bradshaw was expecting.

'Yes, I have been informed. I rely on you to see that they are looked after.' Her eyes rested on Sorrel critically. 'You're looking a little tired, Miss Harris. Perhaps you should take a couple of days off.'

'I would rather work. I'm really very well.'

'Don't overdo things. We can't afford to lose you.' She nodded crisply and went on her way.

Sorrel visited some of the other patients. Most of them were cheerful, friendly young men who looked forward to her company. Two of them asked if she would write letters to their families and it was time for lunch when she eventually left the hospital wing.

After lunch she had a driving lesson with Matthews, then went upstairs to change into a fresh dress. She wanted to look smart for Major Bradshaw's visitor and spent half an hour replaiting her hair. It was a time-consuming chore and she wondered if she ought to think of having it cut short.

It was nearly half-past three when she went into the visitor's waiting room. A young man in army uniform was already standing looking out at the garden with his back to her. She stared at him for a moment, then a tingling sen-

271

sation started at the nape of her neck and she knew him even before he turned round.

'Shima!'

'Sorrel!' His face lit up with pleasure. 'What a wonderful surprise. They told me to wait here for a Miss Harris but I had no idea it was you.'

'I've been here for a while helping with the patients – but you're in the army. I thought you'd gone to America?'

'Did Tarina tell you that?' She nodded and he looked thoughtful. 'She must have got my message then. I intended to go but I settled in Ireland, then the war started and I came back.'

'So you joined up?'

'Yes, for my sins.' His eyes were intent on her face. 'And you're a nurse now?'

'Not quite. I just try to make myself useful – writing letters, fetching and carrying.' She glanced at the little watch pinned to her bodice. 'We ought to go up. Major Bradshaw will be waiting and he likes people to be punctual.'

'I mustn't get off on the wrong foot, must I? They tell me he's a bit of a hero, so I'm lucky to have been assigned to him. It's because he demands the highest standards where his horses are concerned and they think I'm quite handy with them.' He fell into step beside her as she took him upstairs and along the hall. 'You're not married to Jay yet then?'

'No. It . . . didn't work out. We broke up before he joined the army.'

'I'm sorry. I thought you two would make a go of it.'

'We thought so too but . . .' She paused as she realized that he probably hadn't heard the awful news about Tarina. 'There's something you ought to know, Shima. Could we meet later, after you finish with the Major?'

'Of course. Could I take you for a drink – or supper at the inn in the village? I'm staying there and the food is reasonable.'

'Perhaps a drink. We do have to talk.'

'It sounds serious?'

'It is. Too serious to talk about in a few minutes.' Sorrel

stopped outside Major Bradshaw's room. 'Knock and go in, Shima. I shall bring tea in soon.'

His expression was thoughtful and he was obviously concerned about what she had to tell him. 'I've got transport. I'll fetch you at seven this evening, for a meal.'

'All right.' She gave him a little push towards the Major's room. 'Go on, he's expecting you.'

She walked away as he knocked at the door. She had been so surprised to see Shima that for a moment she had forgotten that he had always thought of Tarina as his sister. He would be deeply shocked and angry to learn of her tragic death.

'Tarina dead?' Shima's eyes were coal black as he looked at her in the semi-darkness of the car. 'But how? What happened to her? She was so full of life . . .'

Sorrel explained carefully, telling him about the child, how Jay had taken Tarina to the infirmary and how she had run away.

'They discovered her nightdress in the reeds by the river but they've never found her . . . at least, I haven't been told if she has been found since I left home, but I don't think so.'

'And you say Jake was stabbed to death in a field near the camp?' Shima looked stunned, as if he found it difficult to comprehend. 'Could she have killed him? He was so strong, like a bull. But if she did . . . was that why she took her own life?'

'I don't know,' Sorrel said. 'I've wondered what really happened that night, but I don't suppose we shall ever know for sure.'

'Not if she's dead.'

Sorrel stared at him. 'So you think she might not be? I've always thought it strange that her body wasn't found somewhere downriver. But the nightdress?'

She might have left it there if she simply wanted to disappear.' Shima met Sorrel's worried gaze. 'She was a good swimmer . . . we both are. We had to be – the river was often our only means of washing.'

'But if she's alive, where would she go?'

'I don't know. Unless it was with the father of her child.'

'No.' Sorrel took a deep breath. She hadn't told him quite all of it but he had to know. 'She wouldn't have gone with him. There's more.'

Shima listened as she told him what had led to her quarrel with Jay, and what Fanny suspected. A little nerve flickered at his temple but it was the only sign he gave of his feelings.

'So you believe Richie was responsible – not Jay?'

'Yes, I do now. At first I thought it must be Jay but I've realized since that it wasn't like him to let a friend down. Fanny is sure the child was Richie's and . . . Tarina hinted at something but I didn't understand her at the time. I think now she believed he would marry her.'

'Perhaps. Richie might have lied to her. He must have. Jay wouldn't have betrayed you like that, Sorrel. He loves you.'

'Once I thought he did,' she said slowly. 'But now, I don't know.'

'You hurt his pride,' Shima said. 'He might find that difficult to forgive.'

'Yes, I know. He was always proud and stubborn. Ma says we're too much alike for our own good.'

'You're still in love with him, aren't you?'

'It still hurts,' she admitted and turned her face so that he shouldn't see how upset she was. 'But I shall get over it.'

'Or Jay will. He'll come back to you, when the war is over.'

'No. It's over. He has found someone else. He wrote to Fanny about a girl he has met in Belgium.'

'I'm sorry.' Shima touched her hand. 'Very sorry you've been hurt like this.'

'Forget about me. I'm sorry I had to give you such terrible news about your sister.'

'Tarina wasn't really my sister. She wanted us to be man and wife. If we had . . . but I didn't love her, not in that way. It could never have worked. She would have known and in the end she might have hated me.'

Sorrel choked on something between a laugh and a sob. 'Why do we all make such a mess of our lives? You . . .

274

Jay . . . Tarina . . . me. We've all been cursed, just as Sadie said.'

'Not cursed, that's foolishness. An old woman's babblings. If I knew the answer to all this I would tell you, but I suspect it's merely being human.' He leant towards her, his lips brushing hers gently. He smelt of something soft and woody, reminding her of camp fires and forest clearings. 'Jay was a fool to give you up that easily. If you were mine I would never let you go.'

'Oh, Shima . . .'

The tears spilled over then and he drew her into his arms, rocking her gently, his hands stroking her hair until the sudden storm of grief left her and she was still, then he wiped her cheeks with a clean handkerchief.

She choked on something between a laugh and a sob. 'I'm sorry. I didn't mean to cry all over you.'

'That's what friends are for, Sorrel. I'll always be your friend. Whenever you need me.'

'Thank you.' She blew her nose hard. 'Shall we go and have that meal now? I'm starving.'

'Me too.' His laughter was low and husky. 'I was going to ask if you would like a run into Winchester tomorrow? We could have lunch – perhaps get tickets for a show? I think there's a variety performance at one of the music halls.'

'A music hall?' She looked at him eagerly. 'I would like that, Shima. Very much.'

'Then we'll go,' he said. 'I'm officially on leave, though I have to report to Major Bradshaw once a day. I can go in in the morning then we'll have the rest of the day to ourselves.'

'It was wonderful . . . so colourful and bright. And the music!' They had left the theatre and were walking along the quiet street towards where Shima had parked his car. It was cold but the sky was still light, sprinkled with a trail of stars that lit up the outline of the great cathedral as it brooded over the town. Her head was full of the music she'd heard and she felt relaxed, free of care, as if she were floating on a cloud. 'Thank you so much for bringing me. I loved it all – especially the songs.'

275

'The songs of war,' Shima mused. 'Songs for marching – and for lovers.'

'Yes.' They stopped walking for a moment and she trembled as she gazed up at him. 'I hate this war, Shima. Promise me you won't get killed? Promise me you'll come back afterwards?'

He looked down into her face, his dark eyes seeming to turn to silver in the starlight. 'I'll come back for your sake. I promise you, Sorrel.'

'Shima . . .'

She caught her breath as he drew her close. Their lips touched. At first his kiss was gentle, seeking, but as she melted against him his arms tightened around her and his mouth became hungry, demanding a much deeper response.

'Shima . . .' She breathed a sigh as he let her go at last. 'I wish we . . .'

'No.' He touched her cheek with his fingertips, tracing the line of her jaw delicately. 'Don't say it, Sorrel. I love you. I've loved you for a long time – but it's too soon. I couldn't resist kissing you but it wasn't fair – to either of us.'

'Shima . . .' Her throat tightened nervously. 'You know I've always felt something . . .'

'Jay was there,' he said. 'He was between us. He still is but perhaps when the war is over . . .'

'Yes.' Her chest felt so tight she could hardly breathe. 'If it isn't Jay, I want it to be you. You will keep in touch – come to see me whenever you can?'

'Try stopping me.' He smiled, his teeth white in the starlight. 'We'd better get back before I forget all my good intentions and run off with you.'

She almost wished he would. There was a deep yearning in her, a hungry need for love. She wanted to lie in his arms and feel the tenderness of his loving, to be truly a woman . . . to banish this awful emptiness inside her. Yet in her heart she knew he was right. If they gave into this feeling between them now she might regret it, because a part of her still clung to her dream of being Jay's wife.

'Let's go home,' she said, 'but can we come again? To the theatre – while you're billeted here?'

'Yes, of course.' He smiled at her. 'Perhaps at the weekend if you can get time off?'

'Will you write to me, Shima?' They were taking a little stroll down to the stream before he left. He was driving Major Bradshaw back to camp the next morning and this was their last chance to be alone. 'Just now and then, to let me know you're all right?'

'I'm not one for writing letters, Sorrel. Perhaps a card occasionally so that you know I'm still alive.'

'That's enough. You will take care of yourself?'

'I'll come through, I promise you that.'

She nodded, then kissed his cheek. 'I know you will – somehow I feel it.'

'We'll meet again after the war. Before if I can manage it.' He touched his fingertips to her lips. 'What are you going to do now? Will you stay on here?'

'Matron has arranged an interview for me in London. She knows someone in one of the teaching hospitals and she thinks I could get a place there, to train as a nurse.'

'Yes, I think you would be good at it.' Shima looked thoughtful. 'You have patience and you care for people. You must let me know your new address.'

'Of course I will.'

'Good luck then.' He hesitated, then reached out and drew her close, kissing her tenderly on the mouth. 'You can write to me as much as you like, if you want to?'

'I should like that,' she said, and smiled teasingly. 'And I won't expect you to reply very often.'

'Think about me,' he said, letting her go. 'Remember I love you, Sorrel. I always shall.'

She watched as he walked away, then she went back to the hospital wing to say goodbye to Major Bradshaw. They talked for a while, then he got up and took something from the pocket of his army greatcoat.

'I want you to have this.' She was surprised as he handed her a small velvet box. The corners were worn and it was obviously not new. 'It belonged to my grandmother. I've no one else to give it to, and you've been patient with an old grouch.'

'Thank you.' She opened the box and touched the small gold brooch inside. It was oval in shape and engraved with flowers. 'It's lovely. I shall enjoy wearing it – and I'll think of you whenever I do.'

'Don't give yourself nightmares.' He laughed gruffly. 'I've a gift for Miss Sawle, too. You might give her this for me, if you will?'

'Yes, of course I will.' Sorrel took the box he offered. 'But wouldn't you prefer to give it to her yourself?'

'No, no . . . might embarrass her,' he said, looking odd. 'If you wouldn't mind . . . after I've gone?'

'I'm sure she will be pleased.'

His thick brows drew together. 'I believe you are applying to a training hospital?'

'Did Matron tell you?'

'She mentioned it. You will make a good nurse, Miss Harris, got the temperament for it.' He offered his hand and she took it. 'Goodbye – and good luck.'

'Goodbye, sir. I hope we'll see you again one day, but not as a patient.'

'You may well do so,' he replied with a smile. 'Perhaps when the war is over.'

Sorrel watched as he walked away. His farewell gifts were totally unexpected and she felt as if she were parting from a friend.

Fanny looked surprised when Sorrel gave her her present the next day. She opened the box, exclaiming over the pretty cameo pendant on a fine gold chain.

'That was nice of him,' she said. 'I wonder why he didn't give it to me when I said goodbye to him?'

'I think he was shy,' Sorrel said. 'He said it might embarrass you but I think it was the other way round. He likes you a lot, Fanny.'

'Does he?' She looked surprised. 'I hadn't realized. I shall write and thank him, of course.'

'Yes, you must do that,' Sorrel said. 'Have you had a letter from John today?'

'No – but I had one yesterday,' she said, sighing as she glanced towards the window. 'It has started raining again.'

'So it has.' Sorrel started to leave, then turned to look at

278

her. 'I'm going up to London next week for that interview – why don't you come with me? We could go shopping, or to the theatre.'

'Shima has given you a taste for the high life,' Fanny said teasingly, then became thoughtful. 'Do you think we could?'

'I don't see why not. We could stay overnight and come back on the early train the next morning.'

'We'll do it,' Fanny said. 'It will be exciting, Sorrel, and we're both due for a couple of days off.'

Chapter Thirty-One

Sorrel walked out of the hospital gates and stood looking round her; she felt as if she were dreaming and wondered if she ought to pinch herself to make sure she wasn't.

'You are exactly the sort of sensible girl we are looking for, Miss Harris. I shall make arrangements for you to stay at the nurses' hostel and you can start your training next month.'

The interview had gone much better than she had ever imagined. She was really going to be a nurse – to live in London, a city she had seen for the first time earlier that day when she and Fanny got off the train together.

The noise and the rush of people had confused her at first. Everyone seemed in such a hurry and the streets were full of traffic: trams and cars, lorries, and carts still pulled by horses adding to the general chaos.

'How does anyone ever get across the road?' she asked Fanny. 'It's terrifying.'

The hospital was set in large grounds of its own which gave it a false air of tranquillity; false because within its ancient walls there was a thriving community of nurses, doctors and patients, but outside the roar and bustle of the streets met Sorrel once more.

She had come in a cab for the interview but now she decided to walk a part of the way back to the hotel where she and Fanny were staying. It would be a good idea to get to know her way about before she actually started to work at the hospital. There was plenty of time before she had to get changed for their visit to the theatre that evening, and

Fanny had gone shopping so she wouldn't be waiting for her.

There was so much to see in London, far too much to take in all at once – huge shops with their windows full of exciting things, fine buildings, churches, parks, and the river with its boats chugging slowly past, their decks laden down with all kinds of merchandise bound for who knew where? As yet Sorrel saw it all as a kind of tapestry, not quite real, a little removed from her own experience of life – well-dressed people in their cars and taxis, city girls hurrying to work, street sweepers, costers and the ragged, bare-footed urchins who stared at her hungrily from the doors of terraced houses that didn't look as if they were fit for anyone to live in and ought by rights to have been pulled down years before.

Her wandering steps led her towards the river, through a little narrow lane with uneven cobbles and gutters clogged with rubbish. The smell was unpleasant and she was glad when she emerged into a wider street at the end and saw the bustle of traffic once more. There were several barrows selling fruit and vegetable by the side of the road and a woman with buckets of fresh flowers. A newspaper boy was shouting something about the news from France and she went to buy a paper from him.

As she turned after paying the boy she saw a woman standing a few feet away; she was arguing loudly with a man – a rather flashy man dressed in a striped suit and two-toned leather shoes. Something about the woman made Sorrel look twice and she gasped. Surely that was Tarina! At least it looked like her from this distance.

'Tarina!' she cried and began to walk hastily towards her. 'Tarina . . .'

The woman looked up, her face startled, then she turned and ran into the narrow lane Sorrel had walked down earlier. Sorrel ran to catch up with her but when she reached the top of the lane it was empty and there was no sign of the woman. Where could she have gone? Into one of the houses – or that rather seedy-looking pub she had passed on her way through? She hesitated, wondering what to do next. Should she go into the pub and inquire after Tarina?

She heard footsteps and swung round as the man she had noticed earlier approached. He was staring straight at her, his expression as black as thunder. 'Can you help me?' Sorrel asked, going up to him. 'Please – the woman you were speaking to just now – is her name Tarina?'

'Don't know what you're talking about,' he said, glaring at her angrily. 'Rosie is me sister. You ain't got no right comin' round 'ere frightening 'er. What she does ain't none of your business.' He reached out and grabbed Sorrel's arm. 'You tell your lot we don't want no interference from no do-gooders . . . just keep out of our way or you'll be sorry.'

'I don't know what you mean,' Sorrel said, wrenching away from him. 'I thought she was someone I knew . . . a friend of mine.'

'Rosie don't know you, nor does she want to,' he said, and swore at her. 'Git out of 'ere or you'll feel the back of me 'and! And tell that interfering lot at the Mission that there'll be trouble if they come here again.'

He had obviously mistaken her for someone else. Sorrel backed away from him. He was a coarse-featured, harsh-spoken man and looked capable of carrying out his threats. She walked back to the main street, glad of all the people going about their business. A few minutes later she caught a tram, feeling safer riding than walking. What a horrible man he was! Had she been mistaken? He had said the woman was his sister, but he would not hesitate to lie if it suited him, she was sure.

She was still feeling a bit shaken and breathed deeply as she looked out of the window at the brightly lit shops. She must have made a mistake. It couldn't have been Tarina, of course it couldn't. Tarina was dead. Or was she?

Sorrel forgot about the unpleasant incident when she met Fanny for tea and then hurried up to her room to wash and change for the theatre. She was brushing her hair and humming one of the tunes that were popular at the music halls when the door of her room was thrust open and Fanny came in. Sorrel turned with a smile but it died on her lips as she saw the look on her friend's face.

'What's wrong, Fanny? What has happened?'

'I telephoned Celia to let her know where we were staying...' She gasped as if she found it hard to breathe and Sorrel saw that she had been crying. 'She told me... there was a telegram...'

'Fanny!' Sorrel's heart caught with fear. 'My dearest – tell me. Is it John?'

'Yes.' Fanny's eyes were wild with pain. 'He has been killed in action, Sorrel. Aunt Celia told me his parents rang her... it was a reconnaissance mission in some woods and they walked into an enemy patrol... he was killed instantly. I can't bear it... I can't bear it!'

She rushed at Sorrel, sobbing bitterly as she collapsed in her arms, her whole body shaking with the force of her grief.

'What am I going to do?' she cried. 'I can't bear it. I can't... I can't... it's too cruel. Never to be his wife... have his children...'

'Fanny, my dearest. I'm so very sorry.'

How inadequate that word was. It could never express Sorrel's deep sorrow for her friend's pain, nor could it ease her own grief. Tears filled Sorrel's eyes as she held Fanny, stroking her hair and remembering the shy smile John Parkinson had given her when he'd spoken of his feelings for this young woman. They had only just begun to love and know each other and now it was over, finished before it had properly begun. Life was too cruel!

They sat down on the edge of the bed, holding each other, their tears mingling. It was a long time before Fanny stopped crying, but at last she drew away from Sorrel and wiped her eyes. She stood up and went over to the wash basin to splash her face in cold water. Then she turned to face Sorrel, her features suddenly cold and hard.

'We would have had that night together if it hadn't been for my mother,' she said, and the bitterness in her voice shocked Sorrel. 'She robbed me of that. I shall never forgive her. I hate her.'

'Oh, Fanny.' Sorrel's heart ached for her but nothing she could do or say would bring John back. 'Please don't say things like that. You don't mean it – not really.'

'I do.' Her eyes glittered with anger. 'It's her fault. I shall never speak to her again. Now I'm going to bed. It's too late to get the train home, and I don't feel like going to the theatre.'

'No, of course not. Can't I do something... get you a drink ... anything?'

'There's nothing anyone can do,' she said, 'but thank you for asking. Good night, Sorrel.'

Sorrel watched as she left the room. Fanny was distraught, out of her mind with grief. She didn't know what she was saying. She couldn't hate her own mother: it would destroy her.

Celia was upset for Fanny's sake. She tried to be cheerful but kept looking at her with sorrowful eyes, just as Sorrel's father had at her after she'd broken her engagement to Jay.

'I've telephoned Rebecca,' she told Sorrel a few days after their return from London. 'But she won't come. She says Fanny should go home.'

'She won't go. She's very bitter and angry.'

'My poor dear Fanny. I can't bear to see her so unhappy. It makes me feel ill.'

Celia dabbed at her eyes and went upstairs to lie down. She loved Fanny but didn't know how to cope with her in her present mood.

Fanny was desperately unhappy. She stayed in her room for almost a week, then came downstairs looking pale and red-eyed.

'I shall go mad if I stay cooped up much longer,' she said. 'There's no point in crying. It won't bring him back, will it?'

'No.' Sorrel moved towards her, her hands outstretched, but Fanny stepped aside, shaking her head.

'No, don't pity me, Sorrel. I've accepted it now and decided to get on with my life.'

'Try to think of the good things ...'

'Like what?' Her eyes were empty as she stared across the room. 'Two days ... two wasted days. If we had only taken the chance when we had it, I might be carrying his child. I might have John's child inside me now.'

Sorrel could think of no way to comfort her, so she merely said, 'What will you do? Why don't you apply to train as a nurse?'

'I've thought about it.' Fanny sighed as she looked at her. 'It isn't for me, Sorrel. No, I shall just stay here with Aunt Celia and do what I can. After the war we shall probably travel together.' Her shoulders sagged. 'There's nothing else left.'

'Fanny . . .'

Her mouth twisted in the travesty of a smile. 'We haven't been very lucky in love, have we?'

'No.' Sorrel went to her. 'But we have each other, Fanny. I shan't be far away. We'll see one another often and we can write or phone most days. I promise I shan't neglect you.'

'Yes.' Fanny blinked hard. 'We'll always be friends, won't we?'

'You can come up to town sometimes – and I can come here for weekends when I get time off.'

'Yes, I've still got you and Aunt Celia.' Fanny gave her a bright smile. 'I shall come down for dinner this evening. I've decided to make an effort for Celia's sake. She's terribly upset about all this – it isn't fair to her.'

Fanny's manner was so brittle, so unlike her. But she was doing her best. There was nothing they could do for her but let her come to terms with her grief in her own way.

Fanny drove Sorrel to the station. She had become an accomplished driver over the past weeks and negotiated the bends in the narrow country roads with flair and at considerable speed.

'Well, you're off then,' she said in the new bright tone she used to cover her feelings. 'Off to the big city.'

'I shall miss you, Fanny.'

'Who knows? I might turn up at your hospital with an ambulance one day,' she said. 'I can be useful in that way even if I can't do what you're doing.'

'We don't know if I can yet. I might fail horribly.'

'You won't. Besides, you can always come back to us.' Fanny kissed her cheek. 'I have great faith in you, Sorrel.'

'Take care of yourself.' Sorrel looked at her anxiously. 'You are all right, aren't you?'

'I'm managing,' said Fanny. 'What else can I do?'

Beneath her air of fragility there was a strength none of them had suspected. She was hurting badly but wouldn't just lie down and die – anymore than Sorrel had.

'We're more alike than we realized,' Sorrel said, squeezing her hand. 'Wish me luck, Fanny.'

'Of course I do.'

Sorrel waved to her from the train as it pulled out of the station. Sorrel's heart ached for Fanny and for herself. The future seemed to hold little promise for either of them – yet they were both still young, still eager for life. Perhaps there was yet a way for them both to find happiness.

Chapter Thirty-Two

'Going somewhere special?' Sorrel waited at the head of the stairs as the girl came along the landing towards her. 'You do look nice in that frock. Is it new?'

'Thank you, Jenny. Yes, it is new. Some friends of mine gave it to me for Christmas.' Sorrel smoothed the long, flowing skirt of her evening dress. 'Fanny has invited me to a party. It's being held at a hotel up West by someone she knows and she was asked to bring another girl.'

'Lucky you,' Jenny Benson said, and pulled a face. 'I'm on duty for the whole of the New Year festivities.'

'I worked over Christmas,' Sorrel reminded her. 'But to be honest I'm not really looking forward to this party. I would just as soon go to bed. I'm only going because Fanny would be upset if I didn't.'

'You'll enjoy it when you get there.'

'Yes, I expect so.'

Sorrel ran down the stairs as someone shouted up that a car had come to collect her. The driver opened the back door and she got in, closing her eyes for a moment as he drove away from the nurses' hostel.

She was tired, that was the trouble. It was the last night of 1916 and the war had proved to be bloodier and longer than anyone had imagined. There was a steady stream of injured men passing through the wards and never enough hours in a day to cope with all the work.

Sorrel didn't mind how hard she worked; she didn't mind how many bedpans she had to scrub or the way the disinfectant stung her hands, making them painful sometimes. She had grown used to seeing the most horrendous injuries, to the smells and the long hours – but she hated it when the patients died despite all their efforts to save them. They'd had three deaths on the ward that day . . .

'Well, here we are then, miss.'

'Already?' Sorrel was startled as the driver opened her door. 'Thank you. I didn't realize. I must have been dreaming.'

'Half asleep, I shouldn't wonder,' he said with a grin. 'My youngest girl is in the VADs and she sleeps for twelve hours at a go on her day off. I tell her she's a fool to do it – but I'm proud of her. You girls are doing a marvellous job.'

'Thank you.' Sorrel shook the creases from her dress. 'Happy New Year to you and your daughter.'

'And to you, miss.'

Sorrel went into the hotel. The party was taking place in a large reception suite on the second floor. The lift operator took her up and she could hear music and laughter as she stepped out. She hesitated at the open door, her stomach fluttering with nerves. It wasn't the first of these parties she'd been to on her own. Fanny was always inviting her to some function or other and got upset if she didn't go.

Sorrel's brow wrinkled as she thought about her friend. Fanny seemed to know so many young men these days. Whenever Sorrel saw her there were always three or four of them hanging around – and some of the women she mixed with were what her mother would term a 'fast crowd'. They wore make-up, smoked and drank far more than was good for them.

Fanny was desperately unhappy, of course. She laughed a lot and a stranger might have thought she didn't have a care in the world, but Sorrel knew it was all an act. Fanny was mixed up inside, her grief and bitterness a festering wound that didn't seem to heal.

Sorrel saw her almost as soon as she entered the room. She was laughing, surrounded as usual by an admiring crowd of young men.

'Sorrel!' She waved at her. 'Come and join us.'

'Sorry I'm late, Fanny. I had to stay on at the hospital for longer than I expected because . . .'

288

'It doesn't matter.' Fanny kissed her, then laughed and rubbed the lip rouge from her cheek. 'You know Bertie, don't you? Keith . . . Trevor . . . Paul – oh, and this is Michael Kingston a new friend.'

Something in Fanny's tone made Sorrel look twice at Michael Kingston. He was a man of perhaps thirty dressed in civilian clothes, rather smart with fair hair and extremely blue eyes. Handsome but dangerous was Sorrel's first thought – and those eyes had all the warmth of an Arctic floe. She didn't like him but she thought Fanny might – quite a lot.

'I've met everyone but Mr Kingston,' she said, and smiled because he was a friend of Fanny's.

'Michael, please,' he murmured, clasping her hand in a way she disliked. 'Fanny has told me so much about you, Sorrel. I feel we know each other already.'

'Do you?' She lifted her chin. 'She hasn't mentioned you.'

Bertie laughed and winked at her behind Kingston's back. 'Come and dance,' he said, whisking her away before she had a chance to refuse. 'Can't stand that chap – Ministry Big Wig so they tell me. Seems a cold fish.'

'Yes, that's what I thought.' She looked up at him as they began to dance. Bertie Saunders was one of Fanny's nicest followers and Sorrel knew he was in love with her. 'How are you, Bertie?'

'Fine. Much better. They'll be sending me back soon, I expect.'

'Fanny will miss you. We all will.'

Bertie nodded but looked gloomy, his eyes straying towards Fanny. 'I wish I could believe she would notice – but I doubt it, the way things are.'

'She's fond of you, you know she is.'

'Treats me like a brother,' he said. 'Not quite what a chap has in mind when he's head over heels.'

'Poor Bertie,' Sorrel said teasingly. 'You know she was in love with someone who was killed, don't you?' He nodded and she squeezed his hand. 'Don't give up on her, Bertie. She'll get over it one day.'

'You're a nice person, Sorrel.' He gave her a rueful look. 'Why couldn't I have fallen for you?'

'Because you have far too much sense. I'm a dedicated working girl and besides, I have someone.'

'Just my luck!' Bertie sighed. 'Is he here this evening?'

'No, but I had a card from him this morning. He expects to get leave soon. Perhaps next month.'

'I'm glad for you.' Bertie smiled as their dance ended. 'Make the most of it when he comes.'

'We're going away together,' Sorrel said. 'Perhaps to the sea.'

'Lucky man,' he said. 'I'll get you a drink, shall I?'

'Just lemonade,' Sorrel replied. 'I want to talk to Fanny but I shan't stop much longer. I'm on duty at seven in the morning.'

'Surely you will see the New Year in?' Fanny looked disappointed when Sorrel told her she was leaving an hour or so later. 'We've hardly seen each other all evening.'

'You've been occupied,' Sorrel said. 'Poor Bertie thinks you've deserted him.'

'Bertie is sweet but he wants more than I can give,' Fanny said, looking at a spot somewhere beyond Sorrel's shoulder. 'Michael doesn't.'

'Are you sure about him?' Sorrel asked anxiously. 'I know I shouldn't say this but I don't trust him. He's dangerous, Fanny.'

'Yes, he is rather. Perhaps that's why I like him. I can't hurt him, Sorrel.'

'You're the one I care about. I don't want to see you hurt.'

'It won't happen.' Fanny smiled. 'When can I really see you? We haven't had a proper talk for ages.'

'Shima is coming home on leave soon. He said he might take me to Eastbourne or somewhere on the south coast. When we come back we could call, if that's all right?'

'Of course it is. You know Celia is always pleased to see you. Be sure and come, Sorrel. I miss you.'

'I've arranged to have a week off so we'll spend some of it with you,' Sorrel promised. She suddenly hugged Fanny. 'Take care of yourself, dearest. I must go. I'm nearly asleep on my feet and my taxi should be here.'

'Go on then.' Fanny released her reluctantly. 'But let me know when you're coming so that I'm not driving an ambulance to the other side of the country or something silly like that.'

Sorrel promised she would, said good night to the others and left. Despite all the new friends she had made at the hospital Fanny was the one she cared for most – perhaps because she was Jay's sister.

She sighed as she settled in the back of the car and closed her eyes. Her old life seemed so far away now. Had she ever been that young, naive girl who believed that marriage to the man she loved would bring lasting happiness?

She still thought about Jay sometimes when she was lying in bed at night, wondered where he was, what he was doing and if he was safe. But she thought about Shima, too. He sent her postcards every so often. They were brief, often just one line and his name. He certainly wasn't much of a letter writer – not like Jay. He still wrote long, funny letters to Fanny. Occasionally Sorrel read one but usually she refused to. It hurt when Jay mentioned the Belgian girl he was still seeing sometimes.

Jay had made his choice. There was no point in dwelling on the past. Shima was coming home soon and she wanted to see him. She wanted to see him very much.

'You look wonderful,' said Shima, his expression warm and caressing as he took the bag from her hand and loaded it into the back of the car. 'I've been waiting for this day for a long time. Now I can't believe it has actually come.'

'How did you manage it?' Sorrel asked. 'Most of the men can't get home leave unless they've been wounded.'

'It was Major Bradshaw,' he replied. 'He swung it for me – and asked me to remember him to you and Fanny.'

'He seems such a crusty old thing at first,' Sorrel said with a laugh. 'But underneath he's very kind, and I think he likes Fanny a lot.'

'She writes to him every now and then,' Shima said. 'I see her name on some of the letters he sends, and I can tell when he's had one from her. I think you're right about him liking her.'

'I promised her we would call on our way back from the coast. You don't mind, do you?'

'Of course not.' Shima touched her cheek. 'Whatever makes you happy.'

'Oh, Shima.' Emotion caught at her throat. 'It's so good to see you. So many men come back shattered in mind and body but you – you're just the same.'

'Maybe I've been luckier than most. Major Bradshaw was assigned to headquarters. The Big Brass think he has done his bit and won't send him forward. He'll wangle it in the end, though.'

'Perhaps the war will end soon.'

'I can't see it, Sorrel. Things are pretty grim out there right now, especially for the poor devils at the Front.'

'Don't!' she begged. 'Sometimes I think I can't stand any more suffering. Let's forget it for the next few days, if we can.'

'I want to make this holiday as happy as I can for you, Sorrel.' He moved towards her, taking her in his arms. 'I love you very much.'

'And I love you,' she said, lifting her face for his kiss. 'Let's make the most of our time together. I'm so tired of sickness and pain . . . and of being alone.'

'Then we won't think of it,' he promised, his lips moving softly over hers. 'We won't think of the future at all . . . just of being together.'

'Aren't you cold?' Shima asked. 'That wind off the sea is bitter. You don't want to catch a chill.'

She turned to him, her eyes glowing. 'I love it here,' she said. 'Look at those waves – they're so huge, even from up here.'

They were standing at the top of Beachy Head, having walked up from the town of Eastbourne. Below them the water raged and foamed about the cliffs and the lighthouse looked like a toy as it was buffeted by the angry sea. Behind them stretched the undulating downs and the long slope down to the road. Sorrel's hair had escaped from its usual confines and was blowing in wisps across her forehead. Her cheeks were pink from the cold and she looked beautiful.

'I love you so much,' he said. 'You'll never know how much I've longed for you, my darling. Thank you for giving me this time. I shall never forget it.'

'Let's go back to the hotel.' Sorrel moved closer to him. 'I want to be with you, Shima – really with you.'

'Are you sure?' He looked doubtful. 'I'm not asking for any more than you want to give.'

'I know that, but I want us to be lovers.'

'Sorrel . . . Sorrel, my darling.' He said her name reverently, making it sound like music. 'My sweet, lovely woman.'

Sorrel went into his arms. She was a woman, not a child, and she had a woman's needs. She was tired of being alone, of the empty aching nights when she longed for warmth and tenderness. She needed to be loved, to forget everything in his arms.

It was warm in their room, protected from the storm raging outside. Sorrel lay with her head resting against Shima's shoulder, her eyes closed, the taste of him still on her lips.

His hand moved slowly down the arch of her back and she felt his breath shudder against her hair. 'You're like the best wine,' he murmured. 'You set my senses swimming and I keep wanting more.'

'At your service, sir,' she said, raising her head to look into his dark eyes in the soft light of the fire their host had obligingly lit for them. 'Drink your fill.'

'Wicked, wicked woman,' he said, kissing her forehead then the tip of her nose and finally her mouth. 'How could I refuse such an offer?'

His hands moved over her, caressing and seeking, arousing her to a quivering, aching need that cried out for satisfaction. She moaned as he thrust into her again and again, arching her hips to meet him with a passion that equalled his own.

Afterwards they lay entwined, drifting into a warm, drugging sleep.

In the morning Sorrel awoke to find him lying propped up on one elbow beside her so that he could watch her as she slept.

'What time is it?'

'Past ten. We've missed breakfast but we'll get something out.'

'You should have woken me.'

'You looked so peaceful – and lovely.' He touched her hair, which had spread out over the pillow, letting it fall through his fingers. 'You have beautiful hair. I'm glad you haven't cut it.'

'I ought to,' Sorrel said, and flicked a wisp out of her eyes. 'It takes ages to dry after I've washed it and I don't always have much time.'

'No, I'm sure you don't.' He smoothed his finger over her mouth. 'No regrets about last night?'

'No.' She smiled up at him and stretched like a contented kitten. 'None at all.'

'Good.' He bent to kiss her. 'Shall we go and find some breakfast?'

'Later,' she said. 'Do you think we dare take a bath? There's a notice on the wall asking us to be sparing with the hot water but . . .'

'Then we'll just have to share it, won't we?' He grinned wickedly and pulled the clothes off her. 'Come on, sleepy head, I want my breakfast.'

'I almost wish I hadn't promised Fanny we would call,' Sorrel said as Shima stopped the car a short distance from the house. 'We could have had another day together.'

'We'll have other days,' he promised, and leaned over to kiss her. 'When this is all over, I'll come back and we'll get married.'

'Yes.' Sorrel looked at the simple band of garnets and pearls set in yellow gold which he had given her as a promise. 'When it's all over.'

'It isn't an engagement ring,' he'd said when he slipped it on the third finger of her right hand. 'It's for friendship – and the hope of better things.'

'We'd better go,' he said now. 'Your friends will be waiting. We mustn't disappoint them.'

'No.' She reached up to touch his hair, stroking it back from his forehead. 'Fanny is so unhappy, Shima. She pretends not to be but underneath she is still hurting.'

'You're happy, aren't you?' His eyes were thoughtful as he looked at her. 'You're not . . .'

'Still in love with Jay?' Sorrel shook her head. 'It's over, long over. I love you. Very much.'

'Then I don't mind sharing our last day with your friends.' He started the car again. 'We've got the rest of our lives to look forward to.'

Sorrel had just finished changing for dinner when Fanny came into the room. Sorrel knew as soon as she saw her that something was wrong.

'What's the matter?' she asked. 'You're upset.'

'You know me so well.' Fanny took a small cigarette case from her suit pocket, selected a thin white tube and fitted it into a black holder, then lit it. 'You're so much wiser than me, Sorrel. You warned me, I should have listened.'

'Michael Kingston?'

'Yes.' Something flickered in Fanny's eyes. 'We had been to a party and I suppose I'd had a little too much to drink. He drove me back to my hotel and insisted on seeing me safely into my room. Then he started kissing me and . . . he forced me.'

'You mean, he raped you?' Sorrel's face went white with shock and anger. 'The filthy devil! I hope you went to the police?' She saw the look in Fanny's eyes. 'Of course you didn't . . . you couldn't . . .'

'It was my own fault. I let it go too far before I said no.' Fanny shuddered. 'It was horrible. I feel so dirty . . . so used.'

'It wasn't your fault.'

'But it was,' Fanny said. 'He said I led him on – and I suppose I did, in a way. I wanted to play with fire and I got burned. I have only myself to blame.'

'I still say it wasn't your fault. He had no right to force you, even if you did lead him on a bit.' Sorrel was seething with anger. She would have liked to scratch Michael Kingston's eyes out, or roast him over a slow fire. 'Bertie said he was a cold fish. He couldn't stand him.'

'Bertie didn't like him.' Fanny's voice caught. 'He was in love with me himself.'

Sorrel heard the suppressed sob. 'What do you mean – *was* in love with you?'

'Bertie was killed a few days ago, soon after they sent him back to the Front.' Fanny's eyes held the glitter of despair. 'Of course you wouldn't know. His sister told me on the phone this morning.'

'Fanny! I'm so sorry. He was your friend, wasn't he?'

'Yes.' Her smile was ragged, painted on like a clown's. 'It was just as well I didn't fall in love with him, wasn't it?' Her voice broke as the tears suddenly came flooding out. 'Bertie was such a dear man, so kind and . . .' She lifted her head, her eyes glittering. 'Life is hell sometimes, isn't it?'

'Yes.' Sorrel put her arms around her. 'Yes, it is, Fanny. Sheer hell.'

'Goodbye . . . take care of yourself!' Sorrel waved as Shima dropped her at the gates of the hospital. 'Come back safely.'

She sighed as the car disappeared from sight, then turned as Jenny Benson came up to her.

'First day back?' Jenny asked with a sympathetic smile. 'You look as if you had a good time – lucky you! I saw your friend when he collected you. He's very good-looking.'

'Yes, he is,' Sorrel agreed. 'Are you just off?'

'I've been on night duty,' Jenny said. 'I'm whacked, dead on my feet. Sister Jones was in a terrible mood last night. She never gave us a minute.'

'I know what you mean. She can be a terror, but Sister Norden is worse.' Sorrel glanced at her fob watch, which was pinned to her apron. 'I'd better hurry or I shall be late.'

'See you this evening then. Bye.'

Sorrel waved and hurried into the hospital. The familiar smell met her: disinfectant and . . . what was it? Boiled greens, she thought, wrinkling her nose. Or sickness.

Her wonderful time away with Shima was already beginning to fade, to seem like a dream. Reality had set in with the news of Bertie's death and Fanny's unhappiness.

'You should go home, Fanny,' Sorrel had said before she left Rothsay. 'Make it up with your mother.'

'I can't. Don't ask me to see her.' Fanny had turned her face aside. 'I've had a letter from Jay. He has been on leave but they're sending him up to the Front again shortly. He asked me if I'd seen you recently.'

'Did he?' Sorrel felt a twist of pain inside her. Why did it still hurt when Fanny said things like that? She had told Shima it was over and it was . . . it was! 'I wonder why?'

'I'm sure he still cares about you.'

'No, I don't think so,' Sorrel replied. 'Besides, it doesn't matter anymore. It's over between us. Shima asked me to marry him and I said yes.'

Fanny had looked upset but they hadn't quarrelled over it. Their friendship had grown stronger over the years; they were closer than most sisters, sharing each other's pain and pleasures.

So Jay was going back to the the Front soon, Sorrel thought as she went on duty. She could only pray that he would be safe. She still prayed for him sometimes, just as she did for Shima and all the other young men out there.

Chapter Thirty-Three

Jay paused in the act of pitching straw on to a stack and stretched his shoulders. The sun was warm on his head, making him feel at ease with himself. He was enjoying this break from the war; it was almost like being home again. Louise's family had accepted him as one of them and he spent his leave with them as often as he could. If it were not for the distant boom of the guns he could have forgotten the misery and the hardships of the past months.

'Jay . . .' Louise's cry broke into his thoughts and he turned to look for her. She was running across the meadow towards him, her long hair blowing like spun silk about her face. 'Jay, I have a letter for you.'

He put down his pitchfork and smiled at her. She was so lovely, a breath of fresh air after the stench and filth of the trenches. Now that she was close he could smell the perfume of her skin and it stirred forgotten feelings deep inside him.

'Louise,' he said as she greeted him, her lips just feathering his cheek in a kiss of welcome. 'I didn't know you were coming today.'

'I changed duties with a friend,' she said, laughing up at him. 'A letter came to the house for you so I brought it to you, in case it is important.'

'That was good of you.' He glanced at the envelope, recognizing the writing as Fanny's. 'It's from my sister.'

Louise nodded, seeing the flicker of disappointment in his eyes. She understood what he did not say: that he had hoped it might be from that girl, the girl who had hurt him so badly – the girl Louise hated with all her being.

298

'Shall I go away while you read it?'

'I'll just skim through it,' he said, and slit the envelope open. 'I've almost finished here. We could go for a walk if you like?'

He looked down into her pretty face, then, without thinking about what he was doing, reached out for her, drawing her close. She pressed herself against him, her lips opening in expectation of his kiss. Bending his head he began to kiss her, desperately, passionately, with all the lonely longing and frustration he had kept inside for so many months.

Louise kissed him back, her body moulding into his with a natural abandon that turned Jay's loins to molten heat. He held her away from him as he said in a husky voice, 'I shouldn't have kissed you like that, Louise. It wasn't right . . . it wasn't fair to you.'

'Why talk of right and wrong?' she whispered, her eyes alight with love. 'You need me and I love you. Who knows what will happen tomorrow? Live for today, for this moment . . .'

'Louise,' he groaned, gathering her to him fiercely. 'I want you so much but it isn't fair to you. You know how I feel about . . .'

She pressed her fingers to his lips. 'This is what I want,' she said. 'If this is all I can ever have, it will be enough.' She took his hand, pulling as he hesitated. 'Come with me now. I know where we can be alone.'

It was a misty morning, damp and cold as March often is, just another day in the trenches for thousands of British soldiers . . . until the roar of six thousand German guns heralded the beginning of a terrible battle, a battle that Jay would never forget.

Before it started he was lying on his back thinking about the letter from Louise. How strange that he should never have considered the possibility that she might conceive his child. Those stolen moments in the hayloft last autumn had held a dreamlike quality; he had thought only of snatching at happiness, of easing his loneliness. Louise had begged him to put all thought of the future out of his mind – but

299

now she had written wanting him to commit himself to her and the child.

My father was angry but now he does not mind so much. He says he is ready to welcome you as a son. We could marry and live here on the farm. Papa says . . .'

At that point Jay had screwed the letter into a ball and thrown it away. Surely Louise couldn't really expect that he would marry her and live on her father's farm after the war was over? They said it couldn't go on for much longer, though to him it seemed as if it would never end. Louise had sworn that she would never ask anything of him. She knew . . . she knew that he was still in love with Sorrel. He had told her right at the beginning.

The sudden roar of the guns interrupted his thoughts. He was on his feet as the other men jerked awake. They were used to the distant boom of the German artillery but this was different. As they stared at one another the flap of their makeshift rented accommodation was pulled aside.

'Right, you lot,' the sergeant's voice cracked. 'Start of a busy day. Get yourselves out here on the double.'

'Sounds as if Jerry means business this time,' Jay said. 'What do you reckon, Sarge?'

'How the hell do I know? I'm only the poor bugger who has to look after the likes of you. Sawle, you're on stretcher detail. Pick your team and get yourself up there!'

'Sir!' Jay swung round, running a practised eye over the men. 'Prentice, Johnson, Smith – you're with me. You heard what the sergeant said, move it!'

The bombardment went on for five hours, during which time the mist had settled into a thick fog. Jay and his team wore gas masks as they worked, ferrying the injured to the casualty station. At first it was sheer confusion but then the pattern of the enemy's fire became clear; it was directed mainly against headquarters, signal-centres and battery-positions. They were trying to wreck the communications and cause as much panic as possible.

The fog hampered riflemen, machine-gunners and Jay's

small team alike. The reinforcement of air-defence so desperately needed was out of the question; no planes could take off while the weather was so bad.

In the redoubts of the Forward Zones men were fighting heroically and dying where they stood, refusing to surrender. The men of the 173rd Brigade resisted throughout the morning, some managed to hold out until the next day, but they were not alone in distinguishing themselves. It was against the centre of the 14th and the right of the 36th Divisions that the main assault came, and there that the enemy broke through in overwhelming numbers. Elsewhere the resistance went on, holding out despite the odds.

The Germans were to win considerable success on the Somme that day of 21 March 1918. The following day was equally bad for the beleaguered British army, but by that time the war was over for Jay. He was lying unconscious at the bottom of a muddy trench, a German bullet in his shattered leg.

The last thing he remembered thinking before he passed out was that now he wouldn't have to make a choice between Louise and Sorrel.

Chapter Thirty-Four

She was standing looking out of the window at the dull grey sky; a storm had been brewing all day and it looked as if it might break soon.

'Nurse Harris.' The young doctor tapped her on her arm. He was tall, painfully thin and rather attractive. 'Sister asked me to tell you she would like to see you in her office – at once.'

'Oh, Lord! What have I done now?'

'I don't know – something terribly wicked if I know you,' he said, eyes gleaming with mischief. 'You had better not keep Sister waiting. She has been on the warpath all morning, and from the look on her face it was serious.'

'Wish me luck!'

For the past three and a half years a summons from Sister Norden had been enough to make Sorrel's heart thump wildly. During the first year or two of her training she had been in trouble all too often.

'You are too impulsive,' Sister had told her several times. 'You act independently. Remember, we are a team in this hospital. You must curb your desire to run before you can walk.'

She had tried but it hadn't been easy to discipline herself at first. Her mother was right when she'd told her that she had been spoiled at home, doing much as she pleased once her work was finished, but she had learned to adapt, though slowly and sometimes painfully. This last year or so, however, the requests to visit Sister's office had come less often and she had thought she was doing well. Sister Norden had actually praised her the previous day – but it seemed she was in trouble again.

She paused outside Sister's door, taking a deep breath before knocking. She was instructed to enter, and, when she went in, stood nervously in front of Sister's desk, which was cluttered with piles of reports.

'Ah, yes, Nurse Harris.'

'You asked to see me, Sister?'

She looked grave, her long, thin fingers toying with the pen she was holding. Sorrel's heart sank as she saw her expression. What on earth had she done to upset her? Her mind searched frantically for a breach of the strict rules but couldn't think of anything – unless it was because she had sat a little too long with a young soldier who had asked her to hold his hand until he went to sleep. He had died as he slept, slipping away very gradually and peacefully while she sat by his side.

'I'm very sorry,' Sister said at last, 'but I have bad news for you. You may sit down if you wish.'

'Sister?' The note of sympathy in her voice terrified Sorrel. 'Bad news?' She clung to the back of a chair for support but remained standing.

'Yes, I'm afraid so. A Mr Aden Sawle telephoned. He says he will be at the nurses' hostel to collect you at two this afternoon.'

'Aden telephoned?' Her legs felt odd suddenly and she sat down. 'Is – is it my father?'

'Yes.' Sister looked at her gravely. 'Were you aware that he was unwell?'

'No – at least, I thought he might . . .'

It was two months since she'd been home for her last leave. Her father hadn't seemed his usual self but he had sworn he was fine when she'd left to return to duty.

'Just a bit of indigestion, lass,' he'd said as he kissed her goodbye. 'It's my own fault for eating too much of your ma's dinner.'

'It appears he had a weak heart,' Sister went on. 'He collapsed at his work yesterday and died at home last night. You will naturally want to go home at once.'

'Yes, yes, I must. My mother . . .'

303

Her mother wouldn't know what to do. She hadn't said much good of Sid and might have grumbled at the way he constantly trailed in mud from the yard, but he was her life. May would be like a fish out of water without him, floundering around with no place to go.

'You are excused duty on compassionate grounds,' Sister said. 'Please let me know as soon as possible whether you intend to return or not. While we are not as busy as we were a few months ago – thank goodness! – we always need nurses of your calibre.' She broke off as she saw Sorrel wasn't listening. 'But you can't think of work now. I'm very sorry, nurse. This is a terrible shock for you.'

Death was an everyday occurrence on the wards: young men dying of terrible wounds, children slipping away from them, quietly, pitifully, breaking their hearts because they could do so little for them, women exhausted by continual childbirth and deprivation. They saw it all in the hospital but the death of a loved one was never expected, never easy.

'Yes . . . a terrible shock.'

Sorrel could hardly take it in. Her father dead? It wasn't possible. Not her father. He was too big and strong and solid. He couldn't die, not her father!

Tears blurred her eyes as she left Sister's office. Her father dead . . . it didn't make sense. He had always been there, providing a sense of security and continuity in her life. Yet she had noticed something when she was home. If only he had told her he was ill! But of course he wouldn't. He had never forgiven himself for coming between her and Jay. He wouldn't tell her he was ill because it might have made her feel she ought to give up her job and stay at home.

'Oh, Pa . . . Pa,' she wept. 'Why didn't I realize? Why didn't I know you were so ill?'

She telephoned Fanny from the nurses' home. She knew what had happened and was full of concern for Sorrel.

'I wanted to fetch you myself,' she said, 'but Celia still isn't over her chill and Father said he would come up and take you home.'

'I'm sorry Celia is still poorly,' Sorrel said. 'Give her my love, won't you?'

'She was saying you must come and stay when you can.'

'I was coming next week but . . .'

'Of course,' Fanny said. 'You can't plan anything now, not for a while. Write to me, Sorrel, telephone if you can.'

'Yes . . . when I can.'

Sorrel was thoughtful as she replaced the receiver. Since her unpleasant experience with Michael Kingston, Fanny hadn't been up to town very often. She lived quietly with Celia and refused invitations from all but the closest of her friends, almost as if she had decided that the only way to avoid being hurt was to hide away from the world.

Oh, Fanny,' Sorrel said to herself as she started to pack her clothes. 'Why do things always have to hurt so much?' Tears stung her eyes. 'Pa . . . why did you have to die? I love you. I love you so.'

Aden arrived five minutes early but she was ready for him and waiting downstairs. He took her cases and put them in the back of his car, then opened the passenger door for her. Sorrel blew her nose hard and he touched her hand in sympathy.

'I'm so sorry.'

'I can't believe it,' she whispered. 'He said he was all right – that it was just indigestion.'

'He hadn't been well for a while.' Aden looked at her sadly. 'I think that's why he started drinking again.'

'I didn't know he had. Ma didn't tell me.'

'She didn't want to worry you.' Aden closed her door then got in beside her. 'It hasn't been easy for her these last few months. She's had quite a bit to put up with one way and another.'

'Poor Ma.' Sorrel caught back a sob.

'She asked for you,' he said as the car moved forward. 'I thought it would be easier if I came and fetched you myself.'

'It's very kind of you.'

'The least I can do, my dear. Sid was a good friend – one of the best.'

They talked a great deal on the long drive home. Aden told her about his friendship with her father, about things that had happened when they were both young men.

'We were friends at school,' he said. 'He worked for

305

someone else when he left but when I got on a bit I asked him to come to me and we've never had a cross word in all the years except once ... and that's best forgotten.' He paused and she knew their argument had been over Jay, because Sid thought he'd let Sorrel down. 'Tell your mother she's welcome to stay on in the cottage for as long as she likes. It's her home and yours, too, if you want it.'

He was being very generous. The cottage went with the job and he would be needing someone to take her father's place.

'Thank you,' she said. 'That will be one worry off her mind.'

'She'll be glad to have you back, Sorrel.' He glanced at her thoughtfully. 'Shall you stay now? It looks as if this damned war has almost run its course. You'll be needed at home now, won't you?'

'Yes, I suppose I shall,' she said. 'I haven't thought about it yet – it all happened so suddenly.'

'Well, it's up to you, of course, but I should think you could get a nursing post nearer to home. I'll make some inquiries for you, if you like? I know a few people who might help.'

'I'll think about it,' she said. 'Ma might want me at home for a while, just until she sorts herself out.'

'Give up your nursing?' He looked surprised, then nodded. 'Well, it was just for the war, wasn't it?'

'Yes. At least – I'm not sure.'

At first she had seen nursing as something temporary, just as thousands of other young women had, a way of doing their bit for the war effort, but now she wasn't certain how she felt. It had become a way of life, hard but fulfilling. She wasn't sure how she would feel about living on the farm again.

Aden was silent for a while, then said, 'Jay should be home soon. Fanny did tell you he was wounded about three months ago?'

'She mentioned it.' Sorrel avoided looking at him. 'It was his right leg, wasn't it?'

'Yes. At first they said he was missing and we didn't know

306

if he was alive or . . . but then someone wrote and told us he had been taken to a French hospital.'

'I know.' Fanny had told her Jay was missing and the news had cost her some sleepless nights. 'But now he's coming home. How soon?'

'Next week, we hope.'

'You'll be glad to see him again.'

'Four years is a long time. Rebecca is over the moon, making endless plans. The war is over so far as Jay is concerned. He has been very ill. They thought he might lose the leg but it's healing at last, though he can't walk far yet. We wanted to visit him when they shipped him to a hospital in Portsmouth but he wouldn't let us, said he would rather wait until he was ready to be sent home.'

'A lot of the men are like that. They can't face their families until they begin to feel better.'

Aden drew the car into the kerb and stopped the engine, turning to look at her. 'I suppose there's no chance of you and Jay getting together again?'

'No, I don't think so.' She met his gaze steadily. 'It has been a long time, Aden. We've both changed, we're different people now. Besides, there's someone else.'

She hadn't heard from Shima for a while but she knew he must be all right. If anything had happened to him she would have heard. He had named her as his next-of-kin.

'I should have known there would be.' Aden looked at her sadly and released the brake. 'I'd better get you home to your mother.'

May broke down in tears when she saw her. Sorrel rushed to hug her and they clung to each other, sobbing out their grief.

'Sorrel,' May cried, 'I'm so glad you're home. I need you here, lass. I can't stand to see his chair empty. He was a good man – a good husband to me, despite the drinking.'

'I know, I know.' Sorrel hushed her with a kiss. 'You didn't tell me he was drinking again.'

'What good would it have done? You were getting on so well. We were both proud of you. Sid was thrilled when you

307

got your cap but you'll stay home for a while? You won't go straight back after the funeral?'

'No, of course not. I'll stay as long as you need me.'

'Just for a few weeks,' she said, squeezing Sorrel's hand. 'Until I sort myself out. Rose is all right, she's good company – but she doesn't understand how I feel about your pa. Besides, once Ted comes back they'll want a place of their own.' A look of anxiety came into her eyes. 'I don't know what we'll do about the cottage.'

'Aden wants us to stay here. It's all right, Ma. He won't turn us out. You won't lose your home.'

She nodded but still seemed concerned. 'There's talk in the village. They say Aden has been losing money – through that business of his in Chatteris, the one Richie is supposed to look after. Not that I'd trust *him* in charge of a flea market!'

'Are you saying Richie is to blame? Things haven't been easy for anyone, Ma. It's because of the war.'

'That's as maybe. Sid thought Richie was cheating his father, feathering his own nest.'

'Ma! You shouldn't say that unless you have proof?'

'No . . . Sid wasn't sure enough to say anything.' Tears spilled down her cheeks and May looked suddenly older, as if her husband's death had stolen her vitality. 'And with him drinking, I couldn't say for certain, could I?'

'No – and it would hurt Aden. We mustn't say anything, Ma. Aden was good to Pa, and to me. Look at the way he came up and fetched me himself. Not many would have done that.'

'That's true enough.' She squared her shoulders as if accepting the weight of her grief. 'Folk find fault with Aden Sawle but Sid always thought the world of him. I'll keep my mouth shut about Richie and you'd best do the same.' She took Sorrel's hand. 'You'll want to see your father? He looks peaceful.'

'Yes. I should like to see him alone, if you don't mind?'

'No, I don't mind,' said May. 'We've said our goodbyes but he would want a little time alone with you, Sorrel. You were the light of his life and when you'd gone it just went out . . .'

* * *

308

It was hard to say goodbye to her father but Sorrel's fare-wells were made in private and later she tried not to cry as they laid his coffin in the earth. Rose was crying noisily and so was Mabel but May was dry-eyed. She leaned on Sorrel's arm as they walked home afterwards.

Most of their neighbours came for a cup of tea and a sandwich; they offered help where they could, talked of Sid with warmth and then left. When it was all over Mabel helped with the washing up, then she and Bob went home to their children, who had been cared for by friends.

'I think I'll lie down for a while,' Rose said after everyone had gone. 'I've got a headache.'

'Well, that's that then,' May said as the door closed behind her. 'There's just you and me left now.'

'Yes, just you and me,' Sorrel said. 'We'll be all right, Ma, I promise. We'll be fine.'

'Save all the scraps for the pigs, Sorrel. Bob has been looking after them but he's got more than enough to do. They'll be your job now.'

'Don't worry. I know what to do. I've been away for a while but I haven't forgotten. I haven't forgotten anything, Ma.'

'No.' May sighed as she looked at her. 'You're not a child, are you? Sometimes I still think of you as one but that's silly. You're grown up – quite capable of looking after yourself.'

She looked as if she were wishing herself back in the past and Sorrel's heart ached for her. The last of her youth had gone with Sid and she looked old and weary – worn out by the years and her sorrow.

'I think I shall have a lie down, too,' she said. 'I feel a little tired.'

Sorrel watched as she went upstairs. Ma wouldn't ask her to leave the hospital and come home for good but she couldn't manage alone.

Sorrel got up to look out of the window. So much pain and heartache. It was summer but it felt like winter . . . an endless winter that just went on and on forever.

Chapter Thirty-Five

'Mrs Robinson has just gone,' Sorrel's mother said as she came in from the yard a few days later. 'She was telling me that Tom was home on leave last week. You just missed him.' She sighed and kneaded the dough in front of her. 'I thought once . . . he's never married, you know.'

'I like Tom but I would never have married him.'

'No, I don't suppose you would.' May straightened up and looked at her. 'Would you take some eggs across to Rebecca? Aden told me they need some and our hens have been laying well. We've more than enough for ourselves and most of theirs go to the Ministry.'

'Yes, of course – when I've fed the hens.'

Sorrel had been up early to help her brother with the milking and was feeling too warm for comfort. The sweat was trickling between her breasts and down her back, making her clothes stick to her.

'Rose can see to that,' her mother said. 'I'll make some lemon barley before you go, Sorrel. You look hot.'

'It's going to be very close today. I hope it won't end in a storm again; the one we had last week was bad enough.' Sorrel accepted her mother's offer gratefully. 'I could do with a drink. I'll be down in a minute.'

In her room she doused herself in cool water and changed into a decent dress. She wore a pair of Ted's old trousers and a baggy shirt for working about the yard but she couldn't go out like that: folk would die of shock.

She drank her glass of lemon, then picked up her basket and went out. It was such a lovely day, perfect if all you had

310

to do was lie by the river and dream. It would be wonderful to sit on the bank and dangle her feet in the cool water – or drift idily along it in a boat. If she were at Celia's she might have been boating on the lake.

She hadn't telephoned Fanny yet because she didn't know what to say. Fanny wouldn't approve of her slipping back into her old ways. She would say that Sorrel had a right to her own life. Sometimes she sounded a little hard these days but it was just a way of protecting herself, because she was afraid of being hurt again.

Sorrel wasn't sure what she wanted. For the moment she couldn't think of leaving her mother, not until May had come to terms with her loss. She wasn't sure what would happen if Shima came home ...

Molly opened the door as soon as Sorrel knocked. She looked excited, drawing her inside while she unpacked the basket, obviously wanting to tell her the news.

'Master Jay is home,' she said. 'His father fetched him from the station last evening.'

'Oh ... how is he?' Sorrel felt slightly breathless, which was silly, because it couldn't matter to her that he was back home.

'Not well.' Molly shook her head. 'I never saw such a change in a man. He was exhausted when they got back – went straight up to his room and hasn't moved since.'

'It's probably the shock of leaving hospital after so many weeks. Give him time, Molly. He needs rest and a chance to sort himself out, that's all. They wouldn't have let him come home if he weren't on the road to recovery. They would have sent him to a nursing home where he could be kept under medical supervision.'

'Yes, I suppose so. You'd know about that, wouldn't you, you being a nurse and all?'

'I've seen men look as if they were dying, and be sitting up in bed asking for a kiss a few days later. The human body is a wonderful thing, Molly. You'd be surprised how much punishment it can take at times.'

'You've made me feel no end better.' Molly handed her the empty basket. 'Would you like a cup of tea? It's fresh made.'

'I had a drink before I came,' she replied. 'I'd best get back. I'm glad Jay is home.'

She left the house and walked out of the yard, then ran across the road. Behind the barn at the back of her own house she stopped and leant against the wall, closing her eyes as a wave of emotion flowed over her. The thought of Jay exhausted and ill made her want to weep. She had always kept a picture of him in her mind as he was the day they'd had the contest to see who could carry the most corn. He had been so handsome, so arrogant and sure of himself – so full of life. That was the Jay she had loved so much. She didn't want to think of him in any other way.

'Just a minute, Sorrel!' Bob called as she walked out from behind the barn a moment later. 'You've got a visitor.' He grinned at her. 'Ma wasn't too happy to see him but she asked him in when he said he would wait until you got back.'

'Is that his car parked outside the house?' She frowned as he nodded. 'Who is it?'

'You'll see. He looks different in his uniform, seems they've made him a corporal . . .'

'Shima! Is it Shima?' she cried, and began to run towards the house. 'Shima . . .'

He was drinking a glass of her mother's lemon barley but put it down as she burst in and caught her in his arms, swinging her round and then kissing her.

'Why didn't you let me know you were coming?'

'I wasn't sure when I could get leave. Then this morning the Major told me to clear off for a couple of days – so here I am.'

'You're still with Major Bradshaw then?'

'That's right. It's because of him that I'm here. He went down with a fever so they shipped us both home,' Shima said. 'He was pretty groggy for a while but I think he's getting better now. He's booked into Rothsay for a rest.'

'At least he'll be with friends there.'

'Yes.' Shima held out his hands to her. 'Let me take a good look at you . . . still as lovely as ever.'

'Have I changed?'

'You get lovelier every time I see you.'

'Don't turn her head,' May said as she came back into the kitchen. 'Get out of here, the pair of you. It's too nice a day to waste indoors.'

'Are you sure?' Sorrel was surprised at her mother's tone. 'Don't you want me to help you?'

'Just be back in time to give Bob a hand with the milking this evening.'

'We could go into Ely,' Shima said. 'Have lunch or . . .'

'Take a boat out on the river?' she suggested, feeling a surge of pleasure. 'It's what I've been longing for all day. Wait a moment while I get my things.'

'Perfect.' Shima smiled at her as she trailed her fingers in the water. 'When we were over there I used to dream about being with you, somewhere like this.'

The river was so peaceful, its banks soft and green, fronded with drooping willows and tangled reed beds where fussy moorhens hunted for food. Above them the sun hung huge and golden in a cloudless sky, its heat tempered now by a slight breeze.

'Oh, Shima.' She sighed and closed her eyes. 'It has been such a long time.'

'Too long?' he asked. 'Is there someone else?'

She opened her eyes and looked at him. 'Of course not. I've made lots of friends at the hospital but that's all they were – lonely young men looking for a girl to talk to before they went back.'

'And Jay?'

She hesitated, her eyes dropping before his intense gaze. 'That's all over, you know it is.'

'I heard that he was home.'

'I suppose that was my mother?' She looked at him as he nodded. 'He has been very ill.'

'Yes, she told me. It was odd that we should both arrive today.' He was silent for a moment. 'I should like to see my father while I'm here, but I don't feel like going to the house. Rebecca wouldn't make a fuss about it, but I know how she must feel . . . it must be painful enough for her, just knowing I exist.' He leant on the oars, looking at her with a brooding expression that made his dark eyes seem black.

Sorrel sensed his hurt. 'Oh, Shima.'

A little pulse flickered in his throat. 'You can't get away from it, Sorrel. I'm a bastard and nothing will change that.'

'Don't say it like that! It wasn't your fault. It makes no difference to me.'

'It might to others . . . your mother, for instance. She still sees me as a gipsy brat with a snotty nose and holes in my trousers.'

'I don't remember your being like that at all.'

'It's not far from the truth. I improved as I grew up – used my time with the circus to get myself an education.'

Sorrel laughed as he pulled a face at her. 'You've made me feel better. Everything has seemed so grey and dreary since my father . . .'

Shima's dark eyes were warm and sympathetic. 'I'm sorry. I know you were very fond of him.'

'I loved him – but it's my mother I'm bothered about now. She needs me for a while. I don't know how long it will be before I can think of leaving her.' Sorrel brushed a wisp of hair from her eyes. 'Please try to understand, Shima.'

'I do understand. Besides, I'm still offically assigned to the Major. They won't be sending him back out there and I doubt if they'll split us up now . . . that means I'll be dragging my heels doing nothing in particular for the next few months.'

'What will you do when it's finally over?'

'I'm not sure. Major Bradshaw spoke of buying a place in the country and breeding horses. He wanted me to stay with him as his trainer.' Shima looked beyond her. 'I've a little place of my own in Ireland. I've thought about settling there, but it depends . . .'

She knew what he was saying. He was leaving the future open until she had decided what she wanted to do.

'We said after the war . . . it isn't quite over yet, Shima.'

'No, and if it was I wouldn't rush you,' he said. 'You know I love you, but if you come to me you must be sure. There must be no regrets.'

'Oh, Shima.' Her voice caught on a sob. 'This is unfair to

you. I promised to marry you when you came back and now I'm asking you to wait.'

'No solemn faces,' he said. 'Not today. This is a holiday – let's make the most of it.'

She spoke to Aden that evening. He was working in his garden with his shirt sleeves rolled up and dirt beneath his fingernails. He was surprised to see her but his face lit up with pleasure as she told him why she had called.

'Shima wanted to see you but didn't like to come to the house.'

'I'll pop round in the morning,' said Aden. 'This is wonderful news! I'd almost given up hope of seeing him again.'

'He has to leave tomorrow afternoon but will be pleased to see you before he goes.' Sorrel shuffled her feet, not looking at Aden as she asked, 'Is Jay feeling any better? Molly said he was exhausted when he arrived.'

'He came on the train. I would have fetched him but he insisted he could manage alone. It was too much for him – but I think it was just tiredness.' Aden looked at her consideringly. 'Would you like to go up and see him for a few minutes?'

'No!' Her heart lurched with panic. 'No, I don't think so. You can tell him I asked but I won't go up.'

'Perhaps that's best for now.' Aden scratched his ear, smearing earth on his neck and shirt. 'He seems very quiet – different somehow – but after what he's been through ...'

'Yes. Give him time.'

He nodded, still thoughtful, obviously anxious about his son. 'How's your mother?'

'Better – at least outwardly. She fills her time with work but she misses Pa.'

'It's early days yet.'

'Yes. I'd best get back. You'll be there when Shima comes at about ten then?'

'I'll be there. Thanks for coming round, Sorrel.'

She waved to him and turned away but something caught her eye and she looked up at the bedroom windows. Someone had been watching them. The window was open

315

so whoever was there could have heard what they were saying.

'I'll come down again when I can,' Shima said as they walked along the river bank together. They had been shepherding, more as a way of being alone for a while than out of real necessity. There were fewer bullocks than before the war and they were quickly counted. 'The Major will have to report back once he's fit but I'm fairly certain he'll be assigned to desk duties and I shall probably fill in on supplies or something.'

'At least you've seen your father.'

Aden and Shima had spent an hour or so together in the parlour. May had gone shopping and Sorrel had kept herself busy outside so that they could have privacy.

'And Sadie.' Shima looked grim. 'I went to see her last night. She's had a hard time of it since Tarina died, but Aden said he would do what he could for her.' His eyes met Sorrel's. 'Sadie told me it was Richie's child. He bought her presents and Tarina believed he would wed her.'

'Poor Tarina.' Sorrel hesitated, remembering the woman she had glimpsed in a dirty back street in London at the start of the war. She had never mentioned it to anyone, believing that she must have been mistaken. 'You didn't tell Aden that it was Richie?'

'That's for Jay – or Richie. I simply asked Aden if he could do anything for Sadie, that's all.'

'Why do you bother?' Sorrel asked. 'She wasn't exactly kind to you.'

'She was the only mother I ever knew.' His eyes darkened with the grief of old memories. 'She never loved me but I would not have survived if she had not nursed me after my mother died.'

'No, I suppose not.'

Sorrel could never think of the old gipsy woman without remembering her curses but she had in her way been a mother to Shima, though he must have had more blows than kindnesses from her.

'Keep in touch, Shima – let me know where you are.'

'You'll be seeing me before too long.'

316

'I hope so.' She reached up to kiss his cheek. 'Take care of yourself.'

He drew her into his arms, kissing her tenderly on the mouth. 'Be happy, my darling, that's all I want.'

They walked back to the farm. She watched as he drove away, tears stinging her eyes. Why hadn't she told him that she was ready to marry him now? Why did she feel as if a battle was raging inside her – that she was torn between him and Jay? She wasn't still in love with Jay – that was over, over long ago.

'So he's gone then?' her mother said as Sorrel went into the house. 'I thought you might want to go with him?'

'Would you have minded if I had?'

'Not if it was what you truly wanted. I know I used not to like him but he was with the gipsies then. The army has been good for him, he's improved.'

'Shima was always gentle and generous,' Sorrel said. 'He is my friend and I love him. Anyway, he had to report back to Major Bradshaw. He's still in the army and there *is* still a war going on.'

'He'll have a future with Major Bradshaw, I shouldn't wonder. A decent cottage of his own and a secure job.'

'Perhaps. He hasn't decided yet. He might go back to Ireland or even America.'

'The point is, will you go with him?'

'If you want the truth . . .' Sorrel sighed '. . . I just don't know. I love him but . . .'

'You're not still hankering over the other one?' May sniffed in disgust. 'Well, you'd better make up your mind, my girl, otherwise you'll lose the both of them!'

'Oh, Ma,' Sorrel said, and turned away. 'The things you do say.'

Yet in her heart she knew her mother had spoken only the truth. Shima was understanding and generous but she had hurt him and could not expect him to go on waiting forever.

'Celia is much better,' Fanny said when Sorrel rang her from the post office. 'I thought you would never ring me.'

317

'I haven't had much time.' Sorrel said. 'Shima came to see us. He told me about Major Bradshaw. How is he?'

'Very much better,' Fanny replied. 'I think he was just tired. He has been asked to report back for duty but says he won't be going far away so I shall see him most weekends.'

'That will be nice. At least I think so . . .'

Fanny laughed. 'He is amazingly pleasant these days. We get on very well.' She was silent for a moment, then asked, 'I don't suppose there's any chance of your coming down for a weekend?'

'Not just yet. Ma is beginning to feel better but we're busy. Perhaps in October.'

'I'll look forward to that. I do miss you.'

'Why don't you come home for a while?'

'I do want to see Jay . . .' Fanny sounded odd, a little breathless and uncertain. 'I'll think about it.'

'Isn't it time to forgive her? Couldn't you make the first move, Fanny? She is your mother.'

'We'll see. I must go. Celia wants me. Ring me again as soon as you can.'

She hung up in a hurry. Sorrel stared at the telephone as it went dead. She had broken the rules by bringing up the subject of a reconciliation between Fanny and her mother but she'd had to do it. Fanny would never be happy again until she could bring herself to forgive both herself and her mother.

Sorrel walked slowly back to her home. As she got there she saw a man crossing the road towards her and stopped dead, her heart racing. He was much thinner than she remembered and there were signs of his illness in his face but otherwise he was the same – the same man who had haunted her thoughts for so long.

'Jay!'

They stared at each other, neither of them able to take their eyes from the other's face.

'Sorrel.'

'How are you?'

'Better than I was. On the mend, I think.'

'Good. I'm glad.'

318

Her heart had stopped turning somersaults and she could breathe normally again.

'Would you like to come to the house for a cup of tea?'

'Yes, please, that would be nice. I was coming to see you.'

'Come on then.' She glanced at his leg as he limped beside her. 'Does it give you much pain?'

'Sometimes. I think it will be a good weathervane.'

'At least you didn't lose it. And you're still alive.'

'Some of us had a motto out there: If in doubt run away, live to fight another day. I was just better at running.'

'Oh, Jay,' she said huskily. 'You've never run from a fight in your life.'

'Perhaps not. It's just that when you look at some of the other poor devils, you realize how lucky you are – it makes you feel guilty.'

'I know what you mean, you aren't the only one to feel that way.'

'They say I'm up for a medal but I can't imagine why. I was with the medics for the last show, ferrying the wounded out until I caught it myself.'

'You must have done something special?' He shook his head and, as he obviously wasn't going to talk about it, she changed the subject. 'I've been talking to Fanny. She wants to see you but still won't come home.'

'She's as stubborn as Mother.'

The kitchen was empty as they went in. Sorrel realized they had been talking to cover the awkwardness between them but they lapsed into silence as she filled the kettle and put it on the hob. Then, as she turned back, she surprised a look in Jay's eyes that made her catch her breath.

'Fanny told me you wrote to me. Your letter must have got lost. At least, I never received it.'

'Oh.' Sorrel's heart gave a twist of pain. 'Ma said that was the reason you didn't reply.'

'I would if I'd known.'

'Would you?'

Their eyes met and her heart started on a roller coaster ride.

'Yes, I would. Surely you know that, Sorrel?'

'You went without saying goodbye.'

'I didn't think you wanted to see me.'

'I came to the house to wish you luck but I was too late. You had already left.'

'Father told me. It was his idea that I should come here today.'

'Not yours?'

'I wanted to come but I was afraid – afraid you would refuse to see me.'

'Jay. I . . . that day I was hurt and angry . . .'

'I know I have no right to ask but . . .'

'Please don't say anything, not yet.' Her heart was beating so wildly that she felt as if she were suffocating. She wasn't ready for this. She was confused, scared, too emotional to think clearly.

'It wasn't my child. I tried to help Tarina because she was Shima's friend. I know I should have told you but I was so angry and hurt that you had accepted other people's word above mine.'

'I wanted to ask but you weren't there and your mother . . . I shouldn't have judged you so hastily. I'm sorry, Jay. More sorry than I can ever say.'

They were apologizing now. Why hadn't they been able to talk like this when it mattered? But they were different now, older and wiser.

'You do believe me, about the child?'

'Yes. I've known for a long time. Fanny suspected it and Shima told me that Sadie confirmed it to him. It was Richie . . .'

'Richie!' Jay's face tightened with anger. 'He deserves a thrashing! Not just for Tarina . . . but I can't say more. Father told me in confidence; it's not my business.'

'He has been cheating Aden, hasn't he?' Jay looked at her in surprise and Sorrel knew she was right. 'Don't worry, it isn't common knowledge. Pa suspected something but we couldn't be sure so we haven't said anything.'

'Father is furious. They had a huge row over it and he threatened to cut Richie off without a penny – but he's trying to keep it in the family. We've had to borrow from the bank and Father is fighting to save the business. There's a small mortgage on Five Winds . . .'

320

'On the farm?'

'Nothing to worry about.' Jay stared at his cup as she put it on the table in front of him. 'He's giving Five Winds to me, and the milking herd. He promised me land when I came back and he's keeping his word as best he can. He and Mother will stay at the house for a while but he's planning to sell up most of his property and move to Sutton or Ely. He says it's time he retired so that he and Mother can have more time together.' He paused and looked at her. 'It means I'll be around most days, Sorrel. I shan't be able to afford more than two or three men so I'll be helping Bob myself.'

'Oh.' She digested this in silence. 'Are you up to it yet? I've been helping as much as I can. We could manage for a bit longer.'

'Yard work is too heavy for you. I'll be grateful if you could help with the milking until we get sorted, but you shouldn't have to do the feeding and mucking out – that's men's work.'

'I don't mind.' She hesitated before asking, 'Will you want us to move out of the cottage? Aden said we could stay but if...'

'Of course not. It's your home. I just thought you should know the situation.' He looked awkward. 'I don't want you to be uncomfortable but I can't see any other way...'

'I may not be here for much longer.' She turned away, feeling unable to meet his intense gaze. 'Shima has asked me to marry him.'

'Yes, I'd heard you were seeing him.' Jay pushed away the cup he had not touched and stood up. 'It won't make much difference then, will it?'

'Jay.' She felt compelled to look at him, compelled to tell him. 'We... during the war... everything was so awful and... Shima came home on leave and we...'

'You were lovers, I suppose?' His face had become cold, angry. 'I should have expected it. He always wanted you. He told me he would take you from me if he could.'

'Jay, please don't be like this,' she begged, her voice breaking. 'I thought it was over between us.' She moved towards him, laying her hand on his arm. 'Can't you forgive me? Please, Jay, couldn't we be friends?'

There was a flicker of pain in his eyes as he looked down into her pleading face. 'You want me to say I'm happy for you – is that it?'

'Jay, don't! Please don't look at me like that.'

'How should I look at you?' he asked bitterly. 'You would never let me touch you ... not once. How do you expect me to feel?'

'Jay, I never meant to hurt you. I just wanted you to know the truth.'

'Well, now I do so that's all right, isn't it?' His bitter, sarcastic words struck her to the heart. 'Just don't ask me to your wedding, Sorrel. I'll be seeing you. I dare say we can work together if nothing else.'

She watched as he limped to the door and went out without looking at her again. Why had she felt compelled to tell him the truth about what had happened between her and Shima? Why hadn't she let him say what he had wanted to say at the beginning? Why were her thoughts in such turmoil? She had loved him all her life ... she still loved him, loved him so much that it had torn her apart inside to see that look in his eyes.

Why hadn't she told him that?

Chapter Thirty-Six

'It will do you good to get out of the house for a while,' May said. 'You've been looking down in the mouth for days.'

'Sorry, Ma,' Sorrel apologized. 'I've had something on my mind.'

Jay's parting words of a day or so earlier had hurt her deeply. Since then he had greeted her with a cool nod of the head whenever they passed in the yard and she knew he must hate her. He was refusing to forgive her or even try to understand – but how could she blame him for his attitude when she had not listened to him years before?

'You take care, do you hear me?' May said. 'I think Bob is mad to let you drive his car, but he says you can manage it so it's up to him.'

Bob had bought himself a secondhand Model T Ford with some money his father had left him. He was very proud of the fact that he was one of the few in the village to own a car and Sorrel had been surprised when he'd offered to lend it to her, to take Mabel and Timmy shopping.

'Are you sure you trust me?' she'd asked with a twinkle in her eye when he'd first offered.

'If you can drive Lady Roth's Daimler, you can drive this,' Bob replied with a grin. 'Besides, Mabel wants to go and I haven't time to take her.'

They left little Sarah with Mabel's mother and set out on their big adventure. It was a spanking hot day and there was a large market in Chatteris. Sorrel parked the car well out of the main street in a shady spot.

'Isn't this a treat?' Mabel said. 'So much easier than

waiting for a bus – and more comfortable than the trap. I wish I could drive the way you do.'

'Bob would teach you.'

'I wouldn't dare! I'm not as brave as you.'

They walked round the cluster of market stalls. Most of them were piled high with fresh local produce but there were others selling all kinds of goods from secondhand clothes and books to blue and white pottery. Mabel bought some material for her new curtains and a pair of boots for her small son.

'He'll be going to school next year,' she said as she finished paying for her purchases. 'The years fly by so fast, it's a mystery where the time goes.'

Sorrel was only half listening, her eyes drawn irresistibly to a woman standing by one of the stalls. She seemed to have been affected by the heat and suddenly crumpled to the ground in a heap. Sorrel ran to help her but as she bent over her the woman stirred and opened her eyes.

'Leave me be . . . leave me be,' she muttered fiercely.

'Sadie!' Sorrel hadn't been sure until she was close to her. She looked old, much older than her years, her eyes sunken and dull. 'Sadie, it's Sorrel Harris from Mepal. Won't you let me help you?'

Sadie threw her hands off and struggled to rise but fell back with a moan.

'Don't hurry,' Sorrel said, and used her straw hat to fan the old woman's face. 'You'll be better in a moment – but let me help you.'

Sadie clutched Sorrel's arm and sat up, her dark eyes stabbing at her with hostility. 'Why should you help me?'

'I'm Shima's friend, don't you remember me?'

'I know you.' She dragged on Sorrel's arm as she hauled herself up, her face contorted with pain from the effort.

'Let me help you to that bench over there. You should sit quietly for a while. I'll get you a glass of water.'

Sadie shook her head, muttering something beneath her breath, but allowed Sorrel to lead her to the seat. Mabel came up to them then, carrying a small cup.

'One of the stallholders gave me this,' she said, and handed it to Sorrel. She stood well back, holding Timmy

324

firmly by the hand and the expression on her face made it clear she wanted nothing further to do with the gipsy.

Sadie looked at the water suspiciously then sniffed it. She put the cup to her lips and drank a little, then thrust the cup back at Sorrel.

'Tastes bad,' she muttered. 'Tap water. I never drink tap water, it poisons your insides.'

'Would you like me to take you home?' Sorrel asked. 'We have a car and . . .'

'Leave me be.' Sadie's eyes suddenly focused on her face with a frightening intensity. Her hand shot out and she gripped Sorrel's wrist, her thin brown fingers like wasted talons. 'It's near. I can see it hovering at your shoulder . . . be warned, 'tis near.'

Sorrel felt chilled. It was as if a shadow had moved across the sun, blanking out its warmth.

'What do you mean? What is near?'

'Death . . . death stalks at your shoulder . . . death and pain . . .'

'Leave her alone and come away,' Mabel said. 'She's crazy. Don't listen to her, Sorrel. She's a vindictive, mad old woman.'

'We can't just leave her. She's ill.'

'I'll take care of her.'

Neither of them had noticed the young man who had come up behind them. As she turned Sorrel saw he was tall with a swarthy complexion and black, hostile eyes.

'You're one of her people?' she asked, and he nodded. 'I was trying to help her but she . . .'

'We need no help from your kind,' he said harshly. 'Leave her to me. She's near her time. She'll die soon.'

Mabel pulled at her arm. 'Come on, Sorrel, let's go.'

Sorrel glanced at her and then at the gipsy. Sadie would be best left to her own people and there was nothing more she could do.

'Ungrateful old witch,' Mabel said resentfully as she hurried Sorrel and Timmy away. 'Bob hates gippos and now I know why.'

'She's just an old woman,' Sorrel replied, glancing over her shoulder once more. Sadie's dark eyes were following her and Sorrel shivered. 'She ought to be in hospital where she could be properly cared for.'

'She wouldn't stay if you took her. Besides, she's obviously mad or she wouldn't say such awful things.'

'It isn't the first time. She warned me that I was cursed years ago.'

For a moment Sorrel thought about the first time she had seen Sadie. She had been cursing her . . . and Shima. Tarina had seen blood but it was her own death and that of her child she had foretold. What had Sadie seen hovering at Sorrel's shoulder?

She was aware of a sense of creeping horror. Something terrible was going to happen, something involving her that would bring death and pain.

'You've gone white,' Mabel said. 'You're not letting that crazy old woman upset you, are you?'

'No, no, of course not,' Sorrel forced herself to laugh. 'It was all nonsense. I expect I'm feeling a bit warm, that's all.'

'It's hot enough to make anyone crazy,' Mabel agreed. 'Let's get home. I've had enough shopping for one day.'

'Death hovers at your shoulder . . . 'tis near . . . 'tis near.' Sorrel tossed restlessly on her pillow as the nightmare gripped her. 'Blood . . . the blood will bind us together . . . take care, Sorrel . . . take care.'

Sorrel gave a cry and sat up in bed as she woke from her nightmare. Tarina's face had come to her so clearly in the dream, almost as if she were in the room with her . . . or calling to her.

Shivering, Sorrel jumped out of bed and went to look out of the window. It was just a dream . . . just a dream . . . but as she gazed down to the field behind the house she saw someone standing there looking up at the house.

'Tarina!' Sorrel gasped. Surely it was Tarina? Or her ghost. 'Tarina . . .'

She whirled round, running from the room and down the stairs without stopping to put on her shoes. The rough brick and earth surface of the yard cut into her feet as she raced across it wearing only her nightgown.

'Tarina . . .'

There was no one in the field when she reached it . . . no sign of the figure she had seen from her window. Or had she really seen it? Was it only her imagination because she had dreamed so vividly of the gipsy woman?

Suddenly realizing she was wearing only her nightgown, Sorrel ran back to the house, afraid that someone would see her and think she had gone mad. It couldn't have been Tarina. She must still have been dreaming . . . carrying her nightmare in her mind and making it seem real.

Sorrel gave herself a shake. It was because of what Sadie had said a day or so earlier of course . . . but it had seemed so real.

'Rose has had a letter from Ted,' her mother said as she brought a jug of frothy milk in from the dairy that afternoon. 'He's decided he's not coming back to the farm when he leaves the navy.'

'Oh?' Sorrel looked at her in surprise. 'What will he do then?'

'He has asked about a transfer into the merchant fleet. Rose has been given a choice: she can join him and live at one of the ports or their marriage is over.'

'What will she do?'

May shrugged. 'It's given her a shock, I can tell you.'

'It would.' Sorrel wondered how Rose would feel about her husband putting his foot down at last.

'What about you?' May asked. 'Are you any nearer to making up your mind?'

'Shima is coming this weekend. I may know more after we talk.'

'If Rose goes to join Ted, I might go with her.'

'Why?' Sorrel was stunned by her mother's announcement. 'Do you mean it?'

'Things will never be the same here without your father. With Ted away at sea half the time, Rose will need company in a strange town.'

Sorrel was thoughtful as she went back out into the yard. Was her mother making it easy for her to leave the farm – or did she really want to start a new life somewhere else?

Bob came out of the barn as she began to feed the pigs.

He looked bothered about something as he stood watching her.

'Something wrong?'

'You've just missed Jay.'

'Oh.' He was definitely worried. 'You're not losing your job, are you?'

'No, nothing like that.' He took off his cap and wiped the sweat from his brow. 'It's just that I feel bad about something.'

'Tell me then,' she said, and put down her bucket. 'What's on your mind?'

'Jay said his father had had another huge row with Richie last night. Apparently Aden has spoken of changing his will and now he's made up his mind to cut Richie out altogether.'

'That's not your fault.'

'I'm not so sure. I said something to Aden about you and Jay . . . and about Richie being the father of Tarina's child.'

'You told Aden? Oh, Bob!'

'I thought he knew.' Bob looked stricken. 'It turns out that Rebecca knew all along and when Aden asked her they had a row and Aden went after Richie. Seems all hell was let loose. Sally took the children and went to stay with her mother, though they're back now, and Aden says he's washed his hands of Richie.'

'Oh, no.' Sorrel's stomach churned uneasily. 'I wish you hadn't told him.'

'He was saying he wished you and Jay would make a go of it. I didn't think . . . I'm sorry. I feel terrible.'

'You weren't to know all this would happen.'

'Jay says Richie blames him. Thinks he told their father about Tarina.'

'That's nonsense. Jay has kept quiet all this time – why would he say anything now?'

'Do you think I should go and see Richie? Tell him it was me?' Bob looked uneasy. 'Only I've always thought . . . well, Richie can be a bit odd.'

'What do you mean?' she asked, and as Bob was reluctant to answer, 'Ted said something once about his being mean to the other children at school?'

'It was more than that.' Bob took a deep breath. 'One of

328

the lads brought a kitten to school one day . . . a little stray he'd found and wanted to keep.'

'What happened?'

'Richie said the kitten was his and demanded the boy give it to him. When he refused Richie grabbed it and flung it against the wall. It was killed instantly.'

'How awful. What did Aden say?'

'The lad's father worked for Aden. Richie told him his father would lose his job if he told anyone.'

Sorrel felt chilled. She had always sensed something dark and hidden about Richie but had never suspected anything like this. 'That's sickening. What sort of a person could do something like that?'

'I don't know, unless there's something evil in him.' Bob sucked in his breath. 'There were other things, too – too nasty to talk about – that's why I feel so bad about all this. I think I ought to try and explain to Richie.'

Sorrel shook her head. 'I don't think it would help, Bob. It will probably all blow over in a few days. Aden can't mean to cut him out altogether – and you might make things worse.'

Bob looked relieved. 'You're right. It's between them. I'll keep my mouth shut – it's what I should have done in the first place. I just wish I hadn't spoken out of turn.'

Sorrel wished the same thing but didn't say anything to make him feel worse. All the same, he had made her uneasy. It was foolish but she felt as if there was a shadow hanging over them all. She had a terrible fear that something bad was going to happen.

Shima was in the yard cleaning the hooves of one of the great shire horses that still did most of the heavy work on the farm. Jay had talked of wanting one of the new traction engines but had so far done nothing more about it. Sorrel would be sorry to see any of the horses go; they were wonderful to watch at work on the land and she knew every one of them by name.

As she watched from the kitchen window she saw Jay come into the yard and speak to Shima. There had been a little awkwardness between them when they first met but now they were laughing together, apparently the best of friends.

Sorrel felt a little piqued. Jay was prepared to be friends with Shima – it was Sorrel he could not forgive, who got nothing more than a cool nod in passing.

'You'll have to make up your mind soon,' her mother said from behind her. 'Surely you know which one you want?'

'I don't want to hurt either of them.'

'Then you'll end by hurting yourself,' May said tartly. 'I'm off to Mabel's. She and Bob are taking me out in the car and Rose has gone to her mother's for the day. You'll be on your own so keep an eye on those cheeses for me; they don't seem to be setting as they should. Someone must have put the evil eye on them.'

'I'll see to them.'

Sorrel watched her mother leave. Jay went off across the road and Shima started to lead the horse round the back of the barn to the field beyond.

It seemed strange with the yard and the house deserted. Sorrel took a look at the cheeses; her mother was right, there was something not quite as it should be. It might have been the weather, which was hot and sultry, or perhaps someone *had* put the evil eye on them.

That was silly! She didn't believe in those old wives' tales and wasn't going to let Sadie's warning overshadow her life.

Was it the heat making her so restless? She left the dairy and stood in the yard looking round her as she tried to make up her mind. Should she take a cool bath or . . .

'Sorrel . . . Sorrel Harris.'

Sorrel whirled round as she heard the whispery voice, then stared at the woman who stood just behind her. For a moment she felt faint and her heart raced wildly. It couldn't be! But it was . . . it was . . . and somehow she had always known it in her heart.

'Tarina,' she said. 'It *was* you I saw from my window the other morning, wasn't it? Why did you run away?'

'I was afraid someone might come,' she said. 'I've been watching you for a few days but there's always someone around.'

330

'It was you before,' Sorrel said, suddenly feeling certain. 'You followed me once in the fog in London, didn't you?'

'I followed you several times. I wanted to talk to you.'

'Then why didn't you?'

'You said you would call the police. I was afraid.'

'But I didn't know it was you. You must know I would never harm you, Tarina – I am your friend.'

'Are you? Can I trust you?'

Tarina took a step forward as she spoke, then stopped and caught her breath as if she were in distress. Sorrel looked at her more closely and saw that her face was very pale, her eyes sunken and red-rimmed.

'Are you ill?' she asked, and Tarina nodded. 'Can I help you – will you come into the house and sit down?'

'You can do nothing for me,' she said. Unless . . . can you tell me where I can find Shima? I must speak to him before I . . .' She broke off, a look of alarm in her eyes as someone came round the side of the house. 'I'll come back.'

'Don't go!' Sorrel cried. 'There's no need to be frightened . . .' The words died on her lips as she saw who was coming. 'Richie.' She stared at him in dismay, her heart beginning to beat wildly. 'If you're looking for Jay he . . .'

'I saw him across the fields as I parked my car.' His smile was without warmth and Sorrel shivered as ice trailed down her spine. 'I was hoping to have a few words with you. Won't you ask me in, Sorrel?'

'Yes . . . if you wish.' She went into the kitchen and he followed her inside. There was a brooding menace about him, a strange threat that made her mouth go dry with fear. But he was looking round the room, not at her.

'I haven't been here since old Sarah Green lived in this cottage – but you probably wouldn't remember her. She died when I was very young but I remember . . . I remember everything . . . everything.' His voice had a peculiar, almost muffled, quality and he was clearly in the grip of some strong emotion.

Sorrel didn't say anything. Her stomach was clenching and the sense of impending doom that had been hanging over her all day became so strong that she could hardly breathe.

331

'Would you like a drink?' She managed the words at last. Richie was making her nervous. He was staring at her oddly, as if savouring the moment ... with a kind of suppressed excitement that wasn't quite natural.

'No, I don't think so. This isn't a social call. I've come to give you this.' He took something from his pocket and offered it to her. 'I thought it my duty. It's only right that you should know the truth about him.'

'What do you mean?'

Sorrel felt very cold all of a sudden. Richie seemed so strange. His eyes had a peculiar brilliance she had never seen before in anyone.

'Read that letter. Go on, take it. Read it!'

She took it reluctantly, beginning to feel as if she were in one of her nightmares. She glanced at the envelope and saw it was addressed to Jay and that it had come from Belgium.

'This belongs to Jay. Where did you get it?'

'It was on the tray in the hall when I called to see my mother.' Richie's mouth twisted with bitterness. 'I begged her to help me but she wouldn't listen. She sent me away as usual ... but then she never loved me. It was always him ... him and Fanny ... she took him with her when she went away but she left me behind. Perhaps she'll be sorry one day.' A nervous laugh escaped him. 'I saw the letter and I took it. I've read it and now you're going to ... then you can tell everyone the truth about him. Perhaps she'll love me then.'

'No!' Sorrel cried in disgust. 'I'll give it to Jay but I won't read it. It is his letter and you had no right to take it – or read it.'

'He had no right to tell tales about me to Father,' Richie said, his face pale. 'I'll tell you what the letter says. It's from a girl in France. A girl Jay seems to know rather well ...'

'I don't want to hear this. Go away, Richie.'

'But I want you to know the truth,' he hissed, leaning towards her menacingly. 'Our shining white knight hasn't been so pure and high-minded after all. When I think about the way he lectured me over *her* ...' Something flickered in Richie's eyes, as if he couldn't bring himself to say Tarina's

332

name. 'And all the while he . . .' His voice was rising higher and higher, becoming shrill and unlike his own.

'Please leave!' Sorrel cried. He was ill! Something terrible was happening to him. She ran to the door and wrenched it open. 'Go, Richie. I don't want to hear this.'

'But I want you to read the letter.' He thrust his face close to hers, his manner so threatening and strange that she felt sick. 'Read it, damn you. I want you to know the truth about him.'

'I won't!' She snatched the letter and threw it to the floor. 'Get out of here, Richie. You're jealous of Jay. You always were. You're mean and jealous and . . .'

He grabbed her arm, twisting it so that she cried out in pain. 'You little bitch!' he snarled. 'You will hear it! Jay got a girl in trouble out there and . . .'

She broke away from him, running out into the yard in an effort to escape. Richie came after her. He was so angry! She could see a vein throbbing at his temple and the look in his eyes terrified her. It was as if he had lost control – as if his mind had somehow cracked.

'You will listen!' he yelled, and made a grab at her. She struggled but he was so strong. He held on to her with one hand, at the same time hitting her across the face with the other. 'Stupid bitch! I've lost everything because of you. It's your fault . . . your fault . . .' He was screaming at her now, out of control.

'Richie . . . stop it, please!'

She screamed as he hit her again and again. She fought desperately but he had grabbed her thick plait and she was caught fast as he twisted it viciously. What was the matter with him? He could not really believe it was her fault! But he was beyond reason, lost in some mindless haze of hatred and revenge. He was the architect of his own downfall but must have brooded on his wrongs, letting them fester inside him until they spilled over in this torrent of insane rage.

Sorrel had always sensed something dark and dangerous in him and now anger had stripped away all pretence and she saw him for what he was: ruthless, evil and mad.

His hands were about her throat, his eyes lit by demonic laughter. He was squeezing . . . squeezing . . . driving all the

333

breath from her body, trying to kill her, to destroy what he saw as his enemy.

A shout from somewhere close behind them made Richie's hold slacken. He glanced round, gave an animal snarl and thrust her away from him. Sorrel fell to her knees, gasping and sobbing, but Richie was no longer interested in her.

Jay was limping towards them as fast as his injured leg would allow. 'You swine!' he cried. 'What are you doing to her? I'll thrash you, you bastard. If you've hurt her . . .'

Richie didn't answer. He was staring at Jay as if he had seen the devil, his eyes glittering wildly. Then, as Sorrel rose shakily to her feet, she saw him snatch up an iron bar that was used in the trace harness of the farm carts and lay against a pile of broken tackle. He turned on Jay with a yell of fury.

'You turned Father against me,' he cried. 'We'll see what he thinks when he discovers what you've been doing in France.' He held the iron bar threateningly. 'Come on then, hit me. Why don't you?'

Jay glanced at Sorrel. 'Are you all right?' he asked, and she nodded, unable to speak. 'Go in the house . . . lock the door.'

She shook her head, knowing that she could not leave him alone to face the insane hatred of his brother.

'You've been asking for this,' Jay said. 'Put that bar down and we'll fight fair.'

'Damn you!' Richie lunged at him, catching him on the shoulder with the iron bar before he could move out of the way. He laughed shrilly, a gleeful look on his face. 'I'll kill you, then her, then the bastard. I'll be rid of you all . . .'

'Don't be a fool,' Jay said. 'What's the matter with you? Have you lost your reason, man? I'll fight you but there'll be no killing.'

'You're not so brave now,' Richie muttered feverishly. 'Behold the conquering hero home from the wars – afraid of his own brother!'

'I'm not afraid of you, Richie,' Jay said. 'I've just had enough of killing. I've seen too much death to want yours

334

on my conscience. Give it up, Richie. We can sort out what-ever is upsetting you.'

Richie struck at him again but Jay dodged out of the way. His eyes moved from side to side as he looked for some kind of a weapon to use but there was nothing. He was backing away from his brother, watching him warily... waiting for his chance. Richie lunged at him, hitting him on his shoulder again. Jay gave a cry of pain, then threw himself at his brother. He was trying to grab the iron bar and they wrestled for a moment, then, before Sorrel's horrified gaze, Jay's leg gave under him and he slipped. As he stumbled Richie struck again, catching him a blow on the side of his head. Jay slumped forward and fell to the ground face down.

'Jay... oh, no!' Sorrel screamed and ran forward. 'Jay... Jay, my darling... Jay...'

She knelt on the ground by his side, running her fingers over his face in despair. He was bleeding, his eyes closed, face pale.

'You wicked, evil man!' Sorrel cried as Richie loomed over her. 'You've killed him... you've killed him!'

Richie's eyes held the glitter of madness as he raised his arms above his head and laughed. 'I've killed him and now I'm going to...' He screamed shrilly and Sorrel saw a rush of crimson behind him just as Tarina raised her arm and plunged the long blade of her knife into his arm. 'What...'

Richie went still as he turned and saw her, all the colour draining from his face. Blood was dripping down his arm, staining his shirt crimson, trickling between his fingers. The iron bar dropped from his slack hand as he stared at her, unable to believe what he saw.

'Devil!' Tarina cried, and spat at him. 'I'll kill you as I killed the other one!'

She raised her arm to strike again but in that moment Richie came to life and grabbed her wrist. They struggled and she cried out in pain as he forced her to let go of her weapon. Then his hands were about her throat, squeezing... squeezing.

'You were dead,' he muttered. 'Dead!'

'Stop it!' Sorrel cried, and sprang to her feet. 'Stop it, Richie. Haven't you harmed her enough? She's ill...' She

335

snatched up the iron bar and hit him across the back. 'Stop it . . . stop it!'

Richie's hands fell away from Tarina. For a moment he stared at her and then at Sorrel, seeming bewildered, as though he wasn't certain where he was or what was happening.

'Stay where you are, Richie!' Shima's cool, crisp voice held the ring of command. 'If you attempt to touch either of them again, I'll blow your head off.'

Richie's eyes swivelled to where Shima stood holding a shotgun. 'You?' he snarled, face twisting with hatred. 'The bastard.'

'Tarina – Sorrel!' Shima commanded. 'Get over here behind me. Stay where you are, Richie. Try to come one step closer and I'll kill you. Believe me, I mean it.'

Sorrel and Tarina obeyed instantly. The gipsy woman slumped down on the ground, obviously exhausted by the effort she had made to fight Richie. Sorrel bent down by Jay's side, feeling for a pulse as she watched the tense situation.

'Kill me then,' Richie said. 'Shoot me, if you dare.'

'I would were it not for our father,' Shima said, his eyes as cold as black ice. 'Get out of here before I decide that we would all be better off with you dead. If Jay is dead, you'll hang soon enough.'

Richie glanced down at the still figure of his brother. His eyes had a glazed look about them, as if he were waking from a dream; he stood for a moment, confused and uncertain, then started to back away, shaking his head.

'No . . . no . . . no . . .' he muttered. 'I didn't . . . I didn't kill him.'

Suddenly he turned and ran out of the gate and a moment later they heard his car start up, its wheels screeching as he drove off like a wild thing.

'He's not dead,' Sorrel said as Shima put down the gun and looked at her. 'He's unconscious but he's not dead.' There was a sob in her voice. 'We have to get him to the hospital.'

'I'll get help,' Shima said. 'Tarina . . .' He spun round to look at the spot where she had been a moment before. 'Tarina . . . where the hell did she go?'

'She was probably afraid of being seen by others,' Sorrel said. 'She will come back. Go and fetch Aden. We have to get a doctor to Jay as soon as we can.'

'Yes, yes, of course.' Shima sounded odd but she was intent on pressing her apron against the wound to Jay's temple to stop the bleeding; the blood was turning its spotless whiteness to crimson. 'You stay with him. Do what you can for him. I'll fetch help.'

'Oh, Jay.' Tears trickled down Sorrel's cheeks as she bent over him. 'Please don't die, my darling . . . please don't die. I love you so much. Don't die.'

Chapter Thirty-Seven

'You look terrible,' May said as Sorrel walked into the kitchen. 'Come and sit down, love, before you fall.'

Sorrel had been at the hospital all night, sitting in a narrow, draughty corridor waiting for news. In the end Shima had insisted on bringing her home.

'You can't do anything here,' he'd said when she protested that she wanted to stay. 'Aden will let us know as soon as there is any change.'

'How is Jay?' May asked. 'And where is Shima – didn't you ask him in for a cup of tea?'

'He had something to do,' Sorrel said, and sighed as her mother pushed a cup of tea in front of her. 'Jay was still unconscious when I left.' Her throat caught with emotion. 'Oh, Ma, if anything happens to him . . .'

'Now stop that, miss!' her mother said sharply. 'He had a nasty bang on the head but he's not dead.'

'No.' Sorrel sipped her tea. 'But . . .'

'Bob is blaming himself. He says it wouldn't have happened if he'd been here when Richie turned up.'

'It was Jay he wanted to kill.'

Sorrel felt sick as she remembered the insane rage and hatred in Richie's eyes as he attacked his brother. It must have been building up inside him for so many years and finally it had boiled over, as if the strain of all his problems had become too much for him, plunging him into madness.

'To think of that poor lad in hospital and his leg only just starting to get better.' May looked indignant. 'Whatever must his mother be feeling?'

'Rebecca is with him now.' Sorrel smothered a sob. 'She was in a terrible state when Aden brought her to the hospital. Fanny ought to come home. She ought to be here.'

'You can telephone her later,' May said. 'Why don't you go up and have a sleep? I'll call you if there's any news.'

'Thank you. I think I'll have a bath first. I feel sticky and uncomfortable.'

Sorrel walked slowly up the stairs. Her head ached and she was exhausted by emotion, drained and empty. The events of the previous day seemed like a nightmare – a nightmare from which she could not wake.

She lay in the bath, relaxed by the warm water and thinking how lucky they were to have a proper bathroom. Aden had put it in for them when he built the extension and she had never appreciated it as much as she did now.

After her bath she crawled under the covers of her bed without bothering to put on her nightgown. She was so tired and her head was throbbing but she knew she would never sleep. How could she sleep when Jay might be dying?

She jerked awake when her mother came into the room. 'What's wrong?' she asked. 'Has something happened?'

'Sorry to wake you,' May said, 'but Rebecca is here. She wants to talk to you.'

'I'll get dressed and come down.'

'You'll stay where you are. Just put something on to make yourself decent and I'll tell her to come up.'

Sorrel hastily pulled on her nightgown as her mother went away, fluffing out her hair and sitting up against the pillows. She waited tensely for Rebecca to come in, her hands trembling. Something terrible must have happened if Rebecca had come to see her.

'How is he?' she asked the moment Rebecca walked in. 'He isn't worse?'

Rebecca shook her head. 'No, don't worry. I came to see you, Sorrel. How are you?'

'I was tired but I'm all right now.' She twisted Shima's friendship ring on her finger.

Rebecca hesitated, then sat on the edge of the bed. 'We've never been friends,' she said, 'but that was my fault. I hope that will change in future. I want to apologize for my behaviour towards you in the past – and for what Richie did to you yesterday.'

'I wasn't hurt much.' Sorrel looked at her uncertainly. What must she be feeling? 'It was Jay ...'

'I have you and Shima to thank for Jay's life. I think he would certainly have died if ...'

'Has there been any change?' Sorrel cut in breathlessly. 'Has he regained consciousness?'

'Not yet, but the doctors are hopeful. That is all they will say for now.'

Sorrel swallowed hard. 'I should have done something when they were fighting. But I didn't know what to do.'

'It would probably have happened one day – and I think it was my fault it happened yesterday. Richie came to me for help earlier. He was upset ... angry ... and I rejected him. I sent him away. I should have remembered how jealous and spiteful he could be. If I had helped him none of this need have happened.'

'Richie seemed ... he seemed to have lost all sense of reason,' Sorrel said awkwardly, not wanting to speak more plainly to his mother. 'As if he had lost all control.'

Rebecca nodded and for a moment appeared to sag under the weight of her burden. 'Aden went to look for him last night but he has disappeared. Sally said he rushed into the house late yesterday afternoon, took a shotgun from the cupboard under the stairs and went out without speaking to anyone. He hasn't been home all night.'

'You don't think ...' Sorrel was dismayed. 'He wouldn't ... he threatened to ...'

'Richie might be capable of anything. If he comes here again you must be very careful, Sorrel. Run into the house and lock the door. Send someone to let me know at once. I can control him. I always could.'

'Yes, but I don't think he will come. He believes he has killed Jay ... it was Jay he hated the most.'

'I wanted to warn you myself, just in case. I've known Richie was ... unstable ... for a while. Even as a child there was something ... something dark in his mind. I should have done something sooner but I prayed I was wrong. Whatever he is, he is still my son.'

340

The expression in her eyes told Sorrel just how much it had cost her to admit that her son was mentally ill.

'I'm sorry. It is all so horrible.'

'Yes, it is,' Rebecca agreed. 'I thought the worst thing I could ever experience in my life was when Aden told me my father and his mistress had been murdered but . . .' She paused as she saw the shock in Sorrel's face. 'You didn't know about that?'

'No. I knew there was something, but I didn't know what.'

'I was very young then, younger than you are now. I had been to stay with friends. When I came back Aden was waiting for me at the station. He told me they were dead – Eileen Henderson and my father. Eileen's husband was a butcher. He had used one of his knives to slaughter them as they slept together. Aden brought me to Mepal because I couldn't go home. I married him soon after.'

'Did you love him?'

'At the time I wasn't sure.' Rebecca smiled, looking younger and pretty. 'But I learned to love him very much, despite all our troubles. We often quarrel, because we are both stubborn and proud – but nothing can part us now. Not even this.' She stood up and looked down at Sorrel. 'I must go, but if you want to visit Jay I shall be going to the hospital later. You are welcome to come with me if you wish?'

'Thank you. And thank you for coming to see me.'

'It was the least I could do.'

'It was kind and I am grateful. I'll come round this afternoon, shall I?'

'Please come whenever you feel like it,' Rebecca said with a smile. 'You will always be welcome.'

Sorrel waited until she had gone, then threw back the covers and jumped out of bed. It was time she telephoned Fanny – time she came home.

'I'll come next week,' Fanny promised when Sorrel spoke to her a little later. 'I can't come sooner, but you will keep me in touch? Let me know how Jay is?'

'You know I will. I'll ring as often as I can – but your mother needs you, Fanny.'

Fanny was so stubborn. She wanted to come but she was too proud for her own good – just like her mother.

Sorrel was thoughtful as she walked home. When he dropped her outside the cottage after bringing her back from the hospital, Shima had told her he was going to find Tarina.

'If she's ill, she needs help,' he'd said, looking concerned. 'She wouldn't have come here unless she was desperate. Especially if . . .'

'If she killed Jake?' Sorrel nodded. 'I don't think we should tell anyone about Tarina's part in all this, do you?'

'Not unless we have to,' he agreed. 'Don't worry, Sorrel. I'll find her and I'll let you know what's happening as soon as I can.'

Tarina was ill, Jay was lying unconscious in hospital and Richie had gone mad. It was all so horrible that Sorrel could hardly bear to think about it. Above her the sky was blue and it was a lovely summer's day but she felt as if it was deepest winter.

As she walked into her house she saw that Aden was already there, sitting in a chair by the table. He looked up as he became aware of her and the look in his eyes set her heart racing.

'What's wrong?' she asked. 'Is Jay worse?'

'No – no, it's all right, it's not Jay,' he said, sounding oddly muffled. 'Not Jay . . .'

'Richie?' She knew the answer before he spoke. She had known what was coming ever since Rebecca had told her he had taken his shotgun from the house. 'He has killed himself, hasn't he?'

'Yes.' Aden looked close to death himself. 'He was ill, Sorrel. In his mind. It was my fault. I was too hard on him. I should have tried to understand instead of . . .' He choked on the words.

'You mustn't say that. You couldn't have known this would happen.' She fetched a glass of brandy as he slumped in his chair. 'Drink this. It's good for shock.'

He obeyed her woodenly. He seemed stunned, unable to cope with this further blow. She had never seen him look

342

so broken. It was as if the fire had gone out of him and he had suddenly become an old man.

'Please don't blame yourself,' said Sorrel, kneeling at his side and laying her hand on his. 'You are always so ready to punish yourself.'

'Who else is there to blame?' he asked passing a shaking hand across his eyes. 'Richie was my son. Rebecca will never forgive me for this.'

'She doesn't blame you. She thinks it was her own rejection of Richie's plea for help that drove him over the edge.'

'She's wrong. It was because I told him I would cut him out of my will. Money and possessions meant so much to Richie.'

'You were angry. You would have forgiven him in time. He should have known that . . . he would have known it if he hadn't been ill. I think the darkness was always in him. Nothing either you or Rebecca did could have prevented this in the end. Perhaps that's why Richie decided to finish it: because he knew that the madness was taking him over, because he could no longer control his rages.'

Aden looked at her for a long time, then he wiped the tears from his eyes. 'You're a blessing and a comfort, Sorrel. Thank you, my dear.' He hauled himself up from the chair. 'I have to tell Rebecca. I couldn't face her before but you've given me the strength.'

As he walked to the door she noticed he was limping. 'Have you hurt your leg?'

'I did it a few days ago. It's nothing, just a scratch.'

'Let me look. It might need a dressing.'

'Don't trouble yourself.' He smiled at her. 'Thank you again, Sorrel. I shall see you later.'

Her mother came into the kitchen as Aden went out. 'What was all that about?' she asked. 'I thought it sounded serious so I didn't interrupt.'

Sorrel told her and she looked shocked. May sat down heavily, shaking her head in distress.

'Ritchie dead – by his own hand? It's true what they say, troubles never come singly. Jay in hospital and now this! It's fair taken the wind out of my sails. I feel all of a dither.'

'Have some brandy, Ma.' Sorrel fetched her a glass and

she drank it straight down. 'Now I have to get ready. Rebecca is taking me to the hospital. At least, I think she is.'

'She'll go,' May said. 'I've never known anything stop her yet. She's lost one son but she'll hang on to the other all the harder.'

'I feel for poor little Sally,' Rebecca said as she and Sorrel sat in the corridor and waited for the doctors to come out of Jay's room. 'She's so young to lose her husband – and in such a terrible way.'

'What will she do?' Sorrel asked. 'Will she stay in their house or . . .?'

'I think she will go away,' Rebecca replied. 'Her mother told me she is under sedation at the moment. She is planning to take her to stay with some relatives in Devon. Perhaps that's best. She won't have to cope with all the scandal and the whispering tongues.'

'Poor Sally,' Sorrel said, her eyes stinging. 'It's so awful for her and her children.'

'Yes, but she's young – she'll get over it.' Rebecca touched her hand as she sighed. 'Don't look so anxious, Sorrel. I'm sure Jay is going to get better.'

They had been waiting for nearly half an hour and Sorrel's nerves were stretched to breaking point. What was going on in there? Why wouldn't they let them see Jay?

'I wish they would let us see him,' she said, glancing at the clock on the wall. 'Surely there's no need for them to be in there all this time?'

Usually they were allowed to go in and sit with Jay when they arrived. He had regained consciousness during his second night in hospital but had slipped into a fever and had not been aware of them sitting beside him.

'Do you think he is worse?'

'I'll ask to speak to a doctor.' Rebecca stood up just as the door of Jay's room opened and a doctor came out. 'Ah, here he is at last.'

'Mrs Sawle – and Miss Harris?' The doctor looked at their anxious faces. 'I'm sorry you've been kept waiting but I wanted to speak to you myself.'

'Is he . . . is Jay worse?' Sorrel asked, her throat so tight it hurt.

'Quite the opposite.' The doctor smiled. 'We've completed all our tests now and I have good news for you. Mr Sawle has recovered from the fever and we think he has suffered no lasting damage from the blow to his head. He will need to stay in hospital for a few days and when he comes home he must take things easily for some time – but he should be fine.'

'Thank goodness!' Tears slipped down Sorrel's cheeks. 'I'm sorry . . . it's silly . . .'

'Don't cry.' Rebecca touched her hand. 'You've been so brave all this time. It's all right, Sorrel. Jay will soon be well again. Isn't that so, doctor?'

'As long as he takes it slowly for a while.'

'Thank you.' Rebecca gave Sorrel a little push. 'You go in and see him. I'll join you later.'

'Are you sure?'

'I want to talk to the doctor about the care Jay needs when he comes home. Go in and talk to him, Sorrel. He will be so pleased to see you.'

'Will he?'

Sorrel wasn't so sure. Jay hadn't forgiven her for having told him about her affair with Shima. He might not want to see her now. She took a deep breath and pushed open the door of his room. He was lying with his eyes closed and still looked very pale; the gash on his head was covered by a bandage and there was a bruise on his cheek. His eyelids flickered and then he was looking at her.

'Sorrel . . .' He frowned as if he wasn't sure why she was there. 'I can't remember . . . something about Richie . . . they won't tell me . . .'

'Richie was attacking me and you saved me,' she said, moving closer to the bed. 'You didn't want to fight him but he was . . . he picked up an iron bar and hit you.'

'I know all about that bit,' he said with a wry smile. 'It hurts like hell.' He gazed up at her in silence for a moment, his smile fading. 'What happened after he hit me?'

'Does it matter? Wait until you feel better, Jay. They say you can come out of hospital soon and . . .'

She was standing by the bed. He reached out and grasped her wrist. 'Please tell me,' he said. 'I may have a broken head but I'm not daft. Richie was trying to kill you. Why?'

'He wanted me to read a letter . . . a letter addressed to you from a girl you knew in Belgium.'

'Louise?' Something flickered in Jay's eyes. 'I suppose he had read the letter?' She nodded and a nerve began to throb in his throat. 'She is having a child – my child.'

'Yes, Richie said . . .' Sorrel swallowed hard. 'Are you in love with her? Will you marry her?'

'She married someone else,' Jay said. 'Her father came to see me after I was wounded. He asked me not to try and see her. She knew I didn't love her so she married a man she had known all her life, an older man with a farm of his own.'

'I see.' Sorrel couldn't meet his eyes. 'Then it's over between you?'

'It never really meant anything.'

Sorrel was silent.

'What happened afterwards?' Jay said as the silence became too intense to be borne. 'After Richie hit me?'

She told him, leaving nothing out. 'We haven't told anyone else about Tarina's part in all this,' she said. 'But I know you won't say anything that might harm her. You were always her friend.'

'So Shima saved you?' There was a thread of bitterness in his voice. 'I might have known. It's always him.'

'If it hadn't been for you, he would have been too late,' Sorrel said. 'You were there first, Jay. Your leg let you down, that's all.'

He stared up at her but didn't say anything for several seconds. 'I suppose you'll be going away with him soon?'

'Jay, please,' she said, her throat tight. 'Don't. I can't bear it if you . . .'

'I'm sorry,' he said, and smiled at her in his old way, making her heart catch with pain. 'I was a brute to you the other day. I do wish you happy, Sorrel, of course I do. I hope you and Shima will be very happy.'

'Oh, Jay.' Sorrel couldn't speak further. 'I wish . . .'

'Ah, there you are,' Rebecca said, putting her head round the door. 'You look more like yourself, my darling.' She came to kiss Jay on the cheek. 'The doctor says you can come home in a few days, isn't that good news?'

Sorrel left the room as Rebecca sat on the edge of the bed. If she stayed she would cry again and that would be silly.

Jay was getting better. He would soon be well. Nothing else mattered.

'It's so good to see you, Fanny.' Sorrel hugged her. 'I'm glad you've come home at last – your mother needs you.'

'I came as soon as Father told me about Richie,' Fanny said, looking slightly sheepish. 'I should have come ages ago, Sorrel. You were right and I was wrong.'

'And you've made it up with your mother?'

'We're being very polite to each other at the moment,' she said between a sob and a laugh. 'But I've got some news for you.'

Sorrel could see it was important. 'Tell me then – what kind of news?'

'I'm going to marry Henry Bradshaw. He's taking me to meet his sister and her family next week.'

'Major Bradshaw?' Sorrel stared at her in surprise.

Fanny went pink. 'I know he's older than me but he loves me and . . . I'm very fond of him. I want children and I think this may be my only chance.'

'Oh, Fanny.' Sorrel held out her arms and they hugged. 'I'm so glad. I always knew he thought the world of you.'

'I thought you might say he was too old for me?' Fanny looked at her shyly.

'If you're happy, I'm happy. What did your mother say?'

'She said she was pleased . . . and she asked me to forgive her for coming between me and John that day.'

'Fanny.' Sorrel kissed her cheek. 'I think you have forgiven her at last, haven't you?'

'Yes. It has taken me a long time but I think it has stopped hurting,' she said. 'I shall never forget John, but Henry understands that. He is very kind and patient and I believe we shall be happy together.'

'That's all that matters,' Sorrel said. 'I'm so very glad for you, dearest. So very, very glad.'

347

'What about you?' Fanny asked. 'You and Jay?'

'We're friends, I think,' Sorrel said, turning her face aside so that Fanny shouldn't see her eyes. 'Yes, I think we might be friends at last.'

Chapter Thirty-Eight

'That feels very much better, thank you.' Aden looked at Sorrel ruefully as she finished bandaging his leg. 'I should have let you look at it earlier, it was getting painful.'

'You were very silly,' Sorrel scolded. 'If Fanny hadn't insisted on your having treatment, you could have lost the leg – or worse.'

'Between the two of you, I didn't stand a chance.' Aden smiled at her. 'I know it was foolish of me to neglect it but I couldn't seem to think about anything.' His smile faded and she saw the grief he was trying to hide.

'How did Jay take the news about Richie?' she asked. 'He wanted to know when I spoke to him in hospital but I thought it best if you told him that part.'

'He took it hard,' Aden said with a sigh. 'I think he blames himself. I'm worried about him, Sorrel. He should be getting better but . . .'

'He has been through a lot,' she said, turning away before he saw the grief in her eyes. 'I must go. Tell Fanny I'll see her later.'

The summer had almost gone. Sorrel shivered as she went outside and felt the chill of a misty autumn afternoon. In Europe the news was good; the war was all but over and there was talk of the peace to come . . . so why did she feel so empty and lost?

'How is Aden?' May asked as she went in, and looked relieved as Sorrel told her he was getting better. 'Thank goodness for that. The last thing we want is for him to . . .'

She stopped as she saw Sorrel's face. 'The funeral is the day after tomorrow, isn't it?'

'Yes.' Sorrel went to put the kettle on. 'They couldn't have it before because of the inquest.'

'Richie's wife will be going away afterwards then?'

'Yes, I think so. Rebecca says she's been very brave but she is selling the house and going to live with relatives.'

'That will be best for her.' May nodded. 'Is Rebecca all right?'

'She seems much happier now that Fanny is home.' Sorrel looked at her mother. 'Do you know why she didn't like me? It was because I reminded her of Aunt Ruth.'

'What rubbish!' May was indignant. 'You don't look a bit like her.'

'It's the way I laugh sometimes, apparently. It doesn't matter now. We've become friends.' Sorrel went to make the tea. 'Did you say Rose had had another letter from Ted?'

'His ship is in Portsmouth. He wants her to go down tomorrow – and she has asked me to go with her, help her find a place to live.'

'Shall you go?'

Her mother was thoughtful. 'It would mean missing the funeral – but you and Bob will be there. I don't like to do it but Rose needs me.'

'You do as you think best. Aden will understand.'

'You could stay with Mabel while I'm away. I shan't stop longer than a week, just long enough to get her settled.'

'I'll be all right. I'm not a child, Ma.'

'No, I know you're not.' Her mother looked at her anxiously. 'I wish I could see you settled, Sorrel.'

She turned away. 'I'm fine. Don't worry about me.'

'Is Shima coming for the funeral?'

'Yes, I'm sure he will. Aden rang Rothsay and was able to get in touch with him through Major Bradshaw. He's coming down too, and will take Fanny back with him.'

'And what then?' Her mother looked at her hard. 'Are you going to marry Shima?'

'I don't know,' Sorrel said, blinking as tears stung her eyes. 'I just don't know. I thought I loved him but ...'

350

'If it's Jay you want, you should tell him,' her mother said. 'Never mind your pride, miss. Don't waste your life, Sorrel – and don't marry the wrong man or you'll regret it until your dying day.'

Rebecca was as pale as a ghost as the coffin of her son was carried into the church. Jay and Shima had insisted on bearing part of the load, even though Jay looked as if he might pass out at any moment. They were supported by Aden, Sorrel's brother and two of Aden's labourers.

Sorrel stood with Mabel just behind Sally, her parents, Rebecca, Fanny, and her fiancé. Sally looked as if she wasn't properly aware of what was going on around her. Fanny was crying as they all stood to sing *Abide With Me*. Through a high window a thin, pale sun threw its light over them and Sorrel saw Fanny clasp her mother's hand.

At last it was time to follow the coffin out to the little churchyard. Despite the pale sunshine it was bitterly cold, a rasping wind blowing across the flat land from the river.

Fanny was sobbing into her hanky but Rebecca and Sally stood as they had in church, marble white and motionless.

'Ashes to ashes . . . dust to dust . . .'

After a little nudge from her mother-in-law Sally picked up a handful of dirt, letting it trickle through her fingers onto the coffin. She stood looking down at it for a moment then walked away, passing the other mourners without a glance. Rebecca threw a single rose into the open grave.

'I always loved you, Richie,' she said in a clear, steady voice. 'You never believed it but I always loved you.' Then she turned and followed her daughter-in-law from the churchyard.

'She was crying all night,' a voice said at Sorrel's side. 'She blames herself for all this, you know. Thinks it was her fault because she left Richie when he was a small child.'

'But that can't be true,' Sorrel said. 'Whatever made Richie the way he was came from inside him. Rebecca wasn't responsible.'

'I wish she could believe that,' Aden said. 'Will you come back to the house, Sorrel? It's a meaningless ritual but I'd like you to be there with us.'

351

'If you wish.' Sorrel glanced at Jay, who was standing alone staring moodily at nothing in particular. 'But I won't stay long. I ought to get back and give Bob a hand with the milking.'

'Mother is upstairs in her room,' Fanny said as Sorrel went into the kitchen for another plate of sandwiches to pass round. 'I knocked but she asked me to leave her alone for a while. Would you go up to her? She thinks highly of you and I'm worried about her.'

'I don't think she will want to talk to me,' Sorrel said, 'but I'll see if I can get her to come down.'

She smiled encouragingly at Fanny and went upstairs. Outside Rebecca's door she paused, then knocked. 'It's Sorrel – may I come in?'

There was no reply for a moment and Sorrel was about to turn away when the door was suddenly opened. 'Please come in,' Rebecca said, and smiled at her. 'I suppose Fanny sent you?'

'She was worried. I'm sure you don't really want company. I'll go.'

'No, please come in for a moment,' Rebecca said. 'I did want to talk to you. I would have walked over to see you later if you hadn't come up.'

Sorrel followed her inside. There were some baby clothes folded neatly into piles on the bed. Rebecca saw her glance at them and nodded.

'It's time I got rid of these,' she said. 'I gave most of my things away to children who needed them . . . but I kept bits and pieces. This was Fanny's, of course, and this was Jay's christening gown. And this shawl . . . that was Richie's . . .' Her voice caught on a sob. 'I let him down somehow, Sorrel. Hurt him too many times.'

'You can't blame yourself.' Sorrel moved towards her and then stopped, afraid to offer further comfort. 'We all say and do things we don't mean. Richie was ill . . . he must have known you loved him in his heart. What happened was because of an illness, something in him no one could explain. Even the doctors understand very little about what makes the human mind become ill.'

352

'Perhaps you're right.' Rebecca's eyes were dark with pain. 'But it was about Jay that I wanted to speak to you. He is so desperately unhappy, Sorrel. Can't you find it in your heart to forgive him? Please?'

'I forgave him long ago,' she said, her voice husky. 'He doesn't want me anymore. I hurt him too much for him ever to forgive me. You don't know . . .'

'I hurt my husband once,' Rebecca said. 'When we married I thought I was in love with someone else – but he married my best friend.'

'Celia's husband?'

Rebecca nodded. 'Victor Roth. They were already engaged when I first met him but we were instantly attracted. Of course there was never any question of his jilting her but over the years we continued to feel this mutual attraction and there was a time when he thought he loved me . . .' She sighed deeply. 'Nothing ever happened between us. Celia was my friend and besides I was married – but Aden sensed something and it hurt him badly. We began to drift apart and it almost ruined our marriage. Yet in the end we forgave each other.' She reached out to touch Sorrel's hand. 'If you truly love there is nothing that cannot be forgiven . . . nothing.'

'It is Jay who cannot forgive me,' Sorrel said. 'I would do anything to make it up to him but it's too late.'

'Are you sure?'

'Quite sure.'

'Then I should not have spoken. Forgive me.' Rebecca kissed her cheek. 'I think you might have made him happy.'

Sorrel turned away hastily as the tears threatened to spill over. She went downstairs and out of the house before Fanny saw her. Her emotions were churning inside her, wrenching at her. All she wanted was to be alone so that she could give way to her tears.

'Sorrel . . . Sorrel, wait!' Shima's voice stopped her. 'Sorrel, I must talk to you. Please.'

She turned reluctantly to face him. 'Shima, could it wait for a while?'

He had caught up with her now and stood looking down into her face with that gentle smile she knew so well. 'No,

353

I don't think it should wait any longer,' he said. 'I wanted you to know that I've found Tarina.'

'Tarina . . .' Sorrel took a hold on her emotions, forcing them down so that she could breathe properly. 'How is she?'

'Not well . . . quite sick in fact.' Shima looked grave. 'I took her to a doctor and he says she is in the early stages of consumption.'

'Oh, Shima.' Sorrel forgot her own troubles in concern for the gipsy woman. 'I'm so very sorry. Can they do anything for her?'

'She needs care, good food and a warm climate,' he said, and paused. He reached out to touch Sorrel's cheek. 'That's why I'm going to take her away as soon as I get my offical release from the army. I have some property in Ireland which I have arranged to sell to Major Bradshaw. He will employ a trainer there to help breed his horses and I shall use the money to take Tarina to America. I'll find work there and perhaps one day I'll go into horse-breeding myself.'

'Shima . . .' Sorrel's throat was so tight that she could hardly speak. 'You're going away?'

'Tarina has been through a terrible time since she ran away; she's lived in fear and poverty for years, doing things she can hardly bear to speak of.' He paused, took a deep breath and went on: 'Jake raped her and she killed him. She intended to take her own life but when the water closed over her head she started to fight . . . but she has suffered for what she did. You cannot imagine what she has been through, and she would not want you to know: she is too proud. She needs someone to take care of her or she will die – there is no one else but me, Sorrel. I have no choice.' He gave her a loving, understanding smile. 'Besides, it's best I go, isn't it?'

Sorrel moved towards him. 'I'm sorry. You know I . . .'

'We had a little time,' he said. 'I shall always hold the memory in my heart. We were both lonely and you needed someone to love . . . but it should have been Jay. It has always been Jay, hasn't it?'

She looked into his eyes, then nodded. 'Yes. I do love him. I always shall. I can't help myself.'

'Then don't waste time crying over what can't be helped,'

354

Shima said. 'I love you, Sorrel, I always shall – but I want you to be happy and I know Jay is the one.'

'Shima.' She reached up to kiss him very softly on the mouth. 'Take care of yourself, dearest Shima.'

'Goodbye,' he said. 'I shan't come back – at least, not for years. I've said all my farewells.'

She watched as he walked out of the gate and then heard an engine roar into life as he drove away.

'Oh, Shima,' she murmured. 'I'm so sorry.'

A sound behind her made her swing round. Jay was staring at her, then as she stood motionless he turned and began to walk towards the fields behind the yard. For a moment Sorrel couldn't move, then she called to him.

'Jay . . . Jay . . . wait for me!'

He kept walking, not even turning his head to look at her. She ran after him, her heart racing. She couldn't let him go this time or it really would be too late.

'Jay,' she said as she caught him at last, 'why won't you wait? I have to talk to you.'

'What is there to talk about?' His face was stony, his eyes cold as he stared straight ahead, refusing to look at her. 'I saw you with him . . . there's nothing more to say.'

She caught at his arm, forcing him to stop and look at her. 'We were saying goodbye. Shima is going away . . . taking Tarina to America.'

'You were kissing him.'

The jealousy flashed in his eyes and Sorrel's heart missed a beat. Perhaps he did still care, just a little.

'Just to say goodbye, Jay, that's all. I promise you.'

'You're not going to marry him?'

'No. Shima knows . . . he knows that I'm not in love with him.' She looked up into his face, silently pleading with him to listen – to understand. 'It's you I love, Jay. You I've always loved.'

'But you went with him during the war . . . you loved him then.' His eyes darkened with pain. 'You were lovers, you told me so.'

'Yes, we were. Nothing can change that . . .' Sorrel's voice broke on a sob. 'Can't you forgive me? I know I refused to listen when you tried to tell me about Tarina but I regretted

355

it – and I understand about Louise. I know how you must have felt out there, never knowing if you would be killed on your next tour of duty, how lonely and unhappy you must have been . . .'

'Was that how it was for you?' he asked. 'You were lonely . . . miserable?'

'Yes.' Sorrel lifted her head proudly. 'I was angry, too. Angry with you for finding someone else. Fanny let me read your letters and I knew you had.'

'It was just friendship for a long time.' He seemed to be pleading for understanding now. 'Then, when it happened, I wished it was you. All the time I wanted it to be you. But you . . . you and Shima . . .' Anger and jealousy clashed in his eyes as he stared down at her.

Sorrel's heart sank. He was never going to forgive her. It was useless to try. Rebecca was wrong: some things were unforgivable.

'Then it's no good, is it?'

She stood gazing up into his eyes for several seconds, then turned away. It was no use. No use! Jay would never forgive her. She had hurt him too badly. He must hate her now. She started to run, knowing that the tears were very close.

'Sorrel . . . Sorrel, wait!' He ran after her, catching at her arm and swinging her round to face him. She struggled, not wanting him to see her misery, but he held her fast. 'Don't go. Please, don't go. I'll die if I lose you. I can't let you go . . . I can't!'

'But if you can't forgive me?' she whispered, tears stinging behind her eyes. 'If you can't forget, it would always be between us. Let me go, Jay. It's no use . . . no use.'

'No . . . I swear it won't,' he said, his face working with pain and emotion. 'I'm a jealous fool. I always have been where you were concerned – but I love you. I love you so much that I couldn't bear to go on living if you . . .' He broke off, reaching out to touch her face, his hand shaking. 'Please . . . please give me another chance? Forgive me for hurting you. I love you so much.'

'Oh, Jay.' She looked at him uncertainly. She wanted him, loved him so much, but she couldn't bear it if his love turned to hatred. 'It must be a new beginning . . . no regrets, no recriminations on either side.'

'We begin from today,' he said, and offered his hand, the flicker of a smile on his mouth. 'I'm pleased to meet you, Miss Harris.'

'Mr Sawle.' Sorrel gave a small chuckle then took his hand, feeling the firm clasp of his fingers around hers as he held on tight. 'We *are* different people, Jay. I'm not the naive girl I was and you're more mature, more experienced . . . we've changed because of all that's happened, all we've seen and done.'

'I love the woman even more than the girl,' Jay said, and drew her close to him, his lips touching hers in a gentle kiss that gradually became more demanding. 'I shall always love you, my darling.'

Overhead the clouds had gathered and a few spots of rain had begun to fall. It was autumn and soon it would be winter but in Sorrel's heart all at once it was spring.

She began to smile as she took his hand, pulling at him, tugging him, leading him through the yard and across the road.

'Where are we going?' he asked as she turned her head to urge him on. 'What are you up to, Miss Harris?'

'I'm taking you to my house,' she said, a sparkle of mischief in her eyes. 'There's no one there. We can have it all to ourselves.'

'What are you suggesting, Miss Harris?'

Jay's smile made her heart race wildly.

'Can't you guess?'

'Did anyone ever tell you that you are a minx, Sorrel Harris?' he asked as she drew him into the house and bolted the door from the inside.

'I believe you might have done once.' She tipped her head to one side, her smile teasing and slightly wicked. 'Well, what are you waiting for?'

He caught his breath. 'Are you sure? I can wait – if you would rather?'

'We might have to wait for the wedding for a while,' she said. 'Out of respect to your family. But I don't want to wait for us to be together. We've waited long enough, Jay, haven't we?'

For a moment it seemed as if he could not believe she was real, then he reached out to touch her cheek. 'My beautiful, beautiful Sorrel . . . I've waited . . . wanted you for so long, I'm almost afraid to touch you . . . afraid that you'll disappear into the mist as you did in my dreams.'

'That is all over, my darling,' she whispered. 'All the pain and the killing and the loneliness. You're here with me and we shall be together for the rest of our lives. We shall be happy, I promise you, Jay. This is what I've wanted all my life . . . my own special dream.'

'And mine,' he said, as he gathered her up into his arms. 'My lovely woman. And, come the spring, my wife.'

You have been reading a novel published by Piatkus Books. We hope you have enjoyed it and that you would like to read more of our titles. Please ask for them in your local library or bookshop.

If you would like to be put on our mailing list to receive details of new publications, please send a large stamped addressed envelope (UK only) to:

Piatkus Books: 5 Windmill Street
London W1P 1HF

PIATKUS

The sign of a good book